The Supe

A NOVEL OF WEST POINT

John Vermillion

ISBN: 1511525738
ISBN 13: 9781511525732

Prologue

As a young officer in the cold mountains of Waziristan, Harris Green set out with his platoon to find the route the Taliban was traveling on its way to lay waste to the villages in south-central Afghanistan. He sat in the center of the security perimeter set up at the rest halt, swallowed up by the vastness of this wild place, and while engaged in solitary map study, encountered what to him became satori, a Buddhist state of profound enlightenment. The revelation seemed to him an order higher than epiphany. It was the first time in his life he knew, with metaphysical certitude, he had solved a problem so complex, it was almost unknowable.

Just look around, he thought, *at the infinite possibilities available to the enemy.* They could be using creases, literally numberless, to traverse these mountains.

"I am but a grain of sand on this great beach," he mused. Yet he could place the sharpened point of a pencil on this topographic map and say, "Right here, right here is their route, their way into Afghanistan," although it was just *a* trail, indistinguishable from countless others.

His finding turned out to be brutal truth. While the platoon rehearsed in daylight for an ambush to be conducted with a six-man killer team after darkness fell, a company-sized Taliban force, seventy-five to a hundred bearded men, stumbled directly into them, talking cheerfully among themselves at normal volume, oblivious to any ground threat. It was a savage day. A lot of people sang the hallelujah hymn that cold day. Some hunches, when they feel right, you just do not question, Green had learned.

Partially by virtue of his position and partially because of luck, he had for the second time in his life concatenated an apparently discrete series of events and seen how they ended. In some respects, his matter of present interest was as Einsteinian as the one in Waziristan. Yet he could envisage the solution with equal clarity.

Without his intervention, he was sure that both the United States Military Academy and the country would come to a bad end. Now a General, Harris Green had thought through this for months. For every day of those months, he had seen what was coming and mentally constructed an antidote to the problem. It would require manipulation, a manner of doing business as foreign to his nature as it was unpalatable. There were already enough careerist manipulators ensconced in the Pentagon.

His solution depended upon one man—only one officer in the US military met the requirements Green had in mind, and getting him to agree to the plan was far, far from a sure thing. The man whose services he sought was as stubborn as he was tough. But time was expiring.

Chapter One

Simple Sumbitch

Every combat-arms officer in the US military professes his love for enlisted people and noncommissioned officers. It is a game played, like asking, "How are you?" to a stranger out of politeness, an insincere inquiry. Your objective is for fellow Marine officers to believe you love your Marines. But the officer who loves more than the idea of the Marine is as rare as gadolinium. Simon Pack loved how Marines joked among themselves. How they bragged about nonexistent flashy cars they'd left back home. How their mamas were the best cooks in the world and every meal at home was six courses. How poorly the mess hall compared to mama's kitchen. How they moved. How intensely they played cards, always making the Big Throwdown. How proud they were of dirt and grime accumulated in the field. How, at the kickoff of Pack's career, most were identified as Category IV, or Cat IV, colloquially, indicating exceptions were made to overlook deficiencies in their recruitment packets. The CAT IVs came without high-school diplomas, and typically had finished eight or nine grades. No letter jackets, no proms, no recognizable achievements, maybe a few misdemeanor arrests. But this so-called "simple sumbitch" made a damn fine Marine who, given a little leadership, could do things that would make Ivy Leaguers feel inferior. He could, in a minute or two, assemble and disassemble an M60 machinegun blindfolded. Simon Pack had observed this done so frequently it was not abnormal. He had seen Marines who were assigned an obscure task such as vector control for a unit inspection come away with no deficiencies noted. Watching this simple sumbitch with knowledge in his hands fluoresce and mature and fight like a cornered weasel when called on was to Pack a most wondrous sight. Some learned how to study, and a few even achieved advanced degrees. If he applied the yardstick of "How well did he play the hand he was dealt?" these "simple" fellows often got lofty marks.

The measure of love is what you're willing to give up for it. Pack forsook the status and prestige and honor of choice staff assignments in order to remain more closely attached to those "simple sumbitches." He risked the wrath of his superiors and refused any assignment within a hundred miles of Washington, DC.

Now, military retirement thrust upon him, he had systematically severed all connections to the military community. If he couldn't be among them, part of them, a clean split was the way to go. He didn't want to become the Wise Old House General who retires in proximity to the site of his terminal assignment just so he can repeatedly be leaned on as a guest speaker. Get as far away from the old places as possible, hence Montana. Preferably, in the remote backwoods, surrounded by that state's towering larches, snowy peaks, and rushing, trout-laden streams. Following his wife's untimely death, he could find complete peace only when sleeping on the ground blanketed by the billion-starred sky of the state he considered the most aesthetically excellent in the nation.

Chapter Two

Resolution

Theoretically, I'm the second-ranking person in the US Army: Harris Green, Vice Chief of Staff. In practice, it wasn't that clear. When he was a battalion commander, a lieutenant colonel, he had direct authority over about a thousand people. He relieved them, promoted them, encouraged them, did morning physical training with them, court-martialed them, and punished them for all manner of violations of the Uniform Code of Military Justice. Now, he had direct authority over few but indirect authority over hundreds of thousands. *In those days, I was in the field as much as my troops. It was a large family, but we were a family, and we were happy. We experienced many miseries and many joys, as one. Nowadays, I see little of the field, at most a couple days a year.*

Field, incidentally, is shorthand for combat and tactical exercises and strenuous physical and emotional activity. The field can be hot or cold, dry or muddy, anywhere in the world. *I would prefer that to this, but that's just how it is.* There weren't many senior officers who had good field commands but also were great administrators. If Green could have hidden his administrative talents, he might have.

Most of the time, I hate being here, he thought. Even sitting where he did, wearing the four stars of a Pentagon potentate, he had to admit deep inside, there were scores—no, gotta be honest, magnitudes more than that—of men and women in this building who could run intellectual rings around him. *People whose mastery of material is simply stunning, and whose manners of presentation are more polished than any one I ever gave.* It was a subject of genuine interest for him to ask himself, "How, Harris, did you get this far? Was it luck?"

Granted, I'm the one asking the question, so my opinions are likely idealized. I think it's because I'm a damn direct fellow, and also because I love troops. About the *direct* part, Green wanted the ouzo only, that formidable fluid lodging at the bottom of those Greek barrels. Everyone knew if you were going to brief Harris Green, you had better have completed the distillation process before you got to him. *"Be accurate, be brief, be clear," I say over and over. And you'd better be able to go up to my master diagram and show me where your subject fits into it. Explain why should I care about what you have to offer.*

As he saw it, Green was brutal out of necessity. *I'm not as smart as many of these people, so I make them adhere tightly to the KISS principle: Keep It Simple, Stupid. If I'm going to be pumped to the bursting point with information every day, I damn sure want to understand why and what I'm getting.*

People would be surprised how many senior staff, both uniformed and civilian, love to receive briefings to acknowledge their own importance. *You Service Secretaries in your fine suits, the problem I have with you guys is, you are slow to admit what you don't know. Intra- and interservice cooperation would improve if from the beginning, both sides would lay their information-deficit cards on the table.*

Green did love troops. *I love troops because they are a brilliant part of my country, a country founded on big ideas by brilliant men wiser even than their brilliance. I love it because we made one big mistake (slavery) and white men from the North fought white men from the South in atonement, and killed one another in the hundreds of thousands to overcome it. I love it for its economic vibrancy, though admittedly that occasionally seems out of whack. How is it that a supermodel (I still lack clarity on what that is) has earned $300 million in nine years?* It didn't bother Green in the least that if he were a civilian executive with responsibilities approximating those he had now, he would be taking home multiples of the money he was paid.

Good for them, I say. I'm happy to be an enabler. We remain a land of opportunity. I love being surrounded by young men and women who also so love their country. I am moved far beyond words or tears or normal modes of emotion when these sons and daughters of America give their lives for love of country. The cynics, and there are plenty of them, will say I'm wrong, that these young people sought refuge in the military because their chances of success elsewhere were bleak or nonexistent. But call them "losers" in front of me, and we've got a problem. Cynics, walk in the footsteps of these grand young people, and see how far you go before collapsing of fear or incompetence.

But there are things I do not love about America right now, and right there on top of the heap is me. I don't love me because I haven't had the guts to get to a solution on this big problem before now.

I'll take step one today.

♦ ♦ ♦

It was a Wednesday in the "Tank" at the Pentagon. The meeting was the final scheduled event of Green's day. Like nominal number-twos everywhere, Green did the heavy lifting for his boss, Army Chief of Staff General Wayne Pembrook. Green knew more about the nuts and bolts of the Army in its vastness than any man walking.

Green was grateful to cant the chair back for a joint-popping stretch. Through blinking eyes, he observed the light reflecting from the carpet and heavy drapes that gave the room a pale golden hue. On the walls hung paintings dedicated to each Branch of the military. This elegant room, the Joint Chiefs of Staff (JCS) Conference Room, Corridor 9, F Ring, second floor, was not far from the River Entrance to the Pentagon. The Building, as most who work there call it, was not designed for comfort, but this lair was an exception. Leslie Groves, later to garner recognition as director of the Manhattan Project, attended meticulously to the construction of this behemoth structure in which all Services would coalesce to anticipate, plan, and coordinate field operations.

The Pentagon, the structure itself, is a function-over-form marvel with the last laborers having departed the worksite less than eighteen months after the first laborers strapped on the tool belts. No doubt the injunction to Groves was, "We have a war to get to. Build it quick and make it strong, and give it twice the office space of the Empire State Building."

Joining Green as the last out the door is the JCS Chief of Operations (J3), Marine three-star General Wallace Sweet. Green said, "We've spent most of our waking hours in this windowless hole. I need to talk with you, Wallace, privately. Away from the Building. You and Ralph Rogers. Not looking to piss off the wives, but I'd like this to be guys only. Grill some steaks, pretend we're camping, sit around the fire out back of my place. Could be important."

"Absolutely," Sweet said. "I'll lug some porterhouse unless you wave me off."

"Great," Green said. "See you guys Saturday, any time from midafternoon on. Since I'm taking you away from your wives on your day off, I'll ante up for your wives to have a nice dinner out with Dani. Dani has done this kind of thing for me before, and she'll be happy to drive."

Chapter Three

The Wandering Worker

It would have evolved as it did, anyway, but later. Abe Lincoln started it. As a lawyer for the Illinois Central Railroad, he pressed Allan Pinkerton to form the first railroad police. Early rail companies faced numerous difficulties— assaults against passengers; arson; cargo theft; signal vandalism; ticket fraud; de-railings, stickups, and more. Local law enforcers were ill-equipped and ill-disposed to handle most of these matters. So Abe's prodding paid off, and Pinkerton assembled a band of railroad detectives to protect company interests on their lines and rights-of-way.

In modern America, the seven or so Class I railroads furnish the bulls, or police who patrol most of the one hundred forty thousand miles of rail. To the extent the Great American Public is aware of rail bulls at all, it is likely to know them as foils to hobos. Stories of hobo thrashings at the hands of brutal bulls are legion and real.

Mr. Lincoln did not live to witness hordes of hobos swarming train cars in the years after the Civil War. The "hoe boys," or boys and men of the planting fields, returned from war to find no jobs and their homes destroyed, so they—sometimes with families in tow—packed up and jumped the rails in search of work. Leeching onto railcars occurred in numbers even more vast during the Depression, when some three million people were estimated to ride regularly. The need for a robust bull presence was there. The poorer the economy, the higher the odds illegal ridership was up.

Truth is, not all bulls delighted in bashing hobo skulls. Rail companies do, however, lobby DC lawmakers to elevate penalties for violating existing anti-tramp laws and to draft them with a view toward the draconian. Some railroads still advocate bread-and-water sentences. On the other hand, many bulls are simply railroad employees inclined to be kindhearted to people doing their best to make a living. As long as the hobo does no damage to rail property, he can pass mostly unchallenged and without penalty.

The word *hobo* is held to be connotatively significant. It is imbued with special meaning, one who roves the land in a quest for employment. In the beginning, it suggested people engaged in seasonal harvesting, but today it means a rover who works. They congregated in so-called jungles, for both camaraderie and security. They told tales, sang songs, tried out poems around campfires. Often supped communally. Shared women, along with stories. Occasionally sought arrest for temporary shelter and security, some succeeding ten to fifty times a year.

Rail-passenger traffic withered in the 1960s, as did hobo traffic, thanks to a strong economy. Over the years, freight-moving grew more specialized to achieve greater efficiency in the haul. Locomotives roared with increased power and higher speeds. They morphed into genuine *loco*-motives, crazy with might, one-hundred-twenty-car double-stacks streaking across flatlands at seventy mph, bulling up steep inclines, onward and onward, until crews were capable of changing within a span of sixty seconds. Sucking oneself remora-like onto an open spot on one of these modern monsters is replete with danger, not at all consistent with grabbing the iron handle of the passing chuggers of yesteryear.

But something else apparently withered as well: wanderlust, the call of the Road. In every respect that matters, hobodom has vanished, replaced by cats motivated differently. They are the hobohemians.

The hobohemian shows up at Britt, Iowa, for the annual National Hobo Convention and pretends to have walked in the shoes of the greats. He dines on hobo stew, tells whoppers about where he has travelled and what he has encountered, meanders thoughtfully through the Hobo Cemetery, tours the Hobo Museum. Shoots up and puffs, urinates on property public and private, and will commit damn near any illegality to have this year's King or Queen Hobo crown feathered onto his head.

Meanwhile, the authentic hobo, now numbering in the thousands, is at work somewhere in this vast nation. The wandering worker is the minority. His distant cousin, eight times removed, is the hobohemian tramp, now in the majority. The latter is parasitic in the extreme, the suckerfish on society's outer walls. He plays the system, typically scamming and cadging to replenish his alcohol, drugs, and petty cash. He barks loudest in insisting we refer to him using the respectful *hobo*, but merit the appellation he does not. He spews rum fumes and has no compunction about thieving the last dollar off a fellow traveler. He hasn't the desire to contract for any task involving real labor, skilled or otherwise.

Feign a horrible toothache to an emergency-room doc in southern California, have him prescribe hydrocodone, return the following day claiming no relief, unleash a lachrymose saga about life on the move, and persuade him to issue a three-month supply. Next time you'll have to restock, you might be in New Orleans's Gentilly Yard. Such practice is harder to pull off now than in yesteryear, but it's still done.

When Sheriff Mollison mentioned over coffee at The Sundance that a hobo had been killed down near the rail yard—Sheriff Mollison subsequently amended that to two slayings in four years—, Pack itched to learn more about the people in this encampment. After working days in the building trades, he would drive the Tahoe up the dusty two-track to the cabin, grab a sack of food he had refrigerated that morning, then trudge down the hill on foot to the jungle.

There were sixteen people there, fourteen men and two women. They had accepted him right away. Didn't hurt that he often brought vegetables and meat they threw into communal pots. He had done his research and sensed how fortunate he was that these folks were the real-deal hobos who felt no shame in the life they led. They all worked. The General was astonished when, on his first evening in the jungle, he looked into the firelight-reflected faces of two men he had worked alongside that very day. If you aren't working crops but possess general skills, you get to know where the Home Depots and Lowe's stores are, get there in time for pickups for day jobs, and you put money in your pocket. *Yep*, Pack thought to himself, *I can do this*. He had been clueless that his fellow workers spent nights down here and had no mailing address. How Pack saw it was, maybe he'd found the civilian counterparts of those "simple sumbitches."

He'd most recently worked on an enormous log place perched atop a promontory above the lake. Ponderosa pines, larch, and Douglas firs, paired with a broad, high, ebony iron gate featuring security-coded entrance, shielded it from view from the lake road. It was the Mountain West-chic getaway for a well-known actress of the silver screen. Even in this small enclave of Montana, homes like this were going up by the score, their owners Hollywood vixens and leading men. In interviews, they would say, "I have this little place in Montana to get away from it all: Do all the outdoor stuff; breathe sweet, clean air; recharge my batteries." Actually, they flocked together in Hollywood Northeast, parked their jets at the same municipal airport, timed their infrequent visits to coincide as much as possible, attended the same parties, and occupied essentially the same social circle. They were importing to the country precisely the things in Hollywood they claimed to be running from. Pricey boutique shops bloomed, turning rural Montana towns into replicas of Rodeo Drive.

"A great residence I have helped shape," Pack mused, "effectively wasted."

The two guys in the camp who had been on the homebuilding team were called Memphis Mike and Denver Johnny. They had vouched for Simon Pack in the strongest language. Their duties called for them to be on the job a week or two beyond Pack. By now, they were aware of his interest in learning at firsthand how they rode the rails. They gave him a moniker, Mount Montana, owing to his size. They promised to be his guide as far as Yermo, where he could pick his own way.

Chapter Four

The First Small Step

Most of DC's top military echelon resides at Fort Myer, Virginia, bordering Arlington Cemetery, across the Potomac from the District. It looks much the same as other military installations. Well-ordered, manicured, free of litter, no paint job more than a couple years old. The residences here appear more sturdily constructed than those at, say, Fort Hood, Texas. Most were erected more than a century ago by tradesmen who knew their crafts. Built in the neo-Federal style, in excess of one hundred sets of quarters have brick façades, standing on granite-block foundations. In their early days of life, these quarters characteristically housed the families of two junior officers. After the Pentagon went up in the early 1940s and the virtually anonymous Army post burst to life as the home to the most senior people of all the Services, many of the duplexes were modified into single-family units. The vehicles in the drives tend toward American-made popular stock, not of the newest model year. Luxury brands are eschewed, even for those who can afford them. Better than one in four are SUVs. Many streets have a Jeep or a pickup on them.

Fort Myer has a Commissary, Post Exchange, clothing store, and movie theater. For military professionals, it is a comfortable but unremarkable setting. By civilian standards, it cannot hold its own with the upper-crust neighborhoods of any American community, regardless of size.

At this time of year, residents would not see dense greenery for another month, but the cold hold of winter was losing strength. Ralph Rogers, director of the Defense Intelligence Agency (DIA), was the first to reach Green's address. Sweet followed minutes later. All lived within a quarter mile of one another. Rogers is an Army three-star. The DIA chief might have been part of another Service, but Green would not have invited him to this quiet event were he not Army. Sweet had left Annapolis one year after Rogers and Green left West Point. Green had asked Sweet to come today because the nature of the Marine General's job gave Sweet as much exposure to the Army as to the Marine Corps, and Green figured he would need the support of both those Service chiefs.

Green had ruminated on this meeting with as much care as any combat operation. As he saw it, it was his job. One miscue, and this train would derail, his damn fine career with it. He knew he might go down in flames, infamous. No question about it.

Rogers and Sweet have coordinated: Rogers carried in a mixing bowl of already-tossed salad his wife has prepared; Sweet lugged in the porterhouses he's promised. Green had three huge potatoes ready for baking.

"Look, fellows," Green said, "we don't drink much around here, and all we usually offer guests are water, wine, and iced tea. I learned a long time ago to avoid discussing wine with Wallace in the vicinity, so I bought a cheap bottle of Merlot for whoever wants it, and I have something fine—Knob Creek bourbon—water, and iced tea. Fill your own glasses. I'm aiming to make a dent in the Knob Creek."

Presently, drinks in hand, Green led them to a sitting room of sorts. The large rectangular room at the rear of the house was an addition from what, fifty years in the past? One side of the rectangle connected to the quarters proper. Inlaid book shelving tracked around mullioned windows on three sides. The brilliance of the early Northern Virginia spring swept through the uncovered windows. A broad Persian from Bandar Abbas covered most of the precious old wood floor. Three medium-sized sofas with a coffee table centering them rested within the boundaries of the rug. Each man claimed a sofa. A weighty chandelier—Green could not have afforded had it not been part of the real property—coruscated ominously directly over the table.

Let the Merlot and the KC have their way, Green thought. The stresses of their duties were severe. Green randomly regarded as miraculous his ability to present a semisoldierly appearance, convinced that every week in his job abbreviated his life span by a corresponding period. Seventeen-hour days were routine, and no different for Rogers and Sweet. Pushing paper in the Pentagon was not these guys' idea of a good job, but you didn't complain as long as troops were working in unspeakably difficult conditions combatting Islamic insurgents intent on destroying everyone who did not accept their religion.

Sweet, a proud Marine, occasionally saw a phony reflected back at himself. To numerous gatherings over the years, he had delivered a short speech centered around "heart and balance." He spoke of the need for careful planning and radical focus in order to maximize the duty day. When the day is over, put equal energy into restoring balance in your life: read; think; allow ideas to marinate; question your plans and actions; give to and receive from family; in general, pay attention to your physical, emotional, and spiritual health. At some point in these talks he would insert pertinent historical examples, such as General George Marshall, who as Army Chief of Staff in Washington during World War II would not permit himself to reach important decisions after 1500 hours, fearing the product of a tired mind was unlikely to reap good fruit. As Military Governor of the Philippines, Douglas MacArthur had a standing appointment to meet his wife at a downtown Manila theater at 2100 hours most days. What happened to be playing was immaterial and irrelevant. MacArthur fell asleep soon after sitting down—it was, he believed, a psychic housecleaning. Field Marshal Bernard Montgomery insisted even at the peak of the North Africa campaign that he have an hour of solitude every day. He felt unable to grasp the big picture with clarity until he drank from his "oases of thought."

Valuable though Sweet regarded these pointers to successful senior leadership, he had lied to himself. There was no real balance to his life, and he could safely bet his life it was the same for Rogers and Green. These were Generals occupying three of the most coveted positions in the Pentagon, yet one could argue they had failed in their journeys to acquire the perspective required to best serve their soldiers, sailors, and Marines.

No one in the room questioned civilian direction of the military. The expression goes, "You can't turn an aircraft carrier on a dime." Or in the space of fifty feet. But dammit, most of the civilians working in the Department of Defense (DOD) and the Services came from the groves of academe, bereft of military knowledge, not understanding the issues necessary to win the war against Islamic extremists. They tried to pilot that aircraft carrier as if it were a rubber boat in a bathtub. Their direction was herky-jerky, uncertain, forever shifting. Warfighting doctrine be damned. Most had never heard of Clausewitz, Jomini, Liddell Hart, Sun Tsu, or damn-near anyone else who regarded military matters as worthy of serious theoretical reflection. We don't march, we lurch, the uniformed leaders opined. Green and Rogers and Sweet and every other uniform in the Building could labor sixty-hour days yet fail to advance because so frequently they were effectively thrown back to the starting blocks by new or revised direction from the civilian force. There should be tension between the civilian and the military in the DOD. But the civilian side and the military side were supposed to be checks and balances on one another. More and more often these days, senior civilians just did not consult with their uniformed brothers, and that produced unwanted and unnecessary friction.

The three men sat deep in the sofas, in unintentional mimicry, tumblers teed up in hands atop armrests. Their chat was desultory, skittering hither and yon, the three relieved of the nonstop seriousness of most workdays. None seemed in a hurry to unmask the Vice Chief's reason for bringing them together.

"Too many of our brothers and sisters in the Building, a lot of them wearing uniforms, lack a fully-developed spinal column," Green opined.

"And balls," Sweet added, "if there's a difference. You don't often see big things accomplished by people who back down without a fight. Patton was fond of the expression *'l'audace, l'audace, toujours l'audace,'* I believe. The longer I live, the stronger my conviction you've gotta show the people you're on the field with that you mean business, that you believe in something, that you will not buckle at the first opposition. More of the military guys are getting conditioned to be more like the civilians in the Building."

Harris fetched the Knob Creek and the Merlot, topped off everyone's glasses. "Good to see you appreciate this stuff. I am, as Ralph knows, a seriously knowledgeable oenophile."

This had been a joke between them for years. Rogers could speak intelligently about winemaking and tasting. No way would Green spend so great a portion of his income on the decent wine collection the DIA Director husbanded, no matter its virtues.

Rogers had been in Green's kitchen one time and noticed a cheap bottle, mostly depleted but recorked, on the counter. "How long you had that open?" Rogers had asked.

"Oh, a little more than a week, I suppose," Green had answered.

"Not smart, man. Not smart at all. Dump it."

When Green had admitted he'd picked it up from a sale counter near a Safeway entrance, they had laughed as if that were madly funny. A number of times since, a mere glance at anyone having a glass of wine evoked a similar reaction.

Green knew wine was a hobby of Rogers, but this recorking episode said it was more than that. In fact, Rogers had taken and passed the Court of Master Sommeliers's introductory exam. A dozen years back, he had confided almost sheepishly his desire to one day complete all four levels of the exam.

Scholarly tomes describe the cultural differences among the American branches of Service. By and large, the differences are real. The Navy resists working with the Army and Air Force. The Air Force enjoys its glitzy image and playboy pilots. Marine aviators, who are trained in night-carrier landings, regard Air Force pilots as weak, incompetent, malingering pussies. The Marine Corps Commandant is happy to be called a jarhead in charge of lead-headed, muscle-plated warriors who will attack any position head-on. Also, the Commandant rests easier at night knowing his budget is least likely to be trimmed. The Army—ah, the Army, the Service with the most personnel, is always bruised and battered and slashed by

Pentagon critics, and the bureaucrat inside the Building is disinclined to defend Army interests.

Green and Rogers had graduated in the same West Point Class and roomed together for three or four months at various points. Each knew the other's strengths and weaknesses and how to fill in the other's blind spots. Green could depend on Rogers to render an honest, unbiased reading on any issue. Neither had been acquainted with Wallace Sweet before the Pentagon.

The topics of discussion whipsawed. The grape and bourbon were having their effects, loosening reins on what might be talked about. There was no apparent connection between lines of thought.

Sweet introduced a story his wife recently told him about the hiring of a man to fill a newly-created position, called Assistant Secretary of Defense for Family Affairs. The wife described him as an 'effete gasbag.' With the superior air of a cocksure prosecuting attorney, he asked the military wives on the committee to state what pro-family initiatives they had undertaken recently. Forget that since the day they joined their husbands in the military, they had spent thousands of hours helping families in their commands, all done voluntarily, without pay. And forget that the Assistant Secretary had no military experience, but walked from the university to earn more than a three-star. New positions like this one were popping up frequently these days; in fact, while the budget for the uniformed Services had been slashed by eight percent in the past five years, the hiring of civilians in DOD had risen by that amount over the same period.

The next hour was light locker-room banter, joking and jostling, talking sports, favorite teams, coaching philosophies. Taking advantage of a natural pause, Rogers summarized, "What can I say about a porterhouse that hasn't been said? That was frigging fabulous."

Dishes done and everything put away, Green added, "Give me a simple meal every time. The old classic: steak, baked potato, and salad. Really, that meal was a ten. There's only so good you can get, and nothing's better. Thanks, guys, for bringing the fixings. Nowhere we could've gone would we have gotten a more satisfying meal, that's for damn sure."

Ever the oenophile, Rogers said, "This Merlot is atrocious, by the way. You tried, and I know you paid what you consider a lot for this, but it's rotgut. I'm switching to Knob Creek, my brothers!"

The shirtsleeve afternoon was inching toward windbreaker evening as the sun began its descent over the horizon.

Pointing in the direction of a thick stand of box hedge at the back end of the property, Green announced, "Let's get to it, guys. Why don't you take a latrine break, and by the time you join me, the firepit'll be in full roar."

Chapter Five

Pack On The Road

He knew he had enemies, but he never cared. From the beginnings of memory, he'd done things his way, he supposed because he had to. He never harbored misgivings about his own value. He felt neither inferior nor superior. Life was what it was. After his father's death at Khe Sanh, Pack and his mother lived in a shotgun apartment in the Harbor City neighborhood of Los Angeles. Their putative income was her meager wage from an aircraft-parts assembly-line job. With no government assistance, they were below the neighborhood median wage. It was as ethnically diverse as any section of LA. Racial tensions among the whites, Latinos, Asians, and blacks fueled frequent taunts and physical attacks. Pack was involved often; if you backed away from a fight, you were a dead man walking. Sometimes on the short end of rumbles, he was nonetheless tough and fearless in fighting back. The older boys left him alone once he reached fourteen or fifteen, at which point he could whip nearly any of them individually.

He was industrious and many weeks earned more at honest jobs than his mother did. He called her Mother. Not Mom, or Mama, or a hypocorism. They were close, but in their peculiar fashion. She did not faithfully attend his sporting events. She volunteered for as much overtime as work would allow, so work usually kept her away. But he did not make any kind of deal about it. What was, was. She was in no way solicitous. The neighborhood dustups, she knew, were inevitable, a fact of life.

There were stretches when fine dining meant either spaghetti topped with margarine or macaroni and cheese. Mother never apologized or soured on life. She kept smiling and expressing gratitude for what they did have. At one meal, she'd said, "Simon, you're not a crapehanger, are you?"

He'd replied, "I don't think so, but it would help if I understood what that means."

"Well," his mother had said, "a crapehanger is a gloomy soul. So saying you're not one means you're not gloomy, not a pessimist, that you generally have a positive outlook."

"I guess that's right," he'd said. "I haven't thought about it."

"We have it pretty good, Simon. At least, I do. I'm happy because I am absolutely certain you're going to be a big success and have all the things you want. All the things we do not have, you will have. Look at you. You're the handsomest boy a mother could ask for, somehow you're smart, and you've not gotten tangled up in alcohol or drugs or girls or any other bad things as far as I know. You don't get good grades just because you're a good ballplayer, do you, son? Are some of the teachers taking care of you?"

"They aren't giving me special treatment, Mother. I think I can promise you that. Most of the teachers haven't heard I play sports. I'm just another student."

He hadn't said so, but this woman was the reason he had done well in life so far. He didn't read maxims for inspiration, he didn't much care for locker-room hurrahs, and he loathed the idea of being tagged a Goody Two-Shoes. What drove him could be expressed in a single thought: *Never embarrass my mother through my actions or inactions*. Her example was speech enough for him. She didn't put boundaries around him, seldom gave him explicit instruction and direction.

He reflected on how he had brought up his daughters. He, like his mother, did not read books on parenting. Not even Spock. He loved his girls and they felt it, but he had no desire to sentimentalize. Sentiment, he observed, had once stood in puddles in American statehouses, in newspapers, and on television screens; those puddles had been turned into lakes. America, it seemed, was on a sustained crying jag. He shunned the prospect of negotiating life in perpetual weep.

Jobs on the docks, from crate-carrying to fishmongering, were plentiful. He turned the bulk of his earnings over to his grateful mother, spending what he kept for himself mainly on chocolate bars. He'd buy Mars in the one-hundred-forty-four-count boxes and hide them in a vent above his room. Nutrition, smishen. He didn't care what they said in health class.

He grew big, blessed with unnatural speed, and could outthink slower-witted opponents in every sport he tried. He took his revenge on playing fields and courts. One scout who saw him swing a baseball bat wrote, "Only Henry Aaron's wrists are better. He is Mr. Line Drive." Every major college-football team recruited him. He won the Southern Cal Relays as a senior in two field events. He was talented enough in basketball to make All-City in the tough L.A. leagues. He was just an athlete.

The *Los Angeles Times* selected him as high school athlete of the year in metro LA. When the writer came to his school to present the award, he asked Pack facetiously, "What is it you eat, son, that gives you the power to compete at such a high level in your sports?"

"Chocolate," he answered sincerely, and turned away.

Now, three-plus decades removed from schoolboy days, he figured he still had enough athlete left in him to surf the rails. Finding a stationary train to board was uncommon these days. So, when Denver Johnny and Memphis Mike demonstrated how to develop a rhythm in moving at speed on the flank of a slow mover, he took to it immediately. The hard part was locating a hide spot once he'd jumped aboard. For a man of his size, finding a space to lie out fully wasn't easy.

I don't know a damn thing. How was it I had two grandfathers who worked for the railroads and close to nothing of their experience got passed to me? Why didn't I ask more questions? Why didn't they volunteer information? Yeah, I can tell you the positions they held, but what did they actually do when they went to work? PawPaw was stationmaster of a small freight stop out in the Valley, and I know he was a qualified telegrapher, but what did he do besides send messages? Papa was a roundhouse foreman, which I guess means he supervised repairs, refits, and replacements on cars and engines, but that could be wrong, because he never explained it to me.

No woman was as beautiful to Papa as a steam engine. When "Tales of Wells Fargo" came on, he would sit up on the edge of the chair to get a close glimpse of that steam engine rounding the bend. *I never got a train set for Christmas, but I've always felt I have a special love for trains. No, if that were true, I would know more about them.* Hell, until these guys pointed it out, Pack wasn't aware that cabooses have been largely replaced by end-of-train signaling devices, or EOTs. He didn't know that a great place to hang out if you can manage it is underneath the power unit of a reefer, a nickname for the refrigeration car. Or that usually there is a covered space between the spine and the standing cargo on a spinecar .

The Mineral State shuttles big loads of its output from hard-to-reach locations on short-haul lines to small hubs to larger regional hubs onward to major national hubs. So the three of them got out of the jungle on the Montana Rail Link down to Missoula, from which the possibilities for travel were limitless. Pack made analogies to the military almost immediately. You gathered intel on schedules, which trains were bound for where, and when they were due into the yard. You remained covered and concealed until the last moment. You struck when the enemy's energy was lowest or when his attention was engaged elsewhere. It was an elaborate game of cat-and-mouse. At least, this was how Memphis Mike and Denver Johnny played it, and how Pack would when on his own. This was the old-school way. Some of the hobohemians had in their possession printed schedules that were supposed to be proprietary to the company itself. And they had smartphones from which they scraped useful weather and map data. Theirs was the new-school method, and it made the process of train-hopping, all things considered, more predictable. Whatever your sources, your information was frequently unreliable. *Right there is another similarity to the military*, Pack thought. Then the final, crucial likeness to combat operations: You had to be on alert at all times, but you could experience several days of boredom, with nothing going your way.

The Yermo jungle was as far as imaginable from the Montana encampment. Open spaces, significant military traffic to and from the National Training Center at Fort Irwin and the Marine camp at Twenty-Nine Palms, few areas from which to avoid the bulls. This was the California High Desert, and this time of year, the wind howled perpetually and temps could fluctuate fifty degrees from day to night. This was the High Desert, all right, in more than geography. A quick scan made Pack conclude this was meth-head heaven. Regardless of who the property owner was, why was no entity taking measures to clean this place up? Not many here with high interest in labor and brow sweat.

Memphis Mike said, "Yeah, it looks bad. It is. This isn't Montana. Most of the criminal element practicing this way of life don't have the constitution for going so far off the beaten path as Montana. Gotta look after your possessions, and yourself, real close down here. There's some bad people in this yard."

Denver Johnny went on to explain lots of dirty deals went down in the Yermo yard. Rapes, murders, big-time gambling, all in addition to the drug-dealing. It was remote and had little policing, so it was a natural haven for bad seeds. A few of his acquaintances even claimed there were Islamic-radical sleeper cells that had employed this place as a staging area, but there had been no confirmation of which he was aware.

"Still," Memphis Mike continued, "I have one good memory of this place. Had to be twenty-five years ago. Jumped off a tanker a quarter-mile up the way. An army of bulls spotted me, so I ran like hell. Third track over, two cars were a second away from coupling. I'd seen a 'bo cut in half trying that but went for it, anyway. Let the train block that first wave of bulls is what I was tryin' for. Raced between them couplin' cars a split second before they clanked together. I knowed they had radios, so I had to git the hell away from the yard completely before they caught me. They'd be more of 'em soon. So I made it far as that road over yonder, when I seen a railroad worker in uniform was driving down the company road, on the way out. Motioned for me to hop in, and for some damn reason, I did. Casual as anything, he said if I'm gonna catch another hauler, a good place to set up camp is over there. He pointed out a spot and drove me to a Burger King in town where I could get a cup of coffee. That night, I put up a lean-to in the spot he'd pointed to. When I got up in the morning, there sat a cigar box. Inside were two items: fifty dollars in bills and a Bible. A note in the Bible said, 'God bless you, son. Have a beer on me.' I'll never know, but I'm pretty sure the box come from the guy who saved my ass when he happened to pass by at just the perfect moment."

Pack nodded approval of the report of good fortune. "Where's the Home Depot from here, Memphis?"

"Why, you thinking about stayin' in this pisshole awhile?"

"If you call a few days a while. Gotta put some jack back in my pocket."

"Whatever, man. Nearest one is over in Barstow, fifteen miles west on I-15. Prob'ly have to hitch a ride, but there's lots of highway traffic."

◆ ◆ ◆

The next morning at the day-labor pickup point, the first hirer on scene motioned for Pack to get on the pickup. "You OK with sod layin'?" the portly fellow asked Pack specifically and the hopeful workers generally. Collective nods of assent. "Nine-fifty an hour, eight-hour days. Do good, and I'll put my head behind a more permanent position."

No one moved. The next man selected was a large, dark-skinned man a few years Pack's senior. Pack had seen him over at Yermo and noticed this man commanded respect. The black man thrust a hand at Pack and said, "I present myself as Hard Travelin', sir. Honored indeed to share your company. I espied you in the yard with Denver John and Memphis Mike, I believe it was." So he was acquainted with DJ and Memphis? It would take more than this introduction for Pack to be persuaded that this man's clipped, precise language was not an act. A regular James Earl Jones on the hobo circuit? A man in love with the rumble of his voice and timbre of his laughter?

Pack said, "I'm given the name Mount Montana. And the same excellent greetings to you, Hard Travelin', or would you prefer Mr. Travelin'?"

It took a moment for Hard Travelin' to decide he wasn't being mocked.

Talking on the job wasn't practical. They worked discrete parcels too far apart. The most efficient sod laying was on display for all to see. If you weren't up to the physical demand, it would be evident by lunch break, and you weren't likely to be invited to finish the day. Reports of inadequacy would have been called in to the hirer, and he would have arrived with replacements drawn from the normal day-labor hubs.

On the return ride to Home Depot that afternoon, Hard Travelin' inquired about Pack's 'bo companions. "Haven't known them for long. I trust them, and they've been generous, is what I can say."

"And you, Mount Montana, have just succinctly delivered a ringing endorsement of these fellows. If they are as industrious and reticent as you, I would enjoy their acquaintance. Might you have space for me at your temporary residence?"

Pack answered, "It's not my space, and it's not their space, but you'd be welcome to try out our company. I'm sure you'll find us plenty uninteresting."

"I'll join you with comestibles purchased somewhere along the return line. And let me set the minds of you and your friends at ease. I must vouch for myself. I have led this life for too long, and soon I shan't be able to continue. When you haven't attended to your health since your salad days, it dawns that you'll soon be on the Westbound."

HT, as Pack already was thinking of the man, leaned farther back and inhaled deeply, as if thinking of something rich. "Sometimes we just startle ourselves with the lovely things we say. For instance, Montana, I just called to mind beautiful twin images quite unintentionally. Beautiful, I intend to say, in their own right, because *they* are, having nothing to do with my saying it. It dawned on me, I said. The idea slowly and magnificently materialized as the sun deliberately and marvelously materializes from the eastern sky. Then I believe I said"—he smiled contentedly—"I shall anon take the Westbound. I swear to you, sir, the sweetest words in the hobo language to me concern the image of the Westbound. The interpretation I choose relates to our crossing over into the eternal spaces and embraces of God as we follow the sun out of view on its quotidian course."

Who would have expected a man of the rails to speak in such unusual fashion? Pack thought.

Still, he didn't warm to this fella. *Who's he trying to impress? Why the baroque speech? Character seems fine, though. He appears experienced on the roads, and he's amiable.* The most important reason to cooperate with HT was because even at his age, he'd put in a grown man's day's work. Pack had laid about 40 percent more sod than everyone else but Hard Travelin', who was behind him by roughly 20 percent. *Let's see what happens tonight. Can't keep HT out of our camp, and don't want to, but I'd have appreciated time to make Memphis Mike and Denver Johnny aware we're about to have a chow guest.*

You'd think the genuine hobo's powers of adaptation would rank near the acme on the human scale, but he actually is strongly bound to routines, like dogs, cats, and old people. Was Hard Travelin' an exception to the rule?

♦ ♦ ♦

Travel companions Denver and Memphis said they were OK with a new camper, but they were blah in acceding, like something was on their mind they weren't sharing. After describing Hard Travelin' to DJ and MM, Pack sensed from a moment's hesitation that they were vaguely familiar with HT, likely had seen him on the circuit. He also sensed they wanted to say no, but since it was settled, they agreed.

Pack announced he was assuming fire duty. He had about an hour to scour their surrounds for the materials required for the night. He reached into his backpack and withdrew a poncho liner he'd use as a transporter. Then he pulled out his military-style poncho and neatly placed on it the full contents of his bush kit: paracord, cut into varying lengths; poncho liner; a Leatherman multi-tool; water-purification tabs; small first-aid pack; flashlight; hand-warmers; lighter; matches; flint fire-starter; two canteens with one cup; small hygiene kit; bug juice; compass; an Altoid tin with cotton flats dipped in Vaseline and large pin duct-taped to the inside cover; and a Kindle loaded with books, his concession to comfort and modernity. He knew before setting out he had to recharge the Kindle only once every three to four weeks, and there were always places not far from rail yards where he could attend to that. At the moment he was rereading *The Vicar of Christ.*

The sky out here is a delight, especially this time of late afternoon, Pack mused. Slashed with the lightest of touches of pastels, blues, and reds, the sky looked as if the Maker engaged in afternoon watercolors. The never-ceasing, biting night winds gave it a menacing feel. But one plus in this wild country was you seldom had to worry about covering the fire pits because rains blew through so rarely. It was a land of shimmering beauty, natural home to scorpions and rattlers and coyotes, so why was it a meth-head mecca? First guess was, there just weren't enough lawmen to cover all this territory.

The little campfire had built a nice base of embers by the time Hard Travelin' arrived. With his small kit strapped to his back, he cradled two grocery sacks in his arms.

Before Hard Travelin' could introduce himself, Pack took charge. "Hard Travelin', meet my friends Denver Johnny and Memphis Mike." He showed all three his "I'm playin'" face and added, "They don't have brains, and they don't have brawn, but they're good people."

At that, Hard Travelin' emitted one of his baritone laughs. "If that's the case, we'll get along fine."

Johnny and Mike appeared to loosen up and took the bags from HT.

"What the hell, you know we ain't got refrigeration, Travelin', you expect we can consume all this tonight? This musta took your full day's wage, maybe more."

"I do indeed, gentlemen, expect we shall enjoy this, the product of a single day's labor. Would anyone object to a bowing of heads in giving thanks?"

So, without objection, Mister Hard Travelin' spoke: "Maker of these good men, and every living thing, and every thing that is, let us acknowledge Thy blessings in every detail of their richness. Amen."

HT's method of cooking was to cut up the meat, potatoes, carrots, onions, and mushrooms and wrap each in aluminum foil, which he then situated directly atop the embers. No hobo stew tonight.

With voracious appetites, the men polished off every morsel of main course. Then Hard Travelin' unveiled the grand finale. "This watermelon's not large, gentlemen, out of consideration for our bladders, certainly for my own. A large slice of watermelon would have me urinating the night long."

"So this is your way of tellin' us it's true what they say about black people and watermelons?" Denver Johnny said. He wasn't smiling.

"No, sir, I am afraid that was not my intention. I was perfectly aware, however, you were likely to assume that was my intention. My point was that this little act might help us deconstruct a stereotype right away, and that doing so might encourage us to forget about stereotyping from this moment onward. God placed us all on this big blue ball, and commands us to enjoy its fruits. Watermelon and fried chicken weren't created just for black people, as shrimp and steak weren't created just for white people. I bear no ill will and attach no prejudgments to men of any color."

Memphis Mike spoke: "Point taken. But you didn't need to sermonize me, sir. I ain't held no grudges against the many blacks I've saw in my travels. I coulda been insulted, you see, by the words you just chose. But I ain't. I think you done right by yourself outta the gate. Also, thanks for the great grub. It'll be a long time before I eat another meal good as that one."

"Good, preliminaries are concluded, introductions properly made," allowed Hard Travelin'.

Pack said, "Hard Travelin', can I ask your given name? No racial profiling, just curiosity. Just want to know how far off base I am."

Another chuckle from HT. "You really are new to the life, aren't you, Mount Montana? Don't you know an unspoken but fully understood rule of the Road is we go only by our *nom de hobo*? But this is your lucky day, for I carry little respect for most of our unspoken rules. Before I disclose the facts, what were your guesses?"

"You are from the Deep South, maybe Mississippi or Alabama, and your name is along the lines of Thanopheles."

"Well, Montana, I give you more than half credit. I do indeed hail from Mississippi, Pascagoula that would be, but you are a galaxy or two off with respect to my given name, which is Paul. I don't mind continuing, but I will prefer you gentlemen have the say on that."

Quick glances exchanged, the other three muttered, "Oh, yeah, we'd like to hear your story."

Memphis Mike added, "Stories is part of hoboin', as you know, Hard Travelin'. We want to hear."

"All right, then. My daddy had a small church. I don't know where he got the idea he could call himself 'pastor,' but he did. Had he delved into the Good Book, and cherished what he found there, well…let's just say his nominating himself pastor would have been less objectionable. About the period I went to high school, I had learned on my own enough about the Bible to understand it was not the source of his teaching. He simply strung words together, made things up out of whole cloth. He loved to watch the televangelist frauds like Robert Tilton, Jim Bakker, Ernest Angley, and the others just to learn techniques for opening wallets. I do admit to finding them entertaining myself. They were Elmer Gantrys gone wild.

"The authentic Christian minister possesses faith thick as the crust of the earth. Those scam artists I mentioned were as dust scooting across the surface. My father presented a face of piety to his tiny but loyal flock, quite a different one to my mother, my brothers, and me. He beat us with his fists, cursed us, demeaned us. I did not fight back. None of us incited him. He was a devil-infected man. One day, he inflicted a notably awful beating on my mother. She couldn't walk without gnawing pain for months. I made a plan. I would not execute it till my mother recovered sufficiently. I confided to a brother the specifics, such as they were. In pertinent part, the specifics entailed my sending the family money once I left.

"We drew all our water needs from a cistern. It was deep. On occasion, a problem arose with the functioning of the cistern, during which times we deployed a footstool to peer into the abyss, as it were. To shorten this story segment, I must say once I had coaxed my daddy onto the footstool, I pushed him into that cold, dark abyss. Before he could react, his chin struck the lip of the well most violently, and into it he plunged. I picked up my prepacked belongings and embarked upon my present life, with several stops of some duration along the way.

"As to the name Paul: Whoever might have been responsible for stamping upon me that fine name gave me a grand figure to emulate. Is he the best human in the Bible? He was certainly the most-important man in the early days of Christianity. In his younger days, vices ate through him. He did bad things. Then, on that famous road, he began to turn around, and with himself, the face of Christendom. As an apostle, he was chained, beaten, shipwrecked, and mocked, but never forsook his Christ. He told his acolytes they needed to be above reproach, not open to debauchery, not quick-tempered or violent, self-controlled, upright, and disciplined, not empty talkers. I am totally aware there are some who believe Paul distorted the teachings of Christ, but I am not in their corner."

Pack could read people expertly. He couldn't say exactly what was true and what was false in Hard Travelin's story, but he was certain the untruths were enough to incite wariness on his part.

HT is hard, as his name signifies, Pack thought. *It could be he fit in well at Yermo.*

"That's a good story," Memphis Mike commented, "but hobo camp stories're all lies, ain't they? A hobo by nature don't want no one knowin' who he is. If you'd a killed yer daddy, why wouldn't I believe the law woulda caught up with you a long time ago? You ain't exactly indivisible."

"You're right, Mike." Hard Travelin' let out a long exhale, tiring from the effort of speechifying. In the glow of the fire, his features were clear, seeming to say, "'I'm going real now, dropping all the pretense, all facades of learning and manners."

"Thing of it is, if you was runnin' the law, way back long ago, would you spend the time and money to find a young black who murdered another sorry black whose own wife and child would testify he beat 'em? Wasn't no Sherlock needed to know it was me who done it. But know what?" In the snap of a finger, HT reverted to his other self, the pretentious one, bellowing laughter, sending shock waves through the nippy night air. "Of course, Mr. Mike is correct. In hobo land we tell stories, we fabricate, we concoct, we *act*. We can be who we want to be. We *buuuulshiiit* people we meet 'cause we're born *bullshitters.* The entire Earth is our stage. The audience is seldom the same from day to day. It is also accurate to state that we, gentlemen, are no-things, nonentities, null sets. You don't like that? Well, who's going to mourn your loss if you're gone before this Earth's next belly roll? A handful of hobos?" HT leaned back on his elbows.

After a time, Denver Johnny said, "That last part, about us bein' actors and bullshitters, I'll agree with you. Maybe you thought you were roilin' me, but no, you said the truth in that respeck. But on the same token, I hope you ain't sayin' we're worthless. It's just we don't want no one to get a good bead on us, to know personal details of our lives. We're out here because we don't want to be in no town. No good hobo cares a damn what anyone thinks about *what* he is, but the good hobo cares what *everyone* else thinks about *who* he is.

"Maybe I didn't take your true meaning, HT, but I'm feelin' uneasy here," Johnny went on. "This adult-long journey started out romantic for me, and it still is. My memories will give me a good death, irregardlest of who's at my passin'. That's just a fact. I ain't trying to kid no one. Right now, I could fall onto my back, shut my eyes, and lull myself to sleep with memories of my train trundling down the rails, me looking out on the

Sierras, the Mojave, The Modoc Plateau, the Bitterroots, the Black Rock Desert, the Cascades, the Rockies, and I could go on. I think I've got some worth 'cause of *what* I value. I suppose to some folks the amber waves of grain is corny, too, but by God, I was raised in this great natural cathedral that's America, and it's under the Stars 'n' Stripes I intend to rest. Just 'cause we're BSers, and just because my expiration won't make the news, don't go to question this wanderin' way of life. I'm a 'bo, nothin' to be ashamed of there. I have no shame in tellin' you I finished five grades of school.

"I don't take no pride in sayin' it, and dammit all to hell, I'm sorry this conversation has got under my skin so much. I've blurted out too much a my own bizness. I guess I am riled up, irregardlest of what I said before. You know, HT, I'm thinkin' the Road ain't the only place people pretend to be what they ain't. I'll admit to no recent experience in towns, but what I have saw is about ever'one there's actin' to one extent or another. I would dare to say mosta the people in this nation's workin' to throw off impressions about theyselves that're false. I'm sayin' my ignorant self thinks they's two kinds of phonies: the ones who want to deceive in a little way by protecting their personal information, and the kind who wants ever'one to think they're more than they are. I think you know which side I'll take ever' time. My opinion, hobos do not have a corner on any market in the areas of virtues and vices."

"Very well said, Denver Johnny. Your rebuttal carries the day. I tried to be argumentative, and I succeeded. And you, Mount Montana, anything about yourself you feel like opening up about?" Hard Travelin' prodded.

"Didn't know this was a shrink's office," Pack said. "What I've liked about this life is, you keep your eye on the acts, not so much on the words. I'm sure I could travel happily with a man five years and be content not to know his real name if he didn't want to share it. Long as I know he'd back me up in a fight, because he would understand I don't violate the code.

"If I were you, Hard Travelin', and listened to what I said about acts and words, I might think, *He shot those words right at my gut*. Let's be honest. You seem enamored of your own tones, and you make sentences that sound stylish. But me, I don't care about your eloquence. What I care about, to say so once more, is the sod I saw you lay today. You care about the value of labor. And you expended most of the fruit of that labor on three men you'd barely seen. So, there you go, that's what I have to say for myself."

Any misgivings Pack had about this impressive HT, he decided to keep them to himself for now.

Pack's was the final word. They sank into their separate worlds and drifted into the night spheres, and the fire went dead.

♦ ♦ ♦

He caught the scent of singed flesh and scorched vegetation. In the near distance were slain enemy soldiers by the scores. He could hear the roaring and croaking and hissing of feral life in motion, as if the animal kingdom had just drunk its first cup of Folgers. Water streamed somewhere nearby. He lay on his back, feeling nothing but the rays of a midafternoon sun. His eyes were gluey, but he opened them with mighty effort.

Approaching him was a black man clad as a comic-book Satan, a Grim Reaper come to reap. He sensed before he saw dressings applied, an IV inserted, canteen placed to his lips. The man was not a Satan but an American Master Sergeant Angel of Mercy. A stink of debridement, then back to darkness. The carcasses of soldiers' corpses had mostly vanished, picked over by tigers. He wanted to shoot them, but his body, no part of it, would obey any instruction. A greedy tiger, fierce and merciless, malice in its eyes, paced with mathematical precision to the spot where he lay. The animal began to eat him in square-inch patches. He watched silently and painlessly as his body ever-so-glacially lost its form.

He struggled to wake up. In his hypnopompic state, he asked himself, "Where was it I built my cabin? Was it Two Dot?" That's where his wife had wanted to set up house. No, that was their joke till one day, to convince themselves the town existed, they drove there and almost simultaneously said, "If we ever move again, let's go to Two Dot."

Why can't I focus? I shouldn't have let her out on the roads after the first big snowfall, with the roads looking different from the day before. Back then, the bend was sharp and clear. With the snow, it all looked the same.

Chapter Six

Gotterdammerung

Rogers and Sweet could be forgiven for assuming that Green's get-together involved a list. Published lists are attention magnets for officers and noncommissioned officers. They tell all your peers whether you were selected for an NCO Academy; a First Sergeant's Course; Command and General Staff College; a War College; advanced civil schooling; and most important, whether you were promoted in rank. In some cases, if your name failed to appear on certain lists at certain points in your career, you were subject to dismissal from your service. It's the military's method of saying, "Peter Principle time for you, pal." More and more troops in this military were receiving Reduction-in-Force (RIF) notices, or pink slips. No explanation, just good-bye.

Green would dispel the list idea immediately.

♦ ♦ ♦

They were back from the latrine, and Harris had the fire going, taking the chill off the night air. *This is nice*, each thought as he thrust his feet to within a foot of the fire. The Knob Creek bottle wasn't empty, but Green had an unopened one alongside it should the first be drained. Heavy glasses in hand, they sat soberly around the leaping flames, comfortable but wary, two sets of eyes drawn to the fire and the third almost ready to commence an explanation involving the second satori.

It was Green's time: "First, gentlemen, I have to tell you this has nothing to do directly with either of you. Obviously, the topic's important to me. It's not the kind of thing you can strike up a casual conversation about in the Building. Maybe I have allowed this single idea to germinate in my head to a point I'm irrational about it. I'm depending on you to be the voices of reason. Just follow along, and give me your candid appraisal.

"You guys know I'm a locker-room type of fellow. Grew up opposite-talking, joking around with buddies. Pretty consistently seeing goodness in everyone, smiling inside, doing my best to help others reach their potential, maximize their talents. A few times, life has been ugly, but to me, still noble. Not much nobility has been on display in this great nation lately, and I have been somber and brooding for a damn long stretch.

"I've had weighty thoughts, and I'm sure I'm not alone. Tell me if I've gotten them wrong. So here goes, fellas. What the hell is happening to this country? I can't find a soul in this administration who acts like he loves this God-blessed Republic. And God did bless it. He bestowed upon us wise men at the Founding. Their vision was awesomely comprehensive, and they were endowed with brilliance in the Declaration, the Bill of Rights, and the Constitution. Their successors made mistakes along the way, but our system, with its checks and balances and two-party governance, has generally worked to overcome those failings. America has been a force for good. We have kept the peace, responded to thousands of cries for help, and we have infused capital in foreign lands where there was none. Modern Japan got back on its feet in part by adopting a constitution written by Douglas MacArthur. The Marshall Plan may be the greatest diplomatic achievement of the twentieth century.

"So here I find myself, gentlemen, outdoors, literally, because I cannot know with total assurance that my residence is not being electronically monitored. I'm afraid this is where I am, a man with waning confidence in the political process that controls our national life today.

"President Rozan has done a wonderful job training the voters. It is the frog in the boiling-water thing. Most no longer notice when he acts either unconstitutionally or extraconstitutionally. When we have a President who acts on his own and decides which laws he will or will not enforce, we are no longer a free people but a tyrannized people.

"Let me hit the nub of the matter: We can recite our oath of office by heart. I want to say it slowly: 'I, Harris Green, having been appointed an officer in the Army of the United States, as indicated above in the grade of General, do solemnly swear that I will support and defend the Constitution of the United States against all enemies, foreign and domestic; that I will bear true faith and allegiance to the same; that I take this obligation freely, without any mental reservations or purpose of evasion; and that I will well and faithfully discharge the duties of the office upon which I am about to enter.' We swore we would defend the *Constitution,* not the President, against all enemies foreign and *domestic.* We swore to uphold not the Democrat party, not the Republican party, not anything but the Constitution. Some professors justify the President's unilateralism on the grounds that the Constitution is, or should be, elastic. The fact is, some interpretations of it have changed, but the document itself has not changed. There may even be a General who agrees with the standard academic position.

"I believe we do have to ask ourselves if we believe in the oath we took—or not. Do we?"

Heads bobbed affirmatively.

Rogers spoke softly, deliberately. "You must have a point, Chief."

"I do," Harris said, "but bear with me just a bit longer."

Nods again.

"The Army in particular has been shat upon. Every now and then, the President shows up at a public event to mouth the right words about the military, but that's to camouflage the real damage he's inflicting. Subsidies to Commissaries, upon which many soldiers rely, are being reduced drastically. Lower enlisted soldiers, some of whom are earning minimum wage and some not even, were getting by in a lot of cases because of small price breaks at the Commissary. That single cut turned some of our people, literally, onto the welfare rolls. That chaps me, and it saddens me.

"The Veteran's Administration is rotted through with scandal and is looting taxpayers. Lousy administrators get rich, good doctors and nurses aren't rewarded, and veterans in need either aren't tended to at all or aren't tended to seriously. VA problems are public, but the Administration has no interest.

"The civilian workforce rises, as soldiers, sailors, and Marines, but chiefly soldiers, are handed their pink slips. The civil guys are unionized; the military isn't. Politicians can work with unions, set up a quid pro quo arrangement that usually translates to campaign contributions for the pol in exchange for political support for the union."

Green stood, walked to the woodpile, and retrieved another chunk, placing it gingerly atop the crumbling embers. Rogers and Sweet stood, stretched, and walked into cooler air for a minute or two.

"OK, boss, we're with you. No disagreement so far," Rogers said.

Green went on with his airing of things deeply eating away at him: "Another thing I feel crappy about is seeing myself stand around with other four-stars and proceed blithely on our way while we're placing more and more burdens on platoon leaders and company commanders. When we were in their positions, when we saw training weaknesses, we could insert training, schedule time to work on them. We had some control over the training schedule. As I saw it, the unit I commanded was a learning lab. I could exercise initiative, and just as important, I could train subordinate leaders to do the same.

"Now, if you look closely, you'll see we're developing automatons, check-the-box people. Don't ask questions, lieutenants and captains, just meet the mandatory training requirements, which now consume nearly all their time. And just as entitlement programs have overwhelmed the federal budget, so have sensitivity sessions encroached on the commanders' time. For purposes of this discussion, my thoughts about the subjects of those sessions are absolutely irrelevant. The only point relevant to me is whether we're developing good *soldiers* and good *units.* We need real field training, not classroom sensitivity sessions. What is first and last is being a soldier. I don't care about your inner preferences. Every consideration other than building a supreme fighting force is secondary to me."

"You're right, Harris," Sweet said, head fittingly adroop, "and you're making me feel spineless for failing to protect the interests of our young officers and NCOs. I'll paraphrase your more general question: What the hell have we allowed to happen to our military, which of course includes my Marine Corps?"

Green continued: "Well, I guess that's good, Wallace. At least I appreciate that you admit the errors we've made and still are doing. The WW II Memorial closed on Memorial Day, so that later in the day, the President could speak there. A high percentage of visitors that day were World War II vets who might not have gotten another chance to see it. *Thwap*, slap, right in the mouth."

Green kicked back and took up his glass as Rogers gave the time-out signal to reset the dying embers. He stirred them around and carefully situated three more chunks of wood lifted from the nearby cordage.

"Thanks, Ralph," Green started anew. "That feels a lot better. It's chillier than I thought...here, as well as in the country. As I was saying, the President issues an executive order permitting—no, inviting—illegal aliens to join the US military when just weeks earlier, he ordered a Reduction-in-Force of thirty thousand current soldiers. Some of those RIF notices were handed out on actual battlefields. How can we be accomplices to such treatment of the men we serve? And the damn shame is, I hold no personal grudge against any President. This isn't a political box I want to be pushed into.

"And our Navy is perilously close to being unable to hold the strategic chokepoints around the world. We now have a fleet of a mere two hundred eighty-three ships, down from three hundred thirty-seven in 1999. When I was in the War College, we were headed toward a six-hundred-ship Navy.

"And do not imagine I resist civilian control. I believe in it, and support it fervently. But again, what about the oath? In my mind, we violate it by not opposing the violation.

"They have taken a hacksaw to the Army budget. That's saving by hacking, in this case. It is heart surgery by a sadist. At the same time, it's uprooting ten thousand troops from here to there without strategic direction. Ask anyone at 1600 Pennsylvania to identify the enemy center of gravity or do a two-sided combat power analysis, and not only will he not have a clue what you asked, but he'll give you the evil eye for your impertinence. And let's not confine that specific criticism to the White House. We can say the same about some key decision-makers right there in the Building.

"There was mere passing acknowledgment of the Fort Hood murders, and then to term it 'workplace violence.' And the perpetrator is handled with a soft touch as he renounces American citizenship in favor of Islamic State 'citizenship.' Private Ladenfels abandons his combat outpost and the National Security Advisor immediately alerts the nation that he has performed honorably.

"Four thousand soldiers are dispatched to West Africa to fight Ebola, and fifteen hundred to fight the Islamic State in Iraq and Syria. On the other hand, this White House has worked hard to perfect the use of soldiers as speech props. We live in a world in which the military is either an object of scorn and pity or manipulated for political profit.

"If the time comes that my forecast is proved accurate, you must decide for yourselves what course you will follow, but I ask you to consider following me. I will not participate in the willful violation of my oath. I will have only one option—principled resignation. That is asking a great deal, I am aware.

"I have known each of you for years. You have character and grit. You're smart. By now, I ought to say what I'm asking of you. Two things: What I would term passive support and appraisal of my thinking. I give my word: I will not disclose your names in connection with the plan once you walk out my front door.

"I have a couple of A-one sources in the White House. Their politics aren't mine, but in addition to having access, they're pretty good people. They don't work with one another day-to-day. Just meetings cause them to intersect now and again. One has a nephew in his third year at West Point.

"Remember the much-anticipated national security speech the President delivered at West Point some months back? Editorial rooms across the spectrum gave it low grades. *The Washington Post, New York*

Times, and *Wall Street Journal* agreed it was uninspiring and ludicrous. Others called it icy. Administration aides said the talk was intended to appeal to a nation weary of war. The President told cadets military action cannot be the only—or even primary—component of US leadership.

"In lesser-remarked-upon sections, he spoke, as he has before, about pursuing multilateral solutions for most problems, meaning we abandon our lead position as a stabilizer in this international system. As Kissinger writes"—Green drew a three-by-five-inch card from a breast pocket—"'The attainment of peace is not as easy as the desire for it. Those ages which in retrospect seem most peaceful were least in search of peace. Those whose quest for it seems unending appear least able to achieve tranquility. Whenever peace—conceived as the avoidance of war—has been the primary objective...the international system has been at the mercy of [its] most ruthless member.' But in that speech, the President also raised other points of interest, talking about creating counterterrorism partnership funds coming overwhelmingly from us. Global warming, he claimed to cadets, is and will be, 'the defining problem of our time.'

"Finally, in this line of argument," Green said, "the President described the great national security challenge of negotiating among nations a vague code of conduct. Could it be the mission of the United States Military Academy should shift to negotiating an international code of conduct, and similar endeavors? Sounds ridiculous, but the words *security Academy* have been employed, my sources say."

"Damn!" Sweet yawped. "Let this be proof I was paying close attention, Harris. I let my feet get too close to the fire and burned hell out of them! You, Rogers, owe me for the pair of shoes you've just ruined! Take it easy with that fire, will you?"

The soles were charred, the rubber in fact bubbly and blackened. He removed his shoes and set them back away into the cool air. "OK, boss, no harm done, we're ready for the rest of the story," Sweet said.

Green again took no offense and restarted. "These White House sources report that before leaving office, the President will issue an executive order declaring a change to West Point's orientation and curricula. I think even Texas A&M, for instance, should not be pleased about that. Forget that I know West Point well. It is a vital integument of our society. The degree of discipline and all-round talent required to succeed there are models for America at large. Now is not the time, however, to be sidetracked with a defense of West Point. We have here another case of suffocating a traditional American institution in an extraconstitutional maneuver, and this institution happens to be military and to have contributed in substantial ways to our national life."

"So do you actually think," Rogers interjected, "the President would actually do this? Attempt to overturn a West Point that Presidents Washington and Jefferson imagined and established?"

"Can we take the chance?" Green countered. "One of the outcomes of the aforementioned speech was the President's deepening dislike of the Academy. Who were these insolent, insubordinate cadets who gave him the most anemic of receptions? At the high schools and junior colleges, they cheered and wolf-whistled their admiration and agreement. The latter dug his program, but the cadets' volume setting was a tick above mute. You could see him reaching a boil. Step one was to issue instructions to carve up the Superintendent, the person responsible for what was from all angles a Presidential debacle. Turns out that's a good thing; getting dirt on this Supe was child's play. Lots of us surmised he ought never have been nominated for the job. We have an Inspector General's report that we—of those here, I mean I—should have acted on several months ago. The second outcome was obvious: Destroy the Academy itself, but in distinctly cruel style. In essence, make it a memorial to this President himself, and incinerate its previous history. New mission infused by new ideology.

"I have a plan. I haven't spoken the word *coup*. We've never had to go through one, thank God. Our military, to my knowledge, has never entertained the idea, and I pray to the Almighty we never do. Let me be emphatic about that: I am *not* thinking of a coup. I believe my plan stands a chance of rescuing us, preventing us from further violations of our oath.

Good moment to pause, let me catch up to you on the KC. Feedback, anyone?"

Ralph Rogers spoke up. "I accept your facts and premises in full. You might've been joking about Texas A&M, but I suspect you won't find one Aggie petty enough to regard the re-missioning of USMA as zero-sum. Another election like the last one, and Texas A&M would follow West Point down the same road."

"I've known you at least half my life," Wallace Sweet said to Green, "so you have my unconditional support from the get-go. Tell us what you want us to do."

"OK," Green said. "to your question. The present Supe will get the hell off West Point grounds in about two months, more or less in disgrace. He will be reduced in grade and has had to repay some soldiers of lower rank he took advantage of. I know the idea of calling upon enlisted personnel to perform personal-service projects is repugnant to me. As is a male enlisted soldier who works directly for you found with videos of female cadets in their barracks showers. Inspector General investigation results are close-hold, but I can at least tell you most of the rumors have strong basis in fact. At this point, I don't give a crap about the ignominy he rightly will endure. What I very much care about—and this is where you come in—is who replaces him."

Annapolis grad Sweet asked, "Your Supe's position is now three-star, right?"

"The Superintendent's slot today is a permanent three-star billet," Green replied. "In my day, it was two-star, typically filled by a Division Commander on the rise, people like Westmoreland, Maxwell Taylor, and Eichelberger. Most of the recent appointees have not been warfighters but guys with PhDs who've been in what true warfighters consider less-stressful positions. That's a questionable assertion, granted, but that's how the warfighter looks at it. Today, it's also a mandatory-retirement position; the appointee certifies in writing before taking the job that he will be retired at the end of the tour. The Pentagon civilians thought they were removing politics from the equation, when indeed they may have significantly neutered the Supe by making him a lame duck.

"But not all lame ducks are equal. In the late 1970s, a cadre in DC believed USMA was being ill-led and needed new blood. They pleaded with Andrew Goodpaster to come out of retirement. Goodpaster was known not just in the military, but throughout the government. He had once served as a highly trusted advisor and confidante to President Eisenhower. Department of State solicited his input on foreign policy before going public. General Goodpaster's last duty was as Supreme Allied Commander Europe. Above all, Andrew Goodpaster was a stolid, serious soldier-statesman of unquestioned rectitude. To pick a fight with Andy Goodpaster, you had to be daft.

"In the same sense, I want somebody today who, if you pick a fight with him (a) will fight back and (b) create news in the process."

"Right, right, good point. Who is it?" Sweet asked.

"I'm getting there," Green answered. "But background's important to my case, so let me finish. You are the two people in the Building that my boss, General Wayne Pembrook, trusts most. I know from seeing the man daily. He's going to want to know your opinion on this."

Looking directly at Sweet, Green said, "The Army Chief of Staff is unusual in that he loves the Marine Corps. He really does. I've been in senior-officer schools where they virtually mocked the USMC for not being as doctrinally sophisticated as the Army. You've heard the line: Marines attack frontally, suffer heavy casualties, get great credit. Given the same mission, the Army would have attacked on multiple axes, indirectly, and suffered many fewer casualties. The Army trains smarter, they like to say. I actually think there's more than a grain of truth in that. But we love Marines because you guys breed them to fight; you infuse them with real toughness and loyalty to one another. If the Army claims it's not jealous of Semper Fi, it's lying. Pembrook knows Marines have an advantage in being less than half the personnel end strength of the Army, but still, if he could redo the Army, he would create it in the image of the Marine Corps.

"He had a West Point classmate who did what you did, Wallace, in taking his commission in the Marine Corps after graduation. As you know, if your father or brother served in another Service, you could apply to follow them. Most of the time, the Army agrees, probably because these cases are rare.

"That Pembrook classmate was Simon Pack. His father was killed in the Siege of Khe Sanh in 1968. Pembrook can testify with firsthand knowledge about his deepest admiration for General Pack and about Simon Pack's profound love and admiration for his Marine father. OK, fast forward to the 1980s and 1990s. The Pentagon and Service schools and War Colleges were consumed with the concept of jointness. We discovered in numerous hostile actions how poorly prepared we were to act jointly. The Services in general wanted to fight alongside each other, but discovered—shouldn't have been surprising, but it was—that when push came to shove, they couldn't speak the same language. Doctrine wasn't mirror-image, acronyms differed, equipment capabilities differed, understanding of unit terminologies and capabilities wasn't shared. Then, we discovered gross lack of interoperability among actual communications devices. I know better than almost anyone that this is not a simple problem to solve. We've made progress in aligning doctrine, yes, but regrettably, each Service has been slow to cede control in any area. The progress toward comprehensive jointness and interoperability is, in a word, underwhelming. If we can get Pack in position to clean up his alma mater, we present all Services with a powerful symbol of jointness."

Rogers said, "He was a two-star when he left the Marines, right? What happened?"

Sweet said, "I can answer that. He was a two-star, yes, but he was on the three-star list when he 'Pack-ed' it in. He indeed will have to be promoted before taking the West Point job. I remember the talk, and for a while, the entire Corps was discussing it. Pack had had it with what he called 'The Imperial Generals.' He said he would be court-martialed if he stayed another year. He saw the careerists making inroads in his beloved Corps, and he just couldn't tolerate it any longer. His dislike for these people grew so intense, he just about openly sneered at some of his superiors. The Commandant tried to persuade him not to leave, said it wouldn't be many years before Pack himself was sitting in the Commandant's seat, but Pack thought they were blowing smoke.

"I approve, and approve again, of this choice, Harris, and not because I've had too much Knob Creek. Pack's the man. He was a squadron commander in al-'Anbar. I was involved at the time in another tier-one Special Operations Forces mission inside Iraq, so I can tell you his task unit commanders loved him. I heard the same kinds of stories later in Afghanistan. Troops loved the clarity of his orders, the passion he brought, his authentic love for Marines, and because he spent many cold nights with them in individual fighting positions—foxholes, you might say. And he accompanied guys on every form of urban operation: intelligence gathering, reconnaissance, sniping, clearing buildings, he covered it all. Marines had lots of names for him, but he claimed not to be fond of any of them. I've met him often enough to claim he's the most complete Marine leader I ever met. Once, I was in a banquet hall over at Fort Myer. There must have been fifty officers senior in rank to him, yet he was the center of attention. I staked out a little piece of turf that evening next to a support column from which I could observe the scene. I'll swear that if brass had been cleared from shoulders, an alien being would have pointed to Pack as the one in charge. Didn't talk much. Possessed an air of authority you cannot teach. It's an even-greater endorsement to say his Marines thought they served the best squadron commander in the Corps." Sweet took a break for a Knob Creek refill.

Green said, "There isn't much doubt he was the best lineman in West Point history, a center, maybe the best at his position in America. He was just a huge man, the biggest ever to show up at the Academy. His very presence opened lanes for running backs. Lou Saban by that time had coached the Buffalo Bills, which during that period was known for its great O-line, and he claimed Simon Pack could start in the NFL. His size has always caused me to wonder two things: How in the world he survived boot camp at Lejeune, and how he managed to meet Academy fitness standards, specifically the runs, which in those days, thirty-some years ago, to my understanding were not compromised. He enlisted in the Marine Corps right after high school and served two years. During that second year, he applied to West Point, which is another thing I've wondered about. How are you a top-flight enlisted Marine, and you tell your gunny you want to apply to West Point, and ask if he and the commanding officer can help out? I just have a problem seeing how that scene went down. In any event, the USMC cooperated—to its great credit—and he got the appointment. When he got to USMA, he was far ahead of everyone, in part because he was two years older than most and in part because the Marine Corps had matured him. The man looked like a slab of granite, and nothing seemed to faze him during those first two months at West Point we call Beast. Very reserved. Never appeared to hold a high opinion of himself. Solid student; top quarter as I recall. Went on and got into the Force Recon program, the forerunner to Marine Special Operations Command, which is another mystery, because those slots were guarded carefully, and to allot one to someone who hadn't been in the Marine Corps or the Naval Academy for more than four years is a big deal. As if he had some serious pull, but I don't think so."

Rogers said, "I'm like every other Academy grad of our era. I knew of him but hadn't memorized his bio, as you seem to have. You make him sound virtuous, talented, competent. Did somebody *not* like him?"

Green weighed in on this question: "Marines in general aren't into idolatry, and Force Recon special-ops guys to a man don't seem to be into hero worship. The whole idea of heroes is anathema to most of these men, and a few women also, who do unconventional special operations in support of conventional warfare. Things like direct action; the often-dangerous Visit, Board, Search, and Seize, forcibly boarding ships in the Persian Gulf mainly, but also presumably in the Indian Ocean; and deep reconnaissance. Force Recon is very much SEAL- and Ranger Regiment–like in their methods of airborne, heliborne, submarine, and waterborne insertions and extractions. They preach *team,* not individuals, and they conduct themselves accordingly. It wouldn't surprise me at all, though, if some careerists—and make no mistake, there are some in the Marine Corps—didn't harbor resentment at this officer who seemed to get every plum assignment and to leave admirers in his wake, a veritable Pied Piper.

"But, fellows, I've done my homework on Pack, and I am more convinced than ever that he was pure professional, the absolute anti-careerist. He wasn't satisfied with any but the toughest, meanest assignments. Look at his record, and you'll see it was one hostile environment to another, several in those most highly classified tier-one special-operations jobs: Bosnia, Lebanon...He was there when the Marine Barracks was blown up, leaving two hundred forty-one American servicemen dead. Gulf I, Gulf II, Afghanistan, Somalia, Grenada—and those are the ones we know about. He lived to kill anyone who had practiced murder and intimidation as legitimate combat tactics. Some of those people he is reputed to have killed up close and personally."

Rogers said, "He's an intriguing man from your picture. But you make it sound as if he doesn't bend easily to pressure or, I deduce, follow instructions all that well. So why do you think his style is compatible with USMA's? And what he is up to now? Why he would accept the job if offered? To that I'll add, what does the man who would extend the offer, the Chief of Staff, think about this?"

"Very good questions, all," Green replied with visible respect. "Your add-on question's the most proximately critical, so I'll take it first. The Chief of Staff is wholly unaware of my idea, and I am to a certainty confident he hasn't a whiff of the plan to fundamentally transform West Point." Green was on a roll, speaking without slur or impediment, as if the Knob Creek had actually improved the workings of his mind and tongue. "He is overwhelmed with a long string of decisions facing him right now. From his point of view, I presume to say, who becomes Supe is nowhere on his priority sheet. I'll recommend Pack, but I'll require support. Consultative leader that he is, General Pembrook will seek opinions within a small circle of people he trusts, which is where you come in. My educated guess is, he will not immediately concur with my nominee for a couple reasons. First, it means there would be one less Active Duty Army General Officer to be rewarded, in effect one less chance for advancement for a prominent two-star. The political dimension is not to be understated in this time of troubles when the Chief needs each act and word of support he can muster. The last thing he needs is to be undercut unawares, maybe by a subordinate or two going behind his back to seek support from civilian Assistant Secretaries."

Harris continued, "But before going on to the next part, I want to know what Wallace thinks the head Marine's position on Pack will be. Can't forget he'll have to accede as well, plus maybe get the Chairman's go-ahead, but I think in the end, the latter won't be necessary."

"Well," Sweet opined, "I think the Commandant will endorse the plan with gusto. He's always loved Pack and will be happy to have him reenter the military. He can probably finesse a means of keeping the slot off the Corps's accounts."

"OK, good, *now* to the next part of your question. Why do I think his style's a good fit at West Point, wasn't that it? Truth is, I want Pack because what he stands for is far apart from what this administration perceives West Point stands for. Most of the external influences on the Academy at this moment are deleterious, and I refer especially to pressures exerted by the Board of Visitors. The warrior ethos is dying off, just as the people who desire to transform it into Nothing Special College hoped it would. The Sons of Slum and Gravy—I include the Daughters—need a good, hard shakeup. When a civilian underling in DC orders them to jump, at least two of the big three up there, the Supe and Dean, collectively ask, 'How high?' Pack would be the ohmmeter."

With a nod and wink to Rogers, who had once taught electrical engineering at the Military Academy, he said, "I know you weren't any BJ Alexander (a brilliant EE student and Rogers's classmate) in Cow Juice (the nickname given the junior electrical engineering course), but that dictates restoration of warrior spirit by resisting the current course, pun intentional.

"Further, it means he'll strike back against juvenility and hostility. I know Pack, and I think, *I think,* I see clearly how this will unfold. He takes the job and right away is encircled by ambushers: feminists, professors, administrators, the Pentagon, and ultimately, the White House. He knows you break out of an encirclement by counterattacking one arc of the circle. By the time the White House gets involved, we might have a story of nationwide interest. Who wins if the President takes on General Simon Pack? Don't bet against Simon Pack, folks."

"Wouldn't they fire him before it got that far?" Rogers asked.

"Not a one of them—Secretary of Defense, Secretary of the Army, Chairman of the Joint Chiefs, or Chief of Staff of the Army—would have the balls or, I hope, even the inclination to do it. Remember, in lots of spheres, Pack is revered. Not liking him is one thing; relieving him quite another."

"That leaves three questions: Where is he, what is he doing now, and would he accept the recall?" Rogers asked.

"Maybe he can be persuaded. Personally, I think so. Yeah, I'm confident he can be. Presentation will be the sine qua non.

"He's a semirecluse in northwest Montana, a part of the country several retired General Officers populate. Built a retirement cabin for himself and his wife. Severed contact with the military and about everyone else, too. Turned down job offers from consultants, contractors, and corporations. He might have sat on corporate boards and genuinely been value-added. Sadly, a week into his retirement, his wife was driving on an unfamiliar road that had turned into a snow-covered sheet of ice. Police report said she was trying to avoid an elk, judging from the prints and skid marks. Flipped over an embankment and slammed into a tree fifty feet down the mountain face. Tragic loss.

"Shortly after the tragedy, Pack goes down to his cabin builder, brashly informs the fella he himself can put up houses, do all of it. Wiring? Check. Plumbing? Check. Woodworking? Check. Roofing? Check. Only stipulation Pack insisted upon, to which Bud the Builder puzzlingly consented, was once he wrapped up a job, Pack alone would decide when he would resume his construction career. After six months of laboring at what for him was a pittance an hour, erecting multimillion-dollar log classics, he tells Bud the Builder he's taking some time off and will be in touch. Builder already considers Pack his best craftsman, but a deal's a deal, and he doesn't press."

Sweet said, "I'd heard he intended to settle in Montana, but nothing more. This new information is damn reflective of who he is, I would say. Has he rejoined the builder?"

Harris once more: "No, and how I know that is relevant. Before putting a recommendation on the Chief's desk, I need high likelihood Pack will take it. Wednesday, I asked you to come here today. So, wanting to speak with Simon Pack in confidence, I attempted to reach him Thursday and Friday. Nobody admits to knowing his whereabouts. Bud the Builder says Pack's been away a couple months, and his Tahoe's on the gravel outside the garage, but he says if you know Pack, this is nothing to raise your eyebrows about. Simon Pack is sui generis. Conventional norms do not pertain. His daughters don't have a clue where exactly he might be, either, or so they say, and they sound unconcerned about the situation. Mail's being forwarded to a daughter in Spokane, and she's covering the bills. Seems there's frontier ruggedness of spirit in that family.

"Simon Pack is our man, gentlemen. He has a chance to be a very great deal more than just another in the line of West Point Supes. Unless he surfaces soon, though, we won't know what might have been."

"Don't think it's offensive to ask if you've tried—" Sweet said.

Harris interrupted. "To call or e-mail, right?"

Sweet nodded.

"Well, Wallace, he doesn't own a mobile, and he damn sure doesn't have an e-mail. Odds are, he's on a wilderness trip. He likes to take his kayak into backcountry, where he camps and hikes, the outdoor activities we know he prefers. I intend to be optimistic he will return in time for this egg to hatch. I have a Brit officer friend who would call this enterprise a gapeseed—his word for an idealistic, impossible goal—but I assure you, it is not. Let's hope, a decade from now, we will have been seen as having started a good deed.

"Apologies for talking too much. At least, after the spirits of the day, you're still awake. I didn't anticipate eating so big a chunk of your weekend. Still, business matter aside, I've delighted in your company. Hope you hang around a while longer and top off your bourbon, but if you can't, thanks for dropping by. Your participation was helpful and informs my perspective. Your names will never cross my lips in connection with this."

But Pack wasn't kayaking in the north woods.

Chapter Seven

Vegas-Bound

When Pack shed his bedroll before first light, Hard Travelin' was gone. But so were Memphis Mike and Denver Johnny. What is, is. He had heard stirrings in the dark, but they might've been taking a leak. This wasn't the Marine Corps, and he wasn't a General in charge of them. They weren't obligated to inform him of their comings and goings. The absence of Mike and Johnny would explain their curious expressions yesterday. They had promised to see him as far as Yermo, and they had.

He cleaned up, shaved, hitched his way back to Barstow. Hard Travelin' was in the line of prospective workers again. They were selected in the same order as yesterday, and climbed aboard the same hoopty for the short hop over to the work site. Nobody said a word for the duration.

On the return trip that afternoon, as they were about to split up, Pack said, "Thanks again for the grub last night, HT. I welcomed it. Johnny and Mike did, too, so much so I guess they cut out this morning."

"No surprise there. They don't let the grass grow. Things went kinda sour last night, didn't they?"

"Yeah, I think that's about right. No foul, no harm, though."

"Look, Montana, I have a lot of problems. At the head of the list is inferiority complex. I overcompensated, and I regret it, as I always do."

"I know, HT. I know. You'll be all right." As he said this, Pack pondered how the hobo HT had managed to be so conversant with Christianity. CliffsNotes? Something about the man was inauthentic.

They planted sod two more days. On the job, they worked a large plot together and conversed amiably. They kept their distance at Yermo but plotted to give riding together a shot.

♦ ♦ ♦

From the day you enter the Marine Corps, you learn to use topo maps. Glance at the tightness of the elevation contour intervals to understand the steepness of the incline. Identify depressions, saddles, and ridges. Then one day, after you have gained real proficiency in mapreading, you begin to learn *land*-reading. Real Marines become well-acquainted with the terrain; the best become warm friends. Each fold in the earth has a story to tell.

Pack was a terrain reader par excellence. Looking eastward from Yermo, the untrained eye saw limitless flat desert. Pack observed the subtle markers for declines and inclines. He needn't rely upon the detailed topo maps the rail lines produced.

He asked Hard Travelin', "Feeling strong today?"

"Strong enough, I'm thinkin', for whatever you have in mind."

"What I'm thinking is that sometimes the best chance for latching onto a train is to push away from the yards. Catch a lumbering, long train on a steep uphill, where it has to slow. Am I right?"

"No doubt, Mr. Montana. How far you think we will have to walk before we reach such a propitious point?"

"Ten miles at least. You up for it?"

"I'm already halfway there. Listen up, Mount Montana. I'm a few years your senior, but I take pride in my stamina. I've never been a Weary Willie, if you understand me."

"I've read the term before, but don't know the difference between Weary Willie and Worry Wart. Explain, please."

"A Weary Willie is a hobo who typically is physically run down as a result of late-night frolicking and carousing. I have abstained from all activities that sap body and soul. And brother, it has been a choice not without heavy temptations. When booze and weed and crank have been passed around, I've wanted to hit them more often than not. But I did not, so maybe I didn't desire them that much."

Pack noticed that not a mile into the overland journey, HT was sweating buckets. But Pack had been around enough men in similar situations to know the correlation to general state of health could be tenuous or nonexistent. Some men just sweated much more than others. Not wanting to impugn HT's fitness, he said nothing. Pack decided he would walk a while longer, then pretend he himself needed a short break.

Maybe he could catch HT off guard: "So, is Paul your true given name?"

"Yes, it is, Montana. I suspected that's been bothering you. Paul is my name."

"Thanks, man. I'll say no more about it. It's a good name, and I agree with you about Paul the Apostle."

"What do you say we're just two men walking? Drop the hobo rules. As the Preacher told us, there is a time and a place for everything under the sun. Talking honestly is something I rarely get the chance to do. Campfires actually do not make for good conversation. Ninety percent of what comes from camp talk is egregious exaggeration or outright lie. My Lord, what people will do to fit in," HT said wistfully.

"Stop, now," Pack said. "This is important."

"What is it, man?" HT asked, mouth agape, genuine concern written on his face.

At that, Pack cocked a leg and broke wind loud and long. Pack raised both arms in the touchdown signal as Hard Travelin' laughed so hard he had difficulty drawing a breath.

"Didn't know you had that in you," HT said, and Pack laughed along with him this time.

"Before that"—HT cocked a leg in imitation—"we were on the topic of honest communication. If I'm trekking a desert with no human in sight but you, I'd like to know whom I'm with. What I'm really saying is, we'll likely go our ways once we land in Vegas, so what's the harm in opening up a bit?"

"No harm. Spent most of my life in the Marines. Lost my wife to a car accident last year. Have two great daughters."

"Sorry for your loss, man." Hard Travelin' let that sink in. "How long you been on the trains?"

"Months, not years. Felt with conviction I didn't know my own country as well as I ought to. I'd been away a long time. When I first got back, I stood staring at the grocery clerk when he told me to swipe a card. All that stuff like barcode scanners was new to me. So this was my way of reestablishing contact with America. Of course, out here I haven't seen many scanners. It'll take me a while to assess whether I got what I was looking for."

"You wanted to get reacquainted with America, why didn't you just start driving, talk with folks along the way?" HT asked.

"That's how it's normally done. That suits people, fine, but there's not enough—or maybe better said, the right kind—of life in that for me. I must've been thirty before I had lived long enough to start seeing patterns in my life. The kind of men whose company I most enjoyed, for example. The foundation of my political thought.

"I appreciate a good balance of thinking and doing in a man. In some respects, the internal-cognition engine is more powerful than the internal-combustion engine, and vice versa, depends on the task. I can work with my hands and appreciate others who can, too. But I've seen too many of that type of guy who goes home, pops the first beer, watches sitcoms, and goes to bed. Last book they read was never. People with no powers of discernment or critical thought because they haven't trained their minds how to think. Go to the other pole, I don't appreciate them, either."

HT cut in, "Those are the ones I would pattern myself after. I mean, the ones who can do both, think and act. As a Marine, ever given thought to bin Laden's intelligence, for example? Remember the jokes about him living in a cave, surviving on roots and berries? Man was Al Qaeda, OK, but you have to admire him. Man could think and do. Could say the same for Saddam."

Pack didn't let on how much he wanted to follow up on Hard Travelin's unusual comments. He would at the right time, but for the present let the conversation peter out.

But within minutes HT was urging Pack to explain more of his likes and dislikes.

Pack had scores of malapropisms stored in his head, but offered just a few. "I rarely find misuse of words offensive, just humorous. So I find myself making up taradiddle. Don't care if anyone likes it, long as it makes me smile, laugh even, on occasion."

Hard Travelin' was streaming sweat now but wore a big grin, seeming to be down with Pack's upswell of talk. "Go for it, brother. Let me hear a line or two."

"All right, but let me warn you, I never claimed they're funny to anyone else. Just my personal humor. Here are a few recent constructions: 'Back in the day, I owned the saloon Country's. Before Best Butt Wednesdays, I encouraged the Rear Entrants to use the rear entrance.'"

"I like it, brother. I'm turning my tape recorder on, or would if I had one," HT said with a chuckle.

"The government job interviewer's sizing up another potential bureaucrat, asks, 'What's your favorite animal?' 'The red tapir,' I answer."

"At the very, very, very pricey dining establishment, I fantasize of saying to the waiter, 'I'd like extra origami on that steak.' It's my favorite spice, you see." Hard Travelin' got it all, and for the moment appeared to have shrugged off all signs of fatigue.

"Another silly fancy: I'm staring at the magnificent art of a master glassblower like Dale Chihuly, when in he walks. I feign anger, and roar at him, 'You blew it, mister!'" Pack laughed at his own joke.

With another ten minutes of hard walk left before a rest break, Pack had shut down the talk but not his thoughts. *HT was sending me a message back there*, Pack was sure, *telling me bin Laden and Saddam were admirable. Or he's getting his jollies thinking I didn't pick up on it. Telling me two things: He's smarter than me, and he has connections with some evil people.*

But what the hell, Pack surmised. *I've been wrong a time or two in my life, and also faced down a lot of evil men.*

Back in the moment, Pack pointed to a rock outcropping with a broad awning. "Let's sit in the shade awhile. Short rest break will do us good. Five miles or so lie in front of us."

As he plopped down, Hard Travelin' said, "I don't know what busted your word dam, but you just said a ton. We're not so different. I can profit from the guidance of a wise man like you. What percentage of people do you think would've said, 'like yourself'? I think an apt title for a biography of yours truly is *The Chronicle of a Demented and Uneventful Life Poorly Lived*. It's been these many years, but I believe now I have encountered my cater-cousin. I see enduring memories in our brief relationship, Montana. We are a fit on this long hobo road."

Pack said nothing in return. An image flickered across his brain, an image of the frisson HT appeared to experience when for a millisecond he caught sight of the cash Pack carried in the bottom of his bag. Pack had little to no respect for money. The extent of thought he gave to it was to conclude, as a young man, that the Golden Mean was the ideal with respect to money. Having too much created a basket of potential problems, as did having too little. Earn what you need, and don't worry about the remainder. Before setting out, he'd withdrawn ten grand in cash from his checking account, mostly in twenties, with the intention of dropping anonymous gifts as he saw fit. Johnny and Mike were to have been recipients, but they scooted away in the night, robbing them of his largesse. He had dropped a few hundred to young hard-working diner waitresses. Now he reconsidered Hard Travelin'. He would have to watch his back, maybe not only from an outsider attack, but also from HT. Perhaps Hard Travelin' had multiple reasons for playing up Las Vegas as their destination. And maybe Hard Travelin' didn't like a Marine so much.

"So," Pack said as they laid back in the shade of the ledge, "tell me about Vegas." A half-dozen dust devils blew up not far away. In the far distance, a sweeping dust storm raked across the desert. "Before the wind blows so hard we can't talk."

"For one, it's where I usually reoutfit myself. You see, Montana, between the tourists and the Mob, Vegas has a disproportionately large number of unidentified dead. The morgue throws their possessions out. I take the often-fine threads of their castoff clothing. Two, there is no greater place to dive than in casino Dumpsters—loads of untouched delicacies to be found in them. Three, I am no cardsharp, but I am sufficiently competent on the gaming tables to be able to leave the city flush—enough in my pocket, at least, to provide for the needs of my meager lifestyle for several months into the future. Fourth, and this is happy news for the 'bo, it is the least-fortified city yard in America. If I am not mistaken, security there is under the aegis of the mighty Union Pacific Railroad, so why this is the case is baffling. I haven't spotted a security agent there in many years. Graffiti is ubiquitous on even the highest-value railcars. A lucrative terrorist target, would you agree?"

"Would seem so, HT. I'll tuck that info away." Pack received the information he wanted and hadn't had to ask the question. The evidence that HT was a threat mounted in Pack's mind; HT might have been better served to avoid admission to being a player. *Hubris*, Pack mulled. *How many people have I watched it bring down?*

Pack walked alongside HT so he could see the man's face. "Know what you said back there about let's just be two hobos talking, drop all the crap, and about your liking my busting my word dam? You're right, friend. I feel comfortable now, us talking openly, and that's a big compliment to you, 'cause it took me years with most of my acquaintances. Anyway, I told you I was a Marine. Was for a long time. I was there in the Marine Barracks, Beirut '83, when Islamists murdered two hundred forty-one of my buddies. And I got involved with hunting down some of the Muslims who kidnapped a number of Americans during the 1980s. And much later, I had the pleasure of killing some of the Al Qaeda who murdered, hanged, and burned the Blackwater people in Fallujah in '04. And much more, but that's enough for now. Thanks, friend, for listening. I reckon you're the first person I ever opened up to on that subject. I'm sure you'd have done the same if you had been in my shoes."

HT was flustered, not quickly forthcoming in reply. HT was a quick-draw, but Pack had beaten him this time. HT finally roared with that inimitable chortle that now carried a hostile edge. "Damn right I would've done the same, Montana. Would have killed them all by myself alone if chance came."

The final half-mile was a slog. Down a gently sloping declivity, slow-crawl up a long incline. Their hide spot was perfect. Concealed and covered. No matter the composition of the train, it would have to slow to a speed they could manage. Not many hobos, and probably no hobohemians, would have expended so much energy to assure themselves an excellent mount site. They were prepared.

Hard Travelin' continued as if Pack's monologue of minutes earlier had never happened. "Gotta ration the little water I have left, brother. Train's gotta show up before that dust storm gets here and before my water runs out. Can't tell when the next one comes through."

By late afternoon, the mercury had plunged, and an unusually long train could be seen in the distance. Maybe a hundred thirty, hundred forty cars? As it drew near enough for them to distinguish separate cars, HT said, "Who in hell assembled this train? It is rare you'll see such disparate loads. Don't remember the last time I saw double-stacks mixed with grainers and coal cars. Don't know if you'd call it a junk train or a hotshot. Anyway, my friend, I'll meet up with you on the south end of the Vegas yard. Meantime, I'm going for a sweet double-stack I can get into, stay warm."

Pack grabbed the handle of a passing gondola filled with grain. It was his smoothest mount yet. The approach, the sprint alongside, the sure grip, the rhythm of the swing up, knowing where to find his spot, it was all coming together nicely. He got comfortable in the grainer, and for the next few minutes marveled that here he was, on a damn railcar, gazing up at the winking stars, into the empyrean chamber of the western sky.

◆ ◆ ◆

Hard Travelin' carried a cut-down rail spike in his kit. More than a pound of iron. Five-and-a-half inches long, six inches in circumference, nine-sixteenth inch square shanks, tack-sharp on one end, L-shaped head on the other. When he was a kid watching trains pass through rural Mississippi, he most loved the auto railcars. In those days, the cars were mounted much as they are on big trucks today. Simply ramped up, open to the weather. Crime wasn't as bad in those days, though. Leave them open like that in a rail yard today, and they'll be stripped in no time. Thus, today's auto railcars are covered on all sides, for security most of all. And those types of railcars get locked up.

Hard Travelin' had figured out a way to get inside an auto railcar, which is where the spike came in. Somebody else might know the secret, but he would never give it away himself. Just jam it through the square hole in the wall plate, turn counterclockwise, and open the entry door. Since today's automobiles are loaded with keys in the ignition and doors unlocked, it's a hobo dream. Flatten the seat, and go to sleep, even turn on the A/C or heater. This is how HT rode the distance to Vegas.

Pack leaped off first and casually took up a spot at the south end. As Hard Travelin' had asserted, the security was execrable. Pack's professional training kicked in, causing him to wonder why standards here were so lax. Nothing convincing came to mind right away, but he figured if he bored deeper, he would find tourism, politics, and money tied up in a messy twist at the foundation. Up the tracks, he saw HT shuffling toward him, as he knew HT would.

"Is this where we part company?" Pack asked.

"No way, man. I am just now beginning to realize what a fascinating man you are. I am smart enough to know I have much to learn from you, my friend. Please stay a few additional days, at a minimum. This is Vegas, bro. Enjoy it. I have a proposal," Hard Travelin' said.

Pack replied, "I'm not on a schedule. So let's hear it."

"There's more construction going on in North Vegas than about anywhere. Man with your skills can pick what he wants to do, and very nearly what pay he wants. I can set you up with good people. Or, should you like to go in another direction, I can arrange that as well."

"The museum is generally more interesting with a qualified docent walking in front, is what I think. How is it you are so well read-in on Vegas, my friend?" Pack asked. "And, I hope I don't disappoint by asking what 'another direction' means to you."

"Perhaps I neglected to state straight-up that Las Vegas is as near to a home base as I have. Only the few who love it as dearly as I refer to it as The Meadows. It is a dramatic change from my origins, which likely is a source of that love. As to the other question, I also do not wish to embarrass myself, give you an opportunity to think poorly of me. But we're both aware of human frailties, are we not? I have committed sins of the flesh; I am human. So whatever your desire, I am the man who can give a ready assist."

Pack's reevaluation of Mr. Hard Travelin's character was complete. He had what he needed to know to finish his work in Las Vegas.

Hard Travelin' said, "To your immediate needs, sir, allow me to direct you to a fine washroom. After that, I'll show you a place near Western Trails Equestrian Park where you can set up a nice camp."

"Great. Appreciate your concern. Lead the way," Pack said. He had noticed the "where you can set up camp." HT wasn't planning to be with him.

They were hard upon the park when HT said, "Montana, pardon me, but I can't explain what came over me. Age, I guess. Mind's lacking some these days. Completely forgot about a far superior campsite. The park won't do it. The location I have in mind is as comfortable as you'll find outside The Sands or suchlike."

"Thanks, but this area looks fine to me." He knew Travelin's protest would follow, and it did.

"I won't hear of it. It isn't far from here, and I'll bet a good meal you'll prefer it. My comrades own the place and would be honored for you to rack there for a few days." HT's voice had an insistent edge.

Pack happily acceded to HT's plea. The bed-down site looked to be a closed-to-business auto-body shop. A Pisa-leaning sign read, "Eli's Auto Body and Repair." Two grubby-looking men around thirty-five met HT with man hugs, smiles, hearty laughs. One of them Pack instantly recognized as Somali in origin; he was very tall. Even Pack had to crank his head a bit to see the man face-on. Pack had a former basketball friend who was six-nine, so he figured this gaunt fellow stood about six-eleven. HT called him Joseph, which Pack translated to Yusef. Hard Travelin' said Joseph was his "deputy, so to speak. He knows damn near everything I do, so go to Joseph if I'm out of pocket." The other associate stayed silent.

The rollup door to a two-car maintenance bay worked, despite the garage's run-down appearance, and HT ostentatiously flicked on a bank of fluorescent tubes that also worked. No tools or equipment in sight. Somewhat on the greasy side, but it had a roof, walls, and a functioning toilet. None of it mattered; Pack figured he wouldn't do anything beyond occupying the bay tonight.

Pack said, "I appreciate it, men. We'll sleep sound, Travelin'. You *are* joining me, right?"

"Startin' tomorrow night," HT replied. "Gotta git up wit' my boys. Payin' and collectin'-type things. General catchin' up to do." Not lost on Pack was HT's downshift in speech. He had to talk his boys' language, show his toughness, give no indication of subservience to Pack. "Be back in the mornin' to find you sum work."

The other two guys cocked their heads in a departing salute, and the party of three sauntered away without another word.

Chapter Eight

Death In Vegas?

Once the three were out of view, Pack whipped his pack off the floor and hustled off to the nearest hardware store, where he committed to the most extravagant expenditure of this sojourn. He purchased a dozen large glue traps for rats and a spool of extrafine, super-strong Spidercast fishing line. They wouldn't enter through the rollup door, figuring he would lock it down, as in fact he did. No, they had a key to the side door and would go through the former office area into the maintenance bay.

With this in mind, Pack rigged a two-tiered maze from the fishing line. The lower one extended two feet inside the three walls away from the inside door and ran an inch above ankle height. Pack mounted the next tier one foot inside the three walls and five feet above the floor. Next, he situated each trap so that in the end the pattern was of tessellated tile, so established to follow their likely footpaths. As a Force Recon Marine, you improvised as a way of life. Finally, he set up his sleep covers with filler and laid his sack beside his head. Then he waited.

He reckoned they'd do it between three-thirty and four, maybe even without sleep themselves. The two guys were hard cases, and Hard Travelin' had had plentiful high-grade sleep aboard the train. Four-thirty is a preferred military attack time, when the enemy's biorhythms are most out of sync, but Hard Travelin' knew Pack was an early riser, so Pack anticipated an earlier greeting.

Preparing the room's defenses to the standard he established took until 0200. His senses were fully alert as he crouched in ambush. There was no time to remind himself his body was weary. He willed his mind to rehearse the close-quarter combat about to occur.

Pack hadn't worn a watch in twenty years. If he had trained himself to accurately know the time, he wasn't aware of it. Some might call it training, but he didn't think it mattered how such understanding occurred. Similarly, if he set an internal clock for a 0500 wakeup, nine-and-a-half out of ten times, he awoke at that hour. As a senior officer said on one mournfully frigid night in Bosnia, "You're flesh and bones like the rest of humanity, but how the hell can you even move in this icy universe?" Pack had never acted as if any environmental condition affected him. Some of it had to be illusion, but Pack-watchers were persuaded that even though there were natural laws, there were natural laws that applied to Pack alone.

Before four o'clock, the key turned in the outer door with a low, controlled *snick*. The door eased open almost soundlessly. The first man entered. Hard Travelin' would be last in line, Pack guesstimated. HT was bright enough to regard that position in the file as the dominant one. Ten feet to the frosted glass door opening onto the bay. No flashlight so far, which was best case for Pack.

On the far side of the glass door, Pack breathed slowly through his mouth, exhaling silently, deliberately relaxing muscles, flexing calf muscles with a gradual toe lift. He stood upright at arm's length from the knob, touching it lightly as he pressed against the wall. The first guy's step-through foot plopped more or less squarely on a glue trap. Pack propelled tall Joseph/Yusef forward into the fishing-line garrotes with a wicked forearm shiver. In an instant, he had ahold of Number Two's grimy, smelly shirt, jolting his head into the path of a violent open-palm face strike. Number Two was down cold. Pack stomped his throat with a sturdy boot for good measure. Three or four glue traps pasted Number One, who cried from the multiple wounds inflicted by the nearly invisible filaments. Blood was flowing out of Yusef with each pump of his heart. All this within a couple of seconds, during which Pack had also reached behind him to flick on the fluorescents. Hard Travelin' wore a minatory smirk.

"Told you I had a lot to learn from a sage like you, Big Man. Giving yourself credit for figuring out the enigmatic HT, aren't you? But let me tell you, mister, you don't know me." Voice rising, HT rumbled, "I am a complicated man. I am a complex man. You hear me? I am com-pli-cated, and have done bigger, more important things than your simple soldier's mind can conceive. I will change this country. Real tough, stupid, sol-jer boy, ain't you? You hurt my peeps, I hurt you real bad. But first, I'm *tellin'* you to fetch that roll of yours and lay it nicely in my hand."

Hard Travelin' pulled the cut-down spike from behind his back. "Prob'ly gonna have to kill you." HT figured the cut-down gave him hegemony in this situation.

Pack backed into the maintenance bay, avoiding the traps and rigging, saying, "Get it yourself."

Unable to cock his arm fully for a max-force swing because of the doorway's confinement, Hard Travelin' charged toward the bay. HT could beat down most men, no question of it. But Pack was not most men, and HT had never faced anyone as thoroughly trained in the skills of close combat as Pack. Pack never took his eyes off the spike; as Hard Travelin' thrust the spike as if it were an epee, Pack executed flawlessly two distinct movements simultaneously. As if he were snatching a butterfly in flight, he seized HT's wrist with two hands and twisted the wrist back and down. At the same moment he connected with a hard boot strike to HT's nutsack. The swift combination of Pack's counters crumpled HT to his knees. Hard Travelin' had lost his hold on the spike. Pack seized it and drove it uppercut style into HT's gut. HT's eyes rolled and his breaths grew shallower and more desperate as blood pulsated from a form approaching lifelessness.

"Everyone's complicated in his own way, Hard Travelin'," Pack muttered to himself. "Too bad you didn't have my back."

♦ ♦ ♦

Two dead men, one as good as. Pack took his time calling 911. Having no mobile phone, he had to slow-walk, ribs aching, back to a phone in the convenience store he had spotted during daylight. Personal hobo kit in tow, he had no intention of ever returning to Eli's Auto Body and Repair.

LVPD detained him, took him in for questioning by a fire team of detectives who asked the same questions over and over. The first guys on scene from LVPD were clearly wary of Pack's report. They told him they had discovered just two of the three Pack had claimed were there. Two of the agents were FBI, a fact about which Pack was unaware and unconcerned. Pack didn't get irritated or demonstrate emotion. His answers were the same each time. He left nothing out, altered no fact of his journey on the Hobo Road. Some of their questions baffled him, so he simply claimed ignorance and proceeded. They gave him several hours of solitude and encouraged him to rest. Then they went through the same grind again. All his answers matched.

While in his cell, Pack ruminated on the entire set of events at the garage, and concluded the Feds had gotten involved. They never mentioned that they had retrieved only two men from the scene. Most likely, the Somali had gotten away, in that he seemed most capable of sustaining life. HT was the one the Feds most wanted; Yusef could wait.

Before leaving home, he had stowed his military ID card in a secure location, so throughout the trip, his personal identification was the Montana driver's license. At no point had he divulged his distinguished military past.

Hours after Pack was hauled in, a uniformed cop came to his cell with a short message: "The chief wants to see you, sir. I'm instructed to escort you to his office."

The police chief expressed gratitude and relayed the mayor's request for a photograph with Pack. He asked Pack in the politest manner to stay off the rails, at least until this died down. Right about now, Pack was the most famous hobo in the world.

The following day's editions of *The Sun* and *Review-Journal* carried front-page file photos of Pack alongside a recent shot of Muhamed Ali-Mumen, a.k.a. Elvin Eugene Hawkshaw, a.k.a. Hard Travelin', the leader of Al Qaeda America. The story had already been picked up coast to coast. At this moment, media people of all stripes swarmed Vegas to get their pictures of the crime scene. Pack turned down all requests, including the mayor's. He bought a new head-to-toe set of Carhartt's, and threw in a watch cap and a John Deere cap big enough to pull low. He thought he could pass for a Midwestern farmer. He could rest when he put several hundred miles between himself and Vegas. As the mayor and LVPD chief held their presser, Pack was steering a truck back to Montana. Before leaving the city, he dropped coins in a rack and withdrew a newspaper, which he tossed on the passenger seat.

Hours later, he pulled into a McDonald's around Gardnerville, Nevada, east of Lake Tahoe. He bought two complete meals and set about gobbling them. He spread the Vegas newspaper out on the tabletop. He read: "At around five yesterday morning, Las Vegas police officers were dispatched to a slaying scene where one of the bodies was discovered to be Muhamed Ali-Mumen, known leader of Al Qaeda America. According to the FBI, this man spent five years honing his terrorist talents and ideological underpinnings in Al Qaeda camps some twenty years ago in the mountains of Yemen. Ali-Mumen is believed to have directed terror operations from scores of locations around the country. FBI Special Agent in Charge Robert Atkins said, 'This individual is responsible for a full spectrum of crimes, most notably bank heists, extortion, arson, bombings, and murders. Weeks of investigation will be required to ascertain a reliable number of casualties linked to Ali-Mumen's activities. Although we have brought in many of Ali-Mumen's closest associates over the last decade, he has eluded us. On behalf of law-enforcement advocates nationwide, we thank General Simon Pack for authentic heroism in stopping this war criminal. Make no mistake, Muhamed Ali-Mumen was fighting against American liberty, and he was doing it under the banner of an organization that wants to destroy all things American. I believe the General's valorous conduct will in future be shown to have saved American lives.'

"LVPD spokesmen say new evidence ties Ali-Mumen to the hobo underground. One long-established habitué of the Vegas rail yard wondered whether 'the law mistook Hard Travelin's true identity,' saying the man had always been generous to fellow travelers. Another itinerant acquaintance spoke for several associates who thought Ali-Mumen was untrustworthy and 'probably' guilty of numerous seldom-solved internal 'jungle' offenses. 'We ain't sorry to see him gone, I can tell you that. Whenever I hitch the Westbound one of these days, Hard Travelin' ain't gonna be aboard,' he said.

"Mystery clouds every feature of this story. Three decades ago, the man who stopped Ali-Mumen and his two cohorts, Simon Pack, rose to high prominence in the athletic world. Later, as a Marine Corps officer, his acts of heroism brought additional fame and saw his achievements feted at the White House. He retired from the US Marine Corps as a two-star general less than two years ago. Since going into retirement, he has been out of view, and as of this writing there is no public record of his private life.

"What Pack was doing at any hour in the abandoned auto repair shop remains unknown. Authorities say that the three assailants attacked Pack. They miscalculated, and they got lax. No firearms were discharged, and Pack is said to have only a few cracked ribs.

"One of Ali-Mumen's associates died of a crushed windpipe. Another is struggling for life after incurring the type of lacerations consistent with piano wire or fishing line. One senior law enforcement official said, 'It is very possible, maybe likely, that Simon Pack was operating as an undercover FBI agent.' If he was undercover, why did LVPD release his identity? Or was it leaked in order to bolster the flagging morale in what is increasingly described as a beleaguered agency?

"Whatever his capacity may have been, Pack is uncharged in this case. Major news outlets have staked out Pack's Montana residence, where some journalists have received angry threats from neighbors. One billboard-sized sign several miles from the cabin says, 'Media and Government: Private Property, Leave Us Alone!'"

Pack needed to nap in the truck. On the way out of McDonald's, he was about to toss the paper in the refuse bin, then pulled back and laid it on the nearest table. What is, is.

• • •

Denver Johnny and Memphis Mike were still together way off in Alabama. The Flomaton Yards, just about the center of Universe Hobo. "DJ," Mike said, "we did Montana wrong. My gut and your gut said we shouldn'ta left him alone with that guy."

"What was we 'posed ta do?" DJ replied. "We dint have facts provin' we was right about Hard Travelin', and in my mind prejudicin' Montana wouldn'ta been right, neither. We promised we'd leave him off on his own, which we done. Things worked out. Montana took care of it. Chances are, we'd a been no more'n Job's comforter. We'd a just got in the way, said an' done all the wrong things. Reckon where he's at now?"

As for Pack, his ribs ached; finding a comfortable position was impossible. Sleep came slowly. But it did come, with a big assist from the ample container of pain pills the jail doc back in Vegas had prescribed.

The pack of media jackals would be salivating around his cabin. *Maybe they've already been on my deck, breaking out covered outdoor furniture, throwing butts wherever. Don't get ahead of things. Nothing you can do until you get there and look them in the eye, make them aware they're trespassing, as if the asses don't know. I can stay away until they throw in the towel and go home. Nope, that's no good. I can return straightaway, confront them, try to shoo them off the property. Not bad. Or I can add a day, low-crawl back to northwest Montana, by which time the herd will have been thinned. Read, rest up, get some heat on the ribs. Driving long stretches is not desirable right now. Option three wins.*

Some of the interrogators had asked why HT didn't take him out well before Vegas. The smart one, the local detective first-grade with the knowing eyes, had it figured out. He understood egocentrics bordering on egomaniacal must show their superiority to a worthy adversary when they find one. If HT viewed his victims as ignorant ciphers, people incapable of absorbing the nature of his grandeur, he'd slice them to shreds from the back; such victims couldn't appreciate a complex man like HT. He wanted to experience the thrill of looking into the cast-down eyes of a defeated man of intelligence. Murder must be done according to the code. *He respected me body and mind, so he had to kill me right. I sensed all this almost from the get-go.* Yet HT couldn't have successfully done the deed at any point in the process; Pack was more situationally aware than he could have imagined. *I watched him trying to gaslight me, but actually everyone. There it was, shining bright once more: the overweening pride, the ugly malignancy plain and simple that killed HT well ahead of my schedule. We're all carrying some malignancy inside us.*

What good could Pack speak of Mr. Hard Travelin'? Short answer was not a damn thing. Turns out he had murdered innocents without cause or pause or conscience for years. *Can I say he was smart, that pearl of a compliment? Not up to me to decide, but here's how I see it: Of dot collectors, our supply is long and deep. Mr. Hard Travelin'—high time I begin to think of him as Elvin Eugene Hawkshaw—it would appear was a superb dot collector. But our supply of dot* **connectors** *is short and shallow. Universities are packed tight with the likes of him, that sneering, snorting, dyspeptic professor of the arcane, he who can recite the obscure poem but never quite make out its meaning. This now-rotting flesh I have disposed from among the living, sir, was no kind of dot connector.* Of what Pack called "associative intelligence," the closest definition he could come to 'smart', Mr. Elvin Eugene Hawkshaw was in considerable want. *"Wit"* in the 18th century had a meaning different from ours. To the folks of those days it meant having the developed capacity to make useful associations between apparently unlike objects, people, ideas, etc. Elvin Eugene, yes he did, came up short.

But he had the makings of greatness, did he not? Potential for goodness? The word potential was detritus to Pack. A word so facilely inked onto Marine officer Fitness Reports: "This officer possesses unlimited potential for advancement." *Really? Pay attention to the now. What is, is.* Such an empty word, *potential,* hollow of actual meaning. Something to hide behind. Temporize through the Wonderful World of Potential. Stalk life but never seize it. If by potential, Pack meant Elvin Eugene owned a nice toolbox he could employ for life's myriad assignments, then, yes, he enjoyed advantages. But he was great only in minor key, a footnote to a bio entry on Hitler or Stalin or even Osama bin Laden.

♦ ♦ ♦

The hundred or so citizens who lived within a mile of Pack's hillside cabin did not appreciate the media intrusion. They let Sheriff Mollison know it. He looked at it the same way and promised trespassers would be keel-hauled to his jail. Pack thought their acquaintance might've worked in his favor. Mollison was conciliatory toward the press, saying if Pack ever returned to the cabin, the sheriff would do his utmost to arrange a Q&A down at the town hall. He knew Pack would never agree to that, but his pledge was enough to get them off the hill. Then, too, media budgets aren't as flexible as they once were, and press bosses were not comfortable with indefinitely funding expense accounts. Being unpredictable has its plusses.

So, when at last Pack pulled the rental nobody would recognize into the gravel drive, he was greeted by stillness. The sight of litter made him angry, and there was some left behind by the cheerleaders of the environmentalists, but Pack decided he'd collect it tomorrow and wash his hands of the slobs. *Then I'll call Bud the Builder for a ride to turn in the rental truck—the one-way turn-in fee, I expect, will be jarring to a man of my means—and then I'll plan some kind of self-employment schedule for the next thirty days.* Go to town to reopen mail service. He really didn't have things of importance to do anymore. Just tend to himself and this small plot of ground that pleased him so much. Harvest enough timber to fuel his stoves, feel the muscular joy of chopping and splitting, stacking and hauling. Down in his workshop, he even could fashion some of the wood into what some regard as finely hewn and lacquered sticks of furniture.

Pack's workshop was his Cave of Making, as Auden called such sacred places. He owned a full array of tools: drill presses, sanders, lathes, routers, saws, planers, joiners. He often visited the hardware store in search of an exotic-looking implement whose purpose he did not even know. There was a rare form of delight in coaxing it gently to tell him to what useful means it might be directed. Pack found if he pushed too hard, it wouldn't reveal its secrets. As with many facets of life, straining leads to a poor result.

But first, I need to phone Laura and Alex to let them know their old man's back in the saddle at home. The girls had long ago grown accustomed to Pack's oddities, his unannounced comings and goings, his frequent need for solitude; besides, in their rearing he had largely scrubbed the fret from their natures. An absence of a month or two by their father alarmed them not at all.

Chapter Nine

Contact

The answering machine was a cache of messages, most useless. For a week or two after retiring, he got calls from well-wishers who knew how to get in touch. Mostly pro forma stuff, he knew. He didn't object to the calls, but nonetheless, he switched carriers and deliberately took a new home number. He asked those to whom he gave his new number not to share it. The Marine Corps Commandant and a few senior people at the Pentagon always had access. Harris Green and Wallace Sweet must've gone through Marine Corps HQ, which meant their message was official business. He scanned the message details of the calls. Five total; three from Green, two from Sweet. Two of Green's were recorded before Pack had closed on Vegas, which would seem to rule out a social call of congrats for surviving whatever name one attached to what occurred there. Both of Sweet's came a couple hours following Pack's cuffing, which could indicate either one of the law enforcement bodies had contacted the Pentagon immediately, which was unlikely, or that Sweet was in the dark on Vegas and had something entirely different on his mind. He hit the "Replay" button a few times, listening to tone, tenor, content. The messages inside the messages told him three things: This was quietly urgent, not *official* official business but off the record. The current need-to-know list consisted of just these three, and he should return the calls on their private lines only.

Pack wasn't concerned. He had been the target of numerous allegations and investigations. He was inured to them. If you knew you hadn't violated ethical and moral standards of conduct, or helped create a permissive environment, why worry about an unintentional breach of some pinheaded provision in the Uniform Code of Military Justice?

He knew both Green and Sweet. He would call Green within a day, as a professional courtesy.

◆ ◆ ◆

Everyone in DC received the Vegas story at the same time. Even the principals in the Pentagon, including the Secretary of Defense, stared at their monitors in wonderment. There were so many unaddressed questions that reporters could guarantee themselves employment for as long as they wanted. Over a lifetime, Pack had proved to be a news magnet; the man who actively shunned publicity generated it as few ever have.

Green's instantaneous reaction was that this was a good omen. The essential elements of the story, Green mused, were these: A man already broadly recognized as an unselfish, patriotic Marine who had bled for the country he cherishes had done it again. He stood up to strong anti-American forces, and he felled their leader, struck him dead in almost biblical fashion. He *smote* the man. Some of the more fanciful reporters were asking ruminatively whether this Pack could have risen from the desert floor to slay the satanic Mohamed Ali-Mumen. The man trying to be the hero without a face has one, and the nation is seeing it. *Yes*, Green thought, *many have seen that face before, but now the good news is, there's a fresh generation seeing it for the first time*. The adoring youth who voted this administration into office were angling sharply away from it. And it was more than an inability to find a good job. They had seen love of country evaporating as they had been told by professors and preachers this country is nothing special—well, yeah, it's exceptional, the President gritted his teeth in reply to a question, in the same way Britain's exceptional to the Brits and Ghana is to Ghanaians. Americans of all ages and genders and races and moneyed classes, Green reflected, desired desperately to get out of the grip of gloom and invest their spirits in the best-performing stock on any market: our Founding Principles. *Maybe*

I can't ram Pack into the Superintendency of West Point, but if I can't, this momentary calling attention to who Pack is, and why, is good for the country.

The three who met at Green's residence at Fort Myer got together before a Retired Military Officers Association event in Old Town Alexandria. Rogers said, "I think this uproar in Vegas could hurt his chances as much as it helps, if we get that far. His face and name have new life. Don't you think, for example, that a group like Liberation Links, the frequent disrupter of Congressional hearings, would stand in his way to appointment to any position? He has blood on his hands, they'll say. And I can only imagine what Reverend Wilford will say. In fact, he might be preparing an assault on Pack's good name as we speak, just because. Racial injustice, he'll claim."

"If Simon came along with us, the only men we had to persuade were the Army Chief of Staff and the Marine Corps Commandant," Sweet added. "Now there might be satellite pols who want their names connected, for and against, and they'll try to pressure the two decision-makers. You know General Pembrook best, Harris. What do you think?"

"In my considered opinion," Green seemed to be saying to himself alone, "Wayne Pembrook is a strong leader. He fights battles worth fighting and doesn't engage in those not worth fighting. He will understand in his bones this one is worth fighting, and he'll do the right thing. What will cause his back to stiffen will be opposition to our recommendation. He will support us, gentlemen, and he will obtain the Commandant's approval. This is a sealed deal."

♦ ♦ ♦

Before Pack returned Green's call, Green called again. This time Pack picked up, with his normal drawn out "Ah-lowww."

"Simon, Harris Green here, and I'm relieved more than you know that you answered. Big congratulations for stopping Ali-Mumen, however that happened, but I'm not calling about that. I know you like directness,

Simon, and efficient use of time, so here's the issue: I want your concurrence before recommending the Chief select you to get West Point back on track."

Pack laughed, easy at first, then hard. "Look, Harris, I know all you honchos there in the Pentagon, some better than others. But whose idea of a cruel joke is this? I would have dissuaded my own children from going to West Point, if they had been interested. I don't know who Army football's last game was against, or the game before that. The team is an embarrassment. It's been at least twenty years since I thought West Point produced better combat officers than four or five premier ROTC programs.

"The only time I've been there in forever was as their Founder's Day dinner guest speaker. The Supe, Comm, and Dean stood to lead a standing applause—with crowd cheering as whipped-cream topping—as I took the podium. Within a minute or two, they were choking on their chicken bones as I laced the Academy *de pied en cap*, as you educated people say. If the correct course heading is true north, I more or less said, this Academy is listing to the southeast, and every manjack—even that expression didn't go over well—better examine himself with great care.

"The ballroom was in shock. The three Generals couldn't believe another General, and a Marine guest at that, was in their house, eating their lunch in the open. Someone there erred in not asking for an outline of my comments, but if they had, I wouldn't have given it. So, Harris, I'm not your typical rah-rah alum. I've been pissed at the great USMA a long time. So, no, you gotta be shittin' me, buddy, if you think I want to go there.

"Have you forgotten how many other-than-Army Generals have been Supes? That would be zero. Maybe you guys forgot, I am duly and officially retired from the US Marine Corps. I served long and the record says honorably. I have a damn near perfect life at the moment. I live in a place where the scenery still brings a catch in my throat each new day, and I make enough for beer money. Any other questions?"

"Would you let us give you a ticket to come and sit down with us here?" Green asked.

"I'm not wasting anyone's money. My answer is no, Harris. Besides, I'm over the hill."

"Well," Green replied in what he thought could be an opening, "you and I know whatever you've been up to for months now establishes you're not over any hill. I want to walk into the Chief's office tomorrow, and tell him you need to be the next Supe. Your boss in the Marine Corps will be ecstatic at the chance to bring you back to fix West Point. I'm not into currying favor or begging favors. This is a critical time in our history, Simon, and you are without any doubt the one, the only man who can save West Point. I have no doubt you will. More than West Point is at stake, in my opinion, but that's beyond the scope of this call. I am asking that you be unselfish one last time. We'll figure out ways to take care of your cabin till you return to it. In fact, I promise you, I will travel into territory I've never seen to promise you get the assurances and support you need."

Silence for half a minute. "Simon, you still with me?"

Another quarter minute elapsed. Then Pack said, "Call me a fool and before noon Mountain Time tomorrow. A little deliberate faulty parallelism just for you, Harris. Until then, out."

The line disconnected, but Green felt he had connected. He was hopeful, very much so. *Life is passing strange, how it confounds you*, he considered. But he recollected his satori.

The next day, when Pack answered, he began to talk without formality or preamble. "My answer is a conditional yes. You relay to the Chief that, as has always been the case, he needn't concern himself with ethical shortcomings with respect to my prospective office. I've always been clean, and will be. And tell the Chief don't worry about the budget. He won't get a bloated budget request from me. I'll demand West Point remain the place Sam Sarkeisian or Samuel P. Huntington said never disappoints the tourist. I'll demand it look like the mammy-jammin' United States Military Academy, not the county poorhouse, and I'll ramp up field training, but I'll ask for what we need, and not a penny more. Look me up, see what my record as money-steward is.

"At the same time, I'll go Wild West on anyone up there who doesn't accept that our mission is to furnish the finest officers in the world. I'll be bent on sending to the field officers who know how to conduct military operations and how to win America's wars. Some, judging from what I've observed recently, aren't going to like me. I expect you'll hear some pig-squealing all the way down there. If I'm gonna throw aside the life I have now, even temporarily, to take on a job I never wanted, I'm gonna do it right and I'm gonna do it on my own terms.

"I'll give you a last chance to reconsider this, Harris. I'm not going to be a university president or chancellor. I'm going to be the by-damn Super-intender, and I'm going to *Super-intend.* I'm not going to leave everything up to subordinates. I *will* step on toes. The Association of Graduates will be unhappy I won't be incessantly on the road cadging for donations to various funds. I ain't gonna be the fund-raiser-in-chief, and I will not attend events sponsored by the American Association of University Professors. The Athletic Director, and for that matter, the Army Athletic Association won't like the grenades I'll probably lob in their direction. We must be clear about all I've said.

"One last nonnegotiable condition: You arrange it so there'll be no change of command ceremony. I want him cleared out, bag and baggage, before I step on Academy grounds. Word has gotten out about Norther. I will not exchange the flag with him. He has sullied his office, and I will not be an accessory to it.

"My comments aren't intended to be comprehensive. I just want all concerned to sense my approach to the mission. In a span of minutes, I believe I've said all I care to at this time."

Green said, "General Pack, you may count on our unqualified support. We are indebted to you, and deeply grateful you have agreed to accept. General Pembrook will be in touch shortly. Thank you, General."

Green's analysis of Pembrook's reaction was dead on. There had been some opposition, which only cemented his conviction that the decision to appoint Simon Pack was the right one. Pembrook had privately been sizing up other candidates for several months, but none was as intriguing as this recommendation. After Sweet and Rogers eagerly endorsed the proposal, Pembrook signed off. The Marine Corps happily obliged.

His office empty, Pembrook thought, *I'm proud of this selection. Proud because I could've gone with someone safe, someone who would keep things quiet up there, get a passing performance rating, attract little attention. Instead, I've chosen a man who'll bring positive change, but at a price. Good to be reminded every so often what it feels like to man up. I'll just try to avoid going in the direction of West Point, because if I get too close, I'll surely feel the shock waves.*

Chapter Ten

Strife

Cymbals clashed in the firmament. Thunder rolled through the heavens. Thick heavy summer clouds dumped gobs of rain on West Point. This federal reservation fifty miles north of New York City is a diamond at all times of the year, but it sparkles with multifaceted brilliance in spring and summer, as it did even in this soaker. For the tourist, there is comfort here. The architecture is massive, Gothic, reassuring in its solidity. The sprawling parade ground, the Plain, is as smooth as a golf green. Cadets, whatever their uniform and activity of the moment, convey the sense of organization and discipline. The grass all around the Post in these months smells newly mown, a reminder to most tourists of happy childhoods. To one side of the Plain sits Quarters 100, the Superintendent's residence, a French Quarter–looking pre-Victorian built in 1820 at a cost of $6,670. Overlooking the Plain on the highest ground is the Cadet Chapel, up around Lusk Reservoir and Michie Stadium, which was pronounced "Mikey." Beyond the Plain to the front are the reviewing stands where the public watches the frequent parades. Behind the reviewing stand is Trophy Point, which looks down onto an amphitheater, and farther down, onto numerous athletic fields and facilities, and on to the Hudson River. Visitors pause to examine numerous statues, including those dedicated to the American soldier, Eisenhower, Washington, Patton, and MacArthur.

Last week heralded New Cadet Barracks, commonly termed "Beast." Something along the lines of eleven hundred young men and women will go through about six weeks of rigorous training. If they are able to reach the end of the summer, they will take an oath and be ceremonially welcomed into the Corps of Cadets. During Beast, however, they are New Cadets, not cadets. A quarter of the upper-class cadets form the chain of command that trains the New Cadets. The rest of the upper classes are embedded with Active Duty units around the world; doing field training at nearby Camp Buckner, which is part of the Academy Reservation; or on leave.

Two weeks ago, the outgoing Superintendent relinquished his position to the Commandant, Brigadier General George Bass, on an interim basis. The newly promoted Lieutenant General Simon Pack would arrive next week. Pack's name streams in daily media reports, continuing to rekindle his fame. Every cadet is aware of the man who will take charge. The Firsties, or seniors, will see their third Supe. To them, their Supe has had no material impact on their cadet lives. His orientation, they have been led to believe, is external to West Point. He works the budget, testifies before Washington committees, proselytizes on behalf of Academy interests, tries to keep Old Grads happy. The Corps of Cadets is the bailiwick of the Commandant, the Superintendent a light-year away.

First Classmen Gary Cline and Paul Demetrios share a room on the first floor of the Central Area barracks. Each has done well as a cadet, but at present, both wear the lowly cadet rank of sergeant, indicating that they have no cadet command responsibilities. This accommodation is normal for all football players during the fall season. They are likely to be rewarded come second semester, in January, when football season is over. Recently, the Academy granted football players marginally more athletic-training time during the summer, when every other Division I program is in high gear for the upcoming season. Coach Sumner had lobbied hard with the Athletic Director, who had in turn lobbied former Superintendent Norther for modest changes that would enable players to attain competitive bulk. But Norther was pleased the former coach concurred that cadets of such size and shape would not comport with the image of a male cadet Norther had in mind.

Cline has started as an undersized guard for the past two years. For that position, 290 pounds or more is standard; he weighed 252 at the beginning of last season and finished at 237. Demetrios has decent size for a running back, 208 pounds, but he runs a mediocre 40-best of 4.68 seconds. The football team's record over the two years these men have started is six wins, eighteen losses.

Cline is a preseason candidate for the William V. Campbell Trophy, awarded to the Division I college football player with the best combination of academics, community service, and on-field performance. He says, "Whaddya think Pack will have to say about this football program? It *is* the program, isn't it? Even Coach Sumner hasn't gotten the administration to let us use all the practice time the NCAA allows. We aren't fed as well as our competitors, our lifting routines were primitive until Coach Nasby arrived, our former coaches were bland technocrats, and we probably don't get enough rest. How many of our O-linemen benched over four hundred under the old regime? No, don't answer that, 'cause we know the answer. I can stand getting my brains beat in Saturday after Saturday, but I hate, *hate* the embarrassment of losing three starts out of four. Paulie, you've met my dad and have a feel for his rep around the Army."

In fact, Cline's dad is a four-star Combatant Command Commander—in other words, a very powerful man, and one especially deserving of his rank. Cline continued, "My dad says Pack was the purest illustration of leadership he ever saw in any walk of life. Intense man, I guess. Even with the five-year service commitment of his time, an NFL team offered him a good bonus. Maybe he's lost his taste for football, I've heard that, but either way, I can't imagine he'll be satisfied with the status quo of Army football."

Demetrios said, "Nothing will change. If he were coming in as the new Commandant of Cadets, I'd think he might be interested in this football team. But he's coming in not just as the Supe—someone above football, all sports, most likely—but also as one being pulled out of retirement. Did he ever even think of Army football over there in the Marine Corps? In fact, was he a Navy fan? Instead of dreaming he could be interested in Army football, I'll take wagers on how many times we even see him outside of the occasional parade. Nope, Gary, the miserable state we're in, it hurts me to say, is where we'll stay for one more season at a minimum. The coaches and athletic staff will get paid, we will graduate and move on, and Army football will still be stuck in quicksand."

"You might be right. Your opinion's as good as mine," Cline replied, "but you have to grant the point that General Pack is different from anything West Point will have seen in a long, long time. There's never been a Marine Supe. Don't you wonder what brought all this about? How we are about to have as our nominal leader a man who recently slew two Al Qaeda chiefs, maybe three by now, without a shot fired, in some mysterious operation?"

"Oh, yeah, who here hasn't chewed on that?" Paul Demetrios was spit-shining his low-quarter shoes. He raised one for closer inspection, one hand inside it. Then he lowered it and locked eyes with Gary Cline. "I assumed only people our age in Berkeley or Boulder use the word *surreal*. That's not been a West Point word, but it is now, isn't it?"

♦ ♦ ♦

The Commandant of Cadets paced in his office, no more than fifty meters from Cadets Cline and Demetrios. Brigadier General George Bass was not the very model of the modern brigadier general, with apologies to Gilbert and Sullivan. His forearms were more hirsute than his dome. He looked ten to fifteen years older than his forty-five. His five o'clock shadow appeared at three; he possessed a PhD in pogonotrophy. His normal visage was saturnine.

Slightly less than medium height, just shy of overweight, more dumpy than chunky, George Bass would never flash impressively in a uniform. Profanity was in his nature. Not irreverent, but profane. His dreary dentition was nothing to write home about; unappealing, would you say?, and after a few days of neglecting the ears, they need an angry weed-whacking. Not a handsome man by a long shot, on the basis of appearance alone. Trainloads of peers had glanced at Bass in profile and meditated upon how he could attain any degree of professional success. But he was an honest man, and a tactically and technically proficient infantry officer, and when you lumped all his qualities in Bass's corporeal wrapping, he was beloved by soldiers. He was a blurter, an irrespecter of rank. He had been rudely dressed down many times, but he possessed the uncommon quality of receiving and perceiving all attacks upon himself as impersonal, a quality that imbued Bass with an agreeable equanimity and frustrated his detractors. Some of his bosses from years past were probably just now experiencing strokes from bottled-up rage with Bass. Meanwhile, Bass's health was excellent.

The last twelve months had been grueling and gruesome. As a true leader, Bass deplored the sight of the recently departed Supe. There were days Bass was convinced that man's main concern was the cut of his fingernails and the particulars of the cuticles' lunar phase. Now he had to shake off that dickhead's image, and the man's name with it, he hoped, and zero in on the needs of his replacement, the estimable Lieutenant General Simon Pack.

Bass had never met Pack, but he was energized by the idea of working in the vicinity of a kindred spirit. Too much had been reported about this sumbitch Pack for him not to be a no-shit soldier—he caught himself. *Marines don't say "soldier." They are taught to say "Marine." We'll have to work out an accommodation on what we call—aw, hell, the people here are going to become soldiers, end of story.*

Lieutenant General Norther, the Superintendent whose name Bass wanted to banish, demanded briefings on everything but showed interest in nothing. He was the monarch delighted to confer upon his subjects a wise nod, a slow roll of the head, a furrowed brow, or a faint smile to suggest, "With you, my son, I am pleased." If Dave Norther was the cynosure of all eyes, he was serene and satisfied. The perigee of his performance, as far as Bass was concerned, occurred in February of this year, at the National Prayer Breakfast, an event intended to unify Americans. Under pressure from the New York City chapter of the Convocation of American-Islamic Associations, the caitiff Norther disinvited a retired General who had co-founded Delta Force, as well as a former Marine and head of the Family Research Council, from speaking at the event at West Point. Staging his own protest, George Bass did not attend. Bass was unafraid to show, in a thousand small ways, his total disdain for Norther and the decisions he rendered. A good commander would have relieved Bass for cause, but Norther was too weak for the confrontation it would spawn.

OK, that bastard's purged from memory. Forever. Really. Maybe. I hope so, anyway. A man that ugly, I can't promise I'll never think of him again. He had undercut Bass with metronomic regularity, with ridiculous emphases such as pledging to strengthen ties with Vassar. *Self-discipline, George. Eject him from the game for flagrant fouls of military un-professionalism. Don't allow him to remain on the field. Make him disappear from view.*

It was time now to prepare the landing zone for LtGen Pack's arrival. A knock on Bass's door. "Yeah?" he yelled back, still heated from thoughts of the pusillanimous Norther.

"General," his secretary said, cracking the door open, "the Secretary of the General Staff's office sent this message by courier a moment ago. Said you are to open it immediately."

"Thanks, Sanja." Bass opened the long letter-sized envelope as he normally did, by tearing off one of the short sides of the rectangle. *More efficient that way,* he thought. It read: "George, you may call at your convenience if you like, but it's not necessary. You have my arrival schedule. Plan on two hours alone with me at my residence thirty minutes after I get in the house. Give me a list of what you regard as the most-important items on my calendar for the next forty-five days. I'm thinking those items shouldn't number more than two or three. If they're meetings, attach the minutes of the last two such meetings. I do not want office calls paid by anyone at the Academy. I do a lot of management by walking around. If you are asked before I get there in a week whether I have passed on any guidance, you can say, 'The General says he'll be around to see you. He does not want me to schedule any office calls, because he prefers to visit you on your turf on short notice.'

"Personal for you: I've checked on you, not by reviewing files but by talking with warriors I trust. They tell me you're one of the true breed, so I already am invested heavily in you. I like small staffs, which our new Academy chief of staff understands. If I find any section above authorized personnel levels, it's overwhelmingly likely to get cut. In addition, I like to rely disproportionately on a few workhorses. I demanded a new chief, not because there was anything wrong with the old one, but because I wanted the best damn colonel I can find, and someone I know with whom I can communicate in shorthand. Ditto with the captain aide-de-camp. I intend for you, the chief, and my new aide to work like pack mules crossing the Rockies. And I want you and the chief to spar with me. Speak up if and when you think I'm wrong. I don't want eunuchs and epicenes around me. Unlike a man with whom I recently had an unfortunate encounter, I am not a complicated man. Speak to me directly.

"You can show me a list of meetings Norther routinely took part in, as well as give your best guess at why, but again, I doubt I'll follow suit. I think West Point needs real change, or—I can assure you—I would never have accepted this duty. If you agree with that, you'll also agree that real change demands real *change*. If you're worried that you could be committing professional mutilation by joining me in this crusade, you'd better pick up the phone to me immediately. We have work to do, and we will be scorned by hordes in the doing of it. As you no doubt have figured out, when you get to be a General, you should expect to have no friends. If too many approve of what you're doing, you're probably failing.

"Because you have the only USMA current on-the-ground experience among you, me, and the chief, I'm going to have to lean on you a lot. So, General George Bass, here's your first big assignment from me, and this will constitute the agenda for our private meeting next week: Identify what you believe are the five biggest problems facing West Point, and explain why you think so. (If you want to be modern and call them issues or challenges or just things that are bollocksed up, I don't much care at this point.)"

"Sonofabitch," Bass grumbled approvingly, "Norther spoke Swahili or sumshit I didn't get. I can speak Pack's language."

Even the form of the letter confirmed some of what he'd heard about Pack. Handwritten, in a rock-steady backslant featuring outsized loops in the *h*'s and *k*'s and *l*'s and *f*'s. What would a graphologist make of this careful cursive from a man who had long functioned in a high-pressure world? To begin with, a right-hander like Pack who writes in such backhand is rebellious, almost without exception. The large loops suggest an easy and effective communicator. As a rule, the busier the professional person, the greater the chance his cursive will scrawl into obscurity. The Hummingbird in fact communicates the pride he has in his busy-ness through the inscrutability of his poor penmanship. Pack goes the opposite direction, slaps busy-ness in the face with his carefully crafted cursive.

Bass didn't want to sidetrack himself, but he was fascinated by his amateur analysis. He had observed the evolution of his own handwriting since he was a kid and had never enjoyed the conclusions he had drawn. He changed styles often, not so much because he wanted to as needed to. It's something deep in his head of which he's never gotten control; he was certain of that. Today, small neat forehand—he tells himself this will forever be the style he affects. In three days, he adopts a large, looping backslant. Three more days, and he takes to a large, straight, up-and-down cursive-print combo. With pens and pencils, any and all writing instruments, cheap and expensive, he is similarly unequal to the task of settling on one with which he is comfortable for more than a week.

Bass was a little disheartened that the analytical revelations of these few minutes manifest in some vague sense his inferiority relative to Pack. *Got yourself in a funk; get out of your normal environment and do something.* Bass called the Regimental Tactical Officer running Beast, one of the four in charge of the Corps of Cadets, and announced with a tone of more aggression than normal that he was about to depart his office for an unannounced walk-through of the cadet living area. He wanted only the CQs of the nine companies to accompany him. The CQs, or Charges of Quarters, are duty-rostered cadets who act as the company commander's representatives twenty-four hours a day. They will take notes and write up deficiency reports as required.

No cadet likes to see a commissioned officer in his company area. A commissioned officer is not there to spread good news but to find shortcomings in your performance. And Bass is not just any officer. He is the senior officer in charge of the USCC. The USCC Blue Book lists thousands of offenses for which demerits or a passel of demerits, called a *slug*, may be awarded. The Blue Book is a hefty tome, as is to be expected of a document that has been continuously refined since the establishment of West Point on July 4, 1802. Underwear not folded properly, socks not perfectly aligned, dust on the rear of the locker, bed not sufficiently tight, footgear improperly shined, items in the wastebasket during certain hours, and water droplets in the sink are but a minuscule sample of punishable offenses. Different categories of cadets receive different monthly allocations of demerits. If a cadet has accumulated more than his allocation for the month, he will receive "punishment tours," which normally means having to prepare for and stand special inspections during weekends, then march back and forth across a paved quadrangle adjacent to cadet barracks, with a rifle, at a prescribed pace, all under the supervision of cadet officers. Four demerits over the allocation means four hours marching the Area.

A vicious cycle often ensues: Stand punishment tour inspection, be "awarded" more demerits, get more punishment tours. This is not a fraternity or sorority game to cadets. Getting into a hole is spirit-robbing and hammers at the will to resist. Having the Blue Book thrown at you for four years builds the hard shell essential to surviving the four years of West Point. So word that the Commandant was in the company area is genuinely fearsome. This was midday, so the barracks were nearly deserted, with all the New Cadets at their training sites. Only a few upper-class cadets occupied a couple of rooms on each floor.

General Bass had little interest in laying demerits on New Cadets. That is primarily an upper-class cadre function. His focus was the cadet training cadre performance. He had dictated pages of general observations to CQs, more positive than negative. The most important notes he'd reserve for personal discussion with the Regimental Tactical Officers, and those memos would concern how well the Academy had trained the cadet trainers.

Each year's Beast brings some new misfortune. At least one family will be heartbroken at the news. Last year, with a week left in the New Cadet training, one candidate walked away and disappeared.

New Cadet Bryan Groom had arrived with top academic credentials. He had participated in high school athletics but without distinction. He snapped from the physical and psychological pressures of Beast. Bryan spazzed when required to perform myriad tasks. Upperclassmen called him "Groom Goon" and for several days forbade him to touch his full plate of food at every meal. The mess table trouble began when Groom took more than his one-tenth share when the food was passed around. Beginning at that moment and each meal thereafter, Mr. Groom was made to yell for minutes on end, "I like to dick on my classmates!"

They made him brace against a hallway wall and read for hours from a random book in his loudest voice, during which time his mates were feverishly preparing themselves for the following day. The upper-class cadre was hard on young Groom, but others among his prospective classmates received virtually the same treatment. Bryan Groom simply was unable to cope and should have resigned. Instead, he fled. Days later, after an extensive search, he was found naked in a stark Canadian farm field, a saber run through his gut, an apparent seppuku, at least a gaijin version. Animals had gnawed at his innards. *Unfortunate*, Bass reflected, *but we're making soldiers here, not milksops*. Besides, if the boy had it in him to drive a sharp object all the way through his middle, he should have made it through Beast.

With a single sharp rap, Bass threw open the door to an upper-class room. The occupants bolted to their feet in a position of attention. "Sir, Cadets Cline and Demetrios reporting to the Commandant, prepared for inspection," they said.

"Oh, I doubt that, gentlemen. That you're prepared for inspection. You weren't expecting an inspection, were you? Don't answer. I know you weren't. I'm going to look around, anyway." Bass immediately recognized on the windowsill a generous helping of bananas, apples, bread, sliced roast beef, and Apple Brown Betty dessert. "Well, well, I don't have to search at all. I see water clinging to the side of your sink. I also see you've brought mess hall food back to your room. Did you receive permission to do that?"

"No, sir."

"Why did you do it then? Better be a good answer."

Cline was the designated speaker. "Sir, I brought the food from the mess hall. Cadet Demetrios did not. I brought it for two reasons." Cline hoped the Comm might be willing to drop the subject at this point.

"Mr. Cline, I'd like to hear those reasons."

"Yes, sir. I have a couple of New Cadets I want to see make it through. They aren't getting enough on their tables, in my judgment. Both of these New Cadets were recruited. One for the football team, and the other for the wrestling program. Sir, the fact is that these two, unlike many New Cadets, aren't carrying around any baby fat. These two are both lean and mean already. In any case, we have an Army football team that's twenty-five pounds lighter on average than our lightest opponent. I don't think we need to give our opponents any additional advantage."

"What are their names?"

Cline named them.

"About what portion of what you took out did you give them?"

"About three-fourths of it, sir."

"You know I'm the Commandant of the USCC, which means you know I am, among other things, charged with enforcing the Blue Book and with seeing general disciplinary standards are upheld. What I believe about specific elements of the Blue Book is totally immaterial with respect to my enforcing them. What punishment should I render for this violation, Mr. Cline?" Bass asked.

Cline could see Bass wasn't concerned about the sink water. "The Blue Book calls for six demerits, sir, so that is my answer," Cline answered.

Bass said, "Off the record, I'm going to give you an opinion about carrying food out of the Mess, to wit, I don't give a crap. If you had told me you did not share that food with those two New Cadets, though, I'd have written you up. Good job, Mr. Cline. Kick ass on the field, men. No excuses this season."

Bass felt a lightness in his step as he strode back to his office.

♦ ♦ ♦

The Academy was astir. Pack's star remained bright, as the media strove to quench the public's thirst for the hidden curiosities of the Vegas episode. Hundreds of photos of him from the past featured him wearing either battle dress utilities or an Army football uniform. Bass's favorite was the one showing Pack flattening a Pitt Panther nose tackle. "Is General Pack here yet?" members of the public queried passing cadets. Cadets themselves were eager for a glimpse of the man. The First Captain, the highest-ranking cadet in the Corps, was astonished that just two days from Pack's arrival, there had been no announcement of a reception parade or other ceremony involving cadets.

The other General Officer on post, Brigadier General Elijah Steinberg, who held dual doctorates and served as Dean of the Academic Board, was not at all happy at having been shunned thus far. *By the gods*, Steinberg thought, *Superintendent Ego Pack will rue the day he came in with his high-and-mighty ways and tried to trample on the Academy's raison d'être. I sit at the head of thirteen academic departments, so if he wants a fight, it will be fourteen to one in my favor.* Steinberg steadied a bit as he pondered the strength of his position. *From what I've heard, he's only a few genes removed from a Neanderthal, not a formidable match in a contest of minds.*

Over in the Army intercollegiate athletics offices, no real attention was directed to Pack's arrival. The Athletic Director had been in the job eight years, and was the scion of a well-known AD recently retired from Stanford. Superintendents left him alone, the way he liked it, and he had no cause to suspect this one would be different.

Truth be told, Pack was a virtual unknown to present occupants of West Point. The extant image derived chiefly from his rough-and-tumble exploits. Most harbored a picture of a troglodyte, a man 90 percent physical, 10 percent cerebral. Drill into the essence of Pack, though, and you found a man of reason. Sometime in his twenties, Simon Pack made one of the most influential discoveries of his life: The centrally vital battle ever fought is also the most widely fought, the struggle between passion and reason, heart and head, emotion and intellect. Both powerful forces live in each of us, but one typically predominates. One also typically prevails in national life. In modern America, Pack believed, feelings rule, powerfully so, and that is a dangerous condition. Understanding this primordial conflict explains so much of the world's doings. Just fifty years ago, there was reasonable balance between the two. Nowadays, the public is so conditioned to the natural superiority of emotion that its politicians can safely avoid intellectual defenses of their votes as long as they "strongly feel" they're right. Lieutenant General Simon Pack sat on a high plane of intellectual capacity and clear thinking, but few were aware of it until his rapier mind had disemboweled them. He anticipated engaging in the passion-versus-reason struggle once more at West Point.

Chapter Eleven

Kickoff

General Bass sipped coffee from a rusty-looking metallic canteen cup as he looked from his window onto the Plain, where New Cadets were formed into a dozen platoons of thirty people each. They trained with pugil sticks, doing circuits, martial arts, and drill and ceremony routines. A mazarine sky was the perfect background to the Plain's rich-green carpeting. It was a pleasant scene, soothing to a man of Bass's temperament. There had been the usual hiccups, but on the whole, this Beast was proceeding without serious incident. He could concentrate on the meeting with Pack. Finally, Pack would appear tomorrow. Bass grinned while thinking that he hoped Pack wouldn't need political backing anytime soon. How many requests for meetings with the Supe had he rejected from parasitic mayors, congressmen, a couple senators, even New York's governor? Getting your photo snapped with Simon Pack translated to votes, at least for a while longer.

George Bass had no second thoughts about either his discussion points or his method of delivery to Lieutenant General Pack. All over America, in and out of the military, even in many small businesses, today's standard is PowerPoint at a minimum, and flash-bang presentations in Technicolor with sound effects and intensifying techno wizardry at the top end. Bass had had to assemble and present these types of briefings so many times, he couldn't count them. When subordinates had to brief him, however, Bass insisted on simplicity of presentation but substantive content. He had often reminded his protégés that "simple is to simple-minded as lightning is to lightning bug. Simplicity is a virtue, simple-mindedness a vice, and you had damn well better know the difference."

At the same time, he could recall almost the precise moment he understood the importance of recognizing that people learn in different ways. Some are auditory, some visual, and some kinesthetic. Everyone uses all, but as with passion and reason, one style tends to hold sway. Bass's revelation was that the subordinate's learning style is relatively unimportant; it is the subordinate's responsibility to accommodate the senior's learning style. He therefore needed a quick primer on Pack's relationship with his staff. He had learned what he wanted from the spanking-new Academy chief of staff, the aforementioned colonel that Pack held in high esteem. Colonel Jim Dahl, Bass saw, was simply superior. He was a Marine. Every detail of his uniform and person was as carefully attended to as Bass's was frumpy. Direct, concise, and reserved, Colonel Dahl opined that Pack wanted some simple visuals to outline the overall direction of the presentation, but they could have been on butcher paper, a whiteboard, or a one-page handout. Pack wasn't opposed to pie charts and Venn diagrams and the like, Dahl said, but use them only when they seem the best way to make a point. If it's a map overlay for a combat operation, every military symbol must be meticulously rendered in accordance with the appropriate Field Manual. When Dahl had been Pack's Marine Division operations chief, he gave Pack a pocket Moleskine notebook labeled "Ops and Plans," where Pack used to jot notes. Pack, Dahl said, demanded all briefers be subject-matter experts, susceptible to interruptions, organized, and able to answer questions succinctly. Be organized—lay out the material from general to specific, then back to general—and speak with force and conviction. Never read from prepared copy. Far from being a problem for Bass, this set of requirements was right in his wheelhouse.

Colonel Dahl entered Bass's office, just a few doors down the hall from his own. "General," Dahl said, "I don't think I'm divulging a confidence, but in any case, I was about to inform you. It's not within your normal area of responsibility, but because you are the acting Superintendent, I will tell you that General Pack has directed me to reassign all aides aside from the residence groundskeeper. He wants the chef reassigned to the Cadet Mess. He wants the housekeepers returned to the Housing Office for further disposition. Says he will hire a housekeeper out of pocket. Because it is a national historic site, the residence may continue to be maintained by the federal government, which has a vested interest in the exterior upkeep. If there is a special occasion requiring a dinner at the residence, a cook from Cadet Mess can handle it as needed. Commented he has had plenty of practice buying and eating groceries. His one aide will be the captain. The appropriate staff sections will have made these changes by 0600 tomorrow. The Cadet Hostess, Mrs. Rose, who informs me she has occupied her position for thirty-seven years, is demanding to see him to explain what a mistake he is making. I'll mollify her, but Mother Hen isn't going down quietly."

"Roger, Jim, our Superintendent is already making his mark, and he ain't here yet. I'm all in. I hope you are as energized about getting on with this task as I am. I don't know details of changes about to occur here, but I can for damn sure write home that big change is a-blowin' in the Academy air, and I'm ready to do my part."

Dahl was on the way out when Bass's secretary, Sanja, delivered a message. Sanja was a placid lady, unruffled in anything but emergent situations. "General," Sanja said, "Senator Brandywine phoned. Not an aide. The Senator herself. Said to make you aware there will be consequences if you drag your heels on responding to her. Cursi—"

"Were you about to say she was cursing?"

Sanja blushed. Flames leapt from Bass's bulging eyes. "Did she curse, Sanja? I won't ask you to say the word or words, because you don't deserve to be in the middle of this. But you will tell me if she cursed."

"Yes, sir. In my opinion, it was vulgar."

"Sanja, next time she calls, refer her to Colonel Dahl. Here's a question for you, Sanja, and I'm pretty damn confident you know the answer. Is Senator Brandywine in my chain of command?"

"No, sir, she is not."

"And who do you work for?"

"Sir, I work for you, the Commandant of Cadets."

Now Bass was smiling. "OK, Sanja, we're both fine. You're the best. Keep pluggin'. It's almost time for us to start havin' some fun around here."

Sooner or later, they were sure to have a gunfight at the corral. Senator Kelly Brandywine was a member of the Board of Visitors, or BoV, referred to in 1972 Federal Statutes as "a central governing body of the Academy." Pack undoubtedly had passing familiarity with the Board's role, but it would be Bass's job to direct him to the specifics of the sad state of relations between the Board and the Academy, at least from Bass's perspective. General Norther and the Board had got on well, if not famously. Bass was thankful Pack would have to deal with the fifteen members of the Board, because Bass himself didn't have the patience at this juncture of his career, or the maturity, either. Of one thing Bass is dead-solid certain: Pack will not be the malleable tool Norther was. Yes, a storm is rising.

♦ ♦ ♦

Colonel Dahl phoned the Commandant that Pack's military flight had landed at Stewart Air National Guard Base in nearby Newburgh. ETA at Quarters 100 was forty minutes. "Good, Jim. Captain Cooper has all the keys and has walked through every inch of the place to be sure everything works and is in place? And the tailors are laid on for a fifteen hundred uniform fitting?"

"Check to all, sir. And for what it's worth, the Supe made a fine pick with young Captain Russell Cooper. Sorry for the unsolicited opinion, but there it is," Dahl replied. "Cooper will be by to escort you over once General Pack is settled."

"All right, Jimmy. You just tell that young shitferbrains he better have it together when he meets me, damn it all to hell. I feel like eatin' some captain ass this mornin'."

Bass was clearly in a good mood. Dahl smiled on the other end of the line, and hung up by saying, "I'll be sure to do that, sir."

♦ ♦ ♦

Captain Russell Cooper rapped solidly on the Commandant's door and entered. "Sir, Captain Cooper announcing General Pack is prepared for you. I will wait for you outside, sir."

"No need for that. I'm ready to go." Bass noted Cooper was in the battle dress uniform, no doubt at Pack's direction. What he saw was a tall, solidly built, crew-cut officer in his late twenties in a uniform bearing the Combat Infantryman's Badge, the Expert Infantryman's Badge, the Ranger Tab, and the Pathfinder Badge, indicators of Captain Cooper's drive and competence. Bass picked up his hat and moved past Cooper, asking "How many combat tours?"

"Three, sir."

Profound respect oozed from Bass. Observing that this fit young soldier moved with a marked limp and had trouble maintaining Bass's pace, Bass slowed a little with unstudied subtlety. "I'm proud of you, son," was all Bass said until they were in the Superintendent's study.

Cooper led Bass to the closed door of the study. "Here you are, sir," he said and hitched away in the opposite direction.

Strangely, the first thought to bubble into Bass's mind upon seeing Pack was *Mount Montana*, the *nom de hobo* that had by now become known and thus attached to Pack in the press.

What Bass said first was, "Welcome, General. You look well after the cross-country flight. I'm honored to meet you and glad to have you here, as everyone at the Academy is."

"For a day or two anyway, they might be glad to have me," Pack said with a chuckle, "until we get to work in earnest. I already made mistake number one, George. I wrote you that we would spend two hours together this morning. On the trip here, I thought that what we have to discuss—and I want this to be a discussion, not a briefing—will probably take longer. So if you need a few minutes to adjust your schedule, go ahead before we begin. This is an important use of time for me."

"Sir, I don't need to adjust. I'd be a dumbass for scheduling anything but this today. I am at your service for as long as it takes."

"Fine. First point, please."

Bass handed the Supe a sheet of paper on which were typed five subject headings. He commenced: "Until I announce point two, everything I say will fall under the rubric of 'Leadership.' We say we are the premier leadership laboratory in the world. I don't believe that is true today. It is obscene that many First Classmen graduate with their major leadership experience having been leading parades. What, really, does the cadet company commander do today? Quite a bit of admin crap gets pushed down to him, and he has counseling responsibility, but his real leadership requirements are negligible."

Pack interrupted. "Why aren't you including Recondo training and the rest of the field training at Camp Buckner?" Recondo training is a dollop of Ranger school.

"Buckner is good as far as it goes. It's just not intense enough or long enough. I think of the three physical fitness guidelines: frequency, intensity, and duration." Also, Buckner involved mostly Third Classmen, or sophomores, with just a handful of First Classmen, or seniors, whose main duty was to get the subordinates to training sites where Regular Army troops conducted the training. "And, let's face it, with all the recreational facilities out there, it has the earmarks of a summer camp for rich kids. Even if we agree Buckner training serves its purpose, what other rigorous military training do we give these cadets in the remaining three and three-quarter years?"

Bass paused, then added, "I suggest that one regiment a month should road march from here to Buckner—12.7 miles—on Saturday mornings, under full combat gear. Bivouac Saturday night, march back to Post Sunday morning."

"With sabers, M14s and shiny bayonets?" Pack pushed Bass facetiously.

"Well, you're getting to the point, sir. I want two weapons for every cadet—a marching and parade weapon, and a combat weapon. And I want sufficient combat unit crew-served weapons to service one USCC regiment. M60 machine guns, 81mm mortars, squad automatic weapons, you've got the picture. Get 9mm Berettas for cadet officers. I'll work the details and disseminate them to every swinging Richard and Annie on this hallowed ground. Start in September, the first full month of the new academic year. So I have about six weeks to make it happen."

"George, I think you're trying to make soldiers out of these cadets... I love it. OK, here's what we're going to do: I want real military training involving live-fire on that Saturday. I want First Classmen to plan and execute the whole thing. Route of march, checkpoints, flank and rear security, a genuine training mission. You figure out the details, but I'm thinking it starts as a road march, but concludes in spring with a forced march. The first time out perhaps involves marksmanship, but climaxes later in the year with a live-fire assault course. We'll do the first time through over relatively flat ground, then go to rougher terrain that has nine- to ten-percent grades. The cadet chain will receive postexercise evals from the Tactical Department, who must therefore be integral to the training. But during the training mission itself, Tacs give wide berth to cadet leaders. That includes writing five-paragraph field orders with annexes as needed. This will occur every month of the academic year. I think you know where you'll find me when this kicks off. And, George, I've done this kind of thing before, so I can anticipate virtually every bitch and ramification. Lot of people, for example, gonna have to put their heads together to figure out the arms room piece."

Bass was struggling to restrain his excitement. *This man thinks like a soldier, no doubt about it. The bitching will begin immediately and from four corners, and that's a good thing*, he was thinking. "I like it, sir. I like everything we can do to advance the thinking that our mission is to fight and win America's wars. Period. And that means constant reminders that they are required to close with and destroy the enemy. It means marching to the sound of the guns. It means imbuing a warrior ethos and everlasting respect for the honorable profession of arms. Quartermasters and adjutants general and the other support branches of the Army have their places, and although not every graduate can become a combat arms officer, no graduate of this institution should aspire to be other than a combat arms officer. Which, if I may, leads to my second point."

"Before you get there, George," Pack inserted, "I need you to understand that the directive concerning the monthly marches to Camp Buckner is an illustration of my intent. You exercise initiative within the bounds of that intent, and I'll support you. Footnote: In my mind, concentric initiative is the type that spins around the center core of intent, in direct support of it. But there's the eccentric type as well, which would be like the Earth breaking away from its orbit around the sun. Keep it concentric, and we're OK. Any doubts, let's talk, all right?"

"Understood, sir," Bass replied. Then he plowed on. "I'm going to a second point now, but after thinking this assignment through as closely as I'm capable, I honestly can't say any point is more important than another. It's not *the* second point. They're just totally enmeshed, and it seems to me that without tackling them all together, real change will not ensue."

Pack again: "George, you had to believe I wouldn't have solicited your views merely to make you feel good. I gave myself the same task, of course. I want to learn where and if our views are substantially disparate. And I don't intend to waste time with studies and committee reports. If I believe we've found the azimuth to success, I do intend to start the march toward the goal forthwith.

"As our first Superintendent, Sylvanus Thayer, wrote to his sister, and I paraphrase: I accepted this appointment as a solemn duty, and I am determined to perform it whatever the consequences to me personally or professionally," Pack said. "I am going to put the following in writing, but please listen with care to three principles I have decided upon to direct everything we do at the United States Military Academy. And, George, that is everyone: Director of Admissions, Army Athletic Association, the academic departments...everyone. One: Every facet of Academy life will orient on developing military leaders. Two: Philosophical idealism. Three:

Knowledge defined as the deduction of immutable truths through mental and emotional discipline. Put all of them together, and you get one word: *character.*

"There isn't much difference between you and me. I had two stars, as much by accident as anything, and by dint of fate, have three now. You have one, and most surely will have more, maybe four one of these days. I don't look at myself as the savior of West Point. I could be its destroyer, too, I suppose. I'm just a Marine, but that's saying a lot. I believe in my bones this is a noble profession, and I want to restore reverence for profession to this place. Sometimes institutions inadvertently and unwittingly and imperceptibly begin a slow drift away from what made them great, and someone comes along and rehabilitates and revamps them. I haven't done the latter yet, but that's what I aim to do, with the help of a tough kernel of likeminded professionals. Give me a sec. You know where the head is."

Pack went out and had a word with Cooper. The rich scent of freshly brewed coffee filled this part of the house. He had sent a shopping list ahead to Cooper days ago along with a blank check, so the kitchen was stocked with the staples. From this point on, he would depend on no one for provisions. With two mugs in one hand and a plate bearing sugar, Stevia, and cream, he reentered the study and laid it on a low table between him and Bass.

"Nice, boss," said Bass, "but I won't plan on you being the majordomo on a regular basis. Thanks."

"Yeah, don't plan on it. But, if we're still going an hour from now, I'm going in that kitchen and throw some lunch together, and I'm not a luncheater. Missed my breakfast this morning."

"You don't mind my saying, sir, Captain Cooper can call in a request to the mess hall, and they'll be happy to bring it over. You need a little time to get organized," Bass offered.

"Nope. This is the way I operate. And if I hadn't long ago accepted self-reliance as a way of life, I would have after following Norther into this job. He abused his office, this office, and it's up to me to pour a drum of disinfectant all over that behavior. All right, let's get back to where we were."

"Sir, just before the break, you spoke of reverence for the profession of arms. I think today's graduate lacks that. He doesn't know enough about America's great battles, especially the Army's, or about the heroics of the great Americans who've led our fighting forces. He doesn't know about our traditions in enough detail to enable him to feel them. Ours is an exceptional military, and I think this decade's graduate doesn't appreciate that."

Pack said, "I've worked with six, eight, ten—I don't know how many nations' armies. At some point, all of them would revert to the same excuse: 'If we had your money, we would have as good a military as you. You have equipment we don't have.' After a while, I'd get tired of it and tell them our military is exceptional not because of hardware; but one, because we have systems and procedures for doing things, so if one man goes down, the next up can step in because he has been taught to know the system; two, because we make a heavy investment in training and exercises, and most other countries aren't serious about training in the way we are; and three, because of our faith in our people. No country has a noncommissioned officer corps remotely as good as ours. They are in fact our backbone. We let them make decisions. We demand they make decisions. We're the only country in the world with such decentralized decision authority. In other nations, officers fear if they cede any authority, it's lost forever, and their positions are threatened. And you know what? We don't have enough decentralization in our Marine Corps and Army to suit me, and we probably don't have adequate decentralized decision authority at this putative leadership lab."

Bass remained silent until he was positive Pack was finished.

"General, I understand what you tasked me with. No offense, and certainly nothing personal, for getting into the Dean's business. Since the time we were cadets, *The West Point Atlas of American Wars* has been the standard military history text. It's a brilliant work of scholarship, and may still be of use."

"Oh, I remember the *Atlas*. As a cadet, I wondered who drew those incredibly detailed maps. I wasn't one who could, or wanted, to recite where a particular platoon was at 0737 on a particular day. I was always more interested in the bigger picture," Pack said.

"Well, sir," Bass continued, "I couldn't remember the big *or* the little picture. We studied everything from Thucydides to the Korean War, a comprehensive sweep of history that might be too much so. We might allot more time to personalizing the great battles, digging into what officers and their soldiers were actually doing, what decisions they wrestled with, and the nature of some of the problems they dealt with. I think we ought to study in detail ten great battles, which incidentally might include Ramadi in particular and Anbar in general, after which cadets leave knowing they've wrung significant leadership lessons from them. Lessons that will stick with them."

"That was my point a moment ago, George," Pack reiterated. "Yes, our profession can't be total sterility."

"So," Bass went on, "in the effort to make them understand the carefully selected battles, we dwell more on knowledge of the terrain, the enemy, the hardware and technology, relative combat power, time constraints, how this battle fit into the operational and strategic plan, and so on. For reasons you know but cadets won't until they study it, Kasserine Pass could be one as well. Mine is the concept. Theirs"—he pointed across Thayer Road toward the academic departments—"is the parsing of it. Secondary schools have been teaching for years that we have gotten our asses kicked in all recent wars. Just as there are high school history teachers who still call us baby killers. We can't change history, but we ought to change the manner in which we present it."

Pack said, "OK, we're still synching. How are we doing with respect to teaching our tradition-stunted cadets about the Founding and its meaning?"

"In preparation for this," Bass said, "I checked into multiple sources for an answer as to how much high schools teach about our foundational documents, which to me include the Constitution, the Bill of Rights, the

Declaration, and the Federalist Papers. And I also think we must include our Oath of Office. What I found is, the answer is between zero and five hours, and the five hours might get little beyond having them memorize a few names. In Gwinnett County, Georgia, they care about their students remembering Button Gwinnett signed the Declaration of Independence, but I dare say most of the teachers can't explain what the Declaration stipulated. Who should be more conversant with the Founders' thinking than those charged with defending it? We have to move beyond the junior-high gloss-over. Heck, right now Hillsdale is one of the few institutions that treats this subject with the gravity it deserves. We ought to take a backseat to no one, absolutely no one, in the teaching of this material. As you said, we're making a mistake in assuming incoming high schoolers are well grounded in this respect."

Pack butted in again. "Additionally, we need a closer look at the Uniform Code of Military Justice in the sense of its connection to the Constitution, and how it fits into the overall fabric of American jurisprudence. Our graduates should be able to explain that linkage."

"If I may, sir," Bass interjected, "we have a segment of Congress that wants to lay waste to the UCMJ, and some of them sit on the Board of Visitors, a wonderfully distinguished assemblage you'll be pleased to entertain in the near future. We should allow no one to graduate from this Academy, in my opinion, without being a deep-rooted patriot. Too frequently, patriotism means assuaging our individual and collective guilt from nonparticipation by standing at ballgames to cheer a disabled veteran, or showing an endless grab bag of tricks like having a little girl throw out the first pitch at an MLB game to a figure in full catcher's gear who, when he pulls off the mask, turns out to be her dad who's on leave from a tour in Afghanistan."

"OK, George, our lists have coincided so far," Pack said. "I'll take the next point, which is fraternization. The entire subject is shrouded in legalese. The lawyers have taken over rule-writing in the NFL, and they're mapping out their turf in the NCAA and, yes, here at the Academy itself. I like analogies. If they're deliberately harvested, they have great explanatory power. Every Sunday, we see replays slowed to frame-by-frame speed, in order to ascertain whether the receiver had actual possession at the time he danced out of bounds. Look, if he hung on to the ball and had it even after hitting the ground, I don't give a damn how many times he bobbled it. That's getting strangled in the minutiae mousetrap. Our policy should be clear and direct. To me, fraternization is important as an ethical issue. A cadet should not have an other-than-professional relationship with another cadet who is not a classmate. Period. Another analogy, George: We need the UCMJ because this is the military, not the civilian world, and a different, mostly stricter set of standards should pertain. Similarly, this is the United States Military Academy, not Cal State Fullerton or Minnesota State, and their rules concerning gender and fraternization need not necessarily be ours. Best I can determine, this institution has made no effort to state and defend its interests in these matters. We are the ones with no spine. A subset of this line of thought is the rise of godlessness. In case you haven't followed—and I'm not kidding—an Islamic mosque is planned near the site of the Catholic chapel, and what used to be mandatory chapel attendance on Sundays has been made optional. I object to the idea that West Point is one big lab for the pleasure of the Washington Elect. Now, go on with the next point."

Bass said, "Certainly, sir. We have lost any semblance of balance between the academic departments and the tactical department. The academic side has been ascendant for years, during which period, the military side's position has correspondingly weakened. It is a bad thing that now more than half the academic faculty is civilian. Some on the tactical side believe we have already crossed the point of no return. What's the point of having this Academy if it is not materially superior to an ROTC program?

"Last year during the CBS production of the Army-Navy football game, they gave in-game attention to two West Point players. The first, spotlighted because of academic achievements, stated he will select Military Intelligence as his branch. I've got to say, General, that's just not right. As I said earlier, not every First Classman will get his first choice of branch, but all except the females should strive to be combat arms officers first and foremost. The second player highlighted stated that his goal is to become a marketing manager for a large tech corporation." Bass was disturbed, angry, visibly upset, frothy.

Pack said, "Let's go to the kitchen, get a java refill, see if Captain Cooper can microwave some stuff I lay out. You can keep your place, can't you?"

"Yeah, I can, General. We all have our special ways of solving problems, I guess. Not everyone can be calm and cool. Just because I get hot doesn't make me a hothead."

"This is my reply, George: Perhaps I don't agree with every comma and semicolon of your views, but I've learned one thing about you. You care about this place and the people who populate it. You care about accomplishing the *freakin'* mission of this place, production of the most competent, hardest-working, mammy-jammin' professional soldiers on the planet. Either that, or you're a brilliant bullshitter, and yes, I've encountered one of those recently, too. If I'm not mistaken, he took a spike in his middle parts.

"File this thought away also: We can call ourselves professionals only a day at a time. If we don't actively take steps each day to improve our professional standing, we do in my opinion forfeit our right to call ourselves professionals. This is another way of my saying to you, General Bass, that my spotlight will be on you every day. If you think that's unfair or harsh, you won't have a dog's chance of making it to the finish line with me."

Captain Cooper was standing nearby, ready to help with the microwave lunch. Pack said, "That's a lesson you'd be wise to learn, Russell. Incidentally, tomorrow I might assign you new names, to be used discreetly, of course. The instant you go on my sierra list is the moment I revoke your private name." Pack grinned. "I'm still deciding if you are worth a special name. Take over, Russ. Let's get back in there, George."

Before they started up again, Pack said, "I don't intend to spend a lot of time in my office. This is going to be the primary. I don't want a secretary accounting for every minute of my time, and I don't want people buzzing around outside trying to plead a case. Colonel Dahl is aware and will figure out where the secretary can be of real assistance. All right, then, you were talking about the conflict between academics and tactical instruction. It's not hard to play devil's advocate here and assert the academic-tactical conflict has always been part of USMA history—some might also say the tension is natural. Why should I be overly concerned about it now?"

"With respect, sir, that's a softball question, and you know it. The Thayer system had two critical characteristics. One was reciting every day in every class, or close to it. The other, which I always considered the more important, was the four-year curriculum that was fixed except for a couple of electives allowed in Second and First Class years. I can speak authoritatively and without bias in that I graduated in the lower five-or-so percent of my class. I abhorred most of the classes I was forced to take. Yet, once graduated, I regarded it as the most admirable education system ever devised. I maintained a personal journal for years, and found myself writing many times about the beauty of the Thayer system. I loved the enforced discipline of studying thermodynamics, electrical engineering, lots of physics, and six days of mathematics at two hours a day—these and many more subjects, I never would have volunteered to take. It gave me a little knowledge about many areas of inquiry, and had as a valuable side benefit the stoking of my curiosity to know more not only about them, but also about some subjects I liked from the start but didn't get enough of. The overall result was a dunce like me scored high on the Graduate Record Exam and had no problem with graduate school. And I was not exceptional. You no doubt have the same stories from your Class."

Pack interjected, "Then someone had a brilliant idea to wreck the whole thing."

"Right, sir, someone had an idea that, when implemented, wrought cataclysmic results. That idea was to institute the kind of majors programs most colleges have. You want to be a business major, no problem, or comparative religion, we have that, too—I'm not overstating the point by much. We're a farrago of class offerings. As part of this ugly mess, we ditched class rank. This move was insidious because now cadets have their closest relationships with those they share academic interests with rather than with those who might challenge their thinking. As I see it, getting away from what worked is contributing to the balkanization of West Point. Hell, sir, the entire country is balkanizing a little more each day. So, a natural outcome is a football player saying in front of a national audience that he aspires to be a marketing director. Maybe we cannot stop America from fissuring, but we can stop this Academy from fissuring.

"And West Point's health worsened when various Presidential commissions deemed it in the Academy's interest to have a faculty made up of more than fifty percent civilians. That transformation occurred within a couple years, showing what can happen when there is will behind the decision. Sir, I propose we show the same degree of opposition. The professoriat is the lead dog at the United States *freakin'* Military Academy, and I don't think it's unreasonable to make the case the militariat is in the backseat, just looking out the window, enjoying the view apparently, and keeping its mouth shut. Pardon my crudeness, but the added emphasis was intended.

"Cadets look around and see a binary world, the professoriat on one side and the militariat on the other. Most of the civilian professors, close to a hundred percent—and if I'm honest, I must include the military professors to a lesser degree—do not engage in military activities, nor do most on the tactical side engage in academic activities. We are a house divided, and I doubt it has ever been more pronounced in our history. Change is required in both directions."

Pack took his time before asking a question. "Got it, George. Didn't need to take many notes. You can judge for yourself why not. What do you think about Triple A?" *Triple A* was shorthand for the Army Athletic Association. "Think I need to get involved with them in more than the usual administrative ways, signing off on reports and attending sports banquets?"

"I'm not on firm ground in this area, sir. Your predecessor not only kept me away from any contact with the intercollegiate athletic department, but also forbade me from discussing it, even with him. His attitude about athletics was peculiar. I think he lived in fear of someone on his staff slipping up and criticizing Triple A, and most especially football operations. It was a problem he seemed to believe he could pretend didn't exist."

Pack said, "Do you think Army football is important?"

"I do. I think it is extremely important. Above all sports, its experience is transferable to Army leadership."

Pack said, "I agree. And I want the Athletic Director to see it as I do, that football is *the* sport at the Academy and must be looked at as the only moneymaker we have; it funds every other sport. Unless most of the other coaches really screw the pooch, their jobs are safe. But, oh, yeah, football's premier position is much, much more than a matter of money. My hunch is the Athletic Director and football coach don't need a reminder from me. Coach Sumner has been here one season and was vetted thoroughly. He has won at every level and comes from a coaching bloodline. I think he wants to win as badly as I do. If any damn school in the country should have a great football program, it is West Point. Vignette: At the end of last season, I saw Air Force play Colorado State for the Mountain West Conference title. Air Force was 9–2, CSU 10–1. No question CSU had the better athletes, bigger, faster, stronger at most positions, offense and defense. Yet Air Force ground their faces in the dirt, kicked the shit out of them. It was a sight to behold. Air Force had fiercer will. I understand you have to recruit decent athletes, but my eye tells me every team Air Force played had better talent. Air Force was on a *slightly* lower plane, yet they managed to win ten regular-season games. And they do it at least eight years out of ten. How do those people in Colorado Springs do that, but we can't? In answer, I'm going to put a bow on this morning's session.

"Army football is more important than the most avid fan suspects," Pack went on. "It's important because it puts the million-lumen house lights on everything we have discussed. The most observant, caring fan blames our losing on facilities, recruiting, coaching, and a hundred smaller details. That fan is correct that all those things are determinants in wins and losses, but here's how I see it, General Bass. The United States by-damn *Military* Academy has gone soft. There's gangrenous flesh in its body, and we're going to cut it out, and the patient will probably writhe in pain. There will be outsiders who try to wrest the surgical instruments from our hands, and we'll have not only to subdue them, but beat them back. West Point has gone soft by its too-long accommodation of the inclinations of third-rate intellects. West Point has gone soft by catering to the whims and whines of single-interest constituencies. The prime cause of our loser football program is not coaching or any of the aforementioned other reasons. The Army football team is moribund because the flesh around it is rotting from within. Football here is a symptom of the malady, not the malady itself. The malady is the rot you have ably described this morning, a rot I myself described at a Founder's Day event just a few years ago. If we reverse the misbegotten ways of two decades of Academy nabobs, abetted by gerents in Washington, one of the first signs of healing will come from a resurgent football team. After a messy surgery, we will have as one byproduct the meanest damn football team in Division I.

"One last thing, George. Unless a cadet is walking punishment tours or on one of our monthly exercises, he will be at all home football games. You will see to that, won't you, George?"

♦ ♦ ♦

The following morning, Pack was at the desk in his study reading and making marginal comments on Board of Visitors Reports from the past three years and going through a passel of the Dean's reports, particularly *The Academic Program Strategic Plan*. Colonel Dahl had also left a note reminding him to update the Superintendent's Page on the official website, and to provide keywords that could be expanded into columns he was expected to write monthly for several publications. They would learn soon enough, Pack thought, who worked for whom.

Although Pack hadn't touched a computer since retirement, he could find his way around as well as most. He didn't see what was difficult about any of the programs in the Microsoft Office suite, for example. But he vowed not to get trapped behind a computer, ever. He had a secretary to handle whatever he needed from it. This was one of the few occasions he expected to power it up.

He went to the Supe's Page. *What is the force,* he ruminated, *that can compel a man, a soldier, to submit so timidly to political correctness?* He stared at four paragraphs, at the bottom of which rested a rectangular box containing the acronym *SHARP*. Above this lettering were the words, "Army's Sexual Harassment and Assault Response and Prevention." Underneath it were two Hotline phone numbers.

All four paragraphs were mumbo-jumbo apparently dictated by Pentagon blockheads, replete with gems about "the DOD Office of Diversity Management and Equal Opportunity" and "the Sexual Assault Gender Relations Focus Group's Study." More shocking, Pack read, "The prevention and response to sexual harassment or sexual assault is my number-one priority..."

Pack dialed Dahl. "Jim, take down that Supe's Notes web page ASAP. If I log on at noon, I don't want to see it. Not sure what I'll say, or when, or if at all, but I will not be associated with the present page."

"Roger, sir. Anything else?"

"Yeah, Mrs. Rose, the Cadet Hostess? I'm going to call her, straighten things out, so if that's on your to-do, check it off."

"WILCO, sir," he said, giving the shorthand for "Will comply."

He almost called her then before realizing the time, and that she was a civilian unlikely to be in her office before eight. Instead, there was a faint knock on the front door followed swiftly by a key turning.

Captain Cooper entered, with a "Good morning, sir. I took the liberty of letting myself in with the key you gave me. Figured I could get things moving in the kitchen until you got downstairs."

"Let's go sit down in the kitchen. I need to talk with you. You drink coffee, right? Have some, and hit me with a refill, if you would."

"I do drink coffee. Thank you, sir."

"Never been an aide, have you?"

"No, sir, and I never hoped to."

"If you had been an ADC before," Pack said, giving the abbreviation for *aide-de-camp*, "I wouldn't have wanted you. If you wanted to be here, I wouldn't have asked for you. If you had no combat infantry experience, I wouldn't have wanted you. I do not intend for your career to be damaged in the slightest. This is the time when you would be in the crappiest job of your entire professional life, probably. Between captain and major. Do your best, and all will be well for you, though, trust me."

"Permission to speak, sir?"

"Of course, and if you need to speak with me, no permission needed. You've demonstrated leadership in extraordinarily stressful situations. As such, I expect you possess good judgment. The better leader you are, the fewer lapses of judgment you have. I'm going to trust your judgment. Speak."

"Nothing complicated, sir. I'd just like you to know I'm honored and humbled to have this time at your side. And that within my limits, I'll do my best. I'll do whatever you demand. Most important, sir, is I don't have a career blueprint, that I have to do *x*, *y*, and *z* to assure promotion. I'm not stupid, sir, but neither have I ever called Infantry Branch requesting an assignment. I've been naive enough to believe if I do well on every job assigned, the rest will take care of itself."

"Points taken. OK, onto business. First, I don't want in normal circumstances to call you captain, and I don't want to call you Russ, Russell, or Cooper. I will call you Duck, which dovetails with the second point. You'll be Duck because when you see the duck on the pond, you see the portrait of serenity on the surface but beneath, in the subfusc, Duck might be churning his feet madly. Even when his feet are not churning, he is on alert for what could be either danger or the next meal. Do you take *my* point?"

"Roger, sir. I am Duck."

"OK, the next thing you have to understand is, you are my personal representative at all times. For you, there will never be off-duty time. If you are on leave, you will be mindful that you represent me with respect to your personal standards of conduct. In a real sense, you are an extension of me.

"At times, you'll be on duty for days without a break. You just need to know I'm demanding, but I'll treat you fairly, by my lights.

"Next duty I'm about to describe will depend on your applying sound judgment, so listen up. Napoleon used a lineup of adjutants to perform a function some modern historians have termed 'the directed telescope.' He deployed his corps on extremely broad axes, many miles apart. Communications methods then weren't, it goes without saying, instantaneous. Napoleon sent this squad of adjutants out to different units over stretches of one hundred miles or more. So he gave them general instructions designed to elicit a clearer view of each subordinate command. Let's say he wanted to learn about the state of health in Field Marshal Ney's corps. The adjutant would compile a report detailing desertion rates, number of wounded, wounded who died during treatment, state of sanitation, whether troops and animals were receiving adequate rations, and so on. Explain to me, Duck, some ways in which such an assignment was challenging."

Captain Cooper understood at once. He took but a moment to answer. "Sir, first, the adjutant had to put himself in the mind of the commander, which given the case of Napoleon, was no mean challenge. I'm not an expert on Napoleon, sir, but I remember the words of David Chandler because they leapt off the page and struck me in the face: 'Napoleon Bonaparte was the most competent human being who ever lived.' The adjutant would have to figure out what the Emperor really wanted to know, and develop a supporting plan to acquire it. But the task was incalculably hard because he wasn't the Emperor. He had to be very careful how he dealt with all those corps commanders and their senior people who outranked him. No doubt they resented his presence. He walked a fine line."

"You pass the test on paper, Duck, so to speak. I'm going to put you to the test in real life.

"Now, last thing. I'll let you know when I need you here each morning. Maybe I'll get into texting. You don't have to be here at oh-dark-thirty every day. I'm a lifelong early riser, so I'll be up, but you're welcome to raid the coffeepot whenever you want. We straight?"

"Absolutely, sir. Thanks."

"It's what time now? Still real early. Report to Colonel Dahl at 0700. I've given him some tasks he'll explain to you. I'll be walking around most of the day."

◆ ◆ ◆

A couple minutes after eight, he called Mrs. Rose, the Hostess. Someone else answered. "Who shall I say is calling, please?"

"Simon Pack."

"Right away, sir. Please hold."

"Good morning, General Pack, and welcome, sir. I am Evelyn Rose. How may I help you?"

"Well, ma'am, this might be the first time you've had this request. Can you screen some housekeeper candidates for me? Once you have a candidate, I'd like to come over to your place and conduct a short joint interview."

"I'd be delighted to help. This isn't in my normal line of work, but I'm sure you know that."

Pack interrupted. "Yes, I am aware this falls outside your job description, and I will explore other avenues if you can't support me in good conscience."

"Please, General. If you weren't the Superintendent, I would say, 'Don't be silly.' When would you like me to present a candidate, and what parameters do you have?"

"If you would hire this person, that's sufficient. Good character, discreet—meaning official visitors' privacy must be protected—dependable. As to when, take a week, Mrs. Rose. And thank you."

"You're most welcome. I'll get back to you within the week."

Pack felt sure Evelyn Rose would select the right person.

♦ ♦ ♦

It was time for the walk to Thayer Hall. Duck was to have laid the groundwork for a drop-in on the Dean, Brigadier General Elijah Steinberg. The phone in his pocket was burring. Actually, vibrating and burring. He was unaccustomed to either the sound or feel, the result of which was, he had not answered on numerous earlier tries. *Looks like Duck has called every two minutes for fifteen minutes. Got it this time*, Pack thought. Only a small circle of people knew how to reach him on this new official phone, and if any them called, it was for good reason.

"Pack," he answered.

"Sir, the Dean isn't in his office. He had an offsite meeting scheduled for next week with department heads, plus a few dozen others. General Steinberg rescheduled it for today and tomorrow at Jefferson Hall. The purpose, according to his executive officer, is to review priorities and initiatives for the upcoming year, based on the annual assessment."

"Thanks, Duck. Meet me there, get a seat on a flank where I can see you, and take good notes."

Pack noted a sign-in roster just inside the meeting room door. The last person in was Duck, who was number forty-eight.

The Dean was just bringing the assembly to order and going over the sequence of presentations and Q & A periods. Hearing the side door open, he turned to see Pack and swallowed hard. "Well, ladies and gentlemen, serendipity, it seems, has brought us the good fortune of an appearance by our new Superintendent. I'm Eli Steinberg, and if you would like, we can take the time to allow the department heads here on the main table to introduce themselves."

"No, General, I would not like to do that right now. I probably will intercede at some point in the next few hours, but until then, my only desire is to listen. Carry on."

No one at the table offered a seat to the Supe, who nodded to Duck. Duck already had secured a chair, not one of the plush variety in which the academic heads sat, and waited for Pack to indicate where he wanted it placed. Instead, Pack strode over to Duck, took hold of the chair, and placed it so near the Dean, he could grasp his leg. The Dean was thrown off-kilter, emotionally and very nearly physically.

The Dean occupied most of the first hour providing his views of the Strengths, Weaknesses, Opportunities, and Threats section of the soon-to-be-released Academic Strategic Plan. The second hour was taken up by the first two of the thirteen department heads. They apparently spoke not in alphabetical order, with the head of the Law department first, followed by the head of English and Philosophy. What they had presented, Pack mused, did not differ materially from the current plan. The Dean then announced that, since they had gone long on time, they would reconvene in twenty minutes.

Pack continued to sit, saying softly to Elijah Steinberg, "Take a leak, I'll see you back here in five minutes." It was safe to assume all eyes had been on the exchange. The backbenchers were not about to introduce themselves before their bosses, so they dispersed rapidly into the security of the foyer. The department heads had absorbed every nuance of Pack's effect on the proceedings, and frankly, they seemed shaken by the chill induced chiefly by the Dean. Only three were bold enough to step up to greet Pack with a handshake, a smile, and a welcome.

Pack greeted them reciprocally. They scattered as they observed General Steinberg coming back.

"How are you, General Steinberg?" Pack said. "Thought I would begin by informing you I tag nicknames on those for whom I have special professional regard. For example, that captain over there is Duck. Sort of a special title I judge he has earned. At the moment my name for you is General Steinberg. Not to say you can't earn another name, you understand. But I must tell you, General, the hole you have to crawl out of is deep.

"Let's review: This meeting was originally set up for next week, but you made a last-minute change to today. I wonder why that happened. Three weeks ago, you knew I was inbound yesterday. One of my key people removes himself—or tries to—from my reach just as you had to know I would seek you out. Two: In front of your subordinates, and therefore mine as well, you introduce yourself as 'Eli Steinberg' and do not address me by name. If you knew my history, Steinberg, you would understand I'm not much hung up on protocol. But I am by damn hung up on being a Marine, so until further notice, you will address me as General Pack, giving me the military courtesy I am due. Clear so far?"

"Yes, sir, but—" Steinberg stuttered.

Pack cut him off. "I'm not finished, General. Three: Why are there no decision-makers from across the street in attendance?" he said, referring to the Department of Tactics. "Four: Why was I not invited? When this session reconvenes, I am going to make some remarks, after which this day's program has ended. You will reconvene tomorrow with my guidance in mind, and with your counterparts across the street properly represented. Now, get this thing going again, then hand it off to me."

Steinberg was ashen, angry, momentarily speechless. He drank from his water glass and tried his hardest to collect himself before addressing the group.

"Ladies and gentlemen, our session schedule has changed. General Pack will address you. Once the Superintendent has concluded his remarks, we will adjourn until normal start time tomorrow. I was reflecting during the break that my introduction of General Pack was unsatisfactory. I am absolutely certain you are somewhat familiar with his biography. Stated concisely, he is one of the most distinguished military leaders of this generation. His stamp on Academy athletics is indelible and as bold as any other. He was appointed to his present position by General Pembrook last month. And, as you also are aware unless you are an earthworm, he has been at the center of international media attention since stopping the leader of Al Qaeda America and two henchmen. He was, we are led to imagine, engaged in quite unusual activities during that period. It is a privilege to welcome General Simon Pack."

The three colonels who had defied the herd and stepped out to shake hands with Pack were the first to their feet in applause. The others followed but with less visible enthusiasm. The Supe waved them down. They quieted, and he commanded their full attention.

"Ladies and gentlemen, we have work to do. I don't seek your applause or your plaudits. I seek your acknowledgment that the state of West Point is poor. Assigning blame is not my thing. I came here from what was a grand retirement; I woke up excited to work on projects of my own choosing, living close to a perfect life, by my reckoning. I missed the American Marine and set out to find him in another place, a quest that led me on an unexpected tangent. Then the applicable authorities in the Pentagon urged me for unknown reasons to accept this assignment, and I did, but only after deciding I can accomplish the mission, and deciding the mission needs doing. Not me personally, to be sure, but all of us. You will carry the load of finding and fixing what I believe afflicts the patient.

"When I said West Point is in poor health, I got some quizzical looks. Some take my meaning; others don't. The short, scientific answer for the name of the disease is political correctness. Once you're in its grip, you become weak, listless, sycophantic, ever more susceptible to manipulation. Do you realize how easily you have succumbed to it? Unlikely. It is insidious, slow-growing, more basal than squamous. In this meeting room, there are zero USMA seals but four SHARP emblems. Obliterate all signs of political correctness in each of your domains, ladies and gentlemen, and do it today. Captain Cooper, please remove all four of these banners now, and deposit them in the closest trash can. And I ain't pickin' on your guys, Dean. I was appalled when I opened the Superintendent's web page and found nothing but this crap. It is an Academy-wide infection.

"If anyone is surprised the Superintendent is injecting himself into academic affairs, get over it, because he will. I will not permit sinecures to take root; the ones that already exist are in peril. If you think you have one, I'd advise you to figure out a way to clean it up pronto before I excise it. I told the Commandant yesterday, I smell the rank odor of gangrenous flesh, and as chief surgeon, I will cut it out fiber by fiber.

"I've been here just more than twenty-four hours, and until two hours ago, I was unaware of this meeting. I don't want this to happen again. I want each principal present to have as a checkpoint on every key meeting who from across the street ought to be plugged in, invited to it. I want cross-pollination, not more or longer meetings. The professoriat and the militariat must be abolished and merged into the promilitariat. I have said the same to the others involved.

"Don't waste time in meetings. In the two hours we've sat here, I haven't learned a word that detracted from or added to the Strategic Plan—but not everyone has had a turn, so maybe that judgment is premature.

"I've read your Strategic Plan and all supporting references." This revelation caught at least half the participants off guard. There was more than a smattering of hastily shared glances. He had been on the ground a day, did not know of this meeting, yet he had read our Strategic Plan? Maybe he did give a damn what we do on this side of Thayer Road.

"It is, nearly all of it, a product of clear thinking," Pack continued. "Many parts of it are top-grade. In the main, I approve of what you've done, particularly the passion and persuasive power behind the scholar-warrior argument. And the requirement to produce officers who can seamlessly adapt to unforeseen operational environments. General Steinberg, you and your staff deserve credit for this." Steinberg sat a shade more erect at hearing his name mentioned in union with something positive.

"Now you must every day strive to insure the strategic map is more than soothing words. Empty words weigh nothing and carry no weight. I mentioned something about wasting time. The best use of both our times right now is for me to stop stroking you and start stoking the fire of change. Because I had no foreknowledge I would speak to you today, I do not have notes from my reading, but I recall well enough to pass on the most critical guidance.

"First, you enumerate five strategic goals, maybe six, but five is the recollection. I want you to weed out all the references to diversity.

With respect to the goal of cadet excellence, you refer to *a diverse population of.* You do the same relative to other goals pertaining to educational opportunities and faculty and staff excellence and the professional and collegial environment. We aren't ward heelers in Chicago or borough pols in NYC who have to check that we have to a tenth of a percentage point the correct proportion of races and creeds and religions. We are not one of these proprietary for-profit colleges begging for students. We are after young people who want the tough challenge. We are confident professionals who seek to find and develop the most deserving candidates and cadets, and mold them into officers who may be counted upon to provide a lifetime of service to the country. By the nature and seriousness of our profession, we do not choose our people unfairly. All our blood is red. In the selection and grooming of our people, we will be blind to color of skin. As Reverend King is quoted ceaselessly, we *will* judge our people first and last 'by the content of their character.' We are West Point; we will not be insulted by having our principles challenged. We will not kowtow to and quaver in the face of this interest group and that interest group. We will strive to make this institution the purest meritocracy in America. General Steinberg, you are my point man in coordinating with the Admissions Office and every other organizational arm of USMA that employs similar language. Get it cleaned up.

"The Plan contains a rather lengthy section on Shared Governance. I understand why a brief mention might technically be called for. The NCAA, for instance, does have considerable hegemony in the area of intercollegiate athletics. And the Middle States Commission on Higher Education does indeed have baseline accreditation standards we should meet. But you go further, suggesting the United States Military Academy is under the operational command of multiple organizations. That, ladies and gentlemen, is erroneous. I am responsible for the proper functioning of the Academy. Until such time as I am incapacitated or relieved, I am in charge. 'Unity of Command' is one of the nine Principles of War to which I intend to stay true.

"Penultimate point: The Plan speaks much too broadly of our supporting the Association of American Colleges and Universities Liberal Education and America's Promise initiative. I am quite sure I do not fully support their goals. To the contrary, I am sure some of their goals are antithetical to the Academy's.

"Two concluding points: Eons ago, as a major at the Army Command and General Staff College, I was stunned one day to get called to the office of the three-star Combined Arms Center Commander. Something I had done was brought to his attention, and he regarded it as meritorious. He personally walked me over to the office of the—I don't even recall the man's rank—chief of the Center for Army Leadership to share my insights. The words stenciled on the door, '*Center for Army Leadership*' abacinated me to everything, everything, that occurred that day. I don't remember anything that was said by any of the parties. What I had burned into my mind was the goofy arrogance of a place that called itself 'The Center for Army Leadership.' There were people in that office who truly believed they had been ordained as the final authority on all things leadership. Let's never forget, ladies and gentlemen, that the true center for Army leadership is not in an office but in the field, in the form of sweating privates and sergeants and lieutenants. Point the final, if I may sound anachronistic: I have issued you an assignment for tomorrow's gathering that changes its emphases. Apply yourselves to it. I have in mind additional changes, more profound, relating to the Academic Board, but it is well for me to broach them with General Steinberg in privacy as a start point."

Duck fell in at Pack's side as they exited Jefferson Hall. "OK, Duck, tell me what you took notes about. Leave out names."

"Yes, sir. I took notes about your instructions, and I took notes on expressions and general body language."

"OK, you hang onto those notes. I don't want to see or hear them now, but there will come a time I'll ask to see them. What do you suppose you'll be doing tomorrow?"

"Attending that meeting in Jefferson Hall, sir?"

"You catch on quick, son."

♦ ♦ ♦

There had been no applause when the Supe left the hall. But he had created buzz. The backbenchers were cogitating on what to say if their primaries asked their opinions. What would be the politic position? "Keep it vague," was the most common general view. Something along the lines of "Yes, he was pretty hard on the Board as a whole, but we both know it wasn't directed at us, couldn't be directed at us, because we aren't guilty of the PC-ness he described. Right, sir?"

The department heads ruminated on what tenure actually means at West Point. Not necessarily the same thing as at civilian schools. The tenure system at USMA had to their knowledge never been challenged, but then again, there had never been a Simon Pack here. This guy looked like he was capable of challenging a bison to a fight.

Thus, they stood in stunned silence, few moving, thinking these things. Anon, small pockets began to form, officers in twos and threes, as recognition dawned that their world had just been jolted, if not overturned, thinking, Is my position a sinecure? Have I become sloppy in my ways, arrogant in my thinking? What does this Peking/Java/Cro-Magnon man have in his heart to do to us? Can he get away with whatever he has planned?

Oh, yes, they felt a deep level of concern, but instead put on brave faces, saying, "Just a misunderstanding, probably. The man is so rank-conscious, despite his protestation, that his anger flared at the Dean's perceived gaffe in his too-informal intro. It's likely he already has taken note of his overreaction and is looking for an opportunity to apologize to us."

One small group, however, was singing a different song inside their circle. The department heads of chemistry, history, and physics and nuclear engineering, the three who had broken from the crowd to introduce themselves cheerfully to Pack, were contained in appearance but ebullient on the inside. "Gentlemen," one said to the others, "methinks we have a leader in our midst. Let's see who understands his intent and has the balls and wisdom to follow it. I have been in my present capacity a decade and have recently mulled over folding up my tent to escape the PC madness. Within a span of hours, I have gotten infused with more energy, and hope, than the day I took over my department."

"Yes, yes," Colonel Chemistry replied to Colonel History. One thrust his hand palm down into the center of the group. The other two placed their hands atop his, as if they were team players breaking a pregame huddle.

♦ ♦ ♦

The Supe proceeded from Jefferson Hall to his secondary office. He stopped in the anteroom to present himself to his secretary, Kathy Pillings. They had met often, many years before. "Kathy, please join me in my office," he said with his warmest smile. His smile was genuine. She was his strongest link to the past at West Point.

"Can I get you some coffee, pastries, or something else, General?"

"Both would be nice. I'll have a look at this office." He walked into a room he had been in a time or two as a cadet but recalled vaguely. It was dark, stately, sumptuous in a nineteenth-century manner. Evidence of the twenty-first-century technology rather spoiled it for Pack.

Kathy came in with a tray of coffee and cakes, and set them carefully on the Superintendent's desk. "I am so pleased to see you, sir. And shattered emotionally for some time after Gioia's terrible accident. You were, and still are, Ed's favorite, and how many varsity athletes do you think he has seen come and go? Could it be thousands?"

Ed Pillings was head athletic trainer at West Point and had received scores of awards from fellow collegiate trainers. He was a legend. After freshman year at a major West Coast university, he left to serve in combat as an enlisted infantryman, then was awarded a battlefield commission. After the war, he returned to that same university to graduate. From Pack's point of view, Ed Pillings was a hero, a real man. Just as important, he was a pillar for Pack, the famous football player, the only man besides his head coach to whom he'd ever turned for advice.

"Let me tell you something, Kathy. When Gioia and I retired and set up house in Montana, she had a ton of my sports memorabilia she wanted to put on the walls. Excuse me a sec," he said, taking time to down a chocolate cream doughnut in two bites. "This is a tasty snack, Kathy, and you do coffee good. About the memorabilia, I didn't want it staring at me from the walls. Eventually, we compromised. She could mount what she wanted on the walls of the stairway leading to the basement, but nowhere else. The basement den was pretty much my place. The only football picture I had down there was of two teammates and me in the training room with uniform pads on our legs, cleats on our feet, and tees on top. The fourth person in that black and white is Ed, and I have my arm around him. You tell him that."

Kathy Pillings nodded, smiling, eyes moist, still a beautiful woman in advancing years. "And look where you are now, General. We are so proud of you."

"OK, Kathy. I won't be here long today, but I have some work for you."

She had pen and steno pad at the ready.

"Item one: Set up a meeting with the AD and all head coaches, with Ed as a special guest, on Friday if they can pull it off. Otherwise, get me a couple of options for next week. At their place. An hour and a half should work, the first fifteen minutes alone with the AD.

"Item two: Ask the Dean for time with me in his office Thursday, after regular hours if required. Another hour and a half.

"Item three: As a rule, Kathy, if I give you something out of the ordinary, I'd like it to be kept private. I trust you. OK?"

"Of course, sir. My reputation is good."

"I'd never question you, just said that to guarantee your safety. I'm never going to be safe. In fact, after what happened in Jefferson Hall this morning, I'm pretty radioactive already. Anyway, item three: It's a close-hold research project. I'm not asking for dirt, but the fact I'm looking for information on Board of Visitors members might rile one or two of them up. Some of this information might be filed somewhere already, but if so, I want it organized differently. Make a file on each serving member, with current photo, legislative priorities, work history for at least twenty years back, basic bio data, what he or she plans to propose to the Board Chairman for the next meeting agenda. Then two other sections: one for what they claim their contributions to USMA to be, and another for anything you deem important that wasn't previously included.

"Might seem odd, but I'd like to know where they meet—as I understand it, we have three meetings a year, two here, one in DC—when the meetings are held here, and why that location was chosen. Ask around. Inform Colonel Dahl I have tasked you. He's the only other one in the loop, at least for now. OK?"

"What's my suspense?"

"Ten days."

"If it can be done sooner, it will be. If you'll permit me to revert to the personal again before you go, Ed is happier about your return than I can express. He thinks it will perk up the football program. We know you aren't Cadet Pack anymore, but we still want you to know we'd love to have you over for a meal any time you'd like."

"I'll give notice. My best to Ed. You have my number."

♦ ♦ ♦

His second full day was on the record. He was neither happy nor unhappy. But he felt at peace with himself. He had eaten a healthy meal—fresh salmon, grilled; broccoli; baked potato; a simple tomato-and-cheese salad. Then he had a nice dessert, one of those brick-size Snickers. Washed the dishes, stowed them away. *Let an hour pass, then have two fingers of Blanton's*, he thought. In his walking around through the day, he had organized tomorrow in his head. *Maybe in a month or two I can share my schedule, open wider the door to my intentions, but not yet. Or maybe that day will never come in this job. Better to keep them guessing, not let them get too comfortable. Sinecure-bustin' calls for some bustin'. The Smugly Professors,* he thought, *can see their cocoons being set afire.*

Pack was between books now. He took down the e-reader. He pegged what to order within a half-minute. For a flash, he re-experienced the deep delight he had felt reading those rich-as-that-Blanton's bourbon words of two earlier Daniel Woodrell novels. The last was *Woe to Live On.* So he had the e-delivery of *Winter's Bone* within seconds. He felt near-guilt for the ease of this evening. Before consuming the first sure-to-be delicious sentence of *Winter's Bone*, he wondered if the professors listening today had cause to so regularly marvel at the intricacies of God's handiwork, and to revel in the richness of man's mind as he. He hoped so. Yeah, they must; otherwise, what's the point of it all?

♦ ♦ ♦

Wednesday, Day three of the Pack Experience: Cline and Demetrios were with teammates in the Kimsey Athletic Center weight room, squatting at the moment, spotting one another. The spotter recorded every repetition, every set, every plate added. Each player had his own set of charts up on the wall. The strength coach paid close attention to percentage gains. The previous coach had set great stock in plyometrics, running against resistance bands, leaping vertically, then horizontally against various forms of resistance. Throw in a little isometrics. That coach believed you could win in Division I with small, explosive players. Within some modest weight differential, the coach's philosophy might have proved workable. But the weight and strength spreads were absurdly imbalanced, with the Brave Old Army Team, once a national powerhouse, giving up fifty to seventy pounds a man week in and week out. The still-new coach, Les Sumner, was trying to change that to recruit and nurture bigger players. He laid out a multi-pronged approach to improvement, but a key element was the Old School slinging of more weight under the eye of an assistant coach responsible for strength training. Lieutenant General Norther, the departed Supe, had been singularly unreceptive to Sumner's requests for support.

"Simon's got some kind of meeting with the coaches Friday. Think it's a formality, the usual meet-and-greet?" Demetrios asked Gary Cline.

Cline laughed between grunts, as he was now in the clean-and-jerk sequence. "Simon, is he? He your good bud?" Cline dropped the barbell from his chest to the Tartan surface, bringing the familiar heavy *clank* lifters love to hear. The sweating, the huffing, the grunting, the clanking and clanging, the "Yeah—new PB, my man!" constitute the universal aesthetic of the weight room.

Gary Cline continued. "We've been over this before, Paulie. You think it's a formality, I'm not so sure. We'll just—"

A Firstie lineman they called Bear interrupted with, "I saw my English P yesterday. Proud to say—no, actually embarrassed—I'm one of only a dozen or so cadets total in summer school. Anyway, from his cubicle, I heard others talking about Packman's introduction to the Academic Board yesterday. Asses fried, the way I heard it. Packman kicked ass and took names, went off about PC infecting and infesting USMA. Could be it's just academics he's out to change, though. He can't change it enough to suit me."

Cline loved the Bear, a man whose grades in all subjects always teetered on failure. Bear had shown himself a friend to many and leader to all. Every cadet saw in Bear the great officer he seemed certain to become, and cadets with the highest grades in every subject voluntarily lined up to tutor him.

In stature and girth, Bear and Jesse Bruccoli were matches, but in not much else. Bruccoli was the strongest man on the team; the strength coach thought he might hit the five-hundred-pound benchmark before the season began, in which case he would be the first Army player ever to do so. Jesse Bruccoli was, in terms of national recognition, the best player on the team. But where Bear was gregarious, Bruccoli was reserved. They were at opposite ends on the academic spectrum as well, the lower 10 percent versus top 10 percent. Bruccoli had followed the saga of the new Supe with great interest, and he was fascinated by the possibilities for changing the environment at the Academy. When his teammates looked to him for comment, he said, "From what I read, he's a real hero in a nation starved for them. So I guess if I offered a name off the cuff, it would be something with *Hero* in it. No Simon and no Packman for me."

"OK, guys," Cline said, "we have Simon and Packman, and something with *Hero* in it. Before I forget, here's another nice piece of info: He calls his ADC Duck. So makes sense we should have our own name for him. And by we, I mean the whole Corps. Too much distance between us and them, on the part of both sides, I guess. It's hard to know how these rifts get started. It's not as if we aren't cadets ourselves, after all."

"No doubt," Demetrios said. "The Gulf of Mexico's not as broad as the gulf between the Corps and this team, and that's not good. Surprising how many cadets think we get special privileges, get more to eat, don't have to work as hard for our grades. A few even think the Tacs aren't as hard on us. We know we aren't special. Just wish they could see we are cadets same as them."

"Back to Pack," Cline said. "He was a great player here, and I think out of respect, this team should come up with a name for him. Most companies have underground names for their tactical officers. Why not one for the Supe? Let's plant the seed now, and take a vote when the team's all back together. Another month or so. If, that is, he proves to be any kind of factor in our lives. Think about it. Something silly-endearing, like Pack Mule, or Cold Pack, or Hot Pack. Because, to employ the patois of the gutter, he has done some weird shit, has he not? Or Simon Says? *Mount Montana*'s in the media, but we didn't invent it, so it's no good."

Cline had completed the weight circuit the coach had assigned for the day. "Nice work, Cline. Your chart's looking good, but you can go heavier, quite a bit heavier," the strength coach said with a slap on the shoulder.

Cline picked up his towels and gloves and headed for the locker room. When he got to the door, he about-faced and called for the attention of his teammates. "Everyone does understand I said the name-the-Supe thing out of respect, right? If he does nothing as Supe but sleep all day, I think he'd still have my respect for what he has done. Just want there to be no mistake."

♦ ♦ ♦

The Supe's Chief of Staff, Jim Dahl, sat in his office, thinking of standards he might establish in order to follow the Supe's guidance about paperwork. Great reams of paper require senior leader signatures, and the Superintendency is no exception. Pack refused to sign the bulk of it, saying if he acquiesced, he would become just another Chairborne Ranger (a play on the Army's Airborne Ranger). At first, he said to Dahl, in intentional hyperbole, "If it doesn't have to do with starting or stopping the next war, you sign for me." Then he backed off, advising Dahl to divide all the Supe correspondence into three levels, with *A* being most urgent. Send him only the A stuff, he said, then in partial jest added, "Preferably just the A-One stuff."

Under the Pareto principle, 80 percent of results came from 20 percent of the job, and Pack was putting teeth into his refusal to become deskbound. Colonel Dahl was in the tight circle that could see General Pack was a man on a mission.

"You have experience that corporations spend big for, Jim," Pack told him. "Your judgment's been tested. Exercise that judgment. How does Kit Carson sound to you? You're my great scout, my point man. Nah, still searching for your name. How about Closer? That OK with you? You come in whenever the big inning happens to be. Might be the ninth, might be the seventh. You're a tough one to slap a name on, Colonel."

"Whatever is comfortable for you, General," Dahl had replied with his closed-lip smile.

The Supe prepared to stab the numbers on his new phone to dial Bass. It would be his first outgoing call. Then he recalled everything was on speed dial. He just had to press the "Comm" button.

BG Bass picked up immediately. "Yes, sir, what can I do for you?" Bass said.

"I was just about to ask Sanja how jammed up your schedule is about now, but I'll ask you instead."

"Always can work things around for you, sir. I won't be shoving anyone out the door," Bass said.

"All right, then, I'm out on the apron outside MacArthur, and every cadet on Post seems to be walking by saluting. My arm's gonna fall off if you don't get out here to relieve some of the pressure. I'm staying put till you get here. Let's walk over to my place and have a coffee," Pack said.

"On the way, sir."

Bass observed as they walked that every cadet then occupying a room seemed to be hanging out his window to catch sight of the folk-hero Pack. Everyone with the freedom to do so walked in his direction to see him up close. Pack himself appeared oblivious to the ado. They had navigated back to Quarters 100 with as little aplomb as possible with all eyes on them.

"Go on over to the study, General Bass. I need some caffeine. By the way, I spotted that disease-caked canteen cup you use. Don't have one of those, so porcelain will have to do," Pack said. "How's Beast coming along? You reasonably satisfied?"

"I am, sir. Eighteen dropouts so far, which is about average at this point. The First Beast cadet cadre has acquitted itself well. They have followed the training model of task, conditions, and standards with fidelity, but I would also say this group of upperclassmen has managed to imprint its personality on the process. The Second Beast cadre begins to arrive tomorrow and will take full control in five days. If the next cadre can match this one's accomplishments, we will have had a successful New Cadet Barracks."

"Pretty near inexplicable phenomenon, I've always thought," Pack said, "how and why Classes can differ so much one from another. I suspect that if you did an unbiased analysis of the recruiting and admissions processes, you would find that the people in the Admissions Office in those years had the most influence. I can hear them: 'We've leant too much in this direction or that direction, so we'll compensate this year by going in the opposite direction.' I admired two of the three upper classes above me. One, though, was made up of weak sisters then, dirtbags, to be blunt, and they proved to be dirtbags as officers. We know what happens to our bodies when we try to compensate after an injury by protecting the injured area instead of following the prescribed rehab protocols. We generate another weakness. That was a key point to the Academic Board the other day, Thump. When we stop following established admission standards and introduce a hundred different accommodations to satisfy parties who have no true vested interest in our mission, we'll wind up with weak sister Classes.

"The clock is ticking on the monthly march exercise," Pack reminded him. "It's been two days. Got an update yet?"

"The G-4 is confident we'll get the weapons we'll need. Hundreds of tons of weapons Army-wide are out of commission, in mothballs, since budget cuts have forced troop reductions. Some have been funneled through Homeland Security for municipal police departments, but a high percentage has been turned down over police-militarization complaints. Security for them is a working issue. Acquiring arms room space is essential. We think we can get necessary space in some of the tenant units, but I'll need a week or more, sir. Some things you don't need to get involved in, not yet, at least. On the exercise side, the G-3 is sketching a bare-bones plan—that was my call. The full Corps won't report back for nearly five weeks, so we won't have a functioning cadet chain of command until then. Not much time for them to plan and execute the first one, especially given the requirements of the new academic year. I think your intent, sir, is for cadets to plan these events. That is my intent. So the USCC staff will give them a little push-off for the first one. The cadets take over when they're in place. We'll sync the Buckner exercises with football AWAY games throughout first semester."

"Roger. I'm giving you a wide berth, Thump. Like that name? I wish everyone had such an excellent appellation. Thump. When I need Thumpin' inflicted on someone...No, forget that, I'll do it myself. Let me say again: If I were directly responsible for the USCC, I'd want to be in charge, same as in any other job. But I am in overwatch, ready to provide supporting fires. Ours probably will not be the typical Supe-Comm relationship. I will stay attuned to what is going on in your area of responsibility. I will not be uniquely external-directed; you, the Dean, and a bucketful of others may wish that were the case, but it will not be. If my 'observing carefully' turns into breathing down your neck and smothering you, we'll talk about it. My overriding intent is that we act as a team.

"Listen, Thump, I am acutely aware of my weaknesses. I can sometimes suck the life from the staff, rob them of inspiration, rebuke them with the sting of a scorpion, tromp clumsily through their arenas, seek to make the train move faster than they're able to control. Yes, I know my limitations, and try to be ever alert to their appearance in my professional life. If I fail to detect them now and then, you're the man I want to raise the subject with me. Part of the reason for your name is I want you to be *my* thumper when I warrant it. But there is another side to this coin as well. It's the side the reflection from which in the bright light of noonday tells me I don't have time to allow for the niceties of leader development. I need to deliver a thump, pun deliberate, an ass kick that some may see as brutal. I don't have time for the sluggish subordinate marking time in his cocoon to figure this thing out and get it done. Ever heard of the OODA Loop, Thump?"

"General John Boyd, I believe, sir, US Air Force. He argued that air-combat training should be directed toward getting inside the opposing aircraft commander's decision cycle. By this, he meant observing, orienting, deciding, and acting faster than the bogey. West Point's decision-makers have been victimized by falling into its opponents' decision cycle. Do I have it about right?" Thump asked.

"You have it exactly correct. I doubt I need to spell out all the individuals and agencies who have eaten our lunch, done each OODA cycle faster and with more commitment than we have. A bunch of people here, Thump, have got used to waiting to be told what to do and when, because it's easier that way. 'No worry,' they've convinced themselves. 'I'm resting comfortably in my sinecure, and I don't care a lot if my colleagues, or even the cadets I'm tasked to develop, get axed, belittled, whatever, as long as I remain comfortable in the cocoon.' The irony is that on occasion, the highest form of leadership involves purposely violating the standard principles of leadership. That's where I sit right now. Sinecure-bustin' has to happen, and for it to happen, I must...Here's the analogy: You have a wonderfully sculpted garden of rare flowers that represents an equally crafted chain of command. Problem is, there's a harmful fungus in the soil, and the only means of getting to it is trample through the flower bed. That's me and the chain of command at this time at West Point. I am having to undertake actions normally repugnant to me. Am I making sense?"

"I'm with you. Understand fully. You have to do what you have to do, but without letting the ends justify the means. Everything within the bounds of battle-tested judgment, as I've heard you say, sir." George Bass, a.k.a. Thump, had never met a man in whose judgment he had invested faith in so brief a span. He would go up in flames with Pack without complaint, if it came to that.

They sat in silence for a time, sipping coffee, neither man in the least uncomfortable with it. Then Thump said, "How's that home office situation working out?"

"Very well. Only second thought I permit myself is whether the fence Kathy and the chief have erected is too exclusionary. This institution is lucky, Thump," Pack said slowly, to add force to what followed, "that I don't give a rat's ass that there are those who imagine me abandoning my real responsibilities, which of course would entail my talking with their august selves. No, so far, Thump, I think I have my scheduling about right. But if you ever get wind someone needs a personal audience, and you opine it's in the interest of USMA, speak up.

"My influence, if you can call it that," Pack went on, "seems to be taking a certain shape, one I must admit not to have designed in detail. Time will tell if it continues to form. You and the Dean are handling the operational level, and I will be content to have you do that. If I'm too involved in your business, that's time not spent on the critical aspect of the job I've been assigned to do: Fix the long-term, strategic prospects of the institution. But that's not enough for me. I need to reorganize and reorient this place in the present, which is why it is essential for you, me, and

General Steinberg to be of the same mind. It will require supreme effort on the parts of all three of us to approach the Blucher-Gneisenau and Berthier-Napoleon models of teamwork."

"Right, sir. I guess I'm not as cognizant of my weaknesses as you say you are of yours, but I'm gonna give my all to keep my thick-skulled brain housing group fixed on implementing my commander's intent. Your explanations are…an *illuminating* guide for this dull infantryman."

"I've had enough of you, Bass." Pack expressed love and admiration with that odd humor of his, forever had. "Keep talking like that, and you'll be back to Bass permanently. Thump will have left the building, as Elvis would say. Now get on back to that commodious office suite of yours, and leave me alone. I've got to talk with Duck before the day's done."

Duck had come in with pages of notes he had intended to transcribe. Pack said no, just show me your shorthand code and I'll read it. He had Duck sit there in the study for a few minutes until he felt sure he could understand what the captain had set onto paper just hours earlier. He had presented muscle and bone, leached it of opinion and conjecture, referred to speakers by the offices they represented, not names. Captain Cooper had done the job right, but Pack sent him on his way without compliment.

Darkness had come an hour past, and more. He read the notes several times. The Academic Board's intention to oppose him was evident. He was not displeased, not pleased. He knew the steps he would be forced to take. What had to be, had to be.

♦ ♦ ♦

On a plane just above the dream, looking down on it, he could not remember being part of the ancient world in which he now lived. He had never confronted such a dreamscape. It was a hazy, viridescent Old Testament land comprising ancient tribes. The unrighteous swept across the Earth, conquering everyone before them, like a destructive ill wind. Packs of wolves came at dawn and tore apart the lambs and every animal penned on farms. The righteous were timid, sorely frightened by the power of the wicked. And the righteous starved and thirsted in their craven skins. And the evil people were vain, greedy as the grave, about their strength. They mocked the timid and the righteous, and heaped unspeakable misery and anguish upon them. All around him was commotion, wind and flame and noise and wailing. This could be the state of the known world, he surmised. But he was here, right now, in this awful universe in miniature, and he committed himself to a side in this cosmic battle of good versus evil. The soi-disant righteous cannot credit themselves for goodness until they encourage themselves to impose pain without limit in the struggle to the death.

He believed the God of Jacob would gird him for battle. He desired nothing more than the power to instill courage in his timorous flock, a people gravid with cowardice. If God refused him, he would still engage the enemy. The day came, he stood before his people and cried, "Stand up! Show yourselves to be men deserving the name. Throw off the ways of the sheep, and take up the ways of the lion."

He led them into battle. And he himself was savage in his righteousness, an angry-visaged soldier wielding a sword of burnished steel to lop from human frames every limb and appendage. All the armies of the world had heard his name and feared it. He was the fiercest warrior on this antediluvian Earth, and his people followed him to victories until there was no more rival to defeat.

Smoke filled the camera of his mind. It hung thick and acrid. Then, the greenish, sulfurous world that was, that had been a moment ago, disappeared in a blink, replaced with the Edenic image, at 40,000 feet, of a bluish-hued, sweet-scented, modern West Point. At 1,000 feet, he caught sight of himself, steely-visaged, he thought, but not the angry-visaged man he used to be. The man down below, the other himself now in his field of view, seemed unaware of the many snipers in whose crosshairs he appeared. They bore sandwich boards on their upper bodies, with simple names like Washington, Pentagon, White House, Board of Visitors, and Academic Board. He willed himself to descend, but failed. He tried to scream a warning to the man called Simon Pack, but no sound came.

♦ ♦ ♦

Thursday had dawned. He heard sounds down in the kitchen and got the whiff of coffee. Had to be Duck, a young officer not readily warded off, it seemed. The digital readout said 0437. He's frying some breakfast, too. Not for long. The Supe would ask the housekeeper to freeze a week of meals at a time. At least that many. Thought he might even cough up the jack for a damn upright. Tuesday he would pick someone to manage the residence and be done with it. A captain mustering up breakfast wasn't right, a point he'd be sure to clarify in a minute. Right now, he'd settle for about anyone who could breathe, cook, mop, and dust.

"Good morning, sir," Duck called out as he heard the Supe's footfalls on the landing.

"Good morning to you," Pack returned. "Do not cook for me again. I know you're well-intentioned, but this will not work. Even the faintest suggestion of impropriety on my part is a risk I will not take. Never give the opposition ammo to use against you, Duck. But I did mean what I said about you taking whatever you want when you arrive early, as long as you clean up after yourself. I have no problem with you firing up the coffeepot whenever you see it empty, though. That's a communal resource with communal responsibility."

"Understood, sir, though it's a shame anyone could fault me just for doing what my mother taught me. And for that matter, we often ate communally in the field, people throwing MREs into a mulligan stew. Cooks rotated; rank of the preparer didn't matter. I know you did too, sir. But I understand you well. It won't happen again."

Pack saw that Cooper was embarrassed. *Good, that's part of his maturation.* Never too early or too late to toughen yourself.

"OK, new task. Get to know the company tactical officers. Every one. The Comm has greased the skids. This isn't a giggles-and-grins thing,

Duck. Make a plan before you meet with them, one by one. Learn what you can about their priorities, how much time they spend in their company areas, the state of their interaction with their academic brethren, et cetera. Approach them with professional mien, understand? I want you to know them all. If they invite you to do something, like accompany them on an inspection or watch company athletics, take it. I especially want you to get out to Buckner, because as you know, the Tactical Department has people out there also. A couple of the Tacs out there are from academic departments. Get their views on the plusses and minuses of spending the summer out there away from the classroom. Clear?"

"Roger, sir. Just hope my phone works in the woods, in case you need me."

"Duck, I thought you'd already have understood that if something involves West Point, the Supe gets what he wants."

The Supe thought about those last words to his aide after he had dismissed him. Pack was always confident he would prevail in the current incarnation of the Battle for West Point, but he had never imagined it would result in what would likely be so many bodies left in its wake.

He would have the scheduled private meeting with the Dean in a few more hours, and he had it mind-mapped to his satisfaction. When you know your material and believe in it, too much prep can be waste. If he had forgotten some points of significance, there was a better chance they would come to him in the doing of an entirely unrelated activity. So he called his Academy Chief of Staff, Dahl—he was still having a devilishly hard time finding a name for that un-quirky an officer—to make sure Kimsey Athletic Center is open. He couldn't walk all the way up there to find it locked. "And don't tell anyone I'm coming," he instructed Colonel Jim Dahl. Before he met with the Athletic Director tomorrow, he wanted to be in the proper state of mind.

James Kimsey, USMA '62 and the founder of America Online, pledged millions for this facility. It is 117,000 square feet of devotion to football. It is the Football Place, competitive with any of the football-training palaces in America. Keeping up with the Joneses in this world was tough.

The Nebraska Cornhuskers built a state-of-the-art complex during Tom Osborne's time, and it was regarded as obsolescent when Bo Pelini took control. The Texas Longhorns constructed what they thought to be the standard in their conference, then billionaire T. Boone Pickens decided Oklahoma State would take the lead. Then Phil Knight's Nike money at Oregon won out, and so it goes. Still, Kimsey wasn't built on whimsy. It is a grand four stories: The first consisted of a locker room and sports-medicine center; the second, a so-called strength-development center; the third, a showcase for the greatness Army football was, a gallery of former excellence, a tribute to the Titans of times past; and the fourth floor, a multi-purpose room overlooking Michie Stadium.

Pack wasn't conflicted in beliefs about much, but he was about this emblem of opulence. The reason he had not kept track of Army football over the years was, frankly, that it embarrassed him. A couple of big networks in recent decades had made contracts to televise Army games, and in every game, they zeroed in on the past, meaning until sometime in the seventies. Since that time, there had been little to be excited about, few winning seasons. The whole idea behind this magnificent football complex was that it would enable the Academy to reap dazzling benefits in recruiting. Yet that had not happened. Why did Oklahoma State and Oregon, for example, see those benefits almost immediately, but West Point had not?

Further, this Supe wondered what the demand for these luxurious accommodations in a spartan sport said about the aspiring college footballers. *Heck, places like Highland Park High and Allen High in Texas and Valdosta High in Georgia spend almost as much on facilities as we do at USMA. Probably have a costlier Jumbotron.* Even some NFL players had taken to grousing about the perceived austerity of their locker rooms. *OK, he thought, San Diego, with its leaky pipes and overflowing toilets, might have a case, but none other.* But the high school kid needs a Barcalounger on pile carpeting in front of his locker? Even piped-in music's not good enough; every player must have his own sound system. Does the US Marine Corps attract its people by advertising facilities superior to the other Services? His mind drifted to the locker rooms he had used—a little on the dank side, smelling of jockstraps, sweaty uniforms, liniment, used towels—and he saw romance in the whole ambience. What the hell was wrong with him? His memory carried the one locker room he would pick over this elaborate facility any day. *Maybe I'm too out of touch to argue against Kimsey. Can't deconstruct it, anyway.*

Pack knew the Kimsey layout, so he began his self-guided tour from the fourth floor down. Maybe conduct the Board of Visitors meeting up here? *Could be, but seems too spacious.* Maybe it would inject a bit of needed testosterone into the event. Worth thinking about. He was alone in this upper-level cave and hoped no one had seen him enter.

On the third floor, a cleaning man assumed various postures, getting various angles, to see the vitrine surface he wiped was cleared of fingerprints and other smudges. Pack walked lazily through the floor. He had no need to look closely at the trophies and photographs. He wanted to *feel* the room. At last, the worker looked up, then did a double-take. The man with three stars was startling enough, but *ohmigosh,* standing just down the way was one of the legends enshrined right here in this gallery.

"Don't know what to say, General. Sorry for not noticing you came in. You are Simon Pack, right?"

"The same." Pack proffered his hand, which the man took in two of his own.

"Don't get many days like this, General. Would I be out of place asking for an autograph for my grandson?"

"Not at all, though it's been a while since anyone has wanted it. How old is your grandson, and what's his name?" Pack asked the man.

"You're not gonna believe this, sir, but his name's Simon. And he was named after you, I swear before God. He's a little young yet, nine, but he says he wants to play West Point football like you."

"You don't say...I'd like to do better than an autograph, then. Give me your address, and I'll send you something just for Simon."

"What a day this has been, General! Thank you from my heart." The man searched in distress for something to write on. The Supe pulled a pen and a small Moleskine from an inner pocket. The man wrote his information.

"Good luck to Simon," Pack said. Young Simon and his grandfather would be his guests in the Superintendent's box at a ballgame this season, Pack hoped.

Before entering the Strength Development Center—which he would continue to regard as a euphemism for *weight room*—he paused at a position from which he could peer through the door glass to observe the players working, but from which they could not observe him. He was well aware the team was dispersed at this time of year, in some cases around the globe, but why weren't there more than eight in there? Shouldn't there be momentum of a sort to be gained from having every available player working out at the same time? Not to mention gains from camaraderie and competition? It would be a cop-out to justify so few lifters on the grounds that the strength coach could give more individual attention to the players.

Once he pushed open the door, the players would later tell fellow cadets they "didn't know whether to shit or go blind." Demetrios called the room to attention, a bad idea given that some of the guys were in midlift.

"Continue to work," Pack barked at once, but these cadets were too startled by his presence to carry on normally. "Anyone hurt, tear any muscle, drop a couple hundred pounds on his chest?" Pack gave them his half-grin to defuse the pressure these fellows apparently felt. The strength coach, an under-thirty fellow who looked like a caricature of a Thor action figure, sprinted over to greet the Supe. The lifters, taking their cue from Gary Cline, continued with their assignments for the day.

"Hi, sir, I'm Coach Bob Nasby, in charge of the strength program. I recognize you from the news, of course, and from all those displays on the fourth floor. You look like you could still play."

"Not hardly, Bob, but seeing these machines gets me in the mood. When I played, free weights was about the beginning and end of it. Nautilus was just coming in. I know there are metrics other than poundage on each of the lifts, but how much do you figure we're closing the gap with our opponents? Especially the O-linemen, who must be able to bench press their opponents up and back."

"Frankly, General, when Coach Sumner asked me to take this job, I had no idea what strong headwinds I'd be facing. The previous staff wasn't big on strength and size, as you may know. When I got here a year ago, I told Coach Sumner I thought we were acting irresponsibly by putting players on the field who were at such a disadvantage. We had a disproportionate number of injuries, and I didn't wonder why, with the players' weight and strength disparities. I don't want to get out of my lane here, but what has seemed most important since I arrived is how the football player looks in his Dress Gray uniform and how he's going to pass the Army Physical Fitness Test. That said, we've made great strides, or rather the players have, in terms of strength. Now if we can just add some beef to their frames..."

"That's about how I had it figured," Pack said. "What's your background?"

Nasby seemed a bit shy on the subject. "I played for the Crimson Tide, sir, three-year starter at linebacker. We weren't all mercenaries, as some people on TV try to paint us. I'm from Bessemer, same hometown as Bo Jackson. Most of us who grew up in that state have a strong patriotic streak, me included. So, after serving as a graduate assistant for two years and getting a degree in exercise physiology at 'Bama, I joined Coach Sumner at North Dakota State. When he asked me to join him on this staff, my chest welled up with pride. *Damn*, I thought, *I can do something small for our military*. And that's still how I look at it. I want to be a part of turning this thing around."

"We're going to do that, Bob. Stay on these guys; keep it tough. They want a challenge. Don't lose sight of that. Don't ever feel sorry for them. Why only eight men here?"

"Sorry, sir, don't know the answer to that. I'm led to think Coach Sumner has tried to bring all available together at the same time, but why it hasn't worked out, I can't say," Nasby answered. "But as to keeping it tough, you can bank on that. We still have too many players who think they're giving max effort when they aren't even close. I'm going to need to see more puking before I'm satisfied that they're getting close to the standard I expect. You have a minute to speak to them, General?" Nasby asked.

"I was going to anyway. Gather them over here."

"Listen up, guys, and gather 'round. I don't need to tell you who this is, what he has meant to West Point, and what you can be sure he will mean. Men, General Simon Pack."

Pack looked each player, one by one, in the face, and took his time doing so. They were eager, expectant, wanting encouragement, wearing expressions of supplication for support. In that moment, squinting into those youthful eyes, he knew, even if they had not yet recognized it, that they could become something special for this Academy, the vanguard of change. He spoke to them not more than three minutes. But, oh, the stories they would tell their teammates!

Was it appropriate to cheer the ultimate boss? Nobody considered whether it was. They just did it. All eight—no, nine, because Coach Nasby took part as well—commenced slapping and shoving each other with the delight of four-year-olds opening much-wished-for Christmas presents.

General Simon Pack ambled out, witnessing again the virtue of walking around. There was always a purpose buried somewhere.

If he left right now, he would walk into the Dean's office precisely on schedule.

Chapter Twelve

The Dean Confronts Pack

Ten minutes out from the appointed time, Elijah Steinberg would rather be in the throes of appendicitis. He had pulled the gleaming introduction of Pack out of his ass, and felt he had masked his insincerity brilliantly. This Pack might be edging toward dismantling the academic fiefdom he had constructed meticulously. In a straight-up faceoff, Pack had the advantage of position power, but Steinberg didn't intend a frontal assault. The indirect approach, as Liddell Hart intoned from some musty page of history, was always the better solution. Steinberg planned to array a stronger force than the Supe's. Lee may or may not have been superior to Grant, but the North was stronger than the South. The Academic Board was a voting body, and he thought he could rally a majority to his side on most issues; his kin understood him. Further, the Dean had cultivated relationships with at least half the members of the Board of Visitors. *The BoV is the real power at West Point today*, Steinberg thought, *and that group for damn sure will not be amenable to Pack and his tyrannical methods of governance*.

"I am at a tactical disadvantage," Steinberg reassured himself once more, "but I hold the strategic advantage."

Despite telling himself not to worry about the imminent meeting, Steinberg was still queasy. This Simon Pack could be a brute—he had already witnessed that—and some on the Academic Board had responded favorably to him. Steinberg might indeed carry a majority of the AB, but that could narrow in a hurry if they saw the Superintendent as the one directly controlling their fates, instead of him.

Yes, my majority could dissipate overnight. I have no choice but to play both sides for the present. The word I must keep in the forefront today is "temporize." Trade truth for time. Be pleasant, smile, go along with him. Make him believe he has converted me, then immediately on the heels of his leaving my office, begin to unite my forces.

Steinberg heard his outer office being called to attention by his executive officer, who then showed in General Pack. Shaking hands was not customary is this sort of situation, so Steinberg followed what he hoped was correct protocol in not extending his hand. Smiling, he directed the Supe to one of two identical soft chairs.

"I hope you'll find this chair comfortable, sir. Thank you for the chance to meet so soon after Jefferson Hall."

"OK," Pack said, "let's get to it. That's a good place to start. Tell me about the Day Two proceedings after my guidance on Day One."

"From my perspective, it went well. I observed your aide there taking notes, so I assume he mentioned there was a modicum of resistance from several of our members. Perhaps resistance is too strong a word, so *indifference* might be a better descriptor of their feelings. Depends on the slant your young man put on things. I can assure you, sir, we know our place, and recognize who is in charge. But my Board is made up, as you can imagine, of exceedingly bright, strong-willed individuals who typically have to have reasons for decisions explained to them. They would appreciate my explaining to them, for example, why each will take part in some quarterly tactical march to Camp Buckner and back. Or maybe I misunderstood the message I got to this effect yesterday?"

"Is that a question, General Steinberg?"

"Yes, sir, I guess it is. You see, I cannot imagine you would have promulgated such a decision, realizing we have a number of females, and older people generally, on the faculty. This was not the case when you were a cadet, probably, but it is very true today. Please understand, General, I am merely trying to lift you out of a sticky situation. If I am not mistaken, all our civilian faculty are now unionized and would create a considerable problem for you."

The Superintendent hardly moved a muscle. He gazed placidly at Steinberg. "And your military officers, what do they say?" Pack asked.

"To be frank, sir, they see this as inhibiting their ability to perform their academic duties. It is not sitting well with them," Steinberg said.

"Fine, that's the opening topic. Let's move on to another: What do you have to say about removing all signs of political correctness?"

"Excellent topic, sir. We are in process of taking the steps you desire. We want to follow your instructions exactly, but it seems not everyone on staff agrees about what constitutes PC. I plan to address these questions weekly until we are all on the same page. In the world of these scholars, General, I am afraid not all issues are black and white. They see shadings and nuance the ordinary man and woman do not. I will work my way through the undergrowth that entangles them, but I ask for additional time.

"Let me illustrate these moral vagaries this way. The West Point Honor Code states, 'A cadet will not lie, cheat, or steal, or tolerate those who do.' Has a cadet violated that code by saying he shaved that morning when he did not, if this cadet can go a week without shaving yet show little to no evidence of stubble? Should he be expelled from the Academy for such a picayune white lie?" Steinberg asked. "I dare suggest you might have a tough time deciding that one."

Does he see that what he just said illustrates rather well the difference between him and me? Pack thought. *The cadet didn't shave but said he had. The issue of expelling depends not on significance of the action in question, but on the reason an untruth was communicated. Did he forget he hadn't shaved? Was he trying to avoid discipline? Did he answer without thinking? Did he misunderstand the question?* The Dean emoted about the fairness of the situation while Pack dissected the argument rationally. Reason versus passion.

"I'm getting the picture," Pack said to the Dean. "My turn to raise a point. I'm sure you heard President Rozan say at a presser last week that he's committed to further military budget cuts to 'make the military leaner and stronger,' as he put it. Every President uses the same words, don't they, General?"

Steinberg nodded.

"He means to cut the military *more* than already announced," Pack said. "Do you think West Point will be immune?"

"Certainly not, sir. I'm not the comptroller, but I'm also not naive. And I believe you know I will fight anvil and tong for the interests of the academic departments. You would expect me to do so, I am sure."

"What if I tell you to begin a phase-out of your civilian faculty? That I order you to begin incremental cuts two months from now and be down to one civilian professor per department by the start of next academic year?" Pack asked. "Don't feel obligated to comment yet. We'll have time to wrap it up. You can comment then."

Steinberg was on the ropes. The Superintendent was bull-rushing him, and he had found no way to defend himself. He resented playing the role of the eunuch. This Pack was purposely coercing him to take this role. There was no other way to say it: He hated Simon Pack.

"OK," Pack said, driving forward with the bull-rush, "what's your view of the USMA-sponsored National Conference on Ethics in America? Is that a smart use of funds?"

"Why, yes, sir, I believe it is. Students from seventy-five universities now attend. That nationwide visibility is positive publicity. And captains of industry not only attend, but some lead seminars promoting the importance of ethics in business. Individual Class funds are the source of most of the required financing."

"Have you considered so many schools are represented because, for the students, it represents an all-expenses-paid trip? And USMA does fund part of it," Pack said. "You'll have a chance to respond, Dean, but hear me well. Last year the Superintendent, whose name chokes me, removed one of your department heads for conduct unbecoming. Then, within months, the man who executed the firing is himself the subject of an army Inspector General investigation, the findings of which remain concealed from the public.

"I related the story a day or two ago how appalled I was, offended on behalf of field soldiers, upon being taken to a door that bore the lettering, *Center for Army Leadership*. What we have here is something similar. What we need to do about hosting that conference is stop the pious preaching long enough to get right inside our own walls. Conference on Ethics in America? Please. Everyone associated with this should reflect on its sanctimoniousness. Be, know, do. Does that ring a bell, Dean? Don't answer. We will be a beacon of good because we *are* good and can distinguish good from bad. We will not be a beacon of good by screaming that we are good or by taking out ads proclaiming our goodness. Prepare for NCEA to die real soon." Pack said.

Pack beckoned toward the office outside the Dean's. "Someone out there have a cup of morning brew?"

The Dean was going for the intercom, but Pack repeated the question. "If you do, I will get it myself."

"Or would you prefer a soda or bottled water?" Steinberg asked, suddenly solicitous.

Pack fetched his own coffee, then took a latrine break. He smiled, standing at the urinal, thinking how he did this without thinking pretty often. Buy something to drink at the gas-station convenience store, then go into the latrine, when the reasonable person—the one who gave a tinker's dam about hygiene—would do it the other way around. For a moment, he wondered if he were also smiling because he was pissing all over Steinberg.

No, he concluded, *it is not in my interest for anyone at this Academy to fail, so it cannot be a case of Schadenfreude. If Steinberg is being pissed on, he is doing it himself.*

Pack took the chair again. He wasn't going to be the first to speak this go-round. He scanned the walls and desktop. This place, Pack figured, would place high in the "I Love Me" office-of-the-year competition.

Do I even have a diploma now? Pack reflected. *Pretty sure they all decayed. Where did this man get the time for all these testaments to his learning? If I had these degrees, would I display them this ostentatiously?*

"What else is on your mind, General?" Steinberg asked.

"Two more items I imagine you will take to be of great consequence. First, I am giving you an opportunity to talk me out of a line-item veto."

"You mean," Steinberg said, "with respect to the USMA budget, or the Dean's budget?"

Pack was deliberate with his words. "With respect to neither. I am speaking of a line-item veto over your course offerings. You have a problem with that?"

Steinberg's premeeting resolve was beginning to fade. *I cannot just smile, be agreeable, go along with an attack of this nature.* "General Pack," he began, searching for moderate words to accompany his immoderate mood, "I believe you would think less of me if I failed to defend the people who work for me. Of course, you will expect me to have a problem with such a suggestion. It is the Academic Board, sir, who is charged with every facet of the academic program, and that includes proposing and developing the curricula. Besides, you could not possibly have the time to look into the contents of every course taught in every department. At some point, sir, we have to rely upon the judgment of our subordinates, a theme, I am told, you elaborate upon from time to time. The Board will not approve such a proposal."

"So you are defying me. Am I reading that right, General Steinberg?"

"Please do not misunderstand, sir. I am not a defiant man and would not think of defying you. I am merely trying to explain that this would upset the members of the Board," Steinberg said.

"And it is your job, is it not, to lead the Academic Board to support my intent willingly?" Pack asked.

"Clearly that is so, General Pack, but I do not understand this sudden expression of no-confidence in the academic structure," Steinberg declared, with as much bravado as he could summon.

Pack continued the bull-rush, not at all feeling mercy on Steinberg. Real change demands real change. "OK, maybe you'll find my final point more palatable than the others. Here's a question for you, Dean. Why do we have a system of majors?"

Steinberg had not anticipated any of this. The man was loco, unreasonable by any measure of behavioral sanity. *What the hell?* he wanted to scream at Pack. *What planet did you come from? No, what primeval sludge pit have you crawled from? Who sent you here to destroy my world?* He could feel his hands quivering, but he did not want to call Pack's attention to them by looking down. *Get control of yourself, man. Say enough to get him to leave. Temporize, Elijah! Why didn't you throw back a handful of Prozac, Paxil, or Zoloft before this damn train wreck of a meeting?*

So Steinberg smiled and said, "The origin of the majors program is a Presidential commission's recommendation. The wisdom of that recommendation has been affirmed by every Dean and Superintendent since."

"That may be true," Pack replied, "but I asked you for an answer. Why do you say we should allow cadets to select majors? For the first two hundred years of its history, were West Point and all its leaders wrong? Were Maxwell Taylor and Dwight Eisenhower poorly served by their West Point education? Grant, Lee, Patton? I believe at last count fifteen of the current Fortune 500 companies were run by Academy people, a rather disproportionate representation, all of whom graduated before the majors system was introduced. Were they hurt by the rigidity of their education? I'm asking you for an answer, Steinberg."

Elijah Steinberg looked, and normally felt, fit. He worked out regularly. He had periodic health checkups. At this moment, however, he was a blubbering pustule of a man. This Pack was wickedness incarnate. *I cannot tolerate this abasement, can I?*

"General Pack, kids today don't listen to the music preceding generations listened to. They don't read the types of books we read. The generations you mentioned had their strengths, I'll agree, but today's youth are more sophisticated in most ways and have different educational expectations. They want the full menu, not the Big Mac and fries, and if we do not offer it, they will not give us the time of day. They want choices, and I believe in my heart of hearts, it is our obligation to offer them. Not every young person wants to become educated as an engineer; some want, hard as it is to imagine, a liberal arts degree. All want to feel attached to their surrounds. There is a life out there, a vibrant intellectual life, that cadets twenty years ago probably did not even know existed. When a cadet of that period was fortunate enough to get a date with a Vassar girl, he invariably left her feeling inferior. Those girls were so much more attuned to the greater world. These are kids of the modern world, General, and West Point took the necessary bold step of entering it."

"Steinberg, I have put three principles in writing as my guides to the conduct of our business. One: Every facet of Academy life will orient on developing military leaders. Two: Philosophical idealism. Three: Knowledge defined as the deduction of immutable truths through mental and emotional discipline. They boil down to character. When I see that you have a course on gender studies, I am concerned. When I delve slightly more in depth, I become very concerned when I see the roster of authors represented. I doubt very much that course supports principle one, or two, or three. I doubt very much—no, I am certain—you cannot examine every subject you teach and guarantee it meets the standard of the first principle. And whenever the possibility arises in the hard sciences, I want to see every effort exerted to tie it to the real-world military. If there is doubt, err on the side of fidelity to these principles. Chop away all the undergrowth. I spoke with George Bass about concentric and eccentric initiative; it's not a difficult concept. A man as learned as you will have gotten the difference right away. Your initiative is eccentric, breaking away from the orbit of my intent.

"You are making it difficult for yourself, General Steinberg. I will not get in a pissing match with you. Either you get the Deanship in line with my intent, or perhaps I can assist you in finding another area of work.

"Let's do a quick review, Elijah, a headline version of what we discussed. One, I am likely to exercise a line-item veto soon unless you beat me to the punch in scraping the thick tartar off your academic teeth. Two, I believe the majors program is a countercurrent to cadet teamwork and leadership. It actively works against principle one. You did not provide an adequate rebuttal. What this dumb old general sees when he looks at the academic handbook is a faculty, beginning with you, that has happily acceded to the forces of political correctness. Three, on behalf of your faculty, you seek relief from participation in the road-march and exercise program. I deny that request. As I explained earlier to your outfit, we need to blur the yellow line between all things academic and tactical. Four, the next NCEA will be the last. I reject the National Conference on Ethics in America as elitist and not in keeping with the image of USMA that I want to project. Five, I want to see from you a ready-to-implement plan to cut all but one civilian professor per department. Your suspense for that is two weeks from today. Any questions, General Steinberg?"

Steinberg swiftly decided he would speak his mind. "I must say, sir, you act as if ours is a Firstie-Plebe relationship. As today's kids say, I feel dissed, and I do not say that in good humor. You are blatantly questioning my professional integrity. Don't you think you already have diminished my standing before my chief subordinates?"

"Elijah, I do not care about your feelings. Let that sink in. I am not going to needlessly expend emotional energy over what you correctly perceive as our unbalanced relationship. You are an impediment to what I intend to do to revive this institution's reputation as the best military school in the world. Maybe you have been away from the combat army for too long. I won't ask the last unit you served in, because, Elijah, I have no interest in embarrassing you. And I will not ask why, when you could have gotten into any school in the land, you didn't go to the now-coed Vassar or Columbia or anyplace but West Point. I want to graduate excellent officers, and everything after that having to do with feeling comfortable 'in the greater society' is no matter of concern to me. Worldliness is no substitute for leadership in the midst of battle, and America has no expectation that Vassar will provide battle leaders. That, General, is singularly West Point's job. I'll give you a few days—sorry, I don't have time to slow dance with you about these changes—to think through whether you're boarding the change train or going home, wherever that might be. I'll leave you with your thoughts. I've got work to do," Pack said.

He turned his own thoughts instantly to enjoying the evening in the company of *Winter's Bone*.

Chapter Thirteen

Trust

Friday morning arrived with no Duck downstairs. He was encamped at Buckner until next week. Thump already had passed the news that in less than a day, Duck had done the "Slide for Life," a military version of a zip line, the difference being that cadets climbed a high ladder soaking wet, without safety rigging, then struck the water at high speed. Duck also had completed the rappelling and free climb and assisted one of the 82d Airborne Regular Army noncommissioned instructors with his field-expedient antenna class. The captain didn't need a lot of direction. The Corps of Cadets tactical officers already were getting to know about him by word of mouth.

The Supe's intent was for Duck and the Tacs to develop mutual trust, and Duck did it the Pack way: by example. He hadn't told Duck anything more than get to know them, on their turf, and Duck interpreted the guidance as a real leader does. How many of the cadets and Regular Army officers recognized the pain Captain Cooper lived with every day from a prosthesis that required constant adjustment, and even then, caused swelling and sometimes severe skin irritation? In fact, how many recognized he even wore a prosthetic device? He had been truthful in telling the Supe he had never requested a special assignment from Infantry Branch. But what Pack knew was the state of indescribably high dudgeon young Duck had been in when Infantry Branch told the young officer they had found him medically unfit to continue as an infantry officer. He had chucked it, devil may care, yelling at a man two ranks his senior that the only reason he wanted to be in the Army was to be with infantry soldiers. "I don't want to be Finance or Adjutant General or Transportation. If I wanted to do those jobs, I'd rather be doing them as a civilian! I am an *Infantryman*, and I refuse to have you rebranch me."

"Captain," the lieutenant colonel had said, refusing to pull rank on the then-twenty-four-year-old captain, "I have an ace in the hole: Your USMA grades were good enough to get you into a lot of med schools. You wouldn't be the first to go that route; in fact, quite a few over the decades who could no longer keep up physically let us help them to med school so they could remain in the army. Somewhere around 1980, as an example, we had a lieutenant who graduated first in his West Point Class in physical education. His name's on a plaque outside the old gym. He was on that Merlin Olsen program, 'Survival of the Fittest,' I think it was called, and made it to the final. Anyway, he got knocked off the telephone pole spanning the Snake River and suffered a devastating upper-body injury. Man became a valuable orthopedic doc. Sound good?"

"Sir, I'm going to be released from Bethesda soon. I will relearn how to walk, maybe even run. I can be an infantryman. There's a verse in Revelations that says, 'They did not love their lives so much as to shrink from death.' I do not fear poor promotion so much that I can consent to leaving the infantry. As I see it, sir, the decision is not mine; it is yours, and what you must decide is whether to medically retire me or give me new life in the infantry."

Duck was a groundbreaker, at least in the sense of being a rare case. He had had his days, days he questioned his own judgment, after he got his wish to stay in the infantry. The public saw heartwarming stories on the TV, soldiers recovering from war wounds hobbling along on a smart-looking mechanical device, all of it looking permanent and cheery. The reality remains that prosthetics are to medical advancement as local-weather forecasting is to scientific advancement. One could argue if it weren't for new and horrific injuries to military people during the past decade-and-a-half, there would have been scant advancement in the field of prosthetics since the Civil War. Few understand that each prosthesis is different. Each is slightly different in design, each a product of the intersection of art and science, geometry and drawing. A millimeter shift in the curvature of the brace here or there can mean damage not only to tissue but also to underlying bone. The wearer can feel desolate when for no discernible reason the fit is no longer correct, pain accompanies every movement, and stability erodes. This is especially true if the soldier is no longer in the Army, and must depend on the Veteran's Administration, which may be three hundred fifty miles from his home. The infantry officer—Duck could count them on one hand—who wears a prosthesis is faced with overwhelming challenges, and never knows for certain when his service time will end.

Duck knew no one in medicine, none of the many he had so far encountered, could prescribe a right or wrong way to pace oneself. Some cautioned him to use every step wisely, not overexert himself, because he had only a matter of time before going to crutches or a wheelchair. Others said using the prosthesis—and hence his leg, and the rest of his body, for that matter—as much as possible was a good thing. The body would adapt to the demands placed on it, and grow stronger in the process. Duck accepted the latter opinion, but he knew the medical community really did not have the answers.

The few who knew that Duck had the gizmo attached to a lower leg thought, *Man, he's inspiring, isn't he?* The sober truth was they had no idea.

◆ ◆ ◆

The meeting with Athletic Director Buck Dantoni was uneventful. Pack didn't entertain the idea of replacing the man, but he judged he'd need to reinforce the fellow's spine as time allowed. Not a bad guy, just didn't fight hard enough on behalf of Academy athletics. If Rutgers said, "No football home-and-homes with you for the next decade. We'll play you at Yankee Stadium, but not Michie," Dantoni was inclined to smile and reply, "OK." Rutgers was an example only, but this kind of thing had happened too many times in Dantoni's tenure. In the example, Rutgers essentially got a home game while the diminishing Army fan base got hosed out of a home game. Dantoni struck Pack as a decent man, probably competent in most aspects of his job, but he'd been promoted to a Division I athletic directorship a few years too early. With surer direction, he might be fine. In fact, Pack's predecessor had manifested little interest in, or knowledge of, the intercollegiate athletics department. That had changed, and Dantoni knew it. Pack knew a number of colonels he could call on who could perform suitably as the Army Athletic Director right now, but Buck Dantoni would get a second chance.

They shuffled down the hallway to the room where Dantoni had brought together twenty-three of the twenty-five head coaches. Eight among them were women. Two coaches were away on previous engagements. Head Trainer Ed Pillings was also present, as Pack had requested. They stood as one when the Supe came in. Dantoni's stock elevated a notch as Pack observed the seating arrangement. Pack's seat was at the head of the table. Dantoni himself was perpendicular to Pack's right, Pillings to the left.

"Thanks for coming, ladies and gentlemen," Pack began. "I'm here to offer some thoughts about Army athletics, but permit me to say Corps Squad sports turned out to be incalculably important to my future life. I played on one squad or another more or less year-round. I guess I spent as much time in the training room as anyone ever has. I met a man there, a gruff man, a great man, whose example nourished me immensely. I refer, of course, to Mr. Ed Pillings. Ed, I hope you've been as fine an example to one or two others along the way as you were to me. Thank you for your adult lifetime of service to this institution.

"Now, ladies and gentlemen, I want to say you and I owe Ed. He has had to endure an awful deterioration of our athletic program. It has ripped at his heart, I'm sure. What I want is to repair his heart, and ours, too. But mostly, I want to fix the heart of West Point. In fixing West Point, we fix Ed, we fix me, we fix West Point athletics. In the short time I've been here, I have upset some apple carts. I have made some people angry. I've done a lot of scolding, and I have more to do. It's doubtful I'll stop the scolding for as long as I'm here. But I will not scold the Department of Intercollegiate Athletics, not yet, anyway. See, I have thought about this woeful athletics thing for years, not exclusively in preparing for this post. I'm taking a risk in what I'm saying to you now. I believe the athletic department is culpable only to a minor degree. To the extent you are culpable, I want you to identify and mend. But understand, I am the person most responsible for fixing USMA sports. I have begun the repair process, and I will get the job done. In today's parlance, I've got your back. I expect you to have mine.

"One of the greatest men to occupy the Superintendent's chair, Robert Eichelberger, said of Army football, 'It looks as if we are developing the finest bunch of losers in the world. By the gods, I believe the cadets deserve a football team that will teach them how to be good winners!' The difference between his view and mine involves the root of the problem. The problem he faced was a mirror image of mine, meaning in the sense of oppositeness. I believe the football team needs a cadet corps that will be good winners. Eichelberger went out and got himself a football coach named Red Blaik. I don't need to do that. We have Coach Les Sumner, who has proved he can lead this team to wins if he gets a little support."

Looking directly at Sumner, the Supe said, "Coach, we will talk directly, and you will get my backing. I think the problem is that first, West Point grew soft, then the football team did, then everybody just accepted softness as the new normal. I am demanding the Corps regain its toughness. I call on the football team to set the example. You began to turn the corner last season. In other words, reverse the process that brought this place to where it is. I ask the football team to lead us out of the wilderness. I expect victories—real, not moral—this year. Scoreboard talks, ladies and gentlemen.

"I make no apologies for orienting on football. It is our one and only revenue-producing sport. There probably would be no other intercollegiate athletic programs if there were no football. Every once in a while, someone needs to remind you of that. For that reason alone, every coach in the room ought to be as concerned about winning football as I am. At the same time, I am not concerned about football only—or even chiefly—because it brings us money, but because it is widely perceived to be a combat sport. We are the *Military* Academy, as I have told every audience at West Point. I will deliver that message over and over. We are the potting soil for men and women who can professionally, creatively, and with awful malice destroy America's every enemy. We must be proficient in a combat sport that is a reflection, however murky, of our professional calling.

"Break, break, break: Let me interrupt this message to disclose a revelation to the other head coaches. You are unlikely to be fired as long as you keep yourselves above reproach morally and legally. Be tough, be respectful, but keep your hands off your cadets—in all ways. Can you interpret my saying you're not likely to be fired because of a lack of interest in your sports? Well, yes, you can—if you're stupid. A good number of you coaches have had good success in the past several seasons. Maggie Dixon established what has grown into an annually competitive women's basketball team. The men's basketballers have had more downs than ups since Coach K's departure, but you look now capable of sustaining what got you two years of winning. Lacrosse, another sport I played and loved, is resurgent, but you sit just outside the tight circle comprising Syracuse, UNC, Johns Hopkins, Maryland, and a couple others. You once were in that circle and can break through again. Ladies and gentlemen, I want you all to have the chance to stamp yourselves on this institution as Ed Pillings did on me. That means you stay here a long time. Hockey, you had Jack Riley, and wrestling, you had LeRoy Alitz. Soccer, you had Joe Palone. Baseball, you had Eric Tipton. Men who were greater than their records, though most years their records were good, too. I want every coach here to win and play within the rules, and work your rears off to be the best in your sports. I hope that is clear.

"The hot seat is the one your head football coach sits on. That is a fact, one neither happy nor sad. He provides food and drink for the rest of the people sitting at this table, and for the families for which they provide, and so on. Coach Sumner, I hope you do not read the Army football message board; I have someone do it for me as an occasional pulse check. I am not surprised to read the testimonials of cadets describing the gaping chasm between the Corps and their football team. I won't tolerate that, and I suppose there's some blame to go around on this score. But, coaches, I want every one of you to support each other and see that your cadets do the same. Coach Sumner, work it out so your players get over to watch golf and cross country and all the rest. And Lacrosse, meet Coach Wrestling at his mats and Women's Soccer at her field. Start your team building with your fellow coaches. How about some interaction now? What's on your minds?"

The women's swimming coach said, "Thank you, General Pack. I'm a newbie, been here two years, yet it's the first time besides an all-sports banquet I've ever heard the Superintendent speak of sports. I might speak for the majority in saying I know my sport is just a narrow sliver of Academy life, and my swimmers don't expect much, but I know having a little recognition from fellow cadets would be exciting for them, and probably beneficial. I myself will set the example by getting out to see every sport represented here. And, if I might add, I think it might be helpful to get out to company sports, too. We'll just have to make the time, and we can."

These remarks brought a chorus of, "Yes, yes."

The golf coach said, "I'd like to comment not as a coach, but as a football fan who goes to games." Then he caught himself, saying, "Sorry, sir, no harm intended, but on second thought, I'll keep it to myself. Don't air dirty laundry. My bad."

Buck Dantoni spoke up. "General, I do not know what Coach was just about to say. I do not. But there is dirty laundry, and it is mine, and I'm working hard to get it through the full wash cycle. I'd say we're on about the second spin cycle now. The Michie fan experience will be better this season. New paint throughout the stadium, refurbished restrooms, new vendors with new food offerings. I have a decision paper somewhere in the system for you, sir, about cadets manning some of the concession booths."

"Whoa. Your position for or against?" Pack got cloudy.

"Against, sir. This isn't the place to discuss how this happened, but I don't think they should be doing those duties."

"No decision paper required. Buck, I said your job isn't at risk, but it would have been if I had seen cadets hawking Cokes at a football game. *Todos aqui comprenden, muchachos y muchachas?* You get my intent? Cadets will not be treated as chattel. I will yoke their backs heavy and expect them to bear it, but I will not have them disrespected. Everyone clear on the larger intent? Cadets selling Cokes and hot dogs during football games? That is unconscionable and illustrates a decline in pride of place and mission. And if you had said, 'But the cadets volunteered to sell *x* and *y* in order to make money for some cause,' that would actually be worse. Those cadets and all their leaders do not understand their *duty* at football games is to focus on the game and energize their team. That positively irks hell out of me. Makes us look like a junior high 4-H Club selling cupcakes. No, no, no! One more time: This is the United States Military Academy. We have standards of personal deportment and bearing, even at ballgames!

"But I do have a message for you coaches out of this: Do not mollycoddle your cadets. The last football coach was too damn easy on his players. I do believe he felt sorry for them. 'Poor cadets have to get up so early, study so hard, and have so much going on, I can't be another stress in their lives. Wouldn't be right to use the maximum practice time the NCAA grants.' You've lost them the moment they sense you feel sorry for them. And Buck, get involved to make sure we don't have those cadet sideline reporters talking inanely about how tough the cadet's daily schedule is. Hearing that BS during an Army game on television is as predictable as the sun coming up.

"And since this crowd has revved my engine, I want the sophomoric Black Knight skits expunged, too. Along with the Black Knight himself. We still have the mules, don't we? Cadets spend a lot of time tending to them, don't they? And a certified veterinarian checks them periodically? Who are we afraid of? The SPCA? Ladies and gentlemen, the minority will not rule in these matters. Get some backbone. I want to see those powerful beasts of burden patrolling the sidelines, at least before kickoff—and if we can work them into some other sporting events, look at that also. I don't care if they crap on the artificial turf, or damage an occasional turf square on the sideline. We have a proud history; let's recall pertinent parts of it for the present. I will not say that taking the mules away from regular appearances at home games caused us to plunge, but the two events *were* almost coincident. Texas got pressured to remove Bevo from participating at their games, but have they caved? Hell, no! Board the mules on the train to Army-Navy as well. What is the K9 in a police department, ladies and gentlemen? He *is* a law enforcement officer, correct? He has a badge. So be it with our mules. Let them be an active part of our football *team*. The K9 has a genuine role in the department; so be it with our mules. We will look to them as another source of strength.

"I want an end to excuses, every mammy-jammin' one. I have contemporaries, of various ranks, who like to hide behind the excuse that Army will never catch up to Navy and Air Force in football because coming to West Point means it's more likely the players will go into ground combat after graduation, and neither parent nor son wants that. Sounds reasonable, only it's untrue. Sorry for not having the accurate figures in my head, but I can tell you in 2013, two hundred twenty cadets branched infantry. Just ten were football players. Not good enough. Now look at Navy: They had more football players go Marine ground than we had go infantry. The Navy players are not avoiding combat; in fact, they seek to become part of a tough ground force, and on top of that, many request admittance to SEAL training. Cadets are looking for the rough challenge. They want to be known as the toughest guys on the block. They can be. Football plays twelve regular-season games. Don't tell me we can win one-quarter of them, as has become the norm. No, no, no. This team *can* win all twelve. We can be the meanest damn team in college football."

Pack was narrow-eyed now, forming words with great purpose and intensity, delivering them in a low, throaty voice. "We have it within us to get Army athletics back to their rightful place, and in my opinion, we're the only team around that actually has a rightful place. We were meant to lead. Coaches, elevate your games. The Commandant and I spoke recently about something the Air Force calls the OODA Loop. When that enemy aircraft is bearing down on you, trying to shoot you out of the sky, you observe, you orient, you decide, and you act, and you roll through the entire sequence faster than he can. In football, you don't just play the whole game with a set of plays you designed three days ago, do you? No, you have to be mentally agile. I'm not telling you anything new, but part of this is your Superintendent getting his game face on, too.

"Plan thoroughly. Demand excellence. Don't get stale. Build new networks to land those special people, budding leaders who want—in the face of the vacancy and vapidity of American pop culture—to accomplish things that will set them apart, now more than ever. Outthink the opposing coach. Gain every edge allowed by law. Go into every contest with the aim of destroying the opponent's will to resist. Crush his will. Explain to your teams what they must do, the steps they must take, to achieve that objective. Scoreboard talks, ladies and gentlemen. Excuse walks. When I show up at practices, and I will, do *not* send anyone over to keep me company. I'll figure a way to get information if I need it. And coaches, my reason for coming won't be to boost morale. I'll be there to see how well you're preparing your charges.

"Coach Sumner, I have a question, just from a fan's point of view, and I do not want an answer now, and probably never. It is not my intention to become the football coach. Why do we speak of our Academy as a leader development lab, yet our quarterbacks, I am told, have not had play-calling autonomy since the 1970s? Just curious. I'm not suggesting you change. I know the standard is for the offensive coordinator to make the call, but I wonder if sometimes the man on the ground might have a better feel, and that he might perform better if he were personally invested. Most likely I'm wrong, so take it for what it's worth. I just hope the answer isn't what I'm sure it is most places: that I'm making a whale of a lot of money and will *not* entrust that bankroll to a nineteen-year-old.

"Last point: The life span of orcas and elephants isn't appreciably longer than the time elapsed since we last beat Navy, and I do want to crush them, but I want our new thinking to be, *crush everyone*!

"Let's get back to work."

Chapter Fourteen

Mistrust

In most terms of most presidencies, someone stunningly unprepared is appointed to an ambassadorship. The political-patronage system at work, and it can be ugly. Recently, the President appointed three ambassadors who had never set foot in the countries for which they were headed, and in one case, this is a country of great geographical extent and influence in our hemisphere. Secretary of the Army Fitz Spitshugh fits into this category. He brought bags of coin to the President's party, but his knowledge of the Army is subminimal. It is doubtful he could match a Service with its dress uniform. He once made a pre-Army-Navy game wager with the Secretary of the Navy that the Army's aircraft carrier could beat the Navy's on a hundred-mile race course. Maybe that is apocryphal, maybe not. The man loves the ceremonies, and can read a speech with the best of them, long as the words don't confuse him.

So Spitshugh was taken unaware when one of the Defense Secretary's emissaries personally delivered a handwritten message from the Secretary of Defense himself. The note included a phrase, "Slap a chokehold on West Point" and was signed in the familiar scrawl. It was clear even to the less-than-lustrous brain of Spitshugh that additional clarification was due.

"Chokehold?" he inquired of the Defense Secretary's man.

"Look, Mr. Secretary," the envoy said, "this is straight from the SECDEF to you and straight from President Rozan to the SECDEF. The West Wing despises that place so much, wouldn't surprise me to see them bring a voodoo priestess in to cast a hex on it. The President feels he's been dissed twice while at West Point. The cadets' unappreciative applause after his war speech, and again at the last graduation ceremony, only confirm his suspicions they are out of control, that they think they know more about America's place in the world than he does. And worse, they apparently feel they have the right to demonstrate their disagreement with the Commander-in-Chief. Your job, Mr. Secretary, is to get control of that damn place. So do you understand the mission, Mr. Spitshugh?"

"You can believe that!" Spitshugh fumed. "They can't hate it more than I do, and you can certainly relay that message to the President. I'll slap a chokehold on them the World Wrestling Federation will want to copy."

The SECDEF's envoy thought, *President Rozan couldn't care less if this nimrod collapses deader'n a damn stick in the next hour*, but nodded.

Actually, Spitshugh was wondering why he hated West Point, or why he should. They hadn't done anything to him, and he'd always thought it a lovely place. But, boy, oh, boy, he loathed them now, and by damn they didn't want to witness the fury of Fitz Spitshugh, Secretary of the Army and civilian eminence.

Still, once he was alone, he thought, *Whadda they mean exactly, chokehold?* Spitshugh got few calls from anyone this high in the Defense chain. They all just worked around him, knowing he didn't understand jack, anyway. This was the first time that the Secretary of Defense putatively had asked him to do anything. After a bit, Fitz Spitshugh took to fretting, cogitating about what it was he was supposed to do, anyway. Damn those people, you know you should explain things to people in your chain. Just walk in, drop a Molotov and sprint off. *My heavens*, Spitshugh thought, *I can't be expected to know everything, can I? Don't they even have the faintest notion of what leadership means?*

After much brooding, by early that evening, the meaning of SECDEF's injunction had slowly burrowed into his brain. Chokehold: a move that enabled one to subdue or demand absolute compliance on the part of another. That was what the President wanted. An obedient West Point. A West Point that did not question and always applauded.

Spitshugh had two military aides. Lieutenant Colonel Rita Campbell held down the log side and was his interpreter on maintenance and logistical affairs. Lieutenant Colonel Mike Rynearson handled maneuver force issues. Each believed the hardest part of the job was getting every subject down to Spitshugh's abecedarian level. No matter how low they went, they discovered they had to find a new low gear. They wouldn't remember shit from shinola about the real Army by the time they got away from Spitshugh. Campbell and Rynearson had something else in common: They wanted this assignment to be over yesterday. One time at a Middle East Peace Conference meeting over at Foggy Bottom (why Spitshugh was invited remained clear as mud), Spitshugh directed Campbell to check participants' badges as they entered and to assist the representatives, such as the delegate from Qatar, to lug his briefing materials to his spot at the mammoth round table. To which Campbell replied with a Pepsodent smile, "Sir, you've confused me with a bellhop. I am a commissioned officer, and I am not about to embarrass my Service by performing such duties."

The Honorable Fitz Spitshugh withdrew his instruction with a smile of his own, saying, "Look, Rita, I may be the Honorable Secretary of the Army, but I'm allowed to joke once in a while too, aren't I? Just blowing off pressure with a little humor. What was that song, 'Rita, Rita, Meter Maid?'" Har, har, har, laughed the witless Secretary.

How witless? Both officers were West Point graduates and loyal to their alma mater, yet if Spitshugh knew that, he seemed to have forgotten. He summoned both of them and demanded from them a proposal to follow the SECDEF's directive to "put a chokehold on West Point." Spitshugh had decided that turning to a civilian Assistant Secretary might be embarrassing. Besides, he couldn't trust them to keep the matter quiet. They were to a man and woman blabbermouths. These military people tended to be tight-lipped and unemotional.

"Something's seriously amiss," Campbell said later. "We have to put our heads together on this one. Maybe we go back to Fitz and try to milk more information from him. Tell him we want to be sure we have all available information so we can give him the best recommendations. And we talk with Colonel Peters over at Legislative Liaison, see what we can ferret out. If it's just another political vendetta, we'll have to give a quiet heads-up to West Point through the appropriate channels."

"Timing's funny, isn't it?" said Rynearson. "General Pack just got there. Maybe somebody doesn't like him. But I concur. We might have to decide where our first loyalty lies. When I was talked into this assignment—*coerced* into it, really—I put the best light on it and thought, *You'll be near the political center of the country, get an idea how decisions are actually reached, and on the whole, it might be a glamorous gig.* Wear the expensive Dress Blues I wore maybe once a year before. But I tell anyone who inquires, this is the most deflating experience ever. If there are more than a dozen people in the House and Senate combined who are competent, ethical, sedulous, patriotic, I ain't seen 'em yet. And don't get me started on the pill-swillin', money-grubbin', lyin', cheatin', Lotharios and Lotharias everywhere else in government. After a while, you get sick just breathing the Metro DC air. So, Rita, if I have to take sides, the one I'll be on is crystal clear."

"For starters," Campbell said, "I think we ought not speak further about this until we've independently recounted on paper every detail of that office encounter. We can compare later if we need to. But nothing on a computer. This all has to be handwritten."

"On my way home, I'll stop at Kinko's to make copies for each of us," Mike Rynearson said.

"Think tonight about a proposal we could make to Fitz that both delays the plan and is, figuratively, nonlethal. Some kind of reverse Trojan horse."

♦ ♦ ♦

It was **Friday**. Pack went home and sketched out his next week. It would be different in kind from this week. He had thrown a lot of people into the big pot of warm water and applied the heat. Now it was time to let them stew for a few days. Who would want to jump out or call for help to stop their torment? Their actions would declare which side they took. It is wise to know the enemy order of battle before you engage it full-force. Meantime, Pack would organize himself for the long haul.

He had not yet taken the time to walk through this rambling old residence. He roamed casually, looking at it from the point of view of the builder he was. It was a fine construction, every seam wrought with care. This was not the cabin in Montana but a place he would treat with equal respect. The housekeeper he was about to hire needed to know this was a kind of museum, a historical artifact into whose care he had been entrusted. This was not just another large home in Highland Falls or Cornwall. Douglas MacArthur employed the study much as Pack did, as a primary office. Clearly, MacArthur coexisted without interruption by the many ghosts reputed to this day to have lived in these quarters. In 1972, then-Superintendent William Knowlton permitted a psychic demonologist, Lorraine Warren, to tour the home. The results were never published. No matter; no ghost was moving Pack, nor, he hoped, his new employee.

Pack had no television. He did not miss the blaring box. He would, however, remember to offer to buy the housekeeper a small one for some out-of-the-way location. "Everyone doesn't share my peculiarities," he mused, "and that's a good thing." He instead chose the company of the written word, and always had. Tonight would be three fingers of Blanton's, the lone recliner in the study, the single standing lamp adjacent, which left most of the room in blackness, and a new book for the Kindle. *Winter's Bone* was finished, a fact he rued. The girl Ree in that novel, so spare and gritty, was an example for us all: Be tougher than any and all trying to destroy you and what you love. Bear the pain. Don't let them see your hurt. Be remorseless in fighting back against tyranny.

Pack read a book every few days, and many articles of both personal and professional interest. He avoided analyzing his reading habits, fearing if he did, he would restrict himself by overorganizing. Instead, he floated from genre to genre, historical period to historical period, from one field of learning to another. Ancient history was as interesting as the nineteenth-century British novel, and a Stephen Jay Gould work on evolution as fascinating as a George Will book on Sabermetrics, if Mr. Will got around to it. He had read with appreciation all of Samuel Huntington's considerable oeuvre. But tonight he was headed toward *The Warrior Elite*, a work of nonfiction recommended by his friend Sheriff Mollison. Pack kept an on-deck list of books, but unfortunately, it never diminished. *When I finally go to ground*, he thought, *that might be the biggest regret, not having read them all.*

♦ ♦ ♦

The Germans have a word for it: *Fingerspitzengefühl*, or "fingertip feel." Every Great Captain possesses it. Like that special instinct for grasping the mount bar of a moving locomotive, except *Fingerspitzengefühl* is a highly developed intellectual capacity rare as snow in Havana. Simon Pack had it. He could feel the charge of ions in the dead air of late summer, like sharks and whales have when a tsunami is imminent. He could tell circumstances for him and the Academy were about to change; the gates of West Point were about to be stormed. When, by whom, and by what means he could not define well, just that it wouldn't be long. Unlike the sharks and whales, though, he wasn't running for cover. He was going to pass the weekend checking his body armor for chinks and his weapons for serviceability.

He threw his hobo kit into the bed of the red Tahoe and drove himself to an area of Camp Buckner that would not be used for the summer field training. It was a wooded area filled with fallen trees and other undergrowth. The Environmental Protection Agency must have succeeded in not allowing this detritus to be cleared, he reckoned. A *Forstmeister* could make a good difference in tamping down the fire danger.

He had added a military topo map to his kit. As darkness approached, he laid out a spartan campsite, then began to make a fire. The clouds were gravid, promising a soupy rainfall. When there were gleeds in the pit, he watched them as if they were the essence of life, stared as if each glowing ember held the accumulated wisdom of the ages. In anticipation of the storm, the birds in the trees stopped chirruping and tweedling, and the footfalls of the abundant wildlife fell silent. He blended a lean-to into the foliage, then dug out gutters to channel the water away from his poncho and -liner. Near dawn, he would have morning brew, then set out on a tortuous hike around this lake and maybe another one or two. He knew from long experience that thinking while office-bound is overrated—for him, anyway. He did his best thinking while trekking alone, when solutions came unbidden. Assuming the ideas would flow, he planned to reward himself with a field meal of bacon and eggs and toast and a Snickers. Maybe Pack would pass Duck his grid coordinates sometime tomorrow and let him land navigate over to camp.

"I haven't given him much time out here, but it wouldn't do any harm to see if he has any useful information," he mused.

In countless unnamed remote places, he had had the same thought, felt the same awe as he felt now. *This is the Great Cathedral God hath made.* Twenty miles away sat the Cadet Chapel, home of the largest chapel pipe organ in the world, a building of soaring arches, flying buttresses, ornate stone carvings, and a cross-shaped floor plan, a structure impressive by any standard of architectural excellence. And yet...and yet, nature's design is of a standard no man's work can match.

◆ ◆ ◆

It had been a good sleep. He woke up a couple times to feed the fire, but had had to put effort into nursing the dying embers back to life. Waking up is a necessary feature of field craft, so for a man of Pack's experience, returning to slumber is fluid. His reinforced lean-to had repelled the downpour as well as an $800 North Face rig would. He slowly sipped his canteen cup of scalding coffee, heated a separate cup of water drawn from the lake for shaving, and brushed his teeth. He had always looked fit, with a body that resisted fat deposit. And he felt fit. Most of the Army was stuck on running mile after mile for its daily dose of cardio, but Pack's

Marine units eschewed running, preferring to focus on combat fitness. Forced marching was the centerpiece, but it also included repetitively carrying heavy loads as rapidly as possible over short distances. The rigors of the past three months had kept him in a decent state of combat fitness.

Pack buried the fire pit, loaded his camp gear onto the truck, and set out on a route he estimated would take him eight or nine hours to complete. The rain had passed, and the morning sky was luminous. The surface would remain mud-slicked throughout the day. On one treacherous downhill, he slipped awkwardly, a knee hyperextending painfully. He hobbled to his feet, smiled, and said to himself, "It feels damn good to be alive."

It took him nine-and-a-half hours to finish. At the seven-hour mark, he called Duck, whose then-current location was only about two-and-a-half miles away from Pack's camp. "Bring two MREs," he told Captain Cooper. "And if you see one with the chocolate brownie bar, nab it for me."

As it happened, Duck navigated well and arrived before Pack. He carried a full combat ruck, minus weapon and ammo, which suggested he was carrying roughly thirty-five pounds. His leg hurt quite a great deal. He had wanted to arrive ahead of Pack, so that he could remove the prosthesis, massage the damaged area, and do his hurting in private. These two days had taken a toll. Was he going to be able to hold up for a dozen or more years of this infantry life? He brought out a large tube of quick-dry lotion, applying it after wiping the stump clean and dry. He changed the sock on his good foot, dusted inside the sock and boot with foot powder. Then he dry-swallowed three coated aspirin. Much relieved, he jostled the boot back over the prosthesis before the boss closed on the camp.

Pack limped in an hour later. Captain Cooper said nothing about the muddy clothes and the lurching gait. The General was in high spirits, Duck observed, which was what mattered. He could tell Pack liked being in his present state: sweaty, muddy in spots, happily weary from physical exertion.

"Good to see you, Duck. You bring those MREs?"

"Yes, sir. Meals that actually are ready to eat. I'll have a fire in about fifteen minutes. Need to scout up some fat lighter wood," Duck answered.

"Good, I'm going down to the lake, clean up, change uniform. Fifteen will be about right."

Duck was but a little surprised to catch sight of Pack swimming in the cold, deep, spring-fed lake water. By the time he got back up to the new firepit, Pack was reenergized and exceptionally loquacious and casual. "Lucky I have some backup chow in the truck, Duck. That MRE will not be enough. Good job rounding up enough dry tinder to get this fire moving." Both took the coffee, creamer, and sugar packets from the brown MRE package. "How many cals in the average MRE, Duck?"

"I've read the number before, sir. Around a thousand, I think. No, nearer twelve hundred or thirteen hundred," Duck replied.

"Something like that," Pack muttered. "A helluva lot, anyway. Designed for troops performing tough physical activity. If you ate three a day with low-level physical activity, you'd pack on the pounds in a hurry."

"That's true, sir," Duck commented, "but that never seemed to be a problem with my soldiers. The bigger problem was getting constipated from these things; most guys don't hydrate well enough when eating MREs. Some were impacted so badly, their problem became a medical emergency."

"OK, Duck, this is an interesting discussion, but let's get on to a topic more in line with our military duties. Tell me a few points of interest from your Buckner flyover (he was acknowledging Duck had been with the cadets in their field training just a day or two). Whatever got your attention."

"Roger, sir. First thing I stumbled into was the weekly Tacs meeting with the Buckner Commandant, Colonel Wilkins. There are eight company Tacs, as you may know. Three majors and five captains. Two of the captains are from the academic departments, one from English and one from military history. Turns out, the most energetic and aggressive, seemed to me, were the two who are not permanent Tacs, i.e., the two from the professoriat, as you put it the other day, sir. Both are volunteers and said they badly wanted to be with cadets in this environment. They love what they're doing. Colonel Wilkins, a straitlaced man, as you probably know, sir, said to me afterward that their companies' measurable performance has put them in the running for the Pikeman Trophy for best Buckner company. He doesn't think it's random that his two best companies have Tacs who come from academic departments. Without a word from me, Colonel Wilkins opined it would 'be interesting' to have all eight Tacs come from 'across the street.' Kind of a role reversal that struck me as odd, sir. That's as much as I can report about that, knowing I'm not qualified to draw further conclusions."

"All right, Duck, that's the kind of info I'm looking for. Keep going."

"Hear me out on this one, sir. I don't want you to hear me wrong on this. I was and am sincerely curious about the performance of female cadets. No conclusions, I am afraid, on this one, either. I happened to be at the training site where this one female was leading her platoon through the obstacle course, which I recall from my own experience was a tough nut. All kinds of really hard and dangerous events. I remember, sir, how I felt about being twenty feet off the ground, then having to leap backward and upward to catch hold of the next tier of whatever they call that thing. I don't even know, but I do know it's hairy. Anyway, I'm standing with the company Tac, who tells me this girl—sorry, sir, cadet—is at the top of her Class academically. I've just seen her doing these incredible physical feats involving strength, agility, and emotional control. She led her people through every event, meaning she was the first through every event—it was leadership at work, and I was agog. She seems to be the ideal female of her age. Then the Tac says to me, 'Her brother graduated number one in his Class two years ago.' All this is adding up to some story, least to me, sir. Then he says, 'And she came to me last week to say she is resigning.' Her parents, both Type A personalities, successful businesspeople and very wealthy, have put so much pressure on her to duplicate or surpass her brother's standard, she is rebelling by leaving the Academy. Her parents came out from California to address the company and regimental Tacs face-to-face. They demanded to see the Comm. Colonel Dahl politely turned them away, but not before they had threatened to go to their

US Senators. According to the Tac, the cadet has spoken to everyone in the chain of command and declares her decision final."

Pack considered that Dahl had intervened appropriately, but that he should be prepared for a query from either or both of California's Senators. Duck continued, "I know she has decided, but I just couldn't help but think we have lost a top talent."

"Duck, you and I don't rule the world. That cadet reached a decision we'll never understand, but if she didn't have the heart for officership, it's better she leave now. You must have the heart to be an officer. Regrettably, she does not."

"Understood, sir. The other case of interest also involved a female, one who seems to be at the opposite end of the spectrum from the female cadet just mentioned. Why she is still here, I don't know. Well, I guess I do, but I don't want to acknowledge the truth of my supposition. She is as near the bottom in every category of cadethood as the other young woman was near the top. She happens to be in the same company as the first female. In fact, she is a member of female one's platoon. Atrocious in what I saw, sir, a cadet without guts, and from what the Tac said, without many brains, too. She has made it through a full year plus this summer, which caused me to wonder, *How?* I imagine the Tac answered that when he said she is the Vice President's granddaughter."

Pack made a mental note. *If she's being protected, I want Thump to find out by whom and put a stop to it. That's not how we're gonna operate around here.*

Chapter Fifteen

Blitz

Colonel Jim Dahl seldom went over to Quarters 100, the Superintendent's residence. Most of the paperwork was sent over by courier at a prescribed time daily. They talked often by phone. The Supe occasionally stopped by to clear the table with things Kathy Pillings had organized for him and usually spent some time with Dahl while in the building. Dahl's nickname had become "Golden" because he was a University of Minnesota Golden Gopher alum. Pack liked *Gopher,* but he didn't want anyone to mistakenly believe he was calling Dahl a go-fer. So Golden it had become.

Today, Golden was in the Supe's study for a special session requested by Dahl himself.

"How's the housekeeper, sir? I feel like I should've been more involved in the selection than I was," Golden said.

"You just keep your eyes where they ought to be, Golden, on the big things. In the event you have forgotten, you are supposed to know more about the goings-on of Academy operations than anyone, and I picked you because I judged you can fit the pieces together in order to give me a clear view. I don't want you involved in what was a personal matter, or any of that ilk. But since you're so damn nosey, I'll tell you Evelyn Rose gave me a candidate I think will work well. She *is* working well to date. You saw her on the way in. She presents a neat appearance, she seems to be taciturn, she precooks meals for me—I did get an upright for the basement—she refused my offer to buy a small TV to keep her company during downtimes, and she appreciates the money. Her husband died some years ago, and he left her with what sounds like a great debt that is just now being paid off. I think he owned three restaurants that started to tank when the economy did. They did very well for a long time, then *whap.* Evelyn maintains all the employment documents, so I don't know her age, but seventy-two, seventy-three is my guess. The physical side of the job doesn't present a problem for her, she says. So, yes, I'm happy I hired her. At some point, I might accede to a move into the maid's quarters. In sum, Golden, my house-tending requires no attention from me; it's on autopilot from my perspective. So, what is the big thing you came here to talk about?"

"OK, sir, bottom line up front. Several outside agents are doing hit pieces on the Academy, and judging from the volume and timing of these hits, I think the action is being coordinated. By whom, and from where it is being coordinated, I don't have sufficient facts to express even an opinion. I can give some headlines this morning, but I think you might want me to set meetings with subject-matter authorities, after you've heard me out. I think we clearly need to understand why we're being hit, then figure counters to their actions."

"This doesn't surprise me," Pack said. "I've had the sense this was happening, or about to, almost since arrival. Let me hear what you have."

"Out in the public, articles have been springing up all over the place derogating USMA. A congressman from Tennessee yesterday had a piece in the op-ed section of *The New York Times* titled, 'Is West Point's Time Up?' In it, he quotes fellow Tennessean Davy Crockett, who reportedly said West Point was educating the sons of the rich. You and I know that isn't true, but the *NYT* apparently has no interest in correcting the record. I don't believe there's an accurate sentence in the story, but it doesn't matter, they're establishing a point of view.

"More and more stories are appearing that are highly critical of West Point officers. A prominent social historian, whose leanings are decidedly progressive, claims USMA produces officers who are rooted in codes and programs of the past and are hence unable to deal decisively with twenty-first-century problems. Why not shut it down? he asks. The same man writes, if America wants to be a force for the next half-century, it had better get on board with the idea of a Peace Academy.

"Then Mrs. Pillings ran by me the project you assigned her. Very thorough, by the way. I think you'll be pleased with her work. But some of what she found knocked me out of my chair. At least two-thirds of the Board of Visitors has recently made public statements condemning this institution on so many grounds it's shocking. Sexual harassment by, it would seem, every male cadet toward every female cadet. Everything from accusations of profligate spending to the prevalence of numerous forms of discrimination to lack of leadership at the top to unfair treatment of civilian faculty, and on it goes. Abuse of travel privileges. There are claims the athletic department is guilty of unauthorized use of taxpayer funds. One of the members—who most clearly has a mole planted somewhere near us—charges that you have essentially hired a housekeeper so you might have a mistress with minimal fear of exposure. One of the geniuses on the Board of Visitors says that because we are so poorly led, President Keith Rozan has a duty to grant amnesty to all cadets who have been unjustly punished with more than thirty hours of Area time. I ask myself, What's the significance of the President's micromanaging cadet punishments? What is he up to? I'm telling you, sir, this is breathtaking stuff."

"All right, Golden," Pack said. "We aren't going to get excited. We'll figure this out. Let me think more about this. I'll get back to you. These people are flooding the zone. I'm going to need lots of help on this, starting with you. When we're on defense, I can't make all the tackles even if I wanted to. Don't be afraid to take action if time is short."

"I think I'd be doing you a disservice, sir, if I didn't cover the essentials about the Board of Visitors. Let me contrast how the Commandant thinks it used to be with the present Board. General Bass thinks that when you and he were cadets, West Point was overseen by something very much like a corporate board of directors, whether it was so called or not. They were men and women of action, typically accomplished people from business and finance. But the board included clergy, scholars, and civil-rights proponents as well. If they possessed a political bias, it was not apparent in their reports. They produced a report of their observations of Academy operations, and normally included recommendations to lawmakers about budgetary shortfalls. The dominant tone was positive.

"Then in the summer of 1972, Title IX was signed into law. As a senior leader, you have had to deal with Title IX requirements for a long time, so I won't get into detail about its history. Suffice it to say, many argue it is the most far-reaching piece of legislation of the twentieth century. It began as a guarantor of gender equity in sports. But politicians took one look and saw they could use it to get about anything they wanted. Amendment followed amendment, and soon it was bastardized into a legal leviathan capable of destroying anything in its path. It has become an octopus with tentacles that reach into many areas of academic and commercial life. It was expanded to include access to higher education, career education, education for pregnant and parenting students, employment, learning environments, math and science, sexual harassment, and standardized testing and technology. By the time politicians got through adding protections, every single recipient of one federal dollar feared for its very existence, that it might be sued for failing to meet an obscure provision of Title IX, as interpreted by a Washington bureaucrat. One teacher who claimed he or she wasn't promoted because of gender or racial bias could bankrupt the school with legal fees. The law encouraged grievance.

"Most discouragingly, the government assumed guilt, not innocence, it seemed. West Point was no different. Its board could no longer be trusted to keep the Academy on the straight and narrow. Title IX gave them an excuse to institute a Board of Visitors swiftly. And they did. They made this Board a politician-heavy body. It didn't take long to discern that the party holding the presidency would pack the Board with members aligned with its ideology, and would then, under cover of Title IX, impose that ideology on West Point."

"Do I really need to hear all this now?" Pack could hang tough in these discussions, but only if he knew the reason for them.

"Yes, sir. I won't give on this. You've got to understand this is a politically motivated group, and my analysis says they have their knives out. I need for you to have a mental image of who these people are and what they want," Golden said.

"All right. I'm listening and trying to let the image form," Pack said.

"The BoV consists of four Senators, five House members, and six Presidential appointees. That's fifteen total. Of those, ten are progressives who look at West Point, picture a bastion of conservatism, and want it dismantled. They are not interested in our mission. They just viscerally oppose the concept of an institution like USMA. Fifty percent of cadets and faculty could lean liberal, but that's inconceivable to them. The military by reputation is insufficiently compassionate.

"So, the President scans the nine or ten categories of protections in the current Title IX, and has his staff ensure that the insurmountable majority of the Board are known advocates of each. For example, one category of Title IX is standardized testing and technology. So we have a man to cover that area. This legislator actually introduced a very cleverly titled bill, Take on Extraneous Substandard Testing with Established Structures, or the TESTES Act. As if that bona fide wasn't enough, he's submitted other major legislation, such as officially designating a National Weed-Killing Products Week. Granted, there is no necessary nexus between the TESTES Act and liberalism or conservatism, but more the presumption of guilt that rankles.

"Another member has sexual harassment covered. Senator Brandywine has gotten elected, it's fair to say, pushing that single issue to the exclusion of ninety-nine percent of the other issues facing the country. She is responsible for the omnipresent SHARP signage. She thinks of West Point as sexual harassment central because victimization of women is her meal ticket. She might know that's an outright untruth, but she can never admit it. The Senator says she will use her position on the Board to encourage the complete elimination of gender discrimination and sexual assault in the US military. Many of us read that and believe the assumption of guilt is implicit in the statement. We also see she equates the conditions at West Point directly with those of the Army at large. She uses the BoV meetings as an opportunity to grandstand at the Academy's expense. I know *a priori* that immediately after our meeting, she will call for the nearest scribe to describe to him the scourge of sexual harassment and gender discrimination that exists at West Point.

"And a significant constituency of this administration is the lesbian-gay-bisexual-transsexual element. They found just the person to do their bidding on the Board. A female USMA graduate who has said the senior command at West Point has utter contempt for women. She made a show of being part of the first same-sex wedding at the Cadet Chapel. Now her major role in life as a member of the Board seems to be as a flamethrower at USMA.

"Thanks for bearing with me through that, sir. I hope I have convinced you the Board is out to inflict pain on us. What I am about to conclude this discussion with is of a piece with the unavoidable longueur on the BoV. First, the logistics officer on our staff took a call yesterday from a lieutenant colonel who is an aide to Secretary Spitshugh. I've checked her out, and every report on her glows. I shouldn't have mentioned her job description, because I intended to keep her name out of any future handling of the issue. For the moment, I think it's important to protect her, because she sure seems to have taken a huge professional risk. This officer and another aide, according to her, were directed by the Secretary of the Army himself to devise various methods of 'putting a chokehold' on West Point. This fits with point two, something Mrs. Pillings unearthed, to wit: On at least three occasions, a couple Board members have spoken, in nearly identical words, of 'making significant structural alterations to permanent and tenant units at West Point.' I ask you, sir, what interest would a civilian on the BoV have in that topic, and what knowledge would he or she possess on that topic? Close to none, I would think, unless they are following a script written by another party. Point three, which is another piece of this puzzle, as I see it: The Commandant has been raising hell with our logistics officer for not securing arms room space for the weapons he has requested. Until he gets that space, he can't physically acquire the weapons. What the Comm is at this time unaware of is that at least two of these tenant units—the Military Police and Keller Army

Community Hospital, which have cooperated with this office and USMA for decades—have been told by their parent units in distant locations that they are to sever ties to our organizational structure. Someone high up is directing these things."

Pack was locked in thought, mute. He swiveled his chair away from his chief of staff and tilted it back deeply. He raised a hand above the chair in a gesture approximating a wave, and in low throat said, "Thanks, Chief." Golden took his leave, asking the housekeeper on the way out if she might make the General a special meal this evening.

♦ ♦ ♦

Just a few days of Third Class, or sophomore summer training at Camp Buckner remained. The Supe asked Duck to contact the Tac who had supervised the woman that Duck had referred to as the "perfect" female cadet. Have her standing by at the guard shack near the flagpole at the Buckner entrance. In one hour.

On official duty, Pack was not authorized to drive his personal vehicle. A driver with a Humvee drove him to Buckner. When he caught sight of her, Pack could understand Duck's implication that it was difficult to get past this young woman's physical beauty. In fact, he admired Duck's restraint in not commenting pointedly. She was tall, with dark eyes, lush black hair, extraordinarily fit and well-proportioned, but it was her hue of skin that made her different: tan, marble-smooth, but with a tint of ruby. Exotic, but that descriptor fell gravely short of the extent of her attractiveness. In any event, her looks or lack thereof were no concern of Pack's.

The guard shack had space for a standing desk that resembled a podium and two metal folding chairs. The Tac saluted General Pack with, "Sir, Captain Thomas reporting with Cadet Richelieu, as ordered."

"Thank you, Captain. If you'll stay here at the shack with Captain Cooper, Cadet Richelieu and I are going to walk down this road about a hundred feet." Pack started walking away and over his shoulder simply said, "Let's go, Cadet Richelieu."

Once she fell into step beside him, he said, "I know you didn't have much of a choice in the matter, but thanks for spending some time with me this morning. First, understand I did not come all the way out here to Buckner to try to talk you out of resigning. I have not spoken with your parents, and do not intend to. You are an adult and can decide what you want for yourself. You hardly need someone like me or possibly even your parents to bombard you with their ideas about how you should lead your life. I am going to be very honest with you. Leading soldiers is much like the priesthood; it is a calling. It must be in one's heart. Accepting the special burdens of leadership in an organization that all too often asks its members to sacrifice their all is not for everyone. I, for one, completely understand that if the path you have been on for the past year and a half does not rest comfortably in your heart, then you are making a difficult but correct decision to leave us. In your time here, you have done well, reflecting great credit on you, and I have great confidence that whatever path you choose to follow, you will be very successful.

"Now, I'm going to ask you to be honest with me. I need to understand the truth about what is going on at West Point. I absolutely don't want you to tell me what you think I want to hear. That will do none of us any good. I will put great weight on what you tell me. I am asking you to answer a few questions. Why? Because you probably are more qualified than any cadet to give me honest answers than anyone. You have nothing to lose, so cut loose if you want. What do you say?"

"I am pleased to help in any way, sir. I have no grievance against West Point," she replied.

"As background, Cadet Richelieu, let me make two general points. First, I am here, returned from retirement, because West Point has problems that demand redress. Second, I have little faith in the honesty of politicians or press whose attacks on the Academy are unjust, as I assure there is ample proof a considerable number are. There has been an unprecedented outpouring of anti-West Point sentiment from Washington and national media. Still willing to deal with my questions?"

"More than ever, sir," Richelieu answered.

"One phrase I read frequently is 'war on women at West Point.' What do you make of that?" Pack asked.

"General, I played every girls sport in high school, and it is fact I was about the best in them all. I was valedictorian. I was homecoming queen. My success at that level was almost embarrassing. Lots of guys hit on me, and quite a few did it stupidly. They were often boorish, tiresome, pushy, and I believe the conduct of a dozen or more could be labeled sexual harassment. Some teachers fell into that category as well. The conduct I'm recalling falls short of trying to throw me to the ground, but in my mind amounts to harassment nonetheless. My point in relating what sounds like an ego trip, sir, is that I pretty confidently can claim to have some knowledge on the subject.

"To continue, sir, I can offer my opinion that in the sense of harassment, there is no war on women here. I have never been treated by male cadets other than as I wished to be treated. I have gotten the respect I think I've earned, from both genders. Now, the law of averages will dictate there are immature male cadets, but they have never manifested such immaturity toward me. Vignette, if I may, sir: This very week, we were involved in this field training, and I needed to go to the bathroom. No slit trenches or portable toilets on site. Male cadets from my platoon formed a small cordon around me while I went in the bushes. They faced outward, away from me. I ask if that is disrespectful or respectful, immature or mature?

"There is another dimension of the so-called war on women that I have noticed here, however. You, sir, have at least a few feminist professors on your faculty whose lifeblood is the propagation of lies about this 'war.' This is firsthand knowledge. Were I to bring up the example of the cadet cordon to them, they would reply that mine is an isolated example, but the problem rages in the Army at large. And that it is our job to forever raise awareness of this prevalent problem. It just seems to me, as one whose strongest desire is to succeed on my own merits, that the fewer obstacles women face, the angrier the women's studies professors seem to be. In my opinion, they act as if, when their premises are threatened, their positions as professors are threatened."

"According to an external report, Cadet Richelieu, last academic year, there were ten sexual assault complaints at the Academy. Comment, please." It was a Board of Visitors report, but Pack did not disclose the source.

"I have no knowledge of either the report or the alleged incidents, sir. But I can extrapolate. At any given time, there are six hundred or more female cadets. That would mean one-sixtieth of the female population proffered complaints. That is less than two percent. I'm not saying the incidents did not happen, but it's also not a stretch to imagine that a few of the complainants had selfish reasons for making a complaint. I think it's fair to say there is more pressure on *every* cadet than there is on most students at a state university. At the same time, I doubt we'll ever be perfect with this facet of male-female relations. If the alleged perpetrators are found guilty, then remove them from among us. Period. I need say nothing more on that point. These SHARP signs everywhere you look paint cadets unfairly."

Sensing the conversation was nearing an end, Pack started the return to the guard shack. "Cadet Richelieu, is there anything else you'd like to share with me before you depart? Especially with respect to the fair treatment of any individual or group."

"Well, sir, just two months ago we finished up our Plebe year. I thought it was pretty tough for me and everyone else in the Class. Truthfully, it was a lot tougher for some than for others. The bottom line is that screw-ups—no matter the race, creed, or sex—have a pretty tough time here. The system here is set up to weed out the weak links. But I believe you get a fair shake. A final thought: Some people carry themselves in a manner that demands respect, and they typically get it. Others invite disrespect, and often get it. This is not gender bias, but person bias."

"I think I'll end the questioning here, Cadet Richelieu. Thank you, and I wish you great success wherever you wind up."

◆ ◆ ◆

From the look of things, Brigadier General Elijah Steinberg could've been preparing for a second career in politics. Pack had put him in an untenable position. The Supe had ordered him to have USCC's interests and the Superintendent's interests represented at all Academic Board conventions. On the other hand, Steinberg could not allow outsiders to be in on the vote he was planning. To stand any chance of preserving his parochial interests, he had to present Pack with a fait accompli. Steinberg had not long ago fantasized he could command "his" board to return a 14–0 vote against Pack on any conceivable matter of concern to the professoriat. Now he saw that outcome was indeed fantasy, but he believed 11–3 or 10–4 was readily achievable. He had met with them all individually, some in their quarters up on Professors' Row, others over lunch or in his office or theirs. Tried to be casual and discreet about it, let his self-assurance and confidence rub off on them. Make them understand "we're permanent, he's transient," and we have to stand up to his bullying, ignorant ways.

OK, he thought, *I'd be wiser to implore them to "rise up," which sounds more urgent and dramatic.* Order professors to road march twenty-five miles or more? Every quarter of the damn year? Abolish the National Conference on Ethics in America, one of the jewels in our tiara? *I can't believe I'm even thinking to abolish the system of majors. Wow! Just wow!* Steinberg thought. *While we're at it, Pack, let's just road march all the way back to the Paleocene Era. Why stop at Buckner, 'cause that's for damn sure where you're trying to carry us.*

Steinberg wanted total destruction of the conjoined twins: Pack's precious line-item veto, and the severance from the faculty of all but thirteen civilian professors. *This bastard probably cannot understand the titles of some of the courses, much less class offerings. Can this dunce Pack begin to fathom the mockery, the contempt West Point would have heaped upon us by the larger academic world if his vision were realized? Why would the Middle States Commission on Higher Education even renew our accreditation status after we dump a hundred tons of their brothers and sisters out into the street, casting many of them onto unemployment rolls? A fine thank-you to our learned brethren, I should say. Dear Lord, this lunatic who recently stepped onto our soil must be stopped.*

And who else must step forward at great potential professional and perhaps personal peril to aright this ship Pack was running aground? Steinberg knew his fellows on the Board would surely see the mantle of courage that history beckoned him to don. *Pack is turning our beautiful Academy into a fly-infested dung heap, and who else but I can stop this madman?* If necessary, he would say that Hairball Oracle Bass was suckled from the same diseased wolf as Pack. Steinberg steeled himself for that meeting by telling himself history had chosen him to be the Nietzschean hero. Or would Superman be more apt?

Steinberg had referred earlier to this as an Academic Board convention and used the expression "Special Meeting" as well. *No, ladies and gentlemen, this is what we at the highest levels of corporate and educational governance denominate an "Extraordinary Meeting." My people on the Board will see an Extraordinary Man running an Extraordinary Meeting. Sorry, all concerned, but trust me, it must also be a Clandestine Meeting. Pack, your comeuppance is coming.*

Steinberg's favorite acolyte, Colonel Social Sciences, leapt past Steinberg's executive officer to bob his head into Steinberg's office. "Hey, boss, sorry to interrupt, but I have a question."

"Yes," Steinberg said, "but your technique of barging in lacks professional polish, and is a poor example for even my executive officer. What is it?"

"Dean," Colonel Social Sciences led in slowly, "did you know our Superintendent does not hold an advanced degree? I'm sure many of us assumed we hadn't read it on his bio sheet because he doesn't blow his own horn. But, no, he does not have any degree beyond West Point. In fact, he is—or was—the only General Officer in the entire Marine Corps without one. Probably the only one in the entire Armed Forces. Can you imagine the leader of the United States Military Academy with nothing higher than a Bachelor of Science degree? I should think a member or two of the Board of Visitors might find that interesting as well."

"My supposition was the same as yours. But, knowing this…so what? Who cares?" Steinberg asked.

"Well, sir, I recall a talk you had with me last week. You actually were making a pitch to me. Perhaps I misunderstood, but I thought you were asking for my vote against this line-item veto the Supe wants."

"Let's stop playing, Len. Of course, that's what I was asking, but I cannot be so overt with everyone on the board." This tiptoeing around made Steinberg nervous. "Get to your point. I do have work, whether you do or not."

"I merely believe that if you were to innocently and inadvertently let this information drop to the full Academic Board, it might undermine their faith in General Pack relative to his judgments about academic affairs." Professor Social Sciences was happy with himself, sitting as pompously perched on his seat as if he were uncovering the Rosetta stone.

♦ ♦ ♦

Pack seldom got seriously agitated. At this moment, he was seriously agitated. He called for Dahl to meet him in the secondary. He hadn't called him *Golden*, but *Jim*, so the chief of staff was prepared to get beat up a little, or maybe even a lot.

Pack held several pages of letter-size paper. "Chief," he said, gazing evenly at Dahl, "you have staff supervisory authority over the Director of Admissions. When I read this, I conclude your supervision is lacking. I came over to deliver this face-to-face. You read this, and take whatever action you think necessary. Clear?"

"Absolutely, sir," a ruffled Dahl answered. "I'll take care of whatever it is, and report back to you."

"Nope, don't report back. This one is yours alone, Jim. Just take care of it." Director of Admissions Colonel Joanna Reeder had sent a five-page screed to every USMA graduate with an e-mail address on record with the Association of Graduates, and also to numerous media outlets. *Did she do this solo or with the consent of yet-another member of my staff, the Public Affairs Officer?* Dahl thought. *Who normally gives the go-ahead for such releases?*

Dahl didn't want to read it a second time. He was a pale Minnesotan of Swedish extraction whose skin tinged the faintest pink after three days of total exposure to the summer sun. This woman had colored his head, neck, and ears as only a deep niacin flush can to some folks. With respect to propensity toward profanity, Dahl was General Bass's opposite. Not a soul could recall James Dahl saying something as tame as "pissed off." Yet, he was thoroughly pissed off right now. He couldn't let this momentary condition go to waste.

He summoned Colonel Reeder to his office. She arrived a few minutes later, looking smug, smiling, and cheerful. She failed to knock on Dahl's door or otherwise announce herself.

"You wanted to see me, Jim?" Reeder said.

"Let's try this again, Colonel. Go back out, knock, and wait for my response," Dahl said with that peculiar Scandinavian solemnity.

"Are you really serious, Jim?" she said fatuously.

"Do it, Colonel Reeder. Now."

Reeder did it. Fortunately for her, she did not automatically take a seat. Her smirk had morphed into a frown. Dahl shuffled the papers she had transmitted to a broad audience, not reading but giving that impression, letting moments elapse, making her wait and stew.

"Hear me well, Colonel. I am as piqued as I ever get. Angry, if you want the truth. What I'll say falls into two categories. The first is your blindness to whom you report. That would be me, if there is any doubt, Colonel. I am your rating officer. You know that but seem to have forgotten. You blindsided me. I will snap you quicker than a twig if you attempt to duplicate this stunt. And, as God is my witness, that might still happen.

"The second point is in the category of content," Dahl continued. "Shortly after the Superintendent came here, I spoke to this staff, of which you are part, and explained what is important to him. I took great care in passing on his views, and I am sure I took twice as long to do it as the General himself did. Just to be certain, you understand, there could be no doubt about his intent. I included the necessity for you to discern between concentric and eccentric initiative, and to have that guide your judgment. I spoke of his belief that the root of the problem he is here to resolve is political correctness, that energy- and soul-sapping drive to have this institution align itself with what is in public vogue. This is important, Colonel, so I hope you are lending an ear. The General and I believe that classic West Point, the West Point that *has been* until recent years, has more to give modern American life than modern American culture has to offer West Point. We are abandoning our responsibility to the country if we adopt the slovenly standard of political correctness. Our military life requires us to subordinate ourselves to a duty on behalf of society in the way religion subordinates man to God for divine purposes. It seems to me, Colonel, you are uncomfortable in our military monastery.

"Tell me this, Colonel Reeder: Do you prefer the hubbub of Main Street to the disciplined life of West Point?"

Reeder tried to think fast. She wasn't certain she understood every word from Dahl. She also saw this hyperserious officer was not about to brook a word of protest. She decided to be low-keyed and apologetic. "I regret I have let you down, Chief. I know something of the demands of your office, and I didn't want to trouble you with reading my letter. Once you have defined my error with an example or two, I am sure I can correct myself. I will strive not to allow it to happen again."

"If it should happen again, Colonel Reeder, you may be assured you will leave the Service under circumstances you would not enjoy. I can and would make that happen."

"Understood, sir."

"I got here too late to have prevented what you admitted to doing in this letter. But I will prevent it from recurring. First, you shotgunned this transmission as if you ARE the Superintendent. You speak of the 'phenomenal year we have had with the admission of the incoming class.' You are not the judge of that; I, as your chief of staff, and the Superintendent will decide if we even approve your standards of admission. You have one week to submit the standards by which the next incoming Class will be selected. Second, your standard was wrong, simply, awfully ...wrong. As General Pack has made clear, we throw PC-speak out on its ugly head. This letter is dreck, Colonel Reeder, bureau-idiot, stilted, brown-nosing dreck. Who are you to say women were underrepresented, and their percentage of this class will be elevated to twenty-two percent? Who are you to say we will admit higher percentages of various minorities to bring us in line with the national averages? The soldier operating in shit conditions in far-flung corners of this globe does not care what race, ethnicity, or gender his or her platoon commander is. They want the best qualified and trained persons to be their leaders. Period. If you want to work for one of those proprietary colleges that advertise incessantly on our airwaves, go for it, Colonel. They might hire you. But you will not carry their tendencies to this institution. Do you understand me, Colonel Joanna Reeder? And you will never, ever, undertake a mass mailing again without my expressed approval. We are finished here."

Colonel Joanna Reeder had never in her life been upbraided like this, not even in junior high. This Chief was not to be trifled with. He had roasted her to the point she could hear the fat hissing as it struck the fire.

♦ ♦ ♦

The Supe's marvelous smartphone could be metaphor for Reorganization Week, or Reorgy (hard 'g') Week. It hums and chimes and pulses and vibrates and rings out with vigorous activity. This is the final week of Beast Barracks, and will culminate for the New Cadets with Acceptance Day, when they become cadets in the fullest sense. Last year's Plebes, or Fourth Classmen, elsewhere known as freshmen, return from their summers as upperclassmen and now are eager for the opportunity to right the wrongs they perceived in the last crop of Yearlings, the sophomores or Third Classmen. Everyone has a new part to play.

For much of the week, this ritual directs them inward, away from a summer-long dwelling on teams and units, although their preoccupations of the moment prevent them from recognizing this fact. There are texts to draw, schedules to finalize, uniform insignias of rank to change, chevrons to sew on, new roommates to meet, new rooms to move into, a new chain of command to unveil. All this is done with precision, consummate organization. Cadets walk swiftly from one task to another, crossing paths, weaving, intersecting, but in accord with a master schedule. It is not the state of entropy it appears. In one week, the new academic year commences. On the third day of this eventful week, Superintendent Pack elected to address the full body of the Corps during lunch. He would do so from the place special orders were announced each day. This was the aerie called the Poop Deck. A long roster of distinguished names had spoken from this venue high above the mess hall. From here, one could view the entire cadet Corps. Sounds coming from up here resounded with celestial reverb. Under usual circumstances, three different colors of lights would brighten to announce when each upper class could leave the vast mess hall. First Classmen were allowed to exit first, followed minutes later by the Second Class, and so on. Today, the freedom-to-depart signals would not appear. Pack could take as long as he desired.

He began: "Cadets of the Corps: If you were on this elevated platform, you would see I have no notes. I will speak plainly, and I hope you read sincerity and conviction in what I tell you. Most of all, I hope you will take it as a guide to action.

"The mission at West Point is elegant in its simplicity: To develop leaders of character who will serve as officers in the United States Army.

"My job is to keep the eyes of everyone at West Point fixed on this mission. To better achieve that, I will refocus all Academy resources on the mission, understanding which of our activities support it and which do not. I will foster and increase those activities that support the mission. The changes will affect all classes. The Firsties will receive additional leadership opportunities. Underclassmen will prepare by serving as integral parts of the teams to which they are assigned; you also will get more responsibilities to lead. For more years than you have lived, I have observed this institution selling cadets short. I believe not enough has been demanded and therefore not enough has been delivered.

"West Point has let you down, drifted off course, away from the demands of the primary mission. I have told those who work for me, especially including senior officers, that for a time, there has been about this place the fetid odor of rot, and I am about to wield the Hattori Hanzo sword to clear it away. Indeed, cadets of the Corps, I have already begun the wielding.

"I am imposing new standards on your faculty, both academic and tactical. They will achieve or exceed those standards, or they will be gone. I promise you a tightening of all areas of operation. You received appointments to this place presumably because you are multi-talented. But if you begin to regard yourselves as elite, ladies and gentlemen, I am interested in preventing you from going out there to take over platoons of young Americans who are most definitely your equals.

"West Point is second or third in all the postgraduate scholarship grants, including the most prestigious such as the Rhodes, Marshall, and Olmstead. But I am wholly unconcerned about such academic recognition. Those awards are fine, but because you are achievers, they will flow as a natural by-product of your striving for general excellence. West Point will retain its place among the academic institutions. If I find any cadet who is toiling away to compete for a Rhodes Scholarship, however, I will find you—my standards will give you away—and I will not give you time to burgeon a second longer in the fecund soil of West Point. Your focus must be on your mission: to leave here ready to become a professional soldier in the great American Army. A leader deserving of the respect and support of America's best.

"You will learn a lot from your classes. You will learn a lot from the hundred or more dimensions of cadetship. But remember, you are here to mature into military leaders who can fight and win—hear that again, *win*—America's wars. That is your inviolable mission. I want us to make leaders here who will stand up to the civilian leaders of this nation to tell them, 'We will endure any ordeal in the fight, but we will object on the most strenuous moral grounds that our soldiers are not game pieces to be shifted on a board for your personal gain or aggrandizement.'

"You did not come to the United States Military Academy to do the average. You came here because you wanted to excel for a purpose that matters. You can, and you will. If your heart is in this military life, you will relish the learning of what we teach here. You will relish ascesis, the practice of self-discipline no matter how severe. You will be proud to say your word is your bond, that you think first and resist the temptation to act on emotion, to know you cannot lead from behind or below, that you have the will to accept and accomplish any assignment, no matter the personal cost.

"But what will satisfy most, if my long service is to be relied upon, is the profound sense of honor you will feel in the good fortune of serving on a team made up of some of the finest people on earth. Young troops who will astonish you daily with the feats of which they are capable, and the sacrifices they routinely and willingly make. And noncommissioned officers whose accomplishments every day will leave you grasping for words to describe their excellence. Most, I am persuaded, rise to this challenge because they love being on a team in which people depend heavily on them, and they depend on others knowing they themselves will be supported. It is a people thing. They want to be part of the team, and you will have to play the part of leader. Be ready for it.

"I need this Corps to be a team committed to winning. A team whose members are individually and collectively zeroed in on achieving excellence in all its endeavors. I need you to know with total moral certitude that losing is unacceptable on this plot of earth. Understand me, each and all. The Army football team is the lead representative of our commitment to excellence. Support them with your words and your presence. As time allows, get out to their practices. If we rehearse now to build the type of team we want the Army to be, we can accomplish marvelous deeds. Mark my words: You *are* a member of this Army football team. They will show you and you will show them the way to victory."

Someone commenced a chant until minutes rolled by: "HH, HH, HH." It was presumed to be a football player, but in the cavernous mess hall, it was not possible to know. The football team never conducted the actual vote Gary Cline had mentioned, but they had decided informally to call Pack "the HH," which meant, depending on your interpretation, either Hobo Honcho or Heroic Hobo.

♦ ♦ ♦

Against the backdrop of this kaleidoscopic activity, Brigadier General Elijah Steinberg convened his Extraordinary Session of the Academic Board. The sounds of Reorgy Week, the Dean thinks, will muffle the weak sounds of his Board. To Steinberg, Reorgy Week is a big diversion. No straphangers allowed at this assemblage. First team only.

"Ladies and gentlemen, I call an Extraordinary Session on the rarest occasions, when there is indeed an emergent situation of extraordinary import. Superintendent Pack has petitioned us for the power of a line-item veto. I want you to be certain of his meaning, which is to take away this Board's exclusive control of the curricula. He seeks the power to disapprove of any class offering he finds objectionable. I have asked myself numerous times, 'What does *objectionable* mean to General Pack?' Just as important, ladies and gentlemen, does he possess the capacity to discern what is objectionable or unobjectionable? Before you can operate as a civil engineer, say, in New York State, you must be a licensed, board-certified civil engineer, must you not? You have to be properly credentialed, do you not? Now, fellow Board members, each of us is highly credentialed in his field, is he not? Our quest for the knowledge to walk away with those degrees and licenses and certifications has been arduous and long. We earned the right to call the shots in our departments.

"I will not belittle General Pack. He is a well-meaning man and capable officer. All I am saying is, General Simon Pack is considerably out of his depth on this side of Thayer Road. He does not know what he does not know. Insult not intended, but people, I have on solid authority he doesn't possess an advanced degree, except for the normal tier of military colleges. I had hoped against hope I would not be required to divulge that sensitive information about the Superintendent. I woke up this morning, however, believing its relevance is too strong to conceal from you. How may he competently represent our interests before national academic bodies when he possesses little to no knowledge of our interests?" Steinberg took up his tumbler for refreshment. He felt his talk was having the desired effect on his Board.

"Excuse me, sir," Professor Chemistry called out, "is the meeting format such that we may ask questions and present our views?"

"Of course you can," the Dean replied, "but I had planned for us to do our business expeditiously. Let's not drag this out. What would you like to offer, Chad?"

"That I do not accept your line of thought—which, let me hastily add, says nothing about which direction I cast my vote. Was Steve Jobs even a college graduate? We know he wasn't, but I think he did well. And Bill Gates and others well-known whom I might mention. But let's move away from the special cases, and look at the case of, say, Johnson & Johnson, a multinational mega-conglomerate. It just so happens that the present CEO is descended from this Academy, but for purposes of my comment, that is irrelevant. What would the number-one qualification of such a CEO have to be? As we know, that corporation consists of a bewildering array of company types, so what is that chief qualification? Knowledge of manufacturing processes? How to read an annual report? How to write an annual report? The cost of the chemicals in a bottle of baby shampoo? Or would it be leadership? Knowing how to lead, and how to choose subordinates, and how to set standards, and how to hold subordinates accountable for their performance? Having an eye trained to spot what is important and what is fluff. What is the advanced degree that produces a CEO for Johnson & Johnson? He could have any degree represented in this room, I will argue, or he could have none at all. In my considered opinion, General Pack has a more advanced degree in leadership than any person sitting in this room."

Colonel Chad Kauza continued: "For many years, I've carried a small fold of paper in my wallet. The subject is specialization, and the author is Robert Heinlein. It's quite widely circulated, so you might know it. I've read it a thousand times and can in fact recite it. This is the first time I've had occasion to share it, but I think it's pertinent to this discussion. 'A human being should be able to change a diaper, plan an invasion, butcher a hog, conn a ship, design a building, write a sonnet, balance accounts, build a wall, set a bone, comfort the dying, take orders, give orders, cooperate, act alone, solve equations, analyze a new problem, pitch manure, program a computer, cook a tasty meal, fight efficiently, die gallantly. Specialization is for insects.' There is no question in my mind about the accuracy of my assertion that General Pack comes closest to fulfilling Heinlein's requirements. That is not to say I am prepared to hand him veto authority. Thank you, Dean."

The chairman of Behavioral Science and Leadership spoke next. "Dean, I suppose my input is a question. The Superintendent was quite explicit that we were not to conduct meetings without all principal parties having a spot at the table. I must say, sir, I don't feel good about meeting in secret like this. I don't feel right acting in direct contravention of his wishes. My question is, why are we meeting behind General Pack's back?"

"I can see why you might be concerned, Alice, but hear me out," the Dean said. "First, I do not view his wishes as a direct order. Second, I take full responsibility for this meeting. As Dean, it is solely my responsibility to give General Pack the undiluted and uncensored consensus view of the Academic Board. I am confident when this is over, General Pack will be relieved to know we had the fortitude to exercise what he calls concentric initiative to express our collective opinion on a subject of utmost significance. He will intuitively apprehend the value in allowing us to speak freely on a matter of internal concern. If the Commandant is considering a major Blue Book revision, would the Superintendent be upset that General Bass failed to invite us to join his meeting on the topic? I think not. We are showing him guts, ladies and gentlemen, and quite soon he will be apprised of our decision, whatever it might be. Nothing will be kept from him."

◆ ◆ ◆

Colonel Joanna Reeder had been good for Golden. *BJ and AJ,* he thought with his tight-lipped smile. *Before Joanna, I was in firm control of my responsibilities, just being a strong chief for the Supe. Before Joanna, I was a 1958 Magnavox black and white with flickering screen. After Joanna, I feel like a third-gen hi-def liquid-plasma quartz crystal oofy toofy. The woman got me back on my game. If I know me,* Colonel Dahl thought, *this charge is good for at least a year.*

A couple things had occurred this morning that lent credence to his speculation. First, he and Evelyn Rose had rooted out the mole. The receptionist at the Cadet Hostess's Office, the one who picked up Pack's direct call, had followed Mrs. Rose's trail on her quest to locate an acceptable housekeeper. To her friends and neighbors in Croton, the receptionist had freely embellished the age, sexual attributes, and morals of the housekeeper the Superintendent had hired. Now an entire community had accepted as truth the phony story, as the local newspaper had freely printed the untruths with no effort to corroborate prior to running it. New York's junior Senator, a member of the Board of Visitors named Kelly Brandywine, had the damning information dropped right in her lap in that her staff conducted daily Lexus-Nexus searches to find out this kind of stuff about West Point. Senator Brandywine believed heaven really does drop pearls every now and then. She could use this charge to great effect. A shamed Mrs. Rose fired the offending tattler instantly, then took the further step of carrying her own resignation to Colonel Dahl.

One of the duties of the Cadet Hostess is to train cadets in social graces. Her subjects included ballroom dancing, how and when to write thank-you notes, calling cards, old-fashioned dance cards, how to set the china and silver for a formal dinner, seating arrangements, and appropriate attire in various settings. Such matters having to do with protocol are taught during New Cadet Barracks, and are as much a part of the training schedule as martial arts. Picture Evelyn Rose as a more refined Aunt Bee from Mayberry, and you have her down. In the small world she sat atop, and of which she was exceedingly proud, she had sinned, grievously, and deserved to be dumped.

Dahl saw this lady would continue to punish herself more than he ever could. "Mrs. Rose," Dahl explained patiently, "you will not understand how, but I believe you have unintentionally done the Supe and me a big favor. You are a most honorable lady, and have been an advisor to cadets almost as long as I've been alive. You are important to many people, as much so as about anyone here. So, Evelyn Rose, pick up your worthless resignation statement, and get back to work. The Supe isn't concerned about this. It is old, old news, now cold news. Good day, Mrs. Rose."

Second, Dahl had just taken one helluva initiative, and he damn sure hoped it was concentric. He thought it was time for the USMA logistics officer to bow out of the discussion with Lieutenant Colonel Rita Campbell down in DC. He had linked directly to the two Spitshugh aides and instructed them to advise their boss to employ the Board of Visitors as his vehicle to "slap the chokehold" on West Point. Have *them* tell USMA at the next meeting that tenant units will be unresponsive to the Superintendent's orders; that the Superintendent is shacking up with a mistress; that he can't have the combat weapons he wants; that every form of bias and discrimination is rampant; that Pack is trying to overthrow all signs of modernity and progressiveness. Hell, offenses that hadn't yet been imagined could be thrown on the table. All this and more that they would tell the Secretary of the Army would be OK.

After explaining to Spitshugh that the real power at West Point is the Board of Visitors, Campbell and Rynearson no doubt would have to explain what the BoV is and who sits on it. It was likely Spitshugh had never heard of it. But he would adopt the suggestion right off, they knew, because he could play his big-shot role and talk to some pretty powerful people as if he were an equal. And, most important, he wouldn't really have to dirty his hands. Once that meeting was all over and the mission of smearing the Academy complete, Spitsy-boy could even take credit and most likely receive an even higher appointment from President Rozan. Gimme five!

The most recent bit of morning news had come from the Comm. "G'mornin', Chief. How goes it?" Bass said.

"Fine, sir, having epiphanies for breakfast today. Like some?" Dahl asked. Before the Comm's looming presence, Dahl had been thinking in a serious way about what *having an epiphany* meant.

"Long as they're good, yeah, I would. You haven't had an epiphany about a particular cadet, have you?"

Dahl answered with an expression of puzzlement.

"OK, Chief, it's like this. I'm responsible for the Corps of Cadets, not individual cadets, in order to avoid any semblance of favoritism or special treatment. The individual I'm speaking of recently came to my attention because she spoke with the Supe. She had submitted resignation papers despite having established a high positive profile for herself. This coming back to you? You shooed Mommy and Daddy Big Bucks away, didn't let them in to see me."

"Yes, sir. I know the whole story up until the Supe spoke with her. Don't know details, except that he did not encourage her to stay," Dahl said.

General Bass said, "Well, you may let him know she petitioned to revoke her resignation letter, and I've granted her request. Her Regimental Tac heard her out, and seems to think Cadet Richelieu has had an epiphany of her own. Mother and father are back in California siccing federal officials on us, and brother is in Afghanistan, so it appears she did, as she says, reach the decision on her own. Who knows if the Supe had anything to do with it by *not* asking her to stay?"

"How about this, sir?" Dahl asked. "How about I do not inform the Supe? How about if he learns of it in the normal course of events, or if he doesn't? I will guess General Pack simply believes this is the individual's determination, and whatever she has determined, he will see as right."

Bass gave a thumbs-up and rumbled down the hallway.

♦ ♦ ♦

Back over in Thayer Hall, Steinberg's sub rosa meeting rolled on. He wasn't having an easy time of it. One of the department heads requested a delay of one week, so that the Board might think this over and, more important, make the Superintendent aware it was happening. The Dean was growing frustrated with his own crew. *What has happened to you people just doing as I say?* Steinberg thought, not seeing the irony in that.

Steinberg's discussion-ending closing argument was mostly the truth. "General Pack has given me no room to operate. I either begin to implement his instructions within a day or two, or we vote against him and he feels the combined weight of this Board being cast upon him. Now, ladies and gentlemen, we have tarried here a good deal longer than I intended, so let's get on with the vote to decide whether we give the Superintendent veto authority over what we teach."

It was done in roll-call style, a simple one-at-a-time oral *yea* or *nay* from each member. The final tally after all thirteen had expressed themselves was seven in favor of granting authority to Pack, with six opposed.

The Dean himself got a vote, though. The rules of the Board were clear that to avoid a tie, the Dean's vote shall prevail. These situations seldom occurred; the last time the Dean's vote was needed was eight years ago. Most cases were cut-and-dried. Elijah Steinberg was therefore not happy to find himself in this predicament. He had to cross the majority of the Board. "I vote to deny General Pack the power to dictate what we teach. By the rules of this Board, we do *not* grant veto authority to the Superintendent. This meeting is adjourned."

Two things of some significance took place rather immediately following the vote in Thayer Hall. The first was that Professor Chemistry, a classmate and personal friend of the Commandant, reasoned that if Steinberg could hold a sub rosa meeting, he could, too. He was quick about it, telling the Commandant how the Dean had voted against the Board, and that he had done so against the admonition of the Superintendent.

The second was that Steinberg locked himself in his office and instructed his secretary to allow no communications of any form from anyone. "I am off limits to everyone until I say otherwise."

Once he plopped into his deep, soft, leather chair, he said aloud, "*Scheisse*, what have I just done? I am in deep shit." In blatant violation of General Order Number One, which prohibited alcohol of any type in any work location, Steinberg retrieved a liter bottle of Wild Turkey 101 from a carefully concealed location. Then he commenced to swigging directly from the bottle. Elijah Steinberg knew his damn goose was cooked, jack, cooked real good. Right about now, he would happily switch places with the janitor in Kimsey Center.

Thump gave his boss a heads-up. Pack showed no concern, just said thanks, he'd take care of it. He vacated his present location at the motor pool and moved in the direction of the Dean's office.

Pack got there forty-five or so minutes later. The secretary and executive officer were in a little pickle, as they saw it, but not a big one. They could derail most trains headed into the Dean's office, but the Supe's train wasn't one of them. Besides, the Supe didn't stop to request an audience. He strode to the door, grasped the handle, but found it locked.

"General Steinberg, this is General Pack. Open the door." No answer. Again, "Steinberg, you will pay for this door if I smash it. Open up, now."

Pack detected movement on the other side. Steinberg was stumbling toward the door. Pack turned to the two occupants of the outer office and kindly asked them to keep quiet but take a hike for the next hour.

Steinberg opened the door, a dumb, stupid smile streaking his face. He was sozzled, squiffed. "At the moment, shir," he slurred, "I am an inebriant, kindly begging your pardon and forbearance, *mein jefe*."

Pack pushed him into the nearest chair. "Sit there and don't move, Steinberg. And don't speak, either. I have to make a phone call."

General Pembrook called him back quickly. "Wayne Pembrook here, Simon. What is it?"

"A General Officer matter, Chief. I need to find a new home for the Dean, Elijah Steinberg. I'm using his office phone. He is not in condition to speak at the moment. It's an urgent matter involving family, I think. What you do with him, I don't care, and have no recommendation, but I do request you get him off Post hastily. I am confining him to quarters until then. I would like to make Chad Kauza, professor of chemistry, the acting Dean."

"Done and done, Simon. Sorry about this."

"Yes, I am, too. Damned shame."

Pack poured the Wild Turkey into the toilet and stowed the bottle in Steinberg's briefcase, which Pack expropriated for the time being. He forced Steinberg to drink coffee after coffee, then held his head under the lavatory faucet. After ninety minutes, Pack summoned the Military Police to escort Steinberg to his quarters. At the same time, he placed the man under house arrest.

At his residence that evening, the Superintendent reflected that his contention that West Point had gotten soft most definitely included certain of the faculty as well as the Corps. Of course, that would be true, he further reflected. Wherefrom is their example set? There was malignancy at the apex of the academic chain, but the good news was, he had, as promised, exposed and excised it.

Chapter Sixteen

Safety

After Dean Steinberg's firing, Pack thought he could see a scab forming on the face of West Point. It would be ugly for a time longer, but eventually, it would heal and the scar would fade. He also knew other wounds would come, and he would knit them, and the patient would grow stronger at the wounded places.

Colonel Chad Kauza, the acting Dean, was proving to be no doormat for the Superintendent, and he was no pushover with the professoriat he now ran. He was fair but stern with the people who just weeks ago were his peers. Pack respected Kauza, and the latitude he afforded him attested to that respect. Kauza established a written plan, in elaborate detail, describing the pathway toward accomplishing the Supe's design. There was no one on staff now challenging him. They saw the power of Pack's will.

The USMA staff had figured out that Dahl was one of the best damn colonels in the Marine Corps. He had commanded at every level, and his personnel file suggested he sat in the top 1 percent of his peers. His staff not only followed him now, but sought to emulate his example. Dahl would almost surely receive promotion to brigadier general at the end of this West Point tour of duty.

Positive signs abounded. The weekly Regimental parades were sharper; most of the parade-watching public, maybe all of it, could not detect the microscopic addition of crispness in cadet movements, but the tactical officers, who saw these events more frequently than they wanted, could spot it a mile away. Drill Sergeants in Basic Training Centers around the country exhorted their recruits daily, "Put a little pep in your step, a little pride in your stride, trooper!" Cadets had taken that message to heart at West Point. Why this subtle change? Because Brigadier General Bass operated with more zeal, more pride, and more intensity, and that rubbed off on the tactical officers at the Regimental, Battalion, and Company levels. Bass got his energy from Pack. That's how leadership works. If the McDonald's store manager is a slacker, don't expect clean restrooms and prompt service.

The Office of Physical Education had been on the receiving end of a Pack spanking once he showed up unannounced and let the instructor know the standards had to be tougher. Boxing, swimming, wrestling, martial arts, gymnastics, all tightened up. Despite their grousing, cadets walked straighter because of it. If the instructors in any of these sports sensed fear in their cadets, he or she subjected them to the same brutality repeatedly until they "passed" the test. Pack emphasized the physical aspects of cadetship as they hadn't been since the days of MacArthur.

Even Thump got himself on a self-toughening regimen; he actually looked great in his dress uniform. Everyone else in the Corps of Cadets noticed it, too. Tactical officers, who always took care to present a good military appearance, now did so with greater alacrity than ever. Across the street, every military instructor who valued his duty position began a program to improve his profile and bearing. And the civilian cadre of professors, now aware of the reduction-in-force plan, searched for any edge to maintain their positions, so they suddenly placed a premium on fitness as well.

Pack had visited lots of football practices. He just stood and watched from various perspectives, seldom saying a word. The word had circulated not to interrupt him. The team was highly cognizant he was there, though. Damn straight they were. To them, he was a legend walking the sidelines. Tracing the dimension of his influence was impossible, but it was wide, deep, powerful. There was fight in the team that the coach had not instilled, but the players themselves. They would never say it to their coaches, but they had said it among themselves, a mantra not unlike the unspoken one Pack himself thought as a teenager: *We will never do anything to embarrass our Superintendent. We will fight to our final breath to make him proud of us. We will make the Corps proud.*

Coach Sumner sensed the new spirit, the stronger will to succeed, and was bright enough to have felt and observed the Academy-wide changes in mission focus. He was anything but vainglorious. He did not seek the spotlight or personal recognition. He was about the team, and he was happy to make football part of the greater West Point team effort. By gosh, he also knew enough about leadership to understand all this had followed in the wake of one person, Lieutenant General Simon Pack. So at the conclusion of training camp (Pack had difficulty bringing himself to use the expression relative to college football; that had in his day been an NFL-only term), Sumner took a risk of his own and asked for a meeting with the Supe.

"Sir," Sumner began, "when you spoke the first time to the coaches over in the Triple A conference room, you looked directly at me and said you had the right football coach. I thought, after a 3–9 season and a loss to Air Force and Navy, that's a helluva bold thing to say. In my opinion, of course, you were right. I give you credit for good football eyes. Now it's my turn to be bold, if you'll indulge me.

"I do know what makes a winner in football. This thing is taking shape in accordance with your vision. The Corps is shaping up, and so is this football team, and to be honest, I can't tell who's leading whom, and really don't care. It won't come as a shock to you, I hope, that we're gonna win some games this season. I'd like to provide a summary explanation.

"After that meeting over in the AD's offices, I went back and relayed how I felt to my staff. They were so fired up, I wish you could have seen them. I know for a fact I'm sittin' here sharin' air with one of the best leaders I've ever seen. I feel that, and General, I'm no brown-noser. Your entire football operation is working with a joy and a purpose that just wasn't there last year. And the players, I'm not ashamed to say, idolize you. They see what you stand for, and want to be the image of the warrior you are. Ditto my staff. Does that mean I'm less of a coach, that you get all the credit? No, what I'm tryin' to say," Sumner said in his plain, flat, Southern voice, "is that you have freed me up to be the best coach I can be. You have plowed the ground for me.

"The staff took a fresh look at everything—training methods, relationship between us and players, additional defensive schemes, and making the offense more truly triple, sometimes even quadruple, option. We took another look at what Colonel Red Blaik did to become so successful here. In 1949, as you know, Vince Lombardi worked for Blaik, during which period he said he learned the Blaik principles that he himself used: simplicity and execution. This game is about blocking and tackling, and you succeed by demanding perfection in those things in practice. We've shifted positions for at least half the players, in almost every case with enthusiastic support by the players involved. And, as a result of a player-up suggestion that a year ago would've seemed lunatic, we're gonna try playing some of our best guys both ways. That's risky, because as you know if they get hurt, we've reduced our depth, but if they can make it work, we've increased our depth.

"I'd say the most unusual thing to happen is that we picked up four players from tryouts within the Corps. We coaches said, you know, nearly every male at this place played high school football, so we might have overlooked some fellows right under our noses. Your starting quarterback, sir, is a gamer who has what kids today call 'mad skills,' and he's coming from the ranks of the Corps, from our tryouts. Highly improbable, almost something out of fantasy. What I'm hearing is that the Corps is stoked about this; I'm betting this young man will be the cause of some extrastrong cheering. And equally as improbable, General, is that I'm giving him the reins most of the time. Sometimes we'll intervene by sending in plays, but what we've seen in practice is that players seem to perform a little better when their teammate is calling the signals. We'll see. In any case, you asked the question, and didn't expect an answer, but there it is.

"Coach Nasby's weight program has a number of four hundred-plus benchers and five cadets weighing three hundred pounds or more. Film study proves that tackling and blocking techniques are immeasurably better than last season, and special teams, particularly punting and placekicking, are also. I might be a fool for exposing myself as I just did, but I want to put my reputation on the line right in front of you, *before* we've played a game down. Last thing: I know other teams don't stay static, but I have total faith we'll have improved more than any team we face. Thanks for the time, General Pack, and thanks for supporting me in this quest to get our team back to a place you will recognize as the quality of Army football you knew."

♦ ♦ ♦

Pack had dealt with strong headwinds on every front. There were only six days left in September. He had demanded and gotten the weapons for the march to and exercises at Buckner. The Department of Defense's Installation Management Authority (IMA), however, had turned down arms room space, which actually was available in Military Police and medical unit spaces on Post. The IMA is a fledgling DOD organization made up of civilians imposing severe disruptions on field units because their understanding of the ramifications of their decisions was negligible. This was a piece of the effort to weaken Pack and, by extension, the Academy. Washington thought if he didn't get the space to store the weapons in accordance with existing physical-security regulations, he could not accept them.

Get me the weapons, Pack said, and we'll devise a way to store them. The Supe directed the Commandant and Regimental Tactical Officers to find a makeshift solution. They stored the weapons in lockers situated in company commanders' rooms, and found space in the Reservation magazine to store the extra ammunition. Cleaning supplies went into special lockers in the company trunk rooms in the basement. It was a gutsy move, this tampering with one of the most sensitive issues in the military, weapons security. Let them write us up, Pack said. As I see it, the pricks in DC are violating the regulations by denying us certified weapon storage areas that currently exist, and that in the past have been open to us.

"Look at it this way," he said to Thump, "they are standing in the way of my accomplishing my mission, and that's a dangerous place to be."

Tomorrow was Saturday, and the biggest day yet in the new academic year. The Fourth Regiment would march to Buckner by crossing the Line of Departure at 0600. This means wake-up at 0400 in order to draw and distribute weapons and ammunition. Each cadet would receive an aluminum-foil-wrapped combat breakfast to stuff inside his shirt or ruck to eat as circumstances allowed. Once the Regiment had closed on the assembly area at Buckner, individual squads would move forward to negotiate a live-fire range under controlled conditions. The leaders at West Point had changed the game. Even this course, benign by the standards of a good combat unit, was potentially hazardous. With recently reorganized squads, platoons, and companies, people were unfamiliar with their teammates. An accidental shooting was not out of the question. When this weekend was over, Fourth Regiment would feel a little stronger and a lot more tightly knit.

The Army football team would play its fourth game tomorrow. They are 3–0, having defeated teams that all played in Bowl games last season. It's the most exciting Army team in decades, one that's scoring an average of 39.6 points per game. Three running backs have accumulated over three hundred yards rushing apiece, led by the walk-on quarterback, D.E. Stacy, whose adroitness in distributing the football has begun to attract the attention of future opponents. As Coach Sumner predicted, Stacy is a Corps favorite. Stacy is a direct link between the Corps and football team. How far can this team go? cadets start to wonder. Option quarterbacks absorb hits on most plays, even as they pitch at the last moment. How long Stacy's frame can remain intact, in playing shape, is an open question, given his absence of intercollegiate experience. D.E. is a natural for the position, which calls for sure-handedness, quick feet, rapid reads of the defense, and steady nerves. But it is, above all, a *team*, not a two- or three-man operation.

Tomorrow's game is against Stanford at Stanford. The Cardinal have been a top-15 team for a half-dozen consecutive years. Game time is 1600

Eastern, and if the Fourth Regiment cadets have a genuine complaint about this road march, it is that they are not able to follow the game. At the one-quarter mark of the season, the Corps believes in this team, convinced something special is happening. What Fourth Regiment doesn't know is that Pack and Bass have provided speaker systems to deliver a radio broadcast of the game.

Toward the front of the march formation, in the first echelon, were two hulking figures who maintained perfect noise and light discipline throughout. They did not speak even to each other for the duration. They were Duck and the Supe. Their presence did not and could never escape the attention of the least of the marchers. They had crossed the Line of Departure in darkness, but they could be seen in the before-morning nautical twilight. Moving under the weight of pack and weapon and ammo was child's play to Pack, a deeply embedded bit of muscle memory that let him know in advance how he would feel at five miles, ten miles, or upward of twenty. Decades of conditioning did that.

Back near the tail of the march, from which position he could identify the sick, lame, and lazy, was Brigadier General George Bass. The first to wither were the civilian academicians, as Bass frankly expected. *It's possible the Dean won't have to fire anyone*, Bass thought, *in that these people will be queueing up to resign*. Quite a few made it no farther than two miles out the gate of West Point proper. At about the halfway point, on a sharp upgrade, the first cadet fell back. As he trod past the malingerer, Bass overheard the tactical officer barking. The cadet was the Vice President's granddaughter. *She's on borrowed time*, Bass conjectured. *Will she survive first semester?* His question was Duck's: How had she made it this far? He catalogued a reminder to chat with the Regimental Tactical Officer about this next week. Woe to anyone harboring a favorites' list. But even a possible malingerer could not curtail Bass's enthusiasm for this event, for the correct decision he knew it had been. He and Pack and Kauza were making a respectable team.

For Duck, this march over radically uneven terrain brought pain. With every stumble on the bad leg, he saw stars, literally the stun of bright whiteness, with a momentary questioning of capacity to continue. But this young man had seen horrors in Iraq and Afghanistan. A lifetime of pain absorbed in seconds, and always, always, he remained aware that his fellow soldiers had endured far more, and he could make it.

Five years ago, following extended treatment for a different set of wounds, Duck took two weeks leave. During that time, he'd visited three soldiers whose wounds would not heal for a very long time. He had met them during his own hospital stay. He visited one of these on a Saturday afternoon. A busy traffic thoroughfare ran but a short distance from this room in Walter Reed Medical Center. How many kids speeding by out there preparing for a Saturday night carouse knew of the soldiers their age inside these fences? Or cared for the type of soldier Duck was there to see?

Private First Class Dierdre Jackson had served in a Transportation battalion convoying essential supplies around the theater of operations. Duck crept silently into the room to find PFC Jackson the sole occupant. For more than a year, she had lain here in a full-body cast; the staff probably had lost count of the number of major operations she had undergone. The cast had holes for her mouth, nose, and eyes—otherwise, she was a plaster model of a human. Before her body had been shredded by an improvised explosive device, she'd possessed a kind-looking, beautifully expressive face the color of dark chocolate. The only way Duck knew anything of her appearance was a photo of her in uniform, the only adornment on her bedside table. The duty nurse had relayed a story to Duck that had rent his heart. Her family resided in downtown DC, no doubt less than half-hour from this bed. They had come once or twice in the beginning, then came no more. No one came to see her but a boyfriend, who came every single day without fail.

Duck resolved to sit there until the boyfriend arrived. He spoke her name softly, in case she was awake. She was.

"Is that really you, Lieutenant Cooper? You really remember me?"

"Course I do, Dierdre. Nurse says you're making great progress. Seeing you's the best thing to happen to me in a long time."

"Yeah, they tell me I'm doing good, too, and I want to believe them. But, Lieutenant, it's so hard when you haven't seen sunshine for thirteen months."

He thought maybe she was crying, but couldn't tell for sure. This was so damned sad. "Hey, Dierdre, I thought I'd stay till your next visitor shows up. How about you let me do something for you till then? Or we can just talk if you'd like." That duty nurse had told him Dierdre never complained, never made requests, much less demands.

"It's Saturday, right?"

"Yep."

"Means Lemuel will be here about six. He works three jobs now, I think, but gets up here every chance he can. Good guy, Lem."

"You're wrong about that. He's a great guy, a helluva guy, a gem. You have something there, Dee."

"Yeah, we agree about that. Anyhow, what you asked me 'bout doing something for me? You know what I'd really, truly like? A bowl of vanilla ice cream."

The mess hall shut down early on Saturday afternoons, but Russell Cooper thought, *There's no force on freaking Earth gonna prevent me from getting this gallant young woman who hadn't yet had twenty years of life a bowl of vanilla ice cream.* Call a taxi and have it delivered, Cooper told the nurse.

♦ ♦ ♦

This event had pushed Fourth Regimental cadets bivouacked at Camp Buckner back into 1940s America. With the football game, many for the first time experienced the sublime pleasure of radio, the medium that called for active listening and required the listener to imagine—imagine the field, imagine the sky above, imagine the crowd, imagine the team's position on the field, imagine the coaches and players on the sidelines, imagine even the team's mood. Pack used to love listening to games on the radio as a boy, he and his dad riding in a car, especially the part where the announcer said, "As the second quarter begins, Army will be moving left to right on your radio dial," at which point he'd follow the index markers on the dial as if they were the yard markers. Before the game wound down, darkness would curtain the encamped listeners. When was the last time cadets had been involved in an Army football game in so rustic and innocent a fashion?

Elite leaders know where they should be, and when. It is an acquired sense without which greatness is impossible. To be at the right spot on the battlefield at the critical turning point is an ingredient Great Captains share.

Pack might have traveled with the team to Palo Alto, but the critical time and place was here at Camp Buckner. He had to show commitment to this series of toughening exercises if he expected the entire Academy to benefit from them. He could have enjoyed the trip out and back, and the perks of his office during the ballgame, but that would have amounted to choosing the easier wrong instead of the harder right. Self-abnegation, he wanted cadets to discern, is expected of the leader you aspire to be. The leader must show his followers how to inure themselves to discomfort and privation. This is part of the process. In essence, every cadet and every faculty member is giving up one weekend per quarter that he or she might have enjoyed with family or friends. It might have meant a weekend spent mostly in slumber, trying to recover from a week that had stolen vitality and strength. Or it might have meant much-needed additional study for a cadet in peril academically. To sacrifice, by definition, means giving up something. But in this instance, it also meant giving up something in order to capture something else. That "something else"—as Pack had repeated to himself—was pride in place and mission.

These cadets had completed the day's challenges not much the worse for wear. Nobody got shot, nobody got killed. A few people had to visit the aid station, but that's life in the army. Each platoon was allowed a fire, but with round-the-clock fire watches in place. The fires began early, for cooking and preparing hot compresses. When they were surprised by the sounds of the Army football announcers, the camp stilled, hanging onto every word. If someone conversed in such a way as to interrupt the program, fellow cadets squelched the speaker.

Stanford was rated ninth in both AP and UPI polls. Army hadn't beaten a Top Ten team since dinosaurs roamed, and it didn't look like they would this day, either. Army had won the opening toss and deferred to receive the second half. Stanford's return man pumped up his home crowd by taking the opening kickoff 102 yards for a touchdown and a 7–0 Cardinal lead. What the fans in Palo Alto might've said if they weren't the classiest ones in all of college football: "Pyoo-nee, Pyoo-nee, Arrr-mee," "Go home, losers!" But they didn't; unlike some of the Ivy teams, Stanford people treated Army with dignity from start to finish, as did Army when Stanford came to West Point.

They might have wanted to kick Army in the teeth, though, because the Black Knights led 21–18 at the half. The Army ground game clearly confused and unsettled the powerful Cardinal. Eamon Washington amassed 185 rushing yards, the largest such number Stanford had allowed in thirty-five games. D.E. Stacy was brilliant, but so was the full Army squad. The Stanford offensive line averaged 318 tackle to tackle, and Army's defense around 240, yet the Army defenders shed blocks as if they were equals. The second half played out in similar style. The Brave Old Army team refused to yield. When the final whistle blew, upstart and undersized Army, a 17-point 'dog,' had sent Stanford, a by-damn top-ten team, to the lockers nursing a 45–32 bruising. Army players didn't feel like a 3–9 group any longer. "Say what? We've already collected more wins than a season ago, and we ain't even through September!"

The Fourth Regiment's cheering might have been audible twenty miles away. With the football team leading the way, the Academy was coming together again, the entire place growing stronger at the broken places.

♦ ♦ ♦

Lieutenant Colonels Rita Campbell and Mike Rynearson traced their steps. They had been careful to whom they had spoken about Secretary of the Army Spitshugh's plan to "slap a chokehold" on West Point. This could go down badly for any number of people, including themselves, if it were handled in the wrong way. They knew someone had delivered the message from the Secretary of Defense's office; with a receptionist's help, they learned the name of the man who had handed the mission to Spitshugh. They used Lieutenant Colonel Peters at the Office of Congressional Legislative Liaison for help with determining this man's duties for the Defense Secretary, as well as his connections on Pennsylvania Avenue. But Peters had broken the story for them with the revelation that every time the Defense Secretary's envoy checked into the White House, his appointment was with the senior advisor to President Rozan. Because Peters was in the middle of making administrative arrangements for the Board of Visitors, he discovered that the senior advisor was personally calling the shots on the composition of the Board. Right after the President's big foreign-policy speech at West Point last year, many of the people on the BoV voluntarily moved aside to permit tighter packing by the senior advisor. Moreover, the new appointees each met with the advisor individually over the course of two weeks.

It might not be perfect evidence, but it was sufficient, Campbell and Rynearson opined, to carry the information discreetly to West Point. Their channel in was through Campbell's conduit to the USMA logistics officer. For Campbell to talk within her own logistics channels was normal and would raise no eyebrows. The information was too hot for the logistics officer, whom Campbell swore to secrecy, so he laid out everything he knew to his chief of staff, Colonel Dahl. At that juncture, Dahl instructed that he himself would take over all future communications with the Spitshugh aides.

It was at this point Dahl made the decision to go all in. He explained to Campbell that she was to brief Spitshugh on the efficacy of using the Board of Visitors to achieve his ends. "Go to him," Dahl exhorted, "and have him set up private meetings with the ten members aligned with the White House against the Academy. Let them know your office will do whatever it can to support them. Make sure they see the Secretary as a key player. Go so far as telling the Secretary the meeting is open to the public, and he might want to attend. Better yet, tell him if he plays his cards well, one of the ten will probably invite him in an official capacity."

Actually, Dahl believed, there isn't much of a role for Spitshugh, in that the Board of Visitors will already know more than Spitshugh, but they will see the chance to use him as a fall guy, if necessary, and will welcome him aboard the chokehold train. What Spitshugh knew or didn't know had never mattered, just as long as he had several sacks of campaign funds to hand over. And Spitshugh, well, old Fitz would wallow in the palace intrigue and feel like he's trying on his big-boy pants.

♦ ♦ ♦

"Sir," Dahl said from the chair in Pack's secondary, "we're getting many calls today asking for your comments on an opinion piece in today's *NYT.*" This occurred but two days following the Supe's Poop Deck address. "I'll leave the article with you. The Public Affairs office brought it to my attention this morning. Major Roberts in the Social Sciences Department wrote it. I'd prefer you merely acknowledge receipt from me, and tell me only if you disagree with my method of disposition.

"This Major Roberts works for the Dean, but I would like Brigadier General Bass to discuss the matter with Roberts, with the acting Dean's blessing, of course. This is something you shouldn't have your fingerprints on, sir, in the event this mercurial major might in future claim undue command influence on your part. So I'm asking you to stay away from this, sir, and let us take care of it."

Pack said, "Just be sure Colonel Kauza's prerogatives aren't impinged upon. If he wants to handle it, that'll be his call. And tell the Public Affairs people I have no public comment."

"Clear, sir," Dahl answered.

The subject of Major Roberts's piece was this West Point administration's show of support for Army football. The author, a USMA graduate thirteen years previous, found such a show of "favoritism" reprehensible.

Roberts's view of sports was somewhat Victorian, holding that winning and losing is secondarily important, a distant second, he added, to working up a nice lather on the pitch, then shaking hands good-naturedly with the other boys. Followed by, presumably, "Let's share a pint, mates." Rather Etonish all round. He further found offensive the fact that 60 percent of the Army footballers went through the US Military Academy Preparatory School first. If one is so doltish he must buttress his academic standing through "Prep," Roberts expostulated, he really isn't qualified to be a cadet. This, in spite of the studies showing the percentage of those making General Officer who attended Prep was equal to those who did not. On top of it all, Roberts found mandatory game attendance by the Corps to be an infringement of the cadet's right to privacy. He contended that stamping out mandatory chapel attendance had been a huge step forward, but the ham-handed approach to football was two steps back.

Because the Commandant was lead dog on promoting football interests, Dahl reasoned he was the one best suited to handle this matter. At the same time, Dahl knew there was a possibility Bass would take no action at all.

But, Bass being Bass, insisted upon calling Major Roberts to his office. Acting Dean Chad Kauza willingly consented to Bass's request.

"Major Roberts," Thump began, "let me stipulate your right to speak out in the manner you have. The governing regulation supports you fully. But there is a thing called judgment that is in question. Do you understand?"

"I do not, General. My right is my right, as you have said," Roberts replied. "Either I have the right, or I do not."

Thump continued, "And I have the right to express an opinion unfavorable to a family member close to you, but under any circumstance that would be unseemly. What distinguishes the officer from other ranks is the display of judgment expected of him. You rebuked your superiors here publicly. You did not trouble yourself to raise your concerns in-house. The Army is a team, but you treated your teammates disrespectfully. We are attempting here to rebuild the West Point team, and you are undermining us. You are reinforcing what formerly was the barrier between the Corps and the football team. As you may have heard, we believe Army football is important. And until you are in command here, Major, you will not publicly oppose that view. You are selfish, Major. You have acted as a small man, and I judge you by your actions. Winning is damn important to me. If you aren't devoted to creating a winning culture here, let me know. And by the way, the Army doesn't want you if you don't want to win its wars. Now get out of here, Major Roberts, and know if you aren't with us, you're against us. Think about where your allegiance rests, Major. Go."

♦ ♦ ♦

It is commonly said of both baseball and football, "You build the team from the middle outward," or "You're only as strong as you are up the middle." In baseball, that's the spine running from catcher to pitcher to shortstop to centerfielder. In football, that's the connection between the quarterback and center. The center is like the quarterback of the offensive line; he calls out a special blocking scheme once his line is set and the defense in position. He's exceptionally key in the Army offense, one requiring frequent rushes up the middle to prevent the defense from totally dominating rushes outside the guards. It's a rush-heavy offense that passes fewer than half-dozen times a game. A team doesn't go far in this brand of modern football without a strong, savvy center, and Army had one. A four-year starter, Jesse Bruccoli had gotten the attention of opposing coaches, all of whom gave him special mention in their pregame remarks. No Army lineman in many years—since Simon Pack, to be precise—had as many pancake blocks. Bruccoli had the size, speed, and explosive power of the best centers in college football. Coach Sumner and the Sports Information Office were touting his candidacy for the Rimington Trophy, the annual prize to the best center. *Sports Illustrated* was planning a story on this gifted athlete who also ranked among the top 10 percent scholastically and as a cadet leader. With the team at 7–0 and about to play a 6–1 Penn State team in Happy Valley next weekend, lots of eyes would fall on Jesse Bruccoli. At this moment, however, whether Bruccoli would even travel with the team was problematic.

Major Art Loewens, professor of civil engineering, had two sections, twenty-four students, in his advanced elective course. Loewens's cadets were assigned a take-home, individual work exam in which they had to design a bridge, type of their choice, capable of bearing the weight of two M1A2 Abrams tanks crossing simultaneously from opposing directions. This could be an intricate project. The student was required to show the math of computed stresses at all points on the span, to prepare specifications for materials required, and to keep the bridge within a specified dollar cost. There was, in brief, great latitude for individual work.

When Major Loewens was three-quarters completed with grading, he felt quite proud of the learning that obviously had occurred in his classroom. Some work was of higher quality, to be sure, but every solution was unique. On one project, he encountered a comment—not forbidden—atop the opening page, which read, "On part 2 (c) below, I collaborated with a fellow cadet in making the 'moment' calculation." The cadet reporting this was quite specific. In a case like this, if received credit is cited with precision, it is acceptable. It is also accepted that learning has happened in the collaboration.

The problem was easy to identify. On another project, Loewens encountered a verbatim rendering of the math derivation. But on this project, Cadet First Class Jesse Bruccoli had not made the required statement that he had collaborated or in some manner received or given academic help. Major Loewens notified the chairman of the Cadet Honor Committee at once. It may be safely assumed that near 100 percent of West Point's population, had they known of this closely held affair, hoped this was an innocuous infraction, a blundering oversight by an honorable man. At the swiftly convened hearing, however, Bruccoli dropped his head in shame. He was most sincerely grief-stricken.

Cadet Bruccoli said to the Committee concealed in darkness in front of him, "Members of the Honor Committee, this was no mistake. I do not wish to offer a defense or bring witnesses. I deliberately did not acknowledge the help I got by stating that on the cover sheet. I thought I could get away with it, yet if I had been honest, there would have been no repercussion. I was dumb and dishonest."

The Honor Committee was to a person saddened but had no choice but to forward their finding to the Superintendent for final disposition. Major Loewens had notified the Committee on Tuesday. This was Wednesday.

♦ ♦ ♦

The Honor Committee's report reached Pack in his primary. Golden had toted it over separate from any other papers. "Sir, this one is tough to swallow. Coach Sumner and the football squad leave Friday morning. It is your sad duty to declare if Cadet Bruccoli will go with them. I'll wait for your instructions," Golden said, making a move outside.

"No, sit down over there," Pack said, indicating another chair in the study. "Let me look through this."

Pack read it, started over, read it, started over. What was he looking for? A way out for Bruccoli? Apropos, seemingly of nothing, Pack mouthed to himself, "Like Walt Ulmer said, the problem with the army is, it has too damn many lawyers." Pack thought, *The lawyers would urge me to hide behind the vagaries of some damn legal argument and excuse this fine young man. I have, in fact, multiple legalisms to shield me from challenge, should I let him off.* Others would call this situation a Morton's Fork, where Pack had two clear choices, both undesirable. One choice would weaken the football team, the other would weaken the Corps. He also could send him directly to the army without a commission.

They're all wrong: I have one choice only. "Chief, send Mr. Bruccoli over to the secondary," Pack directed. "Fifteen minutes."

"Aye-aye, sir."

The Supe's secretary, Kathy Pillings, knew what was afoot, and she knew her husband, Ed, regarded Bruccoli highly. She couldn't imagine the Solomonic solution to this one. Presently, Bruccoli showed up, no Tac officer by his side. This big, rugged lineman looked scared and forlorn. He was as nervous as on his first day of Beast Barracks. He knocked and heard the Superintendent order him to enter.

"Jesse," Pack said with authority, "I am upholding the Honor Committee's finding. You are dismissed from the Academy. You will be stronger for this. I don't know how I know that, but I do. I believe you are a good man."

"General Pack, sir, I am ashamed, and I am sorry. I am sorry I will not graduate from the Academy. But, much more, I am sorry I will not have the chance to serve my country as an officer. I love this country, sir."

Pack suspected he would want to help Bruccoli resituate his life. Now he was certain of it. "We will arrange for your expedited admission to another school, one with a good ROTC program, and I'll promise you can join it if you wish. Think about it for a few hours, and let your tactical officer know what you decide. I'd be proud to have you as a son, Jesse."

Jesse Bruccoli's lips quivered, but he did not cry. He held it together, saluted, and made the slow walk back to his room.

♦ ♦ ♦

At least this time, the staff officer knocked and saluted properly. Dahl was weary. He was too tired to make this an ass-chewing to rival the one he inflicted on Colonel Joanna Reeder, the Director of Admissions. For a moment, he considered she actually might be responsible for this FUBAR situation as well.

Standing before him this time, though, was Lieutenant Colonel Dick Wilbur, the Staff Judge Advocate, or chief lawyer. "Colonel Wilbur," Dahl said, "don't you think this still-new command group, starting with me, might like to have been read in on the Cadet Browning Totten case? Doesn't its high-profile nature suggest to you we ought, as a very minimum, to be able to avoid looking stupidly at one another if asked a question about it? If you're even aware of what the Board of Visitors is, you can be certain they *will* raise Totten with us, and that's just a couple months off. Don't you think, Colonel Wilbur, it's kinda important to keep your bosses informed of a potentially flammable situation?"

"Chief, I have dropped the ball on this. When you arrived, I gave you the update on key issues you ordered. I was having a separate paper done on the Totten case, and my man responsible for it was reassigned suddenly because of an emergency family hardship. I lost my grip on it. No excuse, Chief. I'll personally brief General Pack if you think I should take responsibility," Wilbur said with real contrition.

"Of course you're responsible," Dahl replied. "You alone. I'll be honest, I have to wonder what kind of legal representation you offer. Now, within twenty-four hours, I want a clear, concise accounting of the details of this case, including recommendations for action. Get it through that incisive legal mind of yours that this is the kind of festering mess this command group does not want lingering on. If I were the Supe, I would be very, very unhappy—once again—with me. No more, Wilbur. No more."

Cadet Browning Totten referred to himself as a gay secularist. This was his final year at West Point. He was the founder of the West Point Areligious Alliance, a contribution immensely satisfying to him. The list of Mr. Totten's demands was impressive. He advocated to let cadets marry, particularly gay cadets. At the same time, he wanted homosexuals in, he wanted Christians out. There should be atheist chaplains only. Totten spent a good deal of time communicating with the Alliance's parent organization, the Military Association of Temporal Nonconformists. In an interview with *The Washington Post* last year, Totten demeaned "the proudly bigoted culture of this miserable place." He had multiple lawsuits pending against the Academy he attended.

Pack waved everyone off on the Totten case. "Send him to the secondary this afternoon right after classes. I want him alone. Let General Bass know I'll need to close the loop with him afterward." Pack said this to Golden calmly and gently, no emotion evident.

Cadet Totten entered the secondary. Pack returned Totten's salute and pointed to a straight-back metal chair brought in for this encounter. This piece of furniture was an affront to this office, a stick in the eye of its seriousness and style. It was not set up to the front of Pack's desk but touching the Supe's desk at the right. The young man Pack saw was about six-two, wiry and thin, bespectacled. *Maybe the eyeglasses are his fashion statement*, Pack thought. A perceptible smirk of superiority permanently etched his handsome face.

"How're you doing today, Browning? Were you named after Elizabeth Barrett or the Browning firearms company? Probably neither, right, Mr. Totten?"

"That's right, neither. Are you trying to make some point by asking that, General?"

"Mr. Totten, would you describe yourself as an insouciant cadet?"

"Not at all. I have a purpose here that gives me energy every day," Totten said confidently, conspicuously dropping the *sir*.

"Explain, Mr. Totten," Pack said.

"I am a self-assured, determined gay atheist, and I believe I reached this point to change the culture of West Point," Totten answered.

"This 'proudly bigoted...miserable place,'" Pack said, peering down at a quotation attributed to Totten. "Would that be how you stated it?"

"That is correct, General. Those are the words I employed," Totten said, feeling he was holding his own and this Pack wasn't the intimidating figure he was played up to be.

Pack's expression darkened in a flash, and he leaned on his elbows toward Totten, within reach of Pack's meaty paw. In equal flash, he switched the tone and topic of discussion. "Do you know what I did yesterday, Totten? You don't want me to come around this desk, mister. Answer me, and immediately."

"No, sir, I can't possibly know...You probably did many things," Totten said, trying still to maintain his ground, sound strong.

"I separated from the Corps a fine, very fine young man because it was the right thing to do. But it was profoundly hard. I separated a man who loves his country and wants to pay it back for the honor of living in it. I could read it in his eyes. You know, Totten, the kind of young person who might like a CD of patriotic songs for his birthday. Some corny guy like that, who also applies himself academically and is one of the best offensive linemen in all of Division I football. A kind of guy who takes pleasure not in personal accomplishments as much as team accomplishments. But he taught a Sunday School class, so forgive me, Mr. Totten, I'm sure that disqualifies him in your eyes."

"I'd like to know what this cadet has to do with me," Browning Totten said, his courage starting to crack.

"Ever heard of a Biblical book called Ecclesiastes, Mr. Totten? I mean, you being an atheist and all, could be you haven't," Pack said.

"Of course, General. Everyone has."

"OK, Mr. Totten, catch this: The Preacher says to everything there is a season. So this is my point: I am known for being low-keyed, unflappable, calm in crisis. But," Pack said, his face coloring and voice rising, "I shall now take my cue from the Preacher. I am going to let go with you, Mr. Totten. I have witnessed close-up war's savagery, seen men killed and maimed, and came close to both myself a time or two. Seen a lot of soldiers in hospitals, thousands, I reckon. A lot of brave patriots didn't want to go to war but did because they accepted it as their duty. The cadet I separated yesterday is one of those willing to expose himself to great peril on behalf of his fellow Americans. But you, Mr. Totten...I suppose you are familiar with 'The Battle Hymn of the Republic'?"

"Of course, I am," Totten said, confidence draining by the minute.

"Ah, Mr. Totten, I love the conceptual beauty of *terrible swift sword*. I promised when I assumed this position, I would brandish the terrible swift sword of *justice*. And you do not deserve to lead troops in this Army. I would be committing a breach of my office if I let you loose on our soldiers. Your mission, what you prefer to spend your time on, is gay and atheist activism. Have a good time doing that, Mr. Totten, in your civilian life, because that's where you're going. You lack the requisite commitment to our mission, and I therefore must withdraw this institution's commitment to you. Why is it so hard for people to understand I don't give a damn about their inner preferences, but I care everything about the mission? You're leaving West Point because that mission isn't nearly your top priority, Mr. Totten."

"I *am* leaving now. This is unbelievable," Totten said, beginning to lift off his hard chair.

Pack threw a vice grip on Totten's arm, reeling him back to his chair with a jolt. "You'll go nowhere till I'm finished with you, you haughty peacock. The new moon is rising, so I might have cause to beat the dog shit out of you, say you fell off the chair. You're an embarrassment to everyone who has worn the uniform with civic pride. You rank, I'd say, among the top ten on the selfish scale ever to attend this place. You think even the sun revolves around the personal concerns of Browning Totten. Well, mister, the day I arrived here marked the day your attention-seeking life here came to a crashing conclusion. The distraction you have been will be gone by sunset.

"I'll end on a positive note. You never belonged here. The big embarrassment, maybe a bigger one than you, is whatever system of applicant assessment granted you admittance. Thank you for shining the light on a truly broken admissions system that I will fix. Take it to the bank. As long as I'm here, thank the Lord, we'll never admit anyone as deficient at adapting to Academy standards as you.

"Good luck with your lawsuits, Mr. Totten. Let's see what else you've got in your bag of litigious tricks. One discourteous word or gesture attendant to your departure, and I'll have the MPs escort you to the front gate in bracelets, maybe leg irons, too."

Totten rendered no salute, just rose and walked toward the door.

"Halt, Totten!" Pack said in the voice that said he was not to be ignored.

Totten did halt and turn about.

"One last thing. The dollar value put on your education to this point is somewhere between two and three hundred thousand dollars. The drive has begun to recoup those funds from you. That's all."

♦ ♦ ♦

Later that afternoon, Pack plopped himself into a chair in Thump's office. Shaking his head, Pack said, "What the hell was going on here, Thump? For how long has this been going on? I hope that out of my view, or in it if you'd like, you're thumping some heads. Norther had the inmates running the asylum, no doubt of it."

Thump nodded in solemn concert. Nothing more needed to be said. Both thought, *This thumping won't stop soon. The state of the Academy is worse than we suspected. It's time to gather up all the cowboys down at the bunkhouse, tell them we're pennin' up the herd, then we're saddlin' up to round up ever' damn coyote's been pickin' off our cattle.*

Most college teams treat long-snapping for punts as a specialized activity requiring temporary replacement of the normal center. Jesse Bruccoli had been so steady in performing the task, he just stayed in the game to do the long-snapping. As a Plebe, he snapped one slightly above the punter's leaping attempt to corral the ball, but that was the only time he was responsible for a muffed punt.

Army led Penn State 20–14 till the game's final breaths. Both teams' defenses played with passion and intelligence. There had been just three penalties total for both teams, a tribute to coaching and player discipline. Army was only a mild threat up the middle, owing certainly to the loss of their All-American center, but still topped three hundred yards rushing. With thirty-eight seconds remaining, Army dropped to punt from its own fifteen. Bruccoli's inexperienced replacement had performed creditably as a first-time starter, but now the worst scenario unfolded. The center snap skidded a yard in front of the kicker and skipped around the turf for a second or two. An Army player recovered, but it nonetheless went over on downs to the Nittany Lions at the Army two-yard line. Two plays later, with three seconds remaining, Penn State scored the tying points, then won it with the extra point. The final: 21–20 Penn State.

Army had lost for the first time in eight outings on the season. Being removed from the short list of unbeaten teams was painful, but the confidence and resolve of this resurgent team was not shaken. The trip back to West Point was somber but not mournful. Nobody had mentioned Bruccoli's name, and they would not; they felt they could not. The Corps does not learn details of Honor Committee proceedings. Still, cadets had been able to assemble and piece together the facts with little effort. All who knew Bruccoli would miss him as a valuable football player and as an exceptional leader. But another leader surfaced for an encore also. General Pack did not play favorites and did not play to any special audience. The man kept his eye on the mission and his three guides to action. This man is a real force in our lives, cadets surmised, and he means what he says.

At the Supe's direction, the Sports Information Office had requested all media to be respectful of former cadet Bruccoli. Further, the only comment from West Point was "We have great respect for Jesse Bruccoli. So says General Pack." The two announcers in the press booth refrained from saying Bruccoli's name, but the fools in studio at halftime sprinkled feeble innuendos at the former center's expense.

If a single percentage point of cadets mourned Browning Totten's abrupt dismissal, it wasn't detectable. Pack's direct intervention and decisive action, however, were noted and discussed within the Corps. Again, this man Pack, the HH—take your pick, Heroic Hobo or Hobo Honcho—means what he says, and he is damned sure involved in our lives. We know his face by now, and it looks like Leadership.

The **following Saturday in late November** brought the final home football game of the season. Iowa State, this week's opponent, flooded West Point with supporters numbering in the thousands, most having made the trip from Iowa. They were a patriotic throng, manifestly respectful of West Point traditions, a simple fact not lost on an observant Simon Pack, who at this moment sat in the black box seats reserved for the Reviewing Party. Cloudless, uniformly ultramarine and sunny sky, an excellent day for fanfare and football. The entire Corps would issue forth from sally ports in company ranks to wheel around the Plain in a large loop. They would pass in review before today's Reviewing Officer, the Superintendent.

As the lead company streamed through the sally port, General Pack and his small party stood as one, faced left and proceeded down a short ramp before executing a right turn toward the spot from which the Corps would pass in review. During the moment of the slow pivot to the right, Pack was struck by the flicker of an image that distinguished itself in the crowd. Could it have been? In this situation, in his present capacity, he could not turn his head to follow the object he thought had appeared in his line of sight.

For the remainder of the parade, indeed during most of the remainder of the day, Pack mulled the implications of what he had—or maybe had not—seen. The man appeared thinner than last time they were together, but the face and stature unmistakably belonged to Hard Travelin'. Yet Pack had assumed, and law enforcement and media had reported, that HT was dead. After thinking it over, Pack concluded these things: (1) he would speak with someone senior in the FBI to inquire casually about Ali-Mumen's status, living or dead (2) he would not pass information about the putative sighting on to anyone; his evidence was weak, nonexistent really, and there was no need to alarm everyone without cause. (3) had Ali-Mumen intended mass murder, he would have done so. If it was the man he left for dead in Vegas, it was clear to Pack his target was Pack alone. He knew Hard Travelin', knew what made the man tick.

To have called the FBI on the weekend would have been a tacit admission of concern. So Pack waited until Monday. When the Deputy Director learned Pack had called, he rang the Supe at once. "What's up, General? This is Charlie Ramstedt, Deputy Director."

Pack downplayed the seriousness of the call. "Nothing so urgent I needed a call back from the DD of the FBI. On the other hand, I understand this line needs to be secure. Just would appreciate an update on the man with the several aliases. Did you get him?"

"Look, General," Ramstedt said, "I shouldn't answer that, but will, provided we're clear this conversation is related to no one. Can we agree to that?"

"Of course," Pack replied. "I know when to keep my mouth shut."

"Well," Ramstedt began, "if I say the manhunt is still on, that would be correct, but with diminishing resources each day. The volume of blood he spilt on that garage floor says he was mortally wounded. We checked every clinic and hospital in Greater Vegas, and no one matching his description was treated that night. Maybe his associates picked up the body before we got there, or maybe he wound up in the desert where the animals ate him. But without a blood trail, it's more likely his people snatched the body. Yusef al-Siri was dead, couldn't talk, so they left him. The other associate was dead from the moment you stomped his windpipe. Ali-Mumen was still alive, however barely, so his people grabbed him before we got a chance to interrogate him. We think he's dead. Why are you suddenly so interested?"

"Write it off as idle curiosity. Close-quarter combat killings, you don't erase them from memory that easily. Just been thinking about it again recently," Pack said.

"You sure that's all you have to say?" Ramstedt asked.

"One more thing. I was convinced al-Siri was the escapee, as I told all the interrogators, yet no one disputed me. I'm just learning for the first time it was Ali-Mumen who got away, or was whisked from the garage. I think I was owed that information. Then there's the fact that every official in the chain happily told the media Ali-Mumen was mortally wounded. What the hell were you people up to? Why the lie?"

"Damn, General, I really thought you knew. I really did. I'll go this far with you: I opposed the untruth, and the Director did as well. The White House directed the fabrication, telling the FBI and CIA it was a strategic maneuver to draw out Al Qaeda on other fronts. Said it was a national security matter better handled from their end. Personally, I believe they lied to somehow make themselves look better, even if they had nothing to do with the takedown."

Pack said, "OK, I accept that. I was just curious, whereupon I asked a question or two, whereupon I am surprised. Honesty is always appreciated. I'd be grateful for a discreet statement of closure when you reach it. Thanks for the time," Pack signed off.

Chapter Seventeen

The Spike

"The unfailing formula for production of morale is patriotism, self-respect, discipline, and self-confidence within a military unit, joined with fair treatment and merited appreciation from without...It will quickly wither and die if soldiers come to believe themselves the victims of indifference or injustice on the part of their government, or of ignorance, personal ambition, or ineptitude on the part of their military leaders."

—Douglas MacArthur,
Annual Report of the Chief of Staff of the Army, 1933

The second week of December began. A fresh snow had fallen on hard, gelid ground. A funeral was underway at the West Point Cemetery. It was one of the fortunate ones, an old soldier who had lived a life to its natural end. Some of his new partners inside the enclosure of the low, thick stone walls were Brigadier General Sylvanus Thayer, the Founder of the Military Academy; George Washington Goethals, the chief engineer of the Panama Canal, called the biggest engineering project of all time,; George Armstrong Custer, he of the Last Stand; Glenn Davis, the 1946 Heisman winner; General William C. Westmoreland; General Norman Schwarzkopf and his father, Major General Herbert N. Schwarzkopf. Seventeen Medals of Honor are represented among these tombs. "Taps" echoed plaintively through the canyons of West Point's passageways.

Also beside this newest resident of the hallowed cemetery is Colonel Earl "Red" Blaik, one of the most successful football coaches ever. If he could see where Army football had come to this year, he might—he was not given to praise—mouth a few words of congratulations. It was the most remarkable turnaround in West Point's sports history, from 3–9 to 11–1. The Army team, with its mules, mighty Hannibal leading the way, had written a treatise on discipline and teamwork, will and intelligent application of force. There was the head coach, Les Sumner, who demonstrated how a leader sometimes gains power by giving it up. And Bob Nasby, the conditioning coach who made the boys puke. And Ed Pillings, the head trainer, who had decided that he and Kathy would retire to Puget Sound a winner. There was the walk-on, D.E. Stacy, the improbable quarterback and play-caller. And the Bear. And Gary Cline, who just days ago did receive the highest academic honor in college football, the William V. Campbell Trophy. These gallant lads had numbered Air Force and Navy among their victims. A reputable Bowl game would be their reward three weeks hence. The only way this season could have ended in sweeter fashion would have been for Jesse Bruccoli to have won the Rimington. And not to be forgotten were the full cast of coaches in other sports who lent their voices to the Corps's chorus of support. It was estimated that at the daily practices the week of the Navy game, a thousand cadets, virtually every one available, showed up to express their pride in their football squad.

At some instinctual level, most cadets knew the toughening process, still underway and not always pleasant, was the product of the HH's dogged focus on mission. The energy in the classrooms was higher, professors seemed better prepared, and the acting Dean popped into classrooms of every department with regularity. Colonel Kauza was still unearthing pockets of resistance, but he ground them down. For instance, the head of English and philosophy had told him, "We're into the third year of a groundbreaking effort—we meaning myself and a couple of officers in my department—namely, building the definitive concordance to the works of Honoré de Balzac. We are really proud of it, and by the end of the year, we'll have completed this massive contribution to literary scholarship."

"Sir," Kauza stated coolly, "I admit to no knowledge of the skills and effort to create such a thing. But I believe I must ask the question General Pack would ask: Why would you not be doing this work on an American rather than a French author? We are an American institution, and what you are doing seems to me to fall under Pack's category of eccentric initiative. Do we have a point, Jack?"

"You have a point. Teaching some French lit, I think we agree, is fine, but we should in a voluntary project of this type be drawing attention to our native literature. If you'll let me reach the end of this three-year project, I can promise we'll find a major American author who should benefit from similar treatment," the department head said.

"OK, Jack," the acting Dean replied, "I believe we've accomplished a reconciliation. Mission, mission, mission. Incidentally, if there's any doubt, I am convinced to the *n*th degree that your department's role in building the cadet is at least as important as the chemistry department's role. Patriots come in all shapes and sizes, and they exist in countless walks of American life. The hardware store owner's role, the factory floor worker's role, the farmer's role, the medical doctor's role can be just as vital as the soldier's. Most of us military people have immense devotion to our native land, but none of us would ever impugn the devotion many of our fellow civilian citizens have for it also. At the same time, many think as I that the American societal fabric has been rent, but our small jobs, yours and mine, everyone at the Academy, is to begin to stitch it back together in our little corner of the country.

"Appreciate the time, Jack," Kauza said in taking his leave.

♦ ♦ ♦

Pack ordered Duck not to take part in the last two road marches to Buckner. The captain had covered the problem as long as he could, but he eventually reached a point that merely to walk was infeasible. Pack made him remove the prosthesis and show him what condition the leg was in. The stump was an ugly mass of lesions and ulcerations, and what Pack instantly recognized as cellulitis had set in. The Supe called an ambulance from Keller Army Community Hospital. Duck could get better and have a fresh go at walking, but he needed IVs and good wound care right now.

He had lain in a hospital bed two weeks. Pack visited often. He had no plans to find a replacement for Duck. *He won't be up and around much for a while longer*, Pack thought on one such visit, *so I'll put his mind to work.*

Last week, Pack had handed over the imposing set of files Kathy Pillings had so meticulously prepared. Duck studied as if for a serious acting part, which was indeed what it was. The files were under lock and key with Duck, whose formidable assignment was to play each cast member on the "anti-West Point" Board of Visitors. An ambulance with a medical attendant delivered Duck to Pack's study for two hours on each of three evenings. He sat in a special rig with his leg elevated higher than heart and IVs still adrip.

Duck attempted to adopt the persona of each member and hammered the applicable talking points relentlessly. Pack commented little, took no notes, and only a few times requested clarification. Duck worked through the task with his usual industriousness and pertinacity. Pack thanked Duck on the final evening and said to the young officer this had not been make-work. The utter truth was the time spent in the primary with Duck achieved much the same effect as MacArthur's standing appointment at that downtown Manila theater. It amounted to a psychic housecleaning, an event the nature of which let his mind migrate to a secluded place where he might effortlessly assemble his responses to these people who would descend with malicious intent in under forty-eight hours.

The official Federal Notice of the meeting stated that although the meeting would be open to the public, anyone planning to attend must have a valid government photo ID. The irony was delicious; the administration that would not allow photo IDs as a prerequisite to voting demanded one for this meeting. Why? *Could it be that these people of the Board believe their importance should offer them special protections? Whatever,* Pack thought, *it's ironic nonetheless.* Maybe he should hold them to the letter of the law, require them to produce the photo ID before granting access. No, that would be petty. But if the tables were turned, they wouldn't hesitate one Montana second to demand he produce his.

Wednesday, December 19: The Supe was at his residence, about to go out the door, when the taciturn Mrs. Bridgewater said, "General, there's some sort of iron spike laying on the back porch, right by the door. Should it be there? Or maybe you put it there?"

Pack smiled and said softly, "I didn't, but I'm sure there's a good reason for it to be there. Certainly nothing to be worried about. But forget that, Elsa. You just reminded me about my Christmas gift to you. I don't want to see you until the first weekday of the new year. I want you out of here at noon today. I'll have something else for you before you leave. Just wait until I get back."

He's here, Pack thought. *He has moved right onto my turf, damn near into my home. The bastard just dropped off a calling card.* It was a rail spike.

He wanted to remove Mrs. Bridgewater from any potential line of fire, literal or figurative. *Send her home until I get this problem resolved—and I will.* He changed his mind about leaving his housekeeper alone in the residence. He would stay here and figure out his next steps. *Let's review the Academy's physical security: what I see is strong external control at all the entrance gates. To gain entry using a road is hard to do. Internal security is weak, because essentially West Point is a college campus. The rail spike is the key...of course, why didn't I see it before? The bastard used the rails as a mode of travel for years...he had hobo'd his way here.*

Pack phoned Golden. "Chief, get me the best set of Night Vision Goggles you can round up, one with a fresh battery and a spare. I need them by midafternoon. Don't say who you need them for and don't ask me why I need them. Put them in a laundry bag and carry them over yourself."

Golden knew something unusual was afoot, but was in the dark about particulars.

It had been no trick of the eye. He had seen Ali-Mumen. HT had come to kill Pack face-to-face. Last time, Pack took the initiative by preparing a defensive position. This time, he aimed to be entirely on the offensive; he would go after his former rail mate, the terrorist leader. Pack knew where hobos hung out around train stations. Tonight he would begin the prowl, Force Recon style.

By midnight he was dressed ninja fashion. Face blackened, black stocking cap, camouflaged night vision goggles, a six-inch blade sheathed in a black scabbard, and the loaded nine-millimeter he retained from his previous retirement.

The CSX River Line runs along the Hudson and looks up the bluffs toward most of the Academy structures. A tunnel of 2,640 feet, a nice symmetrical one-half mile in length, runs under Thayer Hall, and was bored through the rock facing to avoid a steep uphill climb. On one end of the tunnel rests a fashionable old stone train station and the South Dock and to the north end sits a power station and numerous ball fields. Trees and shrubbery have grown from the crevices in the rock outcroppings lining the west side of the railroad tracks.

Pack started a methodical scan of the terrain along the railroad by starting at the north end, then working south. He covered it thoroughly, including the palisades north and south of the tunnel. Detritus dotted the tunnel, so clearly hobos had sought its shelter. Before wrapping up the search near the train station as the sun rose, a new thought intruded: *He isn't here now. He is coming and going, probably cloaking himself in the New York City jungles. But I do know when he'll be back.*

Chapter Eighteen

Holy Night

> And there were shepherds living out in the fields nearby,
> keeping watch over their flocks at night. **9** An angel of
> the Lord appeared to them, and the glory of the Lord
> shone around them, and they were terrified. **10** But the
> angel said to them, "Do not be afraid. I bring you good
> news that will cause great joy for all the people. **11** Today
> in the town of David a Savior has been born to you; he is
> the Messiah, the Lord. **12** This will be a sign to you: You
> will find a baby wrapped in cloths and lying in a manger."
>
> —Luke 2: 8-12, NIV

The Academy grounds were effectively deserted. Cadets and most faculty had gone away for their Christmas leaves two days ago. Christmas Eve morning brought with it a gentle but steady snowfall that continued peacefully throughout the day.

After finding that spike five days ago, Pack recalled thinking that spotting Ali-Mumen in the parade crowd had not been a trick of the eye. While trekking back to Quarters 100 following the futile effort to locate the terrorist, he had another "eye" word come to mind: *coup d'oeil.* It was rather the opposite of *trompe d'oeil,* or trick of the eye. The former word taken from the French means, roughly, strategic intuition. An Inward Eye that sees the unseen. Pack's Inward Eye saw Ali-Mumen striking tomorrow, on the Christian High Holy Day. He could picture the terrorist thinking about the beauty of what he presumed he was about to achieve. Killing an infidel on any day is good for an Islamic radical, but killing a real Christian infidel on Christmas Day is perfection. Pack was inside Mumen's head.

Pack was so confident he knew Mumen's next move that he did not demur when Laura and Alexandra prodded him to give them a walking tour of West Point. The man he once knew as Hard Travelin' wouldn't shoot him, wouldn't attempt to kill him in any impersonal fashion. It would be by his hand. Indeed, his daughters were at greater risk inside the residence than with him out in the open, Pack figured.

Pack's girls had never visited West Point. They got together and decided to spend four days with their father during Christmas. They looked forward to the Christmas celebration tomorrow in the Cadet Chapel. They were also looking forward to a comfortable Christmas Eve in the cozy Quarters 100. Each wanted to be the fire starter in the spacious fireplace. Pack disappointed them with news that he had to be out for the evening attending to urgent business. They did not understand, but respected him enough not to ask questions. "Please deadbolt the doors once I've left, OK?" They did.

Colonel Dahl had—at Pack's instruction—arranged for MP surveillance during his absence.

Pack went to his secondary, where he had stowed his ninja gear. As darkness fell on West Point, Pack went into stealth mode and disappeared into the shadows leading down to the old train station.

Within daylight's distance of the rail tunnel's south entrance, Elvin Eugene Hawkshaw sat shielded from the snow and warmed himself with a small twig fire. *Don't need a big fire, cause I won't be here much longer. The man was bold to go out walking like that this afternoon.* The terrorist could've brought along some of his men, but he wanted this to be him and Pack. *Kind of nice of everyone to vacate this place to make it easier for me to get to him. Gotta lot of work in front of me tonight, though. Pack complimented me on my sod-laying, but he'd be damn proud of what I'm about to do. Too bad he won't be alive to see me fireman-carry his heavy lifeless frame all the way up the high ground to that cursed church. The infidels coming in all pious tomorrow morning will see his frozen mass right there at the top of the steps in front of the big door. By which time I'll have caught the morning train, or maybe even be all the way back to Gotham. Boys will see I still got what it takes. Then I'm gonna lead them on the Big One, which will be Semtex compared to the 9-11 firecracker.*

Hard Travelin' stroked the cut-down spike as if it were a newborn. Smiling, touching it, fondling it actually. It was the same one Pack had plunged into HT's gut. *Blow would've killed any other man,* he thought with a mixture of pride and hatred. *Count on it: Mount Montana ain't gonna see the sun come up.*

The snow persisted in its descent, layering by the hour. In the stillness abetted by the snow's muffling, West Point seemed vacant of any life form. Only a few twinkles could be observed from serene residences across the Hudson through the night snow. The afternoon train had completed its run several hours ago. The next scheduled through was 6:00 a.m. With the Corps absent, Thayer Hall sat in gothic gloom, not a light from any room. The meager light from the high ground above the old train station emanated from two stanchions in the Thayer rooftop parking area. Lampposts on South Dock and the train station cast but weak, shallow pools of light.

Pack had to follow the road down to the south entrance. Going down the cliffs under these conditions could be done by rappelling, but he did not have the gear. He clung to the bottom of the cliffs as he followed the snaky road down. The snow attenuated the sounds of walking, but also left distinct tracks he could not erase.

Task one was to determine if HT was still in the tunnel. Pack knew HT *could* be somewhere up on the cliffs, but that was so unreasonable he discarded the idea. *He'll stay in the tunnel until it's time*, Pack thought. It was pitch black around the tunnel. He flicked on the Night Vision device thirty feet from the entrance. He saw footprints that were only vaguely visible now. Big prints from a size 13 or 14 boot. His scan inside the tunnel didn't take long. There sat Hard Travelin', clearly his profile, bent over as if he was tying his boots or eating a last meal before setting out.

Before Pack decided to enter the tunnel or lay in wait outside, he could see HT begin to move toward the south entrance. Pack backed away swiftly but quietly, trying to walk in the footprints he had just made. He ducked behind a boulder a few steps away.

HT emerged from the tunnel with force, unconcerned with being detected. Pack could see the vapors of HT's exhalations and hear the crunch of his footsteps. Then...*silence*.

In a speck of time, Pack understood personal combat was about to commence. HT had picked up Pack's footprints, and was making up his mind what to do about the observation. But Pack stepped out before HT moved, and said, "Looking for me?"

"Yes, I am, Mister Mount Montana. I am indeed. Where's your back-up? Got the MPs up the road?"

"No need for that, HT. I take care of the small stuff on my own. What about you? More AQ lurking there in the tunnel?" Pack asked.

"You know that wouldn't be right. My boys wouldn't want me if I couldn't handle you. It's like it was meant to be, I guess, Montana. Just you and me. I gotta tell you somethin' before we get at it, though. You said you loved my sod-layin', said you respected hell outta me for the work I produced...well, that was nothin' beside what'll be required for me to carry your heavy ass up to the Chapel a little later on. Just wanted you to hear that before you die."

No more was said. Pack slid off the night goggles and dropped them beside him. Next he unholstered the nine mill and held it for HT to see, then dropped it onto the snowy ground beside the goggles. Pack took a step toward HT. The Al Qaeda leader emitted a snort and pulled the cut-down spike from behind his back with the same flair he had in the garage. He swung it in an overhanded motion, like a catcher making a peg to second base, as if trying to rip Pack from sternum to pelvis. And this hard carbon spike was capable of doing just that. Except that Pack, enormous as he was, and as slow as one might figure him to be, was much quicker than HT—and he had seen the arc of HT's movement as it was still forming. The sharp tip caught the meat of Pack's deltoid, tearing off a shard of flesh. For less than a second, it hurt wickedly, and had knocked Pack to his back. Now HT held it like a plunger, the plumber about to plunge the guts from Pack. Pack kicked hard, catching the side of the cut-down, causing HT to ricochet facedown to the ground to Pack's right. Before either could get up, both had a grip on the L-shaped head. It was a tug-of-war on the ground, spit spewing from HT's mouth, fire in the whites of his eyes. He head-butted Pack in the nose as blood burst forth. Faces inches apart, HT dropped his head and bit ferociously into the back of Pack's neck. Pack tensed, making it harder for HT to keep the clinch. He dipped his face forward, then snapped his head back, catching HT's nose with a head-butt of his own. Both men were protected from pain by the wild throb of adrenalin. In one mighty surge, Pack wrested the spike from HT's grasp, and looking through blurry eyes, rammed it with all his strength into HT's heart. It was over. This time he did have a mobile phone, and it did work. He called Golden. "Get the Provost Marshal, tell him to secure the body at the tunnel near South Dock, then call Charlie Ramstedt, FBI Deputy Director. Tell Ramstedt that Ali-Mumen wasn't dead, but he is now. Then have some HAZMAT guys come down and clean up the mess. I want to walk back up alone."

It was just after midnight, Christmas now. His loyal chief, Colonel Dahl, was waiting in the secondary. "Just let me get cleaned up, Golden. Stop your damn gawking. Don't call for anybody, don't even think about it. While I'm showering up, call off the MPs over at the residence. When I come out, you can treat me with the Aid Kit that's around here somewhere. You're a Marine, aren't you, Colonel? Sterilize the wound and tape some gauze on the old man, all right? We Jarheads can sometimes be pretty damn capable, can't we?"

Laura and Alex were in bed. He didn't wake them. He went into the kitchen, made coffee, and just sat there, so many thoughts rushing through his brain he thought he couldn't piece two of them into a coherent expression. He went upstairs around seven o'clock to get dressed for church. A glance into the mirror reflected an ugly man, a very ugly man.

The three of them took seats in the front pew, the space reserved for the Supe. Pack was especially grateful for the front row today, as it allowed his countenance to be a lesser distraction. Most had stared involuntarily as he entered. Congregants whispered, even the most reverential, and the Cadet Chaplain himself did a double-take as he took his position. The massive pipe organ bellowed in commencing the service. The opening hymn was "Silent Night, Holy Night."

Gary Cline was at home with his mother Betty in Big Stone Gap, Virginia. Gary was in the kitchen preparing their sumptuous Christmas dinner, at which they would presently be joined by Gary's sister Nancy and her large family. Betty had been cooking all morning, but was getting a few relaxing minutes as she watched a cable news channel in the den. "Gary," she called out, "they're saying something about West Point on the news. Come look!"

Cline let the wooden spoon drop in the mixing bowl, and got to the tv in time to see a still photo of the Supe exiting the Cadet Chapel. Since nearly everyone carries a camera, who knew who might've snapped it? That Pack was unaware of being photographed was evident. "Holy hell!—sorry, Mom—let's hear what's happened to him." Pack's nose looked to be broken, his face was grotesquely swollen, his eyes reduced to slits. A white wound dressing peeked out of his dress uniform shirt collar.

"Mom," Gary said, "let me tell you about this man, but before I do, I need to say, that's the face I want."

Those cadets attuned to the goings-on in the world learned of it that Christmas day. In the minds of most cadets the HH was approaching mythic status. What exactly had happened? The newspeople were vague on details, but most were saying it had been "an unholy night" at West

Point. Damn, how the media loved this Pack! He could keep them employed forever, trying to unpack (one reporter actually said that, un-Pack) all the mysteries that cropped up everywhere he traveled. There was general agreement the dead man was Ali-Mumen, but they had already reported on his death months ago. Somebody lied, that's for damned sure.

Pack watched a little of the coverage for a single reason: he wanted to know who leaked the dead man's identity. It hadn't come from anyone at West Point. Pack guessed it was a nugget let drop from the FBI. Either the Director or Deputy Director Ramstedt was tired of the lies. Maybe both. If pressed, they might even say the original story of Mumen's demise was dictated by the White House. In any case, the President could claim plausible deniability and a specific source would probably never be identified.

Generals Green and Pembrook spoke with Pack, but merely to say they had his back and would support in any way they could. There would be no investigations from the Pentagon, at least from the uniformed side.

The President was in a luxury resort for his holiday, but his aides briefed him on the matter and got to work immediately to form an answer to the question of why the Vegas death of Mumen was apparently untrue. President Rozan once more burned with fury and hatred toward the impertinent General Pack. The President was thinking he had no use for a military officer whose primary mission was to get his grotesque face in the news.

Chapter Nineteen

Gunfight At The Overlook

The Board of Visitors arrived Tuesday afternoon, on this the first full week of the new year. The plushest rooms at Hotel Thayer, the only such place on Post, had been set aside for them. Most of the fifteen and their traveling staff had checked in by early afternoon in order to take advantage of the tony Thayer bar with its cheap prices, certainly by major metropolitan standards. They would spend the entire afternoon and evening alone, then would go from one Department to another to take briefings tomorrow.

President Rozan's staff referred to this group as a CODEL-plus. This meant a Congressional delegation plus other Board members. The designation CODEL-plus was important because tethered to it was an array of federal regulations establishing minimum acceptable levels of such things as accommodations, which could be no less than a junior suite of at least three hundred square feet, for instance. They paraded into the Thayer as VIPs, which most of the fifteen and their staffs well and truly believed they were. An additional reason to get there early, if you were male, was there were ten women and only five men among the Board members, and two-thirds of the staff were women. *Whoa, boy,* thought John Righetti, one of the six Presidential appointees, *Gonna be some good times in the ole Thayer tonight*. If they played the night away and couldn't remember their own names in the morning, who cared? The only thing these one-track-minded military guys would think if the Visitors nodded off once or twice was, *Wow, these dedicated public servants/savants carry a heavy burden, don't they?* All they had to do was listen, nod wisely, and ask a question or two. No, scratch that part about asking a question. Nothing was really required of them. The majority of these people already had their parts of the report written, so what anyone told them during this trip was of no import. *And,* they thought proudly, *this report goes directly to the President, no intermediaries. With just fifteen signature blocks and signatures.*

The venerable hotel's manager had gotten another bid—demand, really—for VIP status within twenty-four hours of the event's start. The manager explained every room was occupied, a thousand apologies to your boss. In the wink of an eye, an angry man's voice screamed into the mouthpiece, "I am your boss, dammit! I am Secretary of the Army Fitz Spitshugh, and if I say I want a room, you better damn well ask if I want the MacArthur or the Eisenhower Suite. I've looked at your website, and now you know who you're talkin' to. Let's chop-chop and ante up. I'm a busy man, hoss."

"Sir," the hotel manager said, "if your assistant will leave a number, I'll see what arrangement is possible and return with a reply as soon as I can. At this late hour, relative to the Board of Visitors' meeting commencement, I mean, this will require some careful manipulation. All right, sir?"

"OK, but listen up, hoss: I didn't get to be where I am by being patient. Know what I'm sayin'? Chop-chop." In the end, civilian eminence Fitz Spitshugh got his way, as was generally the case. Several staffers not yet beyond their midtwenties were sufficiently incensed they would have to double up in rooms that one remarked, "Ain't too special anyways." *Just gag me to death. This sharing (said as 'shearing') might blockade, if you know what I mean, like, my love life this evenin'.*

The mild-mannered Dahl, known as an honest dealer, clean thinker, and fair player, had his own understanding of Napoleon's directed telescope. In that the Supe had appointed him as chief escort for the Visitors' first thirty-six hours, he could not be seen in the Hotel Thayer bar. But he could politely ask a few of the lower-ranking of his staff to amble on down there in civvies and keep an ear to the ground. He picked three people to learn what they could, two males, one female, all captains. Dahl laid out the rules: No alcohol consumption, but you may give the appearance of it. Know their names by their faces, to which ends the captains had to pass a flash-card test. Don't try to find out their backgrounds; being ignorant of your subject is an asset on this job. Don't lie, but be vague if they happen to engage you. Don't let on that you three are acquainted. The one Dahl expected the most from was Tom Leary, a JAG who definitely was Dahl's best trial lawyer. He was like Peter Falk's homicide detective Lieutenant Columbo in getting defendants to give up information, though with Leary there was no contrivance or affectation. He was born a weird dude.

Leary enjoyed a smoke whenever and wherever he could light up. He'd never been inside the Thayer, so his first thought on signing up for this extracurricular activity was whether smoking was allowed. Unmarried, thirty years old, NYC resident all the way through City University of New York and Columbia Law, drinker, tough-talker, this fellow was born for the courtroom. But Tommy Leary was also pragmatic. If the rules said no drinking and no smoking, no problem. He entered the bar around 4:00 p.m. and thought it was safe to assume most of the bar patrons at this hour were CODEL-plussers. It was easy to break down who was who in gross terms. The A-listers sat at tables and expected underlings to pop to attention whenever they wanted to show off, which was often. As the hours passed and got on to around 8:00 p.m., though, Leary figured formalities would fade and serious preening would start to be on display. Lots of seat-shifting would probably happen.

Leary claimed a two-top in good eavesdropping distance of a ten-seat table. Nine of the ten were occupied. He ran the flash cards through his head, and in deliberate fashion, used two bar napkins as paper on which to write the names of these people. If anyone was watching him, he might've been Euler developing a new theorem, so hunched over and intense was he. He wrote: *Kaneesha Griffin, Felicia Ramirez, Gaye Razor, John Righetti, Bill Hartz, Jason Dixon, Judith Bucks, Mary Loosty*, and *Elizabeth Leonard*. The first four were Presidential appointees; the second three, House delegates; and the last two, Senators. They seemed universally aware of Pack, as he was the main subject of their talk.

"I spoke with Sharon Locke before leaving Washington," Ramirez allowed, in high gloat at having been summoned by the senior Presidential advisor, "and she feels, frankly, that this Simon Pack is out of control, shouldn't have been sent here in the first place. Said he seems to think he knows best about everything. Diversity is important to Sharon, I can tell you that, and she feels there is a deaf ear to that particular concern from Pack."

"Dear," Griffin interjected, "I saw Senior Advisor Locke as well. She's 'not at all sanguine about the long-term viability' of this institution, is how she put it, I believe. You think about the life we could inject into some of our social programs—Women, Infants, and Children, for instance—with the money that's wasted here every year. All we do is rile the rest of the world up with jingoists from this place."

Hartz laughed. He was the father of the cheekily named TESTES Act. "Anyone here know about the Thayer system of education these strait-jacketed people use? They test them in some way nearly every day, in every subject. Enough with the tests a'reddy!" bellowed the Long Beach buffoon. "Let 'em learn a little, wudja? Ever thought of joining the twentieth century, West Point?"

Hartz may have been into the bottle a tad early, in that he found this witticism riotously funny, laughing until his damn sides hurt.

"Billy," Senator Kelly Brandywine said sweetly, making her grand entrance and claiming the final seat, "it is the twenty-first century. Thought I'd let you know." Hartz found this riotously funny also, and thus began another bellyroll of guffawing. It was good even to be the butt of a joke by the formidable Ms. Brandywine. Everyone was positively delighted to see Senator Brandywine and told her so.

Kelly Brandywine was the biggest star in the CODEL-plus. Three years ago, she had defeated a three-term incumbent, and instantly became her party's newest heroine and expert spokeswoman on everything from the Iranian nuclear program to Boko Haram to fissures in the polar ice cap. Nothing, absolutely nothing, lay beyond this woman's ken. And so, at this table, there was obvious deference to this Venusian goddess, whom some progressive writers had begun to call "the smartest woman in the world." If mainline members of the media found such a claim to be a little over the top, they weren't heard from.

Truth was, Brandywine was considerably short of an inch deep on nearly every topic of real concern to Americans. Maybe a half-centimeter would be closer to the mark. She said the same things on the same topics all the time. She had memorized the first lines of every sentence in all those campaign briefing books. Nobody seemed to have caught on yet. She could say "START Treaty" without the faintest understanding of its terms. Washington is all about *appearing* to know what you're talking about, she realized right away. Last year, when watching the Oscars on TV, she smiled, thinking she might win if there were such an award for Washington pols. *I'm a better actor than Meryl Streep and Bobby Duvall put together*, she began to think. She had confidence now and would only get better with time.

Senator Brandywine's initial entrance onto the grand stage of national politics had been almost accidental. She'd said something innocuous, boring, and fatuous about sexual harassment to a moronic audience at a third-rate college in her state, and as she herself was about to yawn metaphorically, she received thunderous applause and clucks and clacks. Electricity ran up her spine. She smiled a great gaping smile, the ennui gone, and she let loose an impassioned oration she thought afterward hadn't been witnessed since, oh, say, the Scopes Monkey Trial. Then-candidate Kelly Brandywine imagined, *I have stumbled upon the key that will open the kingdom to me, perhaps all the way to the Presidency.* For the time being, she was content to do President Keith Rozan's bidding in defanging this Military Academy. *And*, she mulled thoughtfully, *every accusation I'll throw at them probably is true, but who cares? The ends—bringing peace on Earth, feeding every hungry stomach in America, achieving perfect social and economic equality—are so majestic that any means—lying, distorting the truth, robbing Peter to pay Paul—are justified. What is to be noted is that my party, more specifically, my followers, care more about those in need than the others.* Passion talks; reason walks.

So it was with little effort that Ms. Brandywine overnight became Ms. War on Women, Wendy One-Note. Everywhere she turned, she saw males harassing females, especially here. "Maybe I should share an observation I had on the way from the gate to this *god-awful outdated hotel.* I saw those drab, gray uniforms, and I saw repression—of those poor cadets' spirits, their intellects, their freedoms, and...their sexual impulses. They are repressed, make no mistake about it, and what happens when you're repressed? That's right; you strike out on your prey. This place creates predators! Little Timmy Timid who's never kissed a girl in his uptight life comes here and becomes Conrad Conquistador! I shudder to think what it must be like to be a female in this Gray Hell. I'm right, and every one of you knows I am. I want you at this table to think hard about the long-term viability of this institution."

The meticulous listener he had trained himself to be, Leary made a note: *Identical words: long-term viability of this institution.* The two speakers hadn't been in the room at the same time. If the first speaker picked this up from Sharon Locke, the second probably did, too. Leary had resided in liberal bastions all his life, and he never felt love for any conservative cause, but he was a fair man. The only reason he was a JAG officer and not practicing in civilian life was to pay back law school expenses. But the truth was, Leary had gotten to like this place, really admire it. He didn't look at it as liberal or conservative. It was to him just a well-ordered mini-society where merit mattered. Many times he had mused that if all of America ran like West Point, our society would be close to perfect. So all this stuff he was hearing from the adjacent table was crap, and these people were about as informed on West Point as a box of rocks. He would like to speak back to these know-it-alls, but that could not happen today. He listened more.

John Righetti said, "I am seriously concerned too many white men are leading combat units. Sociologists are very concerned about this fact. Did you know only ten percent of active duty officers are black? Here's another shocker: Two years ago, two hundred thirty-eight cadets chose infantry, ground combat, as a branch, yet only seven were black."

Bucks admonished Righetti quietly. "Better be careful throwing that argument around. Branch selection is a matter of choice, you know?"

Ms. Brandywine had not lost her place. "If you don't mind, I wasn't finished. I think it is wise for you, my fellow members, to go into this meeting with a plan. And so—"

Leonard, a Senator who was more than a little jealous of the attention Brandywine received, interrupted with modest petulance. "We *have* a plan, Kelly. The senior advisor spoke to each of us, I am led to believe. I think we know the positions we are to take."

Representative Bucks, perhaps the most thoughtful person at the table, surmised that Senator Leonard mentioning this open secret was politically stupid. Who knew who might be listening? That guy nursing a drink at the little table close by was within earshot, but he looked to be engrossed in some personal problem of great moment, so she shrugged him off. Anyway, Bucks thought, *Wake up, Elizabeth, we've gotta be more careful.*

Brandywine had to salvage her position as the Alpha Female here, indeed, the Alpha Visitor, so she jumped back into the discussion. "I am telling you, my study shows beyond doubt women at the US Military Academy must survive in a chilly climate. They have no defenders except us, ladies and gentlemen. We have no higher calling than to protect the welfare of the victims in our society. And in this male-dominated culture, West Point I'm talking about, there is furious, aggressive emphasis on masculinity and violence, and we must suppress it. No, I'll go a step further: We have to stamp it out. When we finish doing what we have to do, there may be no West Point left standing. Regrettable, maybe, but this Hobo Pack or Mount Montana, as some of his adorers call him, had it within his power to get a handle on the problem, but he has done nothing. I'd say he's moved outrageously in the opposite direction. Title IX means nothing to this man, seems to me. There is some chance, I have to tell you, my fellows here, that I might have no choice but to recommend his firing once we're done here. Of course, you're all free to follow your conscience," Brandywine said, clearly implying she was the real leader of this delegation, and everyone knew it.

Leary was practiced in the art of concealing his intentions and covering his tracks. But at this moment, he felt challenged. He understood why Dahl had sent him on this unusual assignment, and his main challenge was to figure out how to "burst capture" the bounty this table was providing. Like the National Security Agency can do with voluminous electronic transmissions, stuff them into a microsecond's space, then play them back at normal speed later, on demand.

♦ ♦ ♦

Not to be forgotten were the five Visitors not aligned with the table of ten. They included the actual, officially designated Chairman of the Board Bob Fairchild, a prosaic name for a seemingly prosaic, albeit wealthy man. Fairchild was a mall developer of national renown. He had graduated West Point more than thirty years earlier. He had been chosen as a shill for the President in that he appeared to have no strong political preferences, and he made no financial contributions to either party. But unknown to everyone on the Board, Fairchild took this job very seriously. If the President were aware of how seriously, he would never have appointed the man.

Fairchild had nodded politely to the President's senior advisor, listened with care, made notes, and received and processed correspondence from each member of the Board. He tried to maintain an open mind. Fairchild accepted no fee for this job he regarded as a duty to nation. He paid his own way because he could. Even the room at this hotel was being paid from his own pocket. Nobody could buy Bob Fairchild. This wasn't a social event to him.

He made a list of the talking points each Visitor and the senior advisor had put forward. Then, over the course of months, he read on these subjects until his eyes were sore. He compiled so many notes, he had material enough for a couple of doctoral dissertations. On each subject, he formed his own conclusion in more or less the same way he adjudicated the efficacy, scope, and timing of his business decisions. Fairchild also was acutely aware of the importance of holding his cards close to his vest, which is why he sat alone at the bar, sipping Diet 7-Up with a lemon slice. *Don't show your cards until the right moment.* If his Visitor mates approached him, he was prepared to claim an urgent cause to return to his room. In his periphery, he observed a figure enter the revolving door from the outside. It was Fitz Spitshugh. Time for that retreat to his room.

Chapter two, same story. Just as Spitshugh had uprooted someone from a hotel room, now he caused a shifting of seats to accommodate him at the big table. He asked Leary if he would move the unused chair from his table over to the big table. Fitz Spitshugh looked expectantly at Leary, eyebrows raised, letting everyone at the big table understand he had made a demand and it would be met. Showing he was more than a power match for anyone at the table. Leary was New York-pissed, but he held himself in check and did as asked. *Get it yourself, you ego-inflated eff,*" Leary was thinking, but if he decked this bag of wind, his reason for being here would have been negated. *Live to fight another day*, Leary said to himself. Leary's courtroom training had rescued him again. Leary wondered who this interloper was; he hadn't been a face in the flash cards.

"How we doin', team?" the suddenly jovial Spitshugh asked. A couple of people around the table hadn't known he was coming and indeed couldn't have picked him from a lineup. "Apologies for not gettin' around to you who reside outside the Beltway, but as Secretary of the Army, I keep a tight schedule, as you would imagine. You folks have any questions for me?"

No matter who surrounded him, Spitshugh's overbearing manner tended to produce uneasy silences. It took a moment for most newcomers to register the extent of his rudeness and pomposity. His behavior, in fact, was so startlingly boorish that many swiftly accepted him as comic-book harmless, like Tom and Jerry setting explosive traps for each other. A man this loggerheaded could surely be outwitted with little effort.

It was up to the levelheaded Congresswoman Judith Bucks to turn the table on Lord Spitshugh, as he seemed to think of himself. "There are a couple considerations in play here, Mr. Spitshugh. First, those of us from DC would like to thank you for the wise counsel you previously extended," she said, even though there was none. "You were probably the first to alert us to the Secretary of Defense's thinking about how we might steer this meeting. Second, however, is the unfortunate fact that you are not a member of the Board of Visitors. I think, if I may boldly advise a Secretary of the Army, it might be time for you to revert to silent partner status. Just advice kindly rendered, please understand. Also, we do have a chairman, Mr. Bob Fairchild, to whom you probably ought to announce your desires and intentions with respect to our meeting. OK, sir?"

Fitz Spitshugh liked the respectful manner in which Ms. Bucks addressed him. She gave him his due. "Yes, that's a fine idea. Where is this Sparefield?"

"All I can say from a look around is Mr. *Fairchild* is not in this room at present, but Reception can assist, I'm sure," Bucks said. Spitshugh clomped away.

"Thank goodness, he's gone," Righetti said. The time was getting on to eight, and he wanted this business discussion to end so he could throw back some real alcohol. As it was, most had already consumed a minimum of four brews or belts, and the slurring had begun. "Can we buzz through some of our key points and be done with this sheariosness?"

Righetti set himself to rollicking again. "Did I jus' say *buzz*? As wha' I wanna be..." Not funny, but Righetti brought forth a wheezy laugh that seemed to start at his toes and erupt from his mouth. "*Har, har, har*!"

"Well," Brandywine began, feeling it was her responsibility to take charge of a group fraying at the margins, "here they are, so consider taking notes."

Leary was ready for the summary. He sat up straight, took a deep breath, and prepared to open the canal to his mind wide, willing it to capture every point.

Brandywine opened her notebook and started talking. Once again, Bucks winced in disbelief. "The Superintendent," Brandywine said, "has formed an inappropriate relationship with a live-in housekeeper. The Superintendent has fired, relieved, whatever they call it, the Academic Dean for apparently nothing more than preserving academic freedom. The same Dean that has enriched and enlightened by bringing in civilian educators with great liberal backgrounds is having his reputation besmirched because Pack is systematically firing them. He brought a ton, really much more than that, of new guns up here, and because they're not stored properly, they could fall into the wrong hands at any time. Remember, fellow Visitors, it hasn't been definitively established that Pack isn't already a murderer." After all, as far as Brandywine could tell, Pack might have *murdered* that unfortunate Ali-Mumen fellow and his friends, no self-defense about it, and the FBI might have made up all those bad charges against them. Would he really care if a few M16s wound up in the South Bronx?

"Pack is a piker," Brandywine said, giving Righetti another opportunity to laugh off a few calories. "At the same time, people, we must admit he's looking more heroic to the rubes out there. He's been in the news so often pixels of his brutish face have burned into computer monitors. He's more or less a university president, isn't he? Have you noticed genuinely educated people assaulting citizens and getting their features pulverized? Women must be protected from brutes like Pack! You'd think this place is a judo for martial mixed arts," she said, interposing and confusing a few words.

"The nutrition program is next to nonexistent—have you taken a look at their menus? Breakfast alone must amount to a couple thousand calories. They eat dessert almost every meal: Napoleon Slice, Apple Brown Betty, fruit compote, fudge brownies. Oh, my! It's distressing they don't follow the USDA nutritional guidelines...I'd say we need to step in to rescue these poor cadets from the hash-slingers that've been on staff two hundred years. And can you imagine the waste? What we could do with that food in the projects of Newburgh. We'll contract out Cadet Mess operations to an approved food-service company, and in the process save money, cut calories.

"He threw out a fine cadet named Browning Totten, a cadet with barely more than a semester left before graduation, only because Pack disagreed with Totten's principled stances on religion and sex. His war on women is relentless, and nobody challenges this 'hero' but us, ladies and gentlemen. I'm exhausted. What say we relax a little? There is one good thing about this frumpy old place. With the gate and MPs to get through, the press hounds are at bay for a day or two, so we ought to take advantage of *that.*"

"Hallelujah, sister!" exclaimed John Righetti. "We are standin' a-churned!"

◆ ◆ ◆

On **Wednesday morning, 0800 hours,** the Board's visit opened: Truth was, by noon, quite a few had been caught dozing. These people, Colonel Dahl observed, could fall asleep anywhere, any time. If the bus transported them from Jefferson Hall to Michie Stadium, your Elizabeth Leonards and Mary Loostys could be sawing lumber within moments of taking seats. Dahl felt he was watching an episode of *The Walking Dead*. A good half of them were enveloped in an alcoholic haze. Torpor followed by stupor. The good steward, Dahl's purpose was to be readily available to address their concerns knowledgeably, and to answer their questions, whether mundane or consequential. Dahl presented only a face of goodwill and good cheer, but he discerned distinctly that a few in the assembly viewed him as a go-fer, not Pack's affectionate Golden.

By Wednesday evening, the Board of Visitors followed the same pattern as Tuesday evening, only with little business talk. Apart from three or four Visitors, they were stupendously incurious. This night Leary took a stool at the edge of the bar, from which he could take it all in while remaining inconspicuous as he pretended to play with his iPad. *Did their per diem cover the spirits they were imbibing?* he wondered. There was a good deal of pairing off, with early beats of feet upstairs. The most interesting was Righetti and Brandywine. Could a war on women be in progress upstairs? The meaning to draw from this lack of interest in the briefings, Dahl believed, was that their individual inputs to their report were already in a desk back at their home offices.

Dahl arranged for his team to meet in his office at 9:00 p.m. Wednesday. They briefed him dispassionately. All in all, it was a sorry state of affairs. *I am sorry my people had to witness this depravity*, Dahl thought. *I gave them ringside seats to the passing of American civilization*. At 6:00 a.m., he would deliver an oral report to General Pack.

The charter coach was waiting after breakfast for the delegation on the apron at the foot of Washington Hall, the Cadet Mess. A wind of better than thirty knots blew an icy drizzle up the Hudson. Colonel Dahl stood by the tall heavy castle-keep outer doors of the Mess. The Thursday morning session was for Board members only at Eisenhower Hall, colloquially called Ike Hall. The Overlook Room at Ike Hall had floor-to-ceiling retractable dividers, making it capable of huddling comfortably fifty to three hundred guests, and the room presented users with an elevated, panoramic view of the Hudson. It is an elegant, wintry scene fit for framing. Place cards in the well-lighted room announced the seating arrangement, and for a little while longer, the precision of the layout would hold, with pens, pencils, writing pads, and water glasses perfectly aligned.

Fairchild opened the meeting by reviewing minutes from the last meeting. He reviewed recommendations from that meeting and the progress in implementing them. It turned into a desultory discussion, colorless, full of halfhearted endorsements, disclaimers, and objections. Clearly, they wanted to move on to New Business. and given the substantial turnover in the Board's composition over the past year, what had happened at this meeting a year earlier might've come from a Glyptodon for as much as these people cared. Meanwhile, the holdovers were offended.

After almost two days with his fellow Visitors, Fairchild was convinced as a group they were whining, shirking, myopic boors bent on settling a score with their perceived enemy, the USMA. Early on day one, Fairchild discerned the majority wanted to leave West Point by Friday morning without ever reviewing their recommendations with the Superintendent. They wanted, in effect, to leave a brief thank-you note patting West Point on the head, then get the hell out of Dodge. He instinctively understood the tools of the trade these elite-level elected politicians used to subdue an opponent: disinformation, gotchas, and backstabs. As they worked to lull Pack into indifference, they prepared the hangman's noose for use by the President.

Fairchild would have none of it. He understood he couldn't change the outcome, but he wasn't going to let Pack be surprised by it. "I will not leave West Point until the Superintendent has been apprised of each and every finding this Board has made. If I have to, I'll brief him myself," he told them, letting that thought percolate in their minds. "But, ladies and gentlemen, be forewarned: You really don't want me to do that. You don't want me to explain your recommendations and what I believe are the shallow, uninformed, and illogical foundations upon which they rest."

With thirty very successful years in corporate life, Mr. Fairchild was no stranger to assessing people. As he now scanned the room after his tough admonition, he saw some Visitors shrinking, abandoning the bravado of two nights before at the Thayer Hotel. And there sat Fitz Spitshugh, forty-five degrees by line of sight, whose face was ghostly wan. Fairchild imagined the Secretary was ruminating on the fact Pack had recently disarmed and slain two, maybe three, very bad men. Down the table, one hundred eighty degrees by line of sight, there looking back at him was a single smirk, a tell that proclaimed, "I'm ready, you chauvinist pig. I'm the smartest, most ruthless person at this table."

Completing his turn of the room, Fairchild said to the smirker, "Senator Brandywine, I believe you could do an excellent job of organizing and explaining the rationale for each of the recommendations the Board of Visitors will be making."

The confident senator replied a simple, "It would be my pleasure."

Fairchild reclined in his Herman Miller ergonomic mesh chair, satisfied he had done all he could to protect his alma mater from this collection of tools. Their combined capacity for hubris was high indeed and would no doubt lead to a poor result for the collective.

The chairman knew his position was similar to the Chief Justice of the Supreme Court in form, if not consequence. Majority opinion ruled. If he was in the minority, he was little more than a toothless emcee. In the end, the public would not much notice if a modern *Marbury v. Madison* were a 7–2 or 5–4 verdict. The Chief Justice was just another vote, in every respect that counted equal to any of the other eight Justices. Fairchild's duty was to render to President Rozan a report that reflected the majority point of view of the Board.

Around the room, in three rows of chairs off to the side sat fifteen concerned citizens who had applied to attend, in addition to the Board's staffers. The ID cards of the third parties had been checked at Washington Gate and a second time before coming into the Overlook Room.

The majority had selected Senator Kelly Brandywine to constellate and consolidate their views. During the gentlelady's harangue, one of the civilian onlookers audibly wept. Fairchild kindly asked if he could help the distressed lady.

Between sobs, the well-dressed, silver-thatched woman replied, "Sir, I don't think that's possible. Ms. Brandywine, have...you...no...shame? Any...at all?" She retrieved her handbag and walked out, leaving all on hand to wonder who she was and what she was talking about.

Brandywine whispered something to the chairman. Fairchild paused, drew in a deep breath, sat up straight, and with clenched teeth said, "Ladies and gentlemen, I must ask you to follow the Board rules, which stipulate no disruptions from observers. The emanation of noise or any form of raucous behavior must result in your expulsion. Thank you for your patience and consideration. Let's all have a comfort station break of fifteen minutes."

"Senator," Fairchild said to Brandywine, "what in the world was that about? Sure seemed to me that was personal."

"No idea, Mr. Fairchild. I might offer a motion to bar the public in future meetings."

"And I'll fight you if you do. We still live in a representative Republic, I believe, though each day I become less certain of it," Fairchild said, and left a red-faced Brandywine in his wake.

The charter coach carried them again to the Cadet Mess. Dahl was his normal sedulous self, making himself available to deal with their concerns. Only a couple of the Visitors, had treated him civilly, Dahl thought. Fairchild, however, sought him out at nearly every break in briefings to ask follow-up questions or to seek clarification on points he had not quite understood. Also not lost on Dahl was Fairchild's unfailing reference to him as *Colonel*. The rank seemed to mean something to Fairchild. Senator Mary Loosty, on the other hand, said to Dahl yesterday, "Jim, Senator Leonard went out on a smoke break thirty minutes ago. Would you go find her and let her know the bus will leave this area in ten minutes?" On behalf of the Supe, Dahl bit his tongue and swallowed his pride, corralling the wayward member of the "most exclusive club in the world," the US Senate. It took him the full ten minutes to find the woman, who had managed to get lost in a parking lot.

Fairchild asked Dahl during lunch if the two of them might go to the waiting bus a minute ahead of the rest of the group. Once outside, Fairchild said, "Colonel, after the afternoon's meeting, I might miss the chance to say I'm embarrassed by this Board's sloppiness. I doubt most of them would make it long working for me. If I've learned anything on this trip it is, well, that the voters of America haven't paid attention to who they've put up for candidates, and it shows. Actually, the better way to say it is as Dr. Johnson did, 'Man requires not so much to be instructed as to be reminded.' Government's run now by the loudest, rudest, most obnoxious is how I see it. Sorry we couldn't have put on a better show for you. Let General Pack know I'll do my best before the report is submitted to the President," he said, not altogether enigmatically.

♦ ♦ ♦

Thursday, 1245 hours,. General Pack was afoot, making his way down the long hill to Ike Hall, no staffers lugging briefing books, rainfall pelting his face and gusts kicking up the tails of his raincoat. This is the Board of Visitors wrap-up session onsite, the one where they invite the Superintendent to hear their summary conclusions and recommendations before going away to assemble the written report to President Rozan.

Bob Fairchild had all in place. "General Pack, on behalf of the Board of Visitors of this year, I thank you for the support of your entire staff. It would be hard for anyone to absorb all the great information we received yesterday, but I can assure you every place we went, we got the kind of nuts-and-blots—excuse me, nuts and *bolts*, I was trying to say—information we asked for. Special thanks to Colonel James Dahl, for whom I personally developed respect and fondness. Just everyone, and I would love to name them all, but we don't have time.

"I feel obliged to explain how the statute says we operate as a Board: I am the chairman, but I am really the coordinator. I possess no particular authority over anyone here. More than anything, I have a duty to put together a packet explaining our responsibilities and constraints. I made sure to explain every applicable regulation, from alpha to omega, minor to major. I provided fact sheets having to do with every area of operations here. In sum, I did my utmost to bring to West Point a Board prepared, meaning informed enough, to do its duty.

"Now, that's the cookie-cutter stuff. Perhaps the most important reminder to you is that the report to the President by custom, by established practice, by precedent, and by the preference of most around the table is nothing more or less than the views of the majority. In the instant case, however, I have decided to take a great liberty I believe is afforded the chair in permitting a dissenting opinion, as is done on the Supreme Court. The views of the minority on this Board strongly diverge from the majority's. The two sides seem not to have differences in extent so much as differences in kind. So, General, I am telling you a minority opinion will accompany the majority's all the way to the President. It might make no difference, or it might cause the President to temper the recommendations of the majority."

This little speech had no visible influence on the majority. They appeared confident the President would ignore any minority opinion. After all, Senior Advisor Locke had essentially already completed the terms of the report by the guidance she'd issued.

"Now, General Pack," Fairchild said in an effort to lighten the mood, "we nuts and bolts—or blots—would like to offer you a place for opening comments before the majority presents its preliminary findings."

"Thank you, Mr. Fairchild," Pack said, "but I have nothing to offer at the moment. I reserve the right to comment before this session concludes."

For the next two-and-a-half hours, each majority member droned on about the crucial importance of enacting new policies relative to his or her focus of interest. These were the same things Leary and his two mates had noted and reported from the majority's loose bar talk. Dahl and Pack could've given this presentation themselves. Pack just waited for a blessed ending. Then he would say what he had to say.

Pack noted that Fairchild had had to step in twice owing to convulsive snoring from a side-bencher. It was a man Pack recognized as Secretary of the Army Fitz Spitshugh, who had long since tired of not receiving glances from the Visitors on the majority side thanking him for having supplied them with their artfully worded scripts. So the Secretary opined he should use his time to recharge for the agonies of his Washington calling. Maybe they weren't expressing gratitude today, but surely they would directly to the Secretary of Defense and Senior Advisor Locke and President Rozan. These people owed him big time, Spitshugh figured, and they possessed the principles and character to toast him in the company of stars. Fairchild, meanwhile, wanted to expel Spitshugh, but feared doing so would redound to bad effect on Pack and the Academy.

The last majority member to speak was, to no one's surprise, the most verbose and impassioned, Senator Kelly Brandywine. "Now, General Pack, the time has come for me to tell you your duty at this moment is to satisfy this Board that you will follow its recommendations to the letter, and to have done so in detail before our next meeting, which is to be held in Washington, DC, on July 6 of this year. We shall now sit back and listen. Thank you in advance."

◆ ◆ ◆

It was over. They had sliced and diced every pillar upon which West Point was built. It was intended to humiliate Pack.

"When I got here, I made a promise to cadets," Pack began. "I told them I would keep my eye on the mission, namely, that this Academy will be the seedbed of combat leaders. I told them we are not here to prepare them for lucrative second careers or to get them a prestigious postgraduate scholarship. We are in the business of preparing the best combat leaders. This must be a place devoted to instilling the qualities of leadership: meaning what you say, keeping your word, looking out for the welfare of soldiers by imbuing them with toughness, and training them under harsh conditions. And you must possess the qualities you expect of your troops. We make them succeed as followers before we allow them to succeed as leaders. We are not a third-rate school, ladies and gentlemen, and we will not adopt third-rate standards. You will succeed here by pushing through what you thought was the upper boundary of your physical, mental, and emotional endurance. You toe lines that would be regarded as unrealistic in many areas of civilian life. This military life is a contest for the strong, and not everyone who attends West Point will find sufficient strength to make it to the end. I told these cadets they would need my stamp of approval before they can walk out this gate. But understand this, Visitors, mine is a proxy stamp only. The stamp of approval is, in the truest sense, a soldier stamp. The people our graduates will serve must give their stamp of approval. Those troops must know we're sending them officers who may be measured against two harsh standards once they're actually out there facing harrowing odds in life-and-death circumstances: Did you get the job done, and how much did it cost?

"I recently expelled two cadets in cases that this Board referred to minutes ago. In the first instance, I released a former cadet named Totten not because of his sexual and religious preferences, as you allege—and parenthetically, I admit to loathing his views—but because he had scant allegiance to the Academy mission. His interests lay outside the boundaries of the Academy mission. You must be selfless to be a good officer; Totten centered his life on personal interests. He could not follow, and he was temperamentally unsuited to lead soldiers. You must believe in the mission, and ever keep it uppermost in your mind, if you intend to graduate from this West Point. I wonder if this Board understands that. If you do not, then nothing we do here can make sense to you.

"The second case involved another ex-cadet, whom I will not name out of respect. What I did was an uncompromising reaffirmation of the Cadet Honor Code. We do not think it is too much to ask cadets to pledge not to cheat and mean it. If a cadet cannot make it honestly, are there not others who would like the opportunity? No one is forced to enter the Academy. To enter is an honor made possible by the taxpayer. Is it too much to expect honor in return?

"In the cases of both cadets, I could have taken the easier route and allowed them to remain as cadets in good standing. In the canons of modern law, there are skirts for us to hide beneath. You and I can justify every action by some technicality, some rule, either written or perceived. Society has adopted the judicial process as its moral yardstick and forfeited common sense and personal responsibility. Legal, however, is not always synonymous with good. I cannot be a relativist. I must do what is right, and I do not use a by-the-numbers approach to tell me what that is. As you proceed through the military life, when you substitute checklists for common sense, you begin to trip over minutiae, which in turn leads to error avoidance and careerism.

"I reject the notion that any group appointed by any President, with ideological agendas and political motivations, should every few years rudder West Point on a different course. I would like this personal view to be on record. If you accept that our mission is to produce the highest-quality officers, then you evaluate us by how well we perform it. Every other concern you have voiced today is ancillary. SHARP, hear me loud and clear, is *not* my number-one priority."

"Now wait just a minute, mister..." Brandywine was in full shrill.

Fairchild cut her down with an even sharper rebuke. "Senator, be quiet. *Now!* You had your say, and I am directing this meeting. It is the Superintendent's stage. Please continue, General."

"My number-one priority is, I say again," Pack proceeded, without a note, "to produce military leaders prepared to fight and win America's wars. Nothing shy of that is acceptable. And while I'm at it, let me say these future leaders we bring aboard did not sign up to be part of various ever-shifting social experiments dreamed up by someone who doesn't know a platoon from a corps. They didn't come here for nanny-state protections. They came here to tackle demands ninety-nine percent of their peers want no part of.

"One of the lessons I learned over my years of service is that as a commander, my staff really isn't those people in the building around me, but the people at the next-higher headquarters. The ones at the next level up are the ones who are supposed to be supporting me. In that sense, I believe I have the right to look at you as my staff, and I should place requirements on you. If I tell you I need *x*, *y*, and *z* to accomplish my mission, and I can demonstrate the requirements are reasonable, you should do your best to serve your country by supporting me. Instead, you are impediments, obstacles in the way of letting us accomplish our mission. Self-abnegation and self-aggrandizement, ladies and gentlemen, are polar opposites. West Point represents one, and you represent the other. It doesn't have to be that way. I suggest you look seriously at placing country over self.

"I am proud to say that character matters here. Most of these cadets entered with the proper ingredients. We forge it, we fire it, we cool it, we freeze it, we temper it, and we turn out a product that's stronger after undergoing the process. I have told cadets this, and I have been true to my word. I defy you to refute my claim that they are proud to be part of the process. I have seen the hardening occur, and it is a pleasing sight to those who value quality over quantity, the premium over the ersatz. We have turned an S curve at a high rate of speed, and yes, I am proud of it.

"Two parting comments: There was in attendance this morning a wonderful lady who sat in a chair over there. Her name is Elsa Bridgewater, and her character is stainless. She has made my residence a home. She works hard to make it so. She prepares food for me, she washes and irons my clothes, she drives across Storm King Mountain in fog and rain and snow, which I would prefer she not. She has not missed a minute of the work for which she is contracted. She is an exemplary worker and an exemplary person. I am indebted to her. One of you—she will not give the name—defamed her reputation this morning. Whoever did so, know that I was advised by Mrs. Bridgewater that she is taking legal counsel to seek one million dollars for defamation of character, and she intends to discuss with counsel the feasibility of meeting with the press to explain what one of you has done to her.

"Finally, I was given a mission upon agreeing to this position, as was every one of my predecessors. My mission remains fixed, and until such time as it changes, formally and in writing, I will not follow any recommendation of this Board that leads me off that path. Thank you, and I wish you the best."

Brandywine seethed. "Point of order, Chairman Fairchild!"

"Go ahead, Senator," Fairchild said.

"As majority spokesperson, and therefore *the* spokesperson, I must inform General Simon Pack that he leaves me no choice but to recommend—in addition to the Report recommendations—that...that to the President, I will say this man must go." She was getting a bit tongue-tied. "That he has to be relieved of his post if we expect our report to be acted upon."

"Do what you must, Senator," Pack answered, unflinching. "You'll join a long line of people who've fought me."

Kelly Brandywine, she of lofty Presidential aspirations, was trembling with fury, already on the way out the door.

Pack knew that as a dutiful subordinate to the Army Chief of Staff Pembrook, he had a responsibility to report what his boss had not yet been told, namely, that the White House had ordered the Board of Visitors to put a chokehold on West Point. He consciously decided against it for the time being. *This is my problem right now, not his*, Pack decided, *and I'll handle it*.

Chapter Twenty

Anabasis

Washington, DC, The White House, January 15: Senior Advisor Locke carried the Executive Summary of the Board of Visitors Report to the President. "Mr. President, the Board has done its job well. I think we can say West Point will no longer be a problem for you once the recommendations are enacted. A couple of unusual aspects I should point out before you sign off on it. One, this Bob Fairchild businessman you appointed violated standard procedure by presenting a lengthy dissent to the majority view. I apologize for having recommended him in the first place. I did not anticipate he would become a thorn in our sides. I suggest you pass right by his verbose meanderings that try to defend the indefensible. He's a mouse dropping. Second, Senator Brandywine was appointed unofficial leader of the majority, and she states in the strongest language that Pack must be fired. This fat-headed General says his mission is fixed, and he will not follow what the Board has told him to do. He is obstreperous, sir, so I agree with Brandywine. We can't have one of these military people standing up to us like this, even if he is popular with the public right now."

"No, Sharon, you don't get this situation, do you? You don't get *me*, do you? Firing him is what an ordinary President would do. Like Truman did to MacArthur. That's the way of a President who lacks confidence. I'm going to bend him to my will. He might have been a big shot in his little military pond, and he might have made the news for those killings in Las Vegas and for being a general weirdo, but I'm going to teach him a lesson. I will torment him by making him enact every little word in that damn report. He will die a slow death. I'll see to it that he presides over the demolition of that Academy—no, not demolition, but that he sees it destroyed piecemeal day by day. I want the process to rip his heart out. West Point mocked me, Sharon, and I will not be mocked. Send me the speechwriters. Three days, almost, until the State of the Union Tuesday night, and I have guidance for them. Also, I want the General Counsel and Chief of Staff in for guidance on the same matter. Within two hours, Sharon, got it? Pack and his people have messed with the wrong dude, Sharon, as they will see. And send a note to the Board I am well pleased with their work and appreciate what they have done on behalf of a grateful nation, standard boilerplate stuff."

"So that I can keep all concerned on the task schedule, Mr. President, I'd like to know your guidance for them," Senior Advisor Locke said.

"Quickly. I don't want this to get past the people I've mentioned. No leaks. I want my General Counsel to assume the lead in writing an Executive Order I will sign the day after the State of the Union. It will state that commencing August next year, in eighteen months or whatever, the United States Military Academy will become the United States Security and Peace Academy. The mission will shift commensurately, emphasizing negotiating skills and a diplomatic Peace Corps sort of thing. Smart power is the future, Sharon. We won't defeat the forces arrayed against us with weapons but ideas. Pack and his people will be responsible for constructing a revised curricula that the Secretary of State and I will approve. And for the speech people, I want this idea of the new Academy to be included prominently in the State of the Union. I want their ideas for wording fleshed out by this time tomorrow."

"Got it, sir. This kind of farsighted thinking is what makes you the President and me the advisor," Sharon Locke concluded.

"And I want something else too, Sharon," President Keith Rozan said, eyes alight, already getting a whiff of conquest, "and it will be my favorite icing on my favorite cake. I want to look into the eyes of that bastard Pack when I tell him what's what. Monday, I want fifteen minutes for the Chairman of the Joint Chiefs, the Secretary of the Army, and Pack. That oughta do it. Screw the rest of them who think they need to be here."

♦ ♦ ♦

Washington, DC, the Oval Office, Monday, January 18: Pack had been invited to the Oval before, had not been impressed then, and would not be now. It was healthier to visit Chernobyl for a month than to stand thirty minutes amid so many radiating so much self-importance. Pack had seen enough of Washington to recognize 95 percent of these self-servants masqueraded as public servants feeding greedily at the public trough. *Better hold tight to your wallet any time you hear one of these people refer to himself as a public servant*, he thought.

Forty-five minutes past the scheduled meeting time, Pack, Pembrook, and Spitshugh were still in a waiting area. Someone finally announced, "The President will see you now," but as she approached the door, she said, "Sorry, false alarm, the President remains occupied." It looked to Pack as if the long wait and the false alarm had been programmed.

After an additional forty minutes, they were ushered in. The President wore his most brilliant smile, as if he had not been this happy to see someone since, well, forever. *The video doesn't do justice to how messed up this man's face is,* the President thought. "Gentlemen," he intoned in his most casual voice, "have a seat. I have important news for you in advance of tomorrow night's State of the Union. As you are aware, I believe American military actions and presence across the globe have contributed to the low esteem in which we are held. It is hard to get things done in a world in which we are the number-one enemy of the majority of the seven billion who populate the Earth. We have the most robust military in the world, we rule the seas, and we have the largest nuclear arsenal, yet we see where all that has gotten us. Military power is no longer the coin of the realm, and maybe never was. If you've ever been to Switzerland, you see the fruits of their nonalignment and their refusal to spend crazily on weapons and bases. What are we doing with a large naval facility on a spit of land in the Gulf of Aden, I ask you?"

The President could argue rhetorically endlessly. The Senior Advisor had instructed them, almost harshly, that this was a listen-only affair. "The new coin of the realm is smart power," the President continued. "We have to maximize Keynesian theories to help the lesser among us, those who haven't been given a fair shake. There is not money to go around, for sure, but more important, we've reached a point in our maturation that we must begin to act as a grown-up in international affairs. We have to be smarter than our adversaries. Our focus must be cooperation, not confrontation. Cooperation requires smart power. I have decided that a vital step toward achieving the full measure of smart power is through all the bright folks at West Point. I want to put your brains to work. I therefore will announce tomorrow a major initiative."

He looked squarely at Pack, hoping to see defeat register in his eyes, to see this large figure reduced to the inferior one he genuinely was. That was, after all, the point of this meeting. The other two men were here as window dressing, nothing more. "Under my leadership, America is safer than she's ever been. As promised, I ended two vicious and costly ground wars. I've brought nearly all our servicemen and women, from the world over, back home. As we now face a much-less-threatening world, this is the perfect time to transform our approach to America's external security." Still focusing his eyes on Pack, he said, turning up the wattage on the smile, "I understand you've been busy killing terrorists, but it's my job to analyze what lies further downrange, well beyond the small threats directly to our front.

"In the twenty-first century, the community of nations has come to believe war is an unnecessary anachronism. Our position of leadership demands that we recognize this new reality. It calls for bold action.

"Therefore, I am today directing the Secretary of the Army to develop plans to fundamentally alter the mission of the USMA at West Point. The new mission to be undertaken by our oldest service Academy will be to develop a diverse group of leaders committed to the attainment of our national interests by peaceful means.

"Waging peace, avoiding war and its horrible costs is the first duty of all patriotic Americans. West Point will continue to provide leaders for America. It is essential that these patriotic leaders are grounded and educated in the theory and practical underpinnings to avoid war and maintain peace through soft power.

"I believe it's time for leaders to learn as much about Gandhi and Bertrand Russell and Dr. King as they do about the kinds of people you expose them to now. So, West Point will become the United States Security and Peace Academy, and all the actions necessary for that to happen beginning with the admission of next year's class will be undertaken immediately. I will issue an Executive Order to this effect on Wednesday morning."

The President's oration did not elicit the reaction he had hoped for. Pack gave no tell, no crinkling at the corner of the eyes, not a millimeter's flinch. It was as if his mind were not even here. He was a tabula rasa, a slab of marble cold as death that gave absolutely no indication he was seated in the office of the most powerful man in the world. Had he willed himself into this transcendental trance, this rude reverie? *He was invited here, for hell's sake,* Rozan fumed.

It was the President whose visage began to mutate. He trained his eyes on Pack, lightning bolts issuing from their sockets. "Get with it, gentlemen. I don't want to hear any protests. Just get with it."

Keith Rozan knew that in some peculiar fashion, Pack had bested him, and his hatred was in full incandescence now. As Pack headed out the door, President Rozan made his signature male-dominance move, grasping Pack's forearm with one hand and slapping his back with the other. The slap on the back was too hard to have been friendly and the grasp too strong, and Pack's fiery eyes told Rozan to get his hands off. In that instant, President Keith Rozan knew he had screwed up horribly in not relieving the bastard.

He nodded them toward the door. President Rozan had no desire to relate the particulars of the meeting to his senior advisor.

President Keith Rozan had appointed this Chairman of the Joint Chiefs, the highest-ranking man in the entire multimillion US force. Few of the most senior people in America's military trusted him. They viewed him as a dupe for the man who appointed him to this high office. The Marine

Commandant, the title given the highest ranking man in the USMC, saw his neutered boss as an insult to the uniform. The Chairman of the Joint Chiefs sometimes returned from a meeting with the President to tell the Army, Navy, Air Force, and Marine chiefs that he had opposed the President on this issue or that, but his claims left them doubting. They suspected, for example, that the President had successfully muzzled him in the instance of an alleged soldier-desertion case in which the public had shown high interest. Pack would have no defender in the office of the Chairman.

Secretary of the Army Fitz Spitshugh, on the other hand, was in festive spirits after the Oval Office encounter. The way Spitshugh analyzed the whole thing, the meeting had been the President's way of recognizing Fitz's special role in orchestrating Pack's and West Point's downfalls. He would tell Lieutenant Colonels Rynearson and Campbell that they had done well in having him lead the Board of Visitors toward a successful result. Also, Spitshugh would say, "I'm telling you, the President looked at me the whole time. I'm not a boastful man, but it was as if the other two in the room didn't matter. I was the center of his attention and—pardon me for saying so—*praise.*" Boring as the trip to West Point was, the Secretary observed that once again he had made the correct decision in going. Bigger jobs were gleaming like diamonds before his eyes.

♦ ♦ ♦

Enroute from White House to Stewart Airport/Air Base, NY: A Coast Guard version of the Blackhawk was the White House's idea of transportation to fly Pack back to New York. Coincidentally, the chopper was designated the HH-60G, no more perfect airframe for "the HH" of West Point. Lots of troops find noisy aircraft easy places to sleep, and Pack was one of them. He had no leadership responsibility on this flight, so he just put a pair of pajamas on his brain, and released it to sleep.

In the hypnagogic state, ideas tumbled madly, as the clothes in a half-full dryer. *He could hear Denver Johnny speaking to him, telling him, "Life ain't all that complicated, Montana. You don't need me to tell you what to do. I heard you tellin' Hard Travelin' sumthin' like, 'In this hobo life, you keep your eye on the acts, not so much on the words.'"*

And he could see young men—already hard as steel from exposure in combat against cruel, evil people who hated America and wanted to destroy it—who could not hide how much they wanted leadership. They wanted to follow someone who could lead them to eradicate evil and deliver them safely back home. He saw the face of childlike innocence. They were telling him the decision he had to make wasn't hard at all. You do what you know is right, sir.

His chin dropped hard to his chest, and with a snort, he awoke. But in less than a second more, he returned to the state where there was no line between fact and fiction, past and present.

He saw his wife looking at him, but beside her was Mrs. Bridgewater, and the faces of both were saying, "You need have no doubts about what is right. We have believed in you, and you have not let us down."

And there was Jesse Bruccoli struggling to push his way into the picture, a young man saying, "You did right by me. You had no problem describing the highlighted route to me."

He saw Duck waiting on the Stewart tarmac, the captain saying, "You let me hold onto my pride. You never felt sorry for me. You are a wise man. This decision is a snap, sir."

And at the end, before real sleep, he saw and heard the Corps of Cadets. He was way up in the sky, and they were from here a mere uplooking humming mass telling him to come home. Just come home, back to them, where he belonged—that was their opinion.

◆ ◆ ◆

Wednesday, 20 January, Washington, DC: The overnights were in, showing the President's speech had garnered thirty-two million viewers, according to Nielsen. It was the second-lowest rating recorded since the Nielsen started tracking it in 1993.

There was much media discussion after the State of the Union about the disproportionate attention paid to the envisioned Peace and Security Academy. A few of the dot-connectors had no trouble surmising this was Presidential petulance run amok, payback for perceived slights by the Academy Superintendent and cadets during the ill-received major foreign policy speech at West Point a year ago. It would take the wiser ones a day longer to learn about the Board of Visitors fiasco a month earlier, but discover it they would. Some few even bothered to question if this had long-term national-security ramifications. Other reporters, though, believed the Commander-in-Chief had a right, even a duty, to stamp out the tacit insubordination of those uniformed elitists at the Military Academy. And this latter group also believed the Security and Peace Academy proposal was brilliant, another move to inject teeth into the "smart power" concept.

Those whose job it was to watch it had plenty to say, but the public had shown little interest in the speech overall, except in what they were hearing about the West Point angle. They didn't seem much to like it. It wasn't that they had so much interest in, much less love for, West Point, but it just didn't feel right. More and more citizens had the feeling the floor they were standing on was getting creaky, and for some, it had already collapsed. *Sumbitch*, thought the man and woman sitting on the stoops and fire escapes in New York City, and the farmer in Iowa hooking up his cows for the morning milking, and the charter boat captain in Florida about to cast off, and the copper miner in Montana and the coal miner in Virginia, and the aircraft engineer in Seattle. West Point's been around since the start of the country or something like that, right, and it seems like it's done its job, so what's this crazy Peace Academy shit all about? Ain't nothin' solid no more.

The three big conventional news channels mentioned the Executive Order, but in the manner they say, "The Dow was down thirty today, but it's still up two hundred fifty for the year." MSNBC and CNN focused on the "outside-the-box brilliance" of the initiative. Fox News and Newsmax were giving it lots of play, discussion, and commentary.

♦ ♦ ♦

Wednesday, January 20, West Point, NY: Pack once more spoke to the cadets from the Poop Deck during their lunch. "Men and women of the Corps," Pack commenced, "last time I spoke from this platform, I said the Academy had not demanded enough and you had not given enough; that I was imposing new standards on your faculty, both academic and tactical; that the Academy had drifted away from its primary mission, the making of combat leaders; that you did not come to this place to do the average; that the highest honor you may receive is to earn the respect of your soldiers because you know your job, because you treat them all with respect, and because you are for them a beacon of integrity and honesty; and that you are committed to winning in every professional endeavor."

Before this speech, Pack had apprised his boss of the White House's intention to take down West Point.

"I had this belief that as the Corps went, so would go the football team. I was right. The change I have been privileged to witness is surpassing wondrous, a glorious sight to this Marine's eyes. Thank yourselves for calling up from down below the power of will to stand tall. You have brought out the luster, polished off the tarnish. I am proud of you, and I am proud to have been your Superintendent for a time. I will carry the fine memory of this time down the back slopes of my mind until I reach the other side, or as my hobo family prefers to say, until I catch the Westbound.

"You are all aware of the decisions made in Washington. There are times, I believe, the leader must willingly put on the crown of thorns. He should show those who follow behind that he cares about the mission he has asked them to invest in. Personal concerns don't matter. You fight for what you believe in. Some of you aren't likely to see the resignation I submitted an hour ago as courageous, but I have heard too many senior leaders give the phony excuse that change is more possible on the inside than the outside. I am taking my stand. I have a life to return to. Fight your hardest, men and women, to become a leader worthy of the name. Be true servants. This nation needs you, urgently. Good-bye."

From most profound silence to thundering Babylon in the flash of a movie frame, the mess hall erupted. What were they saying? Mixed in were chants: "HH, HH, HH!" and also, "No, no, don't go!" It would take a little while for this to sink in, for each cadet to sort out his or her feelings. No speaker from that platform had ever brought up such a state of stupefaction.

Lieutenant General Simon Pack shook the hand of the First Captain of the Corps positioned beside him in the aerie. He descended the narrow stone stairway winding down to the floor of the Mess. Those in the six wings of the sprawling place migrated and merged into the single wing in which the Supe walked. All the cadet sound and fury of a moment before fell away as they pressed in on their leader. He walked without haste, his still-battered head held high. With each stride he made toward those heavy, high, castle-keep doors, the crowd parted in peculiar biblical fashion. They did not follow him down the wide, stone steps toward Quarters 100. Pack heard an inner voice say, "It is not the sound of victory. It is not the sound of defeat; it is the sound of singing that I hear."

Pack told Thump and Duck and Golden and Mrs. Bridgewater he was the Superintendent until the very end, until his resignation was recognized and accepted by General Wayne Pembrook, Chief of Staff of the US Army. In the meantime, he said to Thump, "I'm going camping for a day or two, and you're in charge. Don't call me unless there's a declaration of war."

Thump saluted and said, "Yes, sir," and by damn if there wasn't a tear welling in his crusty damn eye.

Golden, in collaboration with Thump, had exercised initiative again. Whether Pack would call it concentric or eccentric was problematic. They had without Pack's approval invited quite a few press people to the Mess, sensing something of moment would happen. Even *The New York Times* was represented by an especially able reporter. Sal Interdonato over at the Middletown *Times Herald-Record*, a favorite sportswriter of the Supe, was there to put his sports-leavened flavor on the story. From their submissions would bloom a torrent of stories nationally. Newspapers, radio, television all found, to their surprise, a public hungry to learn about the causes and effects of the State of the Union announcement.

By Thursday morning, the Corps was united in its stand. Many cadets claimed they started the petition, and maybe they did, but it blazed from company to company, signed by all but a number you could count on two hands. It said they were resigning as quickly as the documents could be processed. Four thousand cadets, more or less. The cost to them was enormous. Now, at the start of a new academic semester, they would not find another school to accept them, so they would effectively lose a full school year. They were not guaranteed a scholarship anywhere, of course, and most would be unable to afford a top school. The Congressmen and Senators who appointed them were besieged with demands to erase the Executive Order. Stabbing a General is bad enough, but the public didn't see the fairness here. They sided overwhelmingly with the cadets.

President Keith Rozan could not have a Security and Peace Academy, could he, after this January anabasis?

Thump gave Cadet Gary Cline the go-ahead to represent the Corps before the press. There were a hundred, maybe two hundred press people in the Eisenhower Auditorium. Cameras were everywhere; satellite trucks lined the road. There had not been this many credentialed press here since the American Embassy hostages were brought here after 444 days of imprisonment in Tehran.

"My name is Gary Cline, and I am, or was, a First Classman, meaning it's my last year at the Academy. General Pack came to us six or seven months ago, and most of us say we've learned more about what our purpose as cadets and human beings is in that period than in the rest of our lives combined. Wherever you turn, there are plenty of people to educate you about how you ought to live your life, but how often do you witness their teachings in their examples? That's what the Supe did. He taught us the power of example. He stands for self-discipline, self-respect, and patriotism. He believes in us. He believes in America. If he preached, 'Choose the harder right instead of the easier wrong,' he actually did it.

If he said he was going to make cadet life tougher, he did it. If he said he was going to buck up the faculty, he did it.

"There is a lesson in his life, I think, for all of America. We, as a unified Corps of Cadets, have decided not to take the easy course and accept the wisdom of a bad decision from Washington, but to oppose it at great personal cost. What he has done is put a face to real leadership, and I ask, What greater gift could one bestow? In some kind of way, the way we are expressing through a mass resignation, we are giving our lives for him. We believe in him. I hope he does not hear this, but for us he is the one, the only, the genuine Hobo Hero. And we want him back."

General Harris Green, Army Vice Chief, had prepared for this day. He didn't know how Pembrook would handle Pack's resignation request, but Green himself had his mind made up. Pack had set the example, and he would follow suit. He knew it was likely Wallace Sweet and Ralph Rogers would make the same choice as he.

The heat was too much for the Elect down in Washington. They saw that ordinary Americans did give a damn. They cared about the Elect feeling they could dominate the citizenry, order them about like indentured servants in an ancient feudal state. The people used this blowup at West Point as a clarion call to stamp their feet and let it be known, "We *will* be heard. Bring your haughty, cowardly selves out to face us. This is our government, the government of, by, and for the people."

And so, facing the peasant pitchforks, the cowards caved.

President Rozan held a press conference in which his scarce-concealed aim was to walk back his Executive Order. "What I actually said," the President said confidently, "was that I was *considering* a Security Academy. I never said I would follow through on it. And, you know what? The people have spoken, and so I will not even consider the idea over the next eighteen months. I would appreciate if your reporting might be a fraction more insightful in the future."

General Pembrook refused Pack's resignation, but "the HH" had not yet returned from his camping sojourn somewhere in the spaces of Buckner. His decision remained unknown.

Epilogue

Colonel James Dahl was right there, in the middle of it all. He was both observer and participant. With the Corps of Cadets back to work, West Point had restabilized and resumed its normal pace of operation. The estimable colonel kicked back in the recliner in his quarters and reflected on this drama recently acted out. *Who might be said to have been the central figure?* he pondered. *Hero* was not a word he ever used, but perhaps it might truly be apt in this case.

Dahl could not know it might have been General Harris Green, a man of gifted foresight who had two times in his life proved to be a man of extraordinary prescience, a man of mind-bending intellectual prowess, a man whose practiced powers of analysis enabled him to see far in advance how this drama would unspool. Contrarily, maybe what synthesized so simply and smoothly for Green was cosmic accident.

Perhaps it might have been General Wayne Pembrook, Army Chief of Staff, who possessed the courage to break with tradition and appoint a damn jarhead as Superintendent of West Point.

Or perhaps it was Lieutenant General Simon Pack, a Marine who answered some call he intuited but did not know was freighted with significance, as if responding to a dog whistle no other human could hear. A Marine whose unwavering commitment to mission, mission, mission, was the inspiration that lifted West Point from the Slough of Despond. A Marine who unequivocally rejected the second-rate, in every form at its every appearance. A Marine with respect for duty to his country, no matter the cost to himself.

Or perhaps it was the Corps of Cadets, four thousand young sons and daughters of America who experienced a great insight collectively, who showed themselves willing to cast security and personal priorities to the wind in the cause of a much bigger idea, duty to the nation, because they had followed a leader so worthy of emulation.

Or perhaps it was the American people, who stamped their feet with such might the nation shook. And after the shaking, the United States of America settled back onto its *Foundation.* And the citizenry of America was passing pleased with what it had wrought.

About the Author

John Vermillion served in the US Army as a career infantry officer, Airborne and Ranger qualified. He attended all the standard military schools through the War College. Vermillion earned his BS from West Point before adding three degrees.

The author believes the main cause of America's present, pervasive problems is a dearth of leadership throughout society. If the leadership vacuum created our problems, filling the vacuum can solve them. The Supe shows the vast positive influence one genuine leader can trigger.

Like the best leaders he has known, inside and outside the military, Vermillion possesses deep respect for Reason and the stoic code, as does his protagonist Simon Pack.

Made in the USA
Columbia, SC
26 March 2023

14324548R00157